THE GIRL WHO WOULD BE KING

Cover by Stephanie Hans

Cover Design & Book Design by Adam Greene & Kelly Thompson

Title Design by Adam Greene & Susan Fang

Bonnie and Lola "itties" by Meredith McClaren

The type is Garamond. Also used in the print version are: You Are Loved, Futura Book LT, and Tapestry LT.

www.1979semifinalist.com

www.thegirlwhowouldbeking.com

THE GIRL WHO WOULD BE KING

KELLY THOMPSON

NEW YORK, NY

To Adam Greene, **my** superhero.

And to Joss Whedon, who makes all the good things, and inspires most everything I write in one way or another.

PART I:
break away

○

Berks County, Pennsylvania

The car hits the tree going at least fifty miles an hour and I go through the windshield like I've been tossed gently by a hurricane. I land at least a hundred feet from the car on some bright soft grass, barely having missed a tree directly in my path.

Everything is black for a while.

When I open my eyes again all I can see are these vivid green leaves floating casually above me and I wonder for just a moment about their casual ways, trying to understand why certain parts of life just don't care about other parts.

And then the smell hits me.

It isn't serene like the leaves, but assaulting and violent. It fills my nostrils with the same metallic flavor you taste when you suck on your thumb after cutting it way too deep, when the blood is dark and black, not pinkish like a party. My head rolls back under me as my chest heaves up, toward the green in the sky. I turn my head to the side to throw up. Spitting into the grass and leaning up on my elbow a bit, I squeeze my eyes closed as tightly as I can, afraid of what I'm going to see when I finally have to open them again. Tears leak out, hot and wet on my cheeks. The smell of my parents' blood makes me throw up again and again until there's nothing left and I'm just coughing and breathing hard, my small ribcage ready to break from the pressure.

I stand up and look at the bodies still trapped in our new car. My mother's skull is crushed as if she had fallen from hundreds of feet in the sky and hit the ground with only her head, her bright red hair somehow still shiny where it's not matted with blood. They had both been thrown through most of the windshield, but the front of the car is so crumpled that their broken bodies are miraculously both in and out of the car at the same time. The car looks like an accordion, my mother's pale twisted arm lying right where some glossy keys might have been, her silver I.D. bracelet and the broken headlight glistening in the summer sun.

I look from my mother's no longer familiar body to my own. Some of my clothing is torn and there's blood all over both skin and clothes, but no matter how I pull at my shirt and examine my limbs I can't find any cuts in my skin. But my arm is twisted grotesquely. I try to face it forward and it obeys me. It makes a terrible snapping sound and I cry out a little bit, but it stays put when I let go of it. I look up as three big black birds walk around in the trees above. They stare down as if expecting me to speak to them. I don't.

I start to walk away from the car, toward the road, but I turn back and reach for my mother's arm, gently sliding the silver bracelet off her crushed hand. On her pale skin are some small black marks I've never seen before. Three tiny circles and a bird. The images pull on me strangely deep inside for a just a moment before I put the bracelet in the front pocket of my shorts and walk away. The road is dusty and dry and seems extra lonely to me now. I look the way we had been driving, the way home, and then turn the other direction and start running.

I always wake up at the part where I'm running. And I don't remember where I am for whole minutes before it all comes rushing back.

I'm 17, not six. I'm in a home for girls. My parents are dead. My brother Jasper never came to get me. And my name is Bonnie Braverman.

I never scream when I remember these things because I haven't spoken in eleven years.

●

Washoe County, Nevada

Dragging my mother's body to the car is harder than I thought it would be. She'd never looked like much lying around in that threadbare robe on our worn-out couch all the time, so I'd imagined she'd be light, like husks of corn bound together into a person-shape. Of course she isn't dead yet, so maybe that's part of the problem.

The good news is that, although it takes me a at least half an hour to get her out the door of the trailer and into the passenger seat of the car, we live in the middle of freaking nowhere so there's nobody to witness my first bumbling attempt at murder. I try to imagine as I stir up dust and leave obvious drag marks everywhere that if I could see the first murder for any serial killer, it wouldn't look unlike my unskilled attempt today. The bad news is that the longer it takes, the better the chance that she's going to wake up from the deadly cocktail I've fed her. I poured enough Botulinum into her daily bottle of Jack to kill a person twice over, but Delia is not a normal person, and I can feel her struggling against me already underneath her paralysis.

Worrying that the drugs will wear off sooner than expected, I pull an old Dodgers baseball cap over her head, covering her eyes so that I don't have to look them. She has a look that can almost kill, and even under the poison it might be enough to at least murder my resolve. But there's no stopping now. If I stop now she'll kill me herself, or worse, live forever and then I'd never fulfill my destiny. I'm not sure quite when I figured it all out – that Delia has power trapped inside her and that it really belongs to me – but I did. And really? Part of me has always known it. That's how the power feels, like it belongs to me, that even if it once was hers, it's mine now. Whatever. I don't know how I know, I just know. It's taken me a while to get up the guts to actually try to take it though.

Delia has more control over her limbs than I'd like by the time I get in the car with her, but she doesn't have much more time if she's going to do anything about anything, so I'm pretty sure it's all going to work out.

But when we get to the spot I'd picked out, I realize I don't have time for my full speech. I'd planned to take a moment at the edge of the cliff, a moment to remind myself that I'm doing the right thing, a moment of introspection if you will, followed by a long speech. I've seen it in some movies and it always seems pretty cool, but Delia's too awake and I'm too nervous to have time for anything like introspection. Instead, I immediately head to the other side of the car and start shoving her over toward the driver's seat. I'm not sure it matters if it looks like she was driving or not since I don't expect anybody to come looking for her, but I figure it might be a good idea, just in case. I grab a big handful of her robe and push with all my might, shoving her toward the left side of the car. She manages to wrap a couple fingers around a chunk of my hair and I scream and pull away from her violently. She takes a little piece of me with her though.

Her breathing is labored. I go to the driver's side so I can look down on her. I put my hands on my hips defiantly. I'll just give her the cliff notes of my speech. "Delia. You are a total failure. As a mother, as a provider, as a girlfriend, as an employee, as a human, and more importantly, as a god. You've been a really crappy example for me, and I only hope that I can go on to the greatness I expect of myself despite the pathetic standards you've set for me," I breathe out a heavy sigh. "Do you have anything to say for yourself?" There's silence except for her ragged breathing. "Good." I say, after a long pause. I've always thought the best speeches are the ones that have no interruptions or counterpoints so I'm pleased with this result.

It could also be that her tongue is too swollen to speak, which is okay too. I dodge Delia's last wildly inaccurate swing as it comes through the open window, and then lock her arms down with a click of the seatbelt. I jam a piece of wood between the seat and the gas pedal and slam the driver's side door, which has a lovely final sound. I lean through the open window and take the hat off her head so I can kiss her on her sweaty forehead. She tastes like salt. I toss the hat onto the seat next to her before shifting the car into gear, and barely get my arm clear of it as it takes off for the edge of the cliff.

I stand, hands on my hips, watching the car careen off the cliff and wait for the inevitable sound of the crash, or the explosion; I'm not sure which I'll hear first. Strangely, I don't hear either, because before I have a chance to notice any crashing explosions I'm filled with an incredible fire through my whole body. A burning, rotting roar of fire that makes me gasp for air. It's agonizing pain for too long but then a strange warmth takes its place, a warmth I know I'll never have to be without again. A warmth I know I'm right to have killed my mother for.

I had every intention of burning the trailer to the ground but when it comes time to pour the gasoline and light the match, it all seems overly-dramatic and less interesting than I'd imagined it to be. Plus, if I leave everything alone, who knows how long it will be before anything is discovered? Maybe someone will see the flames from the car or maybe they won't. Certainly nobody will be wondering where my mother is anytime soon. She's left such a small mark on the world; I doubt she'll be missed by anyone at all.

Maybe I'll miss her. Sometimes.

I'm only 16; it's okay to maybe miss your mother sometimes, I think.

I stash the gasoline back inside the trailer, lock it up tight and grab my duffel bag from the dusty ground. I tie the bag to the back of my motorcycle and put on the helmet, not because I think I need it but because I don't actually have a license and I figure the fewer flames I throw up the better off I am, at least for now. Besides, it's a badass helmet and I look cool in it.

With my helmet on, my long legs straddling the machine, and my new power humming through my veins, I take off into the sunset. This part does feel like the movie, like what I've imagined. I feel like screaming at the sky, telling the world to watch out, giving it fair warning that Lola LeFever is finally coming to get it.

The world doesn't stand a chance.

o

I run.

I run any time the world will let me. If I had my choice I'd just run through everything, I suppose.

I run as close to the boundary fence of the home as I can. Over the years I've worn a pretty impressive path into the yard. Until two months ago I'd actually taken pride in it, my running path. I hadn't realized there was anything weird about running by a fence, the same path, the same way, day in and day out.

But then we took a trip to the zoo.

The tigers had this beautiful enclosure; there was even a little lake, and I was thinking it looked pretty nice, considering, until I noticed one tiger just walking very fast back and forth through the space. After watching him for a minute I realized he wasn't just walking, but pacing the exact same route over and over again.

He'd worn a similar path into his cage that I'd worn into mine. And I was suddenly sad for both of us, but I also knew I wasn't going to do anything about it. There's something about following rules that is very important to me. I can't really understand it yet, but I hope I will someday.

Even though I know in some way it's like that tiger and his pacing, the running is still good. It makes me feel calm. And it keeps the loneliness away. Maybe it's the same for that tiger. I mean, it's lonely to run; it's a singular activity, but it's supposed to be that way, I think. And, I don't know, the way I see it, there's nothing wrong with feeling lonely when you're supposed to be alone. It's when you're standing in a crowded room and feel lonely that it's really sad, I think. Sometimes, feeling like that makes me want to tear off all my skin.

So yeah. I run as much as I can. And running neurotically by a fence all the time hasn't made me so popular with the other girls. But it was kind of a lost cause with them anyway, I think. They're never mean to me, rather, they just don't seem to understand me, and then from there they just seem to kind of wish I'd stay away from them, and so I do. It doesn't help that I don't speak. The not speaking thing really seems to bother them. I can't blame them. It would probably bother me too. I've tried to find things to say sometimes, but nothing comes. It's just empty inside. Hollow where the words should be. It's felt like that every day since the accident.

That's really how it all started. I just didn't have anything to say for a while after the crash, and then I couldn't think of anything to say, and then I just forgot that I was supposed to be thinking of something to say. And so I was quiet all the time. But that's another reason for the running I guess. Nobody ever expects you to speak when you're running.

A big splashy drop of rain hits me on my wrist and I look up. It's crazy cloudy out of nowhere, the sky looks ready to let loose on me. More cold drops hit my skull and seep into my hair. Running in the rain is even better than regular running. I know I'll be called in immediately though, and sure enough as soon as I finish the thought I look up and see Alice motioning me in from the front door. It's good that it's Alice though, because she likes me more than most of the workers do, and she almost always lets me get another lap in. I hold up my pointer finger to indicate 'just one more lap'. Even from this distance I can see her roll her eyes, but she grins too.

She yells out across the quad. "Okay, but hurry up!" before going back inside. I smile up at the sky and stretch out my legs, really laying into my long strides. I go faster, but never too fast. Never faster than I've ever seen anybody else run. Well, not much faster. I almost laugh out loud in sheer joy at the feeling of the rain pelting my skin, and my muscles humming underneath. It's times like this that I really feel how different I am from everyone else. When I feel like maybe I survived the car accident for a reason. That maybe my destiny is for something bigger than I can imagine.

How someone can wish to be extraordinary and simultaneously wish to blend in and never be seen is something I don't quite understand yet. Like two parts of me battling it out for unknown spoils – one side yearning to be more than I am, calling to something deep inside me that I don't understand, the other side hoping to disappear into the wallpaper and never have to say a word.

Because if I'm the same then the car accident can't be my fault.

If there's nothing extraordinary about me it can just be one of those horrible things that happen. Horrible things happen everyday and I am not unique. Why is that idea so comforting?

So though I want to be the same as every other person that ever drew breath, because it means maybe I'm innocent, something eats away at me on the inside. Shaking its head and clucking its tongue at me, chiding me, reminding me that I've always known there's something very much 'not the same' about me. When that voice rises to the surface I push it down. I bury it in my running strides, repeating to myself 'the same'.

The same. The same. The same. The same. The same. The same. The same.

I come in a minute later, soaked, my feet covered in mud from my wet and quickly eroding path. Alice sighs dramatically like I have just killed her.

"Ack! Bonnie! Get upstairs and change now, before anyone sees you." I shake off the extra water next to her like a dog, splattering her with hundreds of icy drops. She screams and runs away in mock terror. "Get, Bonnie!" she says. I laugh soundlessly and bound up the stairs to the sleeping quarters.

It isn't until I'm changed into clean jeans and a sweater that I realize our trip to the library will surely be canceled because of the rain. I throw myself onto my bed, frustrated, and pull out the three books I've been re-reading since our last trip. Without a trip to the library this week, I'm stuck with the same three books I finished almost two weeks ago. I put them back under the bed and head over to the ancient stacks of community books and comics in the corner bookcase, hoping I'll find some gem that I have somehow missed in years of poring through the piles that rarely change. With the exception of the few comic books, I've read each book on the shelves at least half a dozen times. I frown at the comics, something I've had little interest in over the years. A handful of *Archies* and a *Betty & Veronica Double-Digest.* I've read most of them, but get bored with the stories quickly, and with Betty and Veronica, who I want to like, but who both somehow seem exactly the same but with different hair colors, and also nothing like me. There are also some comics "classics" that are mostly illustrated comic versions of books, like *Moby Dick*, *Crime & Punishment*, and *Treasure Island*, but having already read the real things I can't drum up much interest in the faded pictures and word balloons.

But today, while digging through the books a bit desperately, I come across a handful of comics I've never seen before. It seems impossible that they've been here all this time and I've never noticed them, because when I look at them there's this beating in my chest that can't be ignored. How could I have missed the tremble in my hands when they touch the vibrant pages? Maybe someone recently added them to the shelves? It's possible. It happens sometimes. I can't think of an explanation and I no longer care. I grip the handful of comics to my chest and take them to my bed, face flushed, heartbeat pounding in my fingers and toes.

And my world just breaks wide open as I read the pages. SUPERHEROES!

I read all the superhero comics one after another and then start again, feeling more unity with the brightly colored images than I ever would have imagined possible. Maybe I'm really not 'the same' and maybe that isn't so bad after all.

●

I don't make it to Los Angeles.

I headed there by way of Las Vegas since I'd never seen it before, but once I see Vegas, there's no way I'm going to miss out on it. The lights get me from go – like some crazy carnival for grown-ups. Coming over the hill on my bike at dusk and seeing those lights, like a bright, sexy mirage illuminating the whole sky and pounding back the blackness of the desert, I'm hooked already. It's as if those colored lights alone can help make me into something new and exciting. And that feeling makes it pretty easy to give up on heading any further west, which is funny because L.A. is like all that's been in my head since the very beginning, since I'd begun to know there was anything outside of Reno, which had basically sucked balls. But I forget L.A. the second I see those lights. Maybe it's destiny.

Starting over somewhere always sounded really intoxicating to me, and really easy, but I hate to admit that despite the power I'm holding onto inside me, I'm a little nervous when it actually comes time to make my move. I've been stealing from Delia – God knows who she'd been stealing from – for years, and I have a huge wad of cash, some of it stuffed in my bra and some buried in my bag, so I know I have plenty of time to figure things out, but I'm shocked to find myself almost afraid. I killed my own super-powered mother less than nine hours ago, what on earth is there to be afraid of?

When I cruise my bike into a random motel parking lot and take off my helmet, I'm assaulted by noise. It's like the volume on the whole world has been turned all the way to the right. Or maybe so far that the damn knob has broken off. I put my hands on my ears instinctively. No wonder our trailer was in the middle of freaking nowhere. I shake my head and close my eyes trying to block everything out. But I refuse to live in the middle of nowhere like Delia, so I'm just going to have to gut it out. I pull my hands away and cringe as the sounds tumble around my brain, fighting for dominance. After a few minutes I'm able to push enough stuff away that I can at least stand and walk. It's not like the noise gets any less really, just that my body is learning to compensate for it or something. It's still annoying, but I can live with it if I have to.

I check into the cheap motel attached to the parking lot, and I'm not even asked for my fake I.D., which I'd gone to a certain amount of trouble to get, including letting a creepy guy feel me up, pre-powers of course; there's no reason to have to let anyone do that to me ever again. I'm super irritated that nobody even cares to see it. Once in my room I don't have a goddamn clue what to do. I have this exciting, new feeling coursing through my veins, and the road trip has allowed my mind to wander into awesome fantasies, which when I step off the bike and into the real world, suddenly seem less likely.

Sure, I have all this new power, but really what can I do with it and still stay under the radar of the authorities? The last thing I want is to land in the hands of some FBI morons, or worse, end up in some secret government lab being experimented on. I totally believe that shit happens. I've seen the movies to prove it. So what can I do with my power, which I am literally itching to use, without drawing too much attention to myself? I figure there are plenty of things I can get myself out of, a locked police cruiser for example, maybe handcuffs, but I didn't bother to take the time to figure out what my limits might be. What will happen to me if someone shoots me with a gun? Had Delia ever been shot before? I have no idea.

Whatever. I'm not looking back anymore. I'm going to experience life like Delia never did, I'm going to eat it all up, taste everything, and spit out what I don't like, and I'm not going to wait. It starts tonight, nerves and second guesses be damned.

I unzip my duffel and rifle through it until my hands hit some silky fabric. I pull out the cat suit and hold it up in the dingy light. It glistens like a snake even under the cheap bare bulb. Instantly I feel better. I briefly consider unpacking but then decide it's better not to get too comfortable and drop the bag on the floor and kick it under the bed.

I strip naked, pull on the skintight black suit, and zip it up from my belly button all the way to my neck. The sleeves reach past my wrists and onto my hands, leaving just my thumbs and fingers free. I pull on my knee-high black combat boots and lace them up, wrapping the excess laces around my calf and double knotting them at the top. I look at myself in the mirror. I look like the goddamn Catwoman. It's awesome. I tie back my long dark blonde hair into a tight ponytail and then push it under the suit before pulling on the hood, which fits nicely and leaves only the oval of my face visible. I feel amazing. I walk around the room a couple times in front of the mirror, practicing. I even try a funny little prancy Catwoman-like walk, but it looks ridiculous and so I just go back to walking normally.

I still look awesome.

I unzip the suit a bit and put my hotel key inside a small hidden space above my breastbone and zip it all back up. I sit on the hotel bed fully decked out and wait for it to get later; it's not even midnight. I'm about to turn on the TV when I see the flimsy folded piece of paper sticking out of the back pocket of my jeans on the floor. I pull the soft paper out and read it again.

Delia,

I know you'll kill me to get it. I thought maybe I'd be angrier about it — but somehow it just makes sense. I can't really blame you — I did it too — killed my mother to get it — and she fought me, as I'm sure I'll fight you, and you'll fight your own daughter someday. But I just thought I should say, I forgive you; it's not your fault. It's the disease calling out to you like a siren — the same way it called to me more than twenty years ago. You can only resist it so long — and once it has you — well, I hope you deal with it better than I did. I love you anyway, though I suppose I was terrible at showing it. Try to forgive yourself.

Aveline

I'd found the letter three days ago, while digging through Delia's dresser looking for a push-up bra. I'd looked for push-up bras a zillion times before though and had never seen it. I don't know if she put it there for me to find, or what. Maybe she knew this thing, whatever it is, was coming and couldn't bear to write her own letter to me? That's fed up if it's true, but whatever the explanation, the words knocked me on my ass the first time I read them, if only because I realized with certainty, my eyes drifting over the letter, that I was planning to kill her. It didn't seem like a reality until I saw the letter though. I've read it dozens of times since then. The paper, already old and worn where Delia probably held it hundreds of times herself, is almost as smooth as the cat suit fabric. And now, I'm sitting in a hotel room in Vegas three days later, having done it, having killed her. And I've gotten her power, just as she had from her mother, a grandmother I'd never met, Aveline.

The disease, Aveline called it.

I'm not wild about that word.

I fold up the letter, which seems to absolve me, and put it on the dresser. I don't feel very absolve-y. I sit on the bed thinking about everything that's happened in my life until now, waiting for it to be late enough — dark enough — to go out. It's a long time and I'm not sure how much I like being alone with my thoughts like that. A few days ago maybe it would have been easier, but now it almost feels like I'm not alone. Certainly a lot of my thoughts seem new and strange. Next time I'll just turn on the TV.

I slip out of the motel as quietly as possible. Ironically, the lights that had seemed so appealing now seem like a horrible idea, since despite the late hour, it's lit up like freaking noon outside. I make for the darkness of an alley, hoping I'll blend in better. Once there I relax a bit, but am disheartened to realize that any antics I pull will need to be in the less exciting neighborhoods of Vegas and away from all these bright lights. I have no big plans, but I still want to have them.

At first I just walk around the quiet, deserted streets trying to think of an epic idea, but nothing comes, and so after another hour with no ideas, I decide to rob the first decent-looking jewelry store I see. As luck would have it, the first good shop has a ridiculous, blingy diamond necklace on display. It has no business being left out and not covered up; even I, with my tenth grade education, know this. Someone's probably getting fired over leaving it out, because that necklace is mine now. I know it like I know my own name. I stand at the window for a few minutes making sure there's no cage that's going to trap me once I'm inside, because I've totally seen that happen in movies. I check the street like a thousand times, making sure nobody is around, and once I'm sure, I pull on the metal security gate, snapping it open with ease. Once the glass is exposed, I send my elbow through it as hard as I can. The glass comes crashing down all around me as the alarms break into the quiet night air. I reach into the opening and pull a second set of metal gates open, snapping the padlock in the process. It has taken less than ten seconds. I jump inside the window and hop out onto the store floor. I keep my head down in case any cameras are looking my way and reach out and snatch the necklace off the headless display mannequin. With my prize still dangling from my hand I dive out the window and roll onto the pavement like a freaking Olympic gymnast; I almost wish for crowds to cheer me on.

And then I hear the sirens above the security alarm.

O

Visions of powerful superheroes dance around behind my eyes and my imagination flies out of the room and around the whole world. But my fantasies are soon interrupted by yelling in the back yard. At first it sounds only like teenagers chatting but it ramps up and something about the tone sends a chill down my spine. I roll off my bunk and lean against the open window nearby. The only staff is far away, out of normal hearing distance, and the small cluster of girls are near the house. Now the voices have turned to shouting. At first their grouping is so tight I can't tell who is who, or what's happening, but then a dark-haired girl named Jenny comes flying backward out of the circle and lands on her back roughly. The pack gets eerily quiet and two of the girls go to her aid, but she brushes them off and stands up on her own. Her defiance ignites a spark of admiration and respect in me. She walks back to the group, and two of her other friends are still standing there, mouths open, stunned. I think briefly of going down but am intrigued and impressed by Jenny's bravery. I want to see what she'll do next. Sharon looks to be the one that pushed her. She's new and has been making trouble since day one, but I'm glad to see someone's over it and not afraid to stand up to her. Unfortunately, Jenny is rewarded for her bravery with a slap. The slap shocks even me. It seems like the kind of thing an adult would do, not kids in a yard. Jenny is still recoiling from the impact when Sharon tears a silver chain roughly from her neck. Jenny shrieks and her friends spring into action. Watching them is the first time I've ever really longed for friends in a tangible way. There's something so passionate about their loyalty. They're no match for Sharon, though Hannah is tiny and delicate and goes down easily with a hard shove; Margaret, a little taller and sturdier takes a punch to the abdomen and ends up catching her breath on the brown grass. The other two just get mowed over as Sharon runs from them, shoving Jenny into the side of the building. Then they're out of my sightline and so I race down the stairs barefoot to see if I can help.

Before I can get there however, Jenny comes running into the building in tears, her four girlfriends closely on her heels. She dashes past me into the sleeping room, her friends whispering as they follow. When they get to the room they're talking all at once and so fast and through so much screeching and tears that it's hard to understand what had happened. Sharon had apparently tossed the locket onto the roof of the building, which seems like some kind of backwards miracle, as the roof is quite high – very high actually. It would have had to catch some horrible, fateful gust of wind to land on the roof. My heart sinks. I know there's no chance the staff will get it back. The one ladder in the shed is far too small to make it to the roof. I sit on the bed quietly watching Jenny, wishing I had acted faster, sooner, more bravely, as she had.

Her grief probably seems indulgent to some, maybe even to her friends trying to comfort her; they've all had tragedy or they wouldn't be here, but sitting on my bed I can't help putting my hand in my pocket, feeling my mother's silver I.D. bracelet, and aching for Jenny with my entire being. I feel the letters of my mother's name, which are now hard to make out from years of me tracing the engraving with my thumb unconsciously, as if it would help connect me to her. I know I have to do something for Jenny, even if it means breaking the rules. A superhero would behave this way; a hero helps whether the problem is great or small, even if it breaks the rules. And maybe some rules are different than others. Who says the rule about curfew should be more important than a rule about stealing? My mind hammers at the question and I feel deeply, alarmingly confused by it. But if I'm honest, my heart is racing, telling me there's certainly one that is more important. The women in the pages of the comic books speak to me in the same way I sometimes imagine my mother does, whispering at some greatness that I can't believe in, let alone conceive of. But today, today something has clicked and I feel different. I feel sure that I'm the only one who can help Jenny.

That it's almost my destiny.

I wait until almost three in the morning. Jenny's muffled crying had died down into an exhausted sleep hours ago, but sometimes the staff stay up well past midnight and so I lie here, eyes wide open, plotting. Finally I throw back the covers and creep to the door in my t-shirt, jeans, and tennis shoes. It's raining outside, which is both good and bad. The sound of the rain and the obscured moon will make it easier for me to go unnoticed, but everything will be wet and slippery, and very dark. I edge down the stairs and past the sleeping woman at the front desk. They're always asleep. I go out the side kitchen door, which is the door the girls always use when they sneak out. By the time I get to the shed at the far end of the yard I'm soaked to the skin.

I try the door but it's locked. I rise up on my tiptoes and peek through the dusty window on the side of the shed and try opening that, but it's locked as well. I look back at the building, looming over me in the rain, all the windows dark, water falling off the roof in huge sheets.

It looks big.

I jiggle the door again. And then I try something I've never tried before. I push on the handle with all my strength. The metal comes snapping off in my hand and the door swings open. I gape at the handle, my mouth half open in surprise. I lay the piece in the grass and mud, positioning it in such a way that it could have conceivably just broken and fallen off. Inside the mildew-scented shed, I grab the ladder. If I'm lucky, it will get me to the first floor, cutting a quarter of the distance. On the way out the door, with the metal ladder tucked under my arm, I take a flashlight, checking quickly that it works by accidentally shining it in my eyes and temporarily blinding myself.

So far I'm terrible at this.

When the starbursts of light clear from my vision I stand in the rain looking back at the building. It looks bigger than big, it's foreboding and dark and just huge. I'd always thought of it as just some rather unimpressive stocky brick building. A little sad and rundown, but not overly impressive. It's only four stories tall but now it looks epic. It looks like the hardest thing to climb on Earth, and I feel tiny, wet, and powerless.

I leave the ladder on the grass and head around to the short side of the building, where there are only two windows on each of the four floors. I had thought this would be the best place to climb since people are less likely to hear or see me, but looking at it now I realize that once I run out of ladder I will have absolutely nothing to grab hold of. The brick-face is almost completely smooth, and slick with rain, it's impossible.

As I head back to where I've left the ladder, my mind racing, grasping for options, I notice the corner of the building has bricks set out slightly from the wall. I don't know what they're called or why I've never noticed them before, but they are set into the corner almost like the tiniest of steps. The lip of brick is little more than half an inch and wet like everything else, but at that moment, to me, it looks like a built-in brick ladder reaching all the way to the roof. I break into a huge smile, but rain hits me in my teeth and eyes and so I shake it off and get back to business.

I position the ladder next to the corner, along the short side, where I'm less likely to be heard, and climb up. Climbing takes two seconds and part of me wishes it took longer so that I won't have to start the hard part so soon. I push the flashlight deeper into my pocket and creep to the edge closest to the house corner. The metal shifts in the mud under my feet. Damn it. I reach out with my right arm before the ladder can send me flailing onto the yard, and position my fingers along the edge of the brick lip. I do the same with my left hand until I'm just hanging there about fifteen feet up, my feet dangling. I try to put my feet on the brick lip, but it's far too small. I should have taken off my shoes. With my toes, perhaps I could have gotten some grip on the tiny edge. I think about trying to get back on the ladder and doing just that, but just as I think it the ladder starts to fall. I squint my eyes shut and grimace, anticipating the inevitable crash, but with everything so wet and mushy the sound is muffled, and the ladder, blissfully, doesn't close up on itself, which would surely have been loud. Instead it just lays there ineffectively on its side. I think how lucky I just got and then chide myself for celebrating while I'm hanging off the edge of a building, fifteen feet in the air, in the rain, by my fingertips.

In a way I'm not sure what to do now, as the task I've set for myself seems impossible, but then my arms start without me. My arms do all the work as my legs dangle uselessly below me and I marvel at them, as they seem to be on autopilot, just moving me up brick by brick. The next time I look down I'm at least three floors high and passing a bank of windows. It's funny because my arms feel like they belong to me more than ever before…kind of the way my legs feel when I run, and so I just let them do it. My arms and I are at the top in no time. Both my hands grasp at the metal gutter, pulling me up and over the edge. The gutter gives a little, but holds.

I stand up on the roof as the rain bathes me and I feel like a whole new person, like a person I knew was lurking inside, but hadn't known how to talk to, until now. It's amazing.

So now I just have to find a tiny silver locket in the rainy dark. No problem. I turn on the flashlight and decide to just start circling the roof from the outside and working toward the center. But just as I begin I slip on a loose shingle. When the first one breaks free several more join it – sliding out from under me and taking me with it. I shoot off the edge of the roof toward dark oblivion.

If I hadn't spent the last eleven years not speaking I know I would have screamed.

Instead, I reach my hand out instinctively as I go over the edge, and catch a couple more crappy shingles that crumble under my grasp. The gutter is my last hope, and I manage to snag it but the weight of me falling is too much for it and it pulls away from the edge of the house with surprising speed. I think there's no way not to go down, but my body tells me otherwise. My weight swings with the motion of the detaching gutter and when it bends back toward the building again I leverage myself up and back onto the roof, barely. Holy. Shit. That's the only thought in my head, about a thousand holy shits.

The flashlight has rolled into an intact part of the gutter and when I slide over to retrieve it I see the locket and chain, glistening in the flashlight's beam. I reach out and pocket it like a kid that just found the freaking Holy Grail. But as I stand up and survey the damage I've done I realize this is going to raise serious eyebrows. Part of the gutter is torn away from the building and at least two dozen shingles have either broken or fallen off the house entirely. The damage will be visible from the yard. I look around for a solution; there's nothing. The building is like a lonely island in the yard, the nearest tree at least a hundred feet away. As I stand there, knowing I'm screwed, lightning strikes a warehouse down the street. I watch it, transfixed. Both because I've never seen lightning hit anything before, and also because it seems like something ridiculous out of a cartoon. But it gives me an idea.

I walk to the chimney on the south side of the house; there's a direct line between it and where the shingles have crumbled and the gutter has broken. I position myself behind and slightly above the chimney. I bite my lip in horrible anticipation and strike my fist at the bricks. It hurts like hell but it does break apart. My hand is torn up and bleeding a little but I hit it a few more times anyway, trying my best to make the chimney look 'struck by lightning'. I then position some of the bricks and broken stone on the roof in a random falling pattern toward the gutter. I even jam two of the bricks into the gutter to make things look more feasible. Then I drop a few to the ground, making sure they hit the grass quietly and not the concrete loudly. Satisfied with my cover-up I head back to the side of the building where I came up, only to realize, stupidly, that I have no way down.

I look around helplessly. I don't think even my amazing 'auto-pilot' arms have the hand-strength to get me back onto that tiny stone lip. Would I survive the jump? It's four stories. If I survive, what would I break? Everything? Nothing? I sit down on the roof, drawing my legs up to my chest, and as the rain pours down I bury my head against my knees, breathing deeply, trying to be smart. After a few minutes I stand up and carefully walk around the roof edge. The ground on the south side of the building is the softest and wettest.

I'll jump from here.

I can't decide if I should take a running start, putting distance between the building and myself or if I should just jump from a standing position on the edge. I chew my lip and walk to the middle of the roof. Before I can talk myself out of it, I start running for the edge.

When my feet leave the roof it's the most alive I've felt since before the accident.

●

I'm more than six blocks away and moving at a speed even I thought impossible when the police cars finally screech to a halt in front of the jewelry store. But I can still hear car doors slamming and guns being drawn, voices shouting. I smile. I can't help it, it's funny. Now at a safe distance I put the necklace on and hide it under my cat suit. I decide to run some more. It feels good, almost like I imagine flying might feel.

Everything is going to work out fine.

I stop by my motel and grab a sweatshirt to better cover up my sweet new necklace that matches nothing I own and head toward an all-night diner for a celebratory feast. The feel of the silver and diamonds grazing my neck is exciting and I smile like a kid with a giant lollipop. I slide into a big cushy booth and order a coffee – I've never had one before but it seems like the right thing to do – the grown up thing. I also order something called the "super grandest slam" breakfast, which they serve 24 hours a day. Partway through gorging myself, a waitress – not mine, but another one whose nametag reads Felice – comes by to refill my coffee. I nod even though I'd kind of hated the stuff, and as she pours it to the top, I wince.

"Nice necklace," she says casually. I look down and see that it has partially slipped out of the neck of my sweatshirt. I gulp down some pancakes.

"Uh. Thanks. It's my grandma's."

"Uh-huh," she says, walking away.

An hour later, after two rounds of pancakes and just as I'm getting ready to leave, the same woman, but now in street clothes, slides into the booth with me without saying a word. I look at her one eyebrow cocked and she points to a muted television above the diner's counter. The necklace I just stole is already on the freaking news. She smiles across the table at me.

"I think we should talk," she says. I try to remember I have superpowers and look right at her but say nothing. "You want to explain?" she asks.

"Not to you, bitch." I'm happily surprised that this response shocks her.

"Bitch? You really wanna go there?" she asks, raising her voice. I decide that while I know I can kill her and maybe even everyone in the restaurant without breaking a sweat, I had warned myself just last night to be careful about these kinds of situations. It's best to stay away from the authorities as long as possible. At least until I know what I'm really capable of.

"Sorry," I mumble, choking on the words. "I'm leaving." I throw a twenty on the table to cover my multiple meals and the tip. She grabs my arm as I get up and I sling it away from her powerfully. She's more shocked at this than my ballsy comeback of a moment ago. "Don't freaking touch me," I hiss and walk out the front door. A block later I have practically forgotten about her when she sidles up beside me. She's got dark hair and eyes and now that I'm standing I can see she's shorter than me by nearly a foot and having trouble keeping pace with my long legs.

"You got the wrong idea, honey," she says, catching her breath.

"Oh really?"

"Yeah. I'm impressed. I mean not so much at your crappy choice of words and obvious temperament issues, but you're just a kid – who are you working with that you managed to snag that necklace? Or did you just luck out and find it in the street somewhere?" She lets her sentence dangle there in the air like a challenge and I turn on her, crossing my arms. I know the smart thing is to tell her I found it, but what can I say, I'm pretty proud of my first score.

"What do you think?"

"I think maybe you've got some talent and I should introduce you to some friends of mine," she says. I look at her hard, trying to read whether or not it's a trap, but I can't really tell. I'm not sure if it's a good idea, but I'm also not sure I have anything to lose. I'm trying to figure out what I am, what I want to be doing, and what my life is going to be about, and if she and these friends of hers mess with me or double-cross me, I'll just kill them and move on. As Delia always used to say, you don't make an omelet without breaking a few eggs. Actually it had always annoyed the crap out of me that she said that since she never freaking cooked and I would have happily eaten an omelet, but I'm starting to understand that maybe she wasn't talking about cooking. Felice hands me a card with the name of some Spanish restaurant I can't pronounce on the front. There's an address and a phone number. I raise an eyebrow at her and turn it over. On the back is her name and ten o'clock written in black ink.

"Just come," she says, turning and heading back to the restaurant as if she's in no hurry whatsoever. I watch her go and then crumple up the card and toss it over my shoulder.

But I've already memorized the address.

○

I hit the ground and go into a crouch, my hands and feet sinking slightly into the soft ground. The feeling of being alive doesn't leave me. In fact, as the mud seeps into my shoes and through my fingers I feel deeply connected to it, not just the earth, but to everything. The world feels bigger and yet smaller because of this new connection. It feels important in some unspoken way. I stay there for a long while, just feeling it.

When I finally move again I put everything back to how it was and sneak back in the kitchen door and lock it up. Upstairs, I take off all my clothes, careful to put both my mother's bracelet and Jenny's necklace on the sink edge and rinse the clothes and my shoes in the sink, so that they are only wet and not dirty. I wash my busted up hands, wincing as the water runs into the tears where the bricks cut into my knuckles. I clean off my body and then both my bracelet and Jenny's locket. Looking inside Jenny's locket I see what was more important to her than anything: two tiny photos that are by some miracle barely damaged. They look like they could be her parents. I think of all the things I would do if only I could have a picture of my parents and Jasper.

I look up and catch a glimpse of myself in the dark mirror. I'm always shocked by how much I look like my mother – the same long arms and legs, broad shoulders, red hair, pale skin, and smattering of freckles. My eyes are dark blue like hers but my mouth is a little wider, lips thicker. I guess if I can't have a picture it's nice to carry her around on my face. I just wish there was some of my father in there too.

When I go back into the sleeping room I put my clothes under the bed, hoping they'll dry a little before morning, and the last thing I do before collapsing in exhaustion is place Jenny's locket in her sleeping hand, which is cupped perfectly, as if waiting for it. I think, despite my fatigue that I won't be able to sleep with all the excitement of the night and worry about having to hide my damaged hands from the staff, but my body takes over and I'm asleep almost instantly.

I dream of my mother.

It's the first night since my parents died that I don't dream about the accident and I've never been happier to have a different dream. But it's confusing. She looks different than the memory dream I always have, almost older somehow, and standing there alive instead of lost to me. I'd almost forgotten how tall and strong she always looked, slim, but never delicate. Her skin seems delicate though, like clean sheets of paper sewn together.

I'm pushing on her in the dream to hold me, to keep me, to love me, but she slips away from me; gently, like a loving mother to an impatient child, but there's an insistence in it that worries me. It feels like there's a purpose behind it, rather than just some casual thing my mind would imagine. She's shaking her head at me softly, and she looks, not sad, but concerned. She puts a hand on my shoulder, as if to steady me, to link us; I don't know why because I'm too busy drinking in her smell, like earth, and rain, and a hint of lavender. I ask her dozens of questions that all sound like 'why.' She cannot hear me, or she chooses not to answer. Her eyes become wild, frantically searching the blank horizons around us for something. Occasionally, she looks back at me as if to comfort me, but there is no comfort in the worry that lines her face.

Finally her distance gets to me in the dream, the blind happiness of seeing her before me is overrun with the frustration that she will not hold me, will not take me in, will not speak to me. My face starts to crumble, emotion breaking through, despite my efforts to contain it, and my eyes flush wet with salty tears. I never cry except for in my dreams and it angers me that I'm incapable of crying without her around, and that she should elicit such a reaction in me. I don't want tears to be what I feel when she's here; I want it to be love, and maybe peace.

But there is no peace here.

She leans down to me, taking my shoulders in her hands, as if sensing my frustration, but when I look at her face it's not an apology, it's a demand. She is as frustrated with me as I am with her, and that makes me even angrier.

But then I see.

I see what it is that is causing her face to knit up with worry. Behind her, what once was a desolate horizon is a giant, pulsing river threatening to overflow and nearby a car engulfed in flames. At the very edge of my vision I see wolves running in a long silvery line on the horizon and a lonely cow with big soulful eyes stares at me from beneath a charred tree. The images make no sense. The wind kicks up, dust and dirt swirling around our feet, rising and stinging my arms in a frenzy. A storm builds all around us.

She tries to speak to me, but no words come out, just her lips moving, with no sound, as if someone has forgotten her soundtrack. One of the words lost on her lips looks like 'coming'. She glances behind her and turns back to me and mouths it again. COMING. I follow her gaze to try to understand what might be coming but all I see is desert and the strange thunderstorm continuing to build. Cracked barren ground stretches for miles in front of us, darkening to an almost black as the clouds swirl. Lightning strikes brighten the sky like day in disorienting blasts. They come one after another with a relentlessness that makes me wince. The sky seems to cry out as it pulls itself apart, breaking into thousands of storms, as if even the storms themselves are confused and unsure. Strands of my mother's hair blow into her face and she turns again to scream at me without sound.

From the clouds above us, emerges a giant black bird – a crow maybe – and she flies above me, nearly swiping my face with her inky black wing. I watch her, transfixed. The lightning in the distance causes a glistening flicker on her thick body. With a crack of thunder the crow splits into three. The trio circle above me as if preparing to feast on my limbs, alive or dead. The rain begins in earnest now, drops falling into my eyes as the storm ratchets up another notch. The sky darkens to an even deeper shade of blackened blue and the crows split again and again and again until they are hundreds, flying above me like a jet-black undulating carpet. It looks like something from a horror movie, but I'm not afraid. I feel my mother's fingers taking my hand and I see she's as transfixed by the bird-sky as I am. I look back to the birds and feel part of them – part of something I don't understand – as we fly with great purpose toward the heart of the storm, me linked with the birds, the birds linked with me. I don't want to go where they're going but I don't get the feeling I have a choice.

When I open my eyes I see Jenny, sitting up in her bed, her locket pressed to her chest. She looks up at me suddenly, her eyes wet with relief and happiness. She knows; I don't know how she knows it was me, but she does. I smile at her, silently confirming her suspicions. She smiles back as if to assure me that my secret is safe with her. I know I've made an ally. I don't think it will change how my life is here, but it's comforting in some small way. And my chest swells with an emotion I'm not familiar with…happiness? Pride? I'm not sure what it is, but I suddenly feel compelled to do things that will make me feel this way all the time, which gives me pause, since that seems dangerous too. Surely it's no coincidence that the dream of my mother has come only after my good act. But what about the storm on the horizon she's clearly trying to warn me about? Does the danger come only if I keep doing these things, or will it come regardless? What is the danger that's actually coming? For the first time in my life I'm beginning to have a true sense of something greater than myself, something larger that I never could have imagined existed. It's as if I'm getting just the tiniest taste of it and it's both thrilling and frightening.

●

I come in wearing street clothes but with my sweet cat suit on underneath, just in case. I left my new necklace in my motel room this time. Felice motions me over to a table with four other guys. Two of them are old; one Spanish-looking and one an average white guy with a big gut, the other two have dark hair and their backs to me. I walk up to the table and Felice smiles. "This is her," she says to the four men, who seem not the least bit impressed. The pair who had their backs to me are younger than the others, and the youngest is surprisingly cute, which makes me oddly nervous.

"What's your name?" the white guy with the gut asks.

"Lola," I say. The entire group chuckles. I really don't know what the hell people think is so damn funny about my name but I get this reaction a lot. "You got a problem with my name?" I ask, crossing my arms. Felice stands up.

"No, no," she gestures to her seat. "Sit down. I'll get you a drink. What do you want?"

"A beer is fine," I say, pretending I drink beers every day and not taking the offered seat. She leaves and I look at the white guy that asked me my name. "What's your name?"

"Melvin," he says with a straight face.

I crinkle my nose. "And you're making fun of my name? Jeezus." The entire tone of the table changes in an instant. Nobody is smiling and the hairs on my arms prick up in warning. After a long silence that feels like some kind of old Western standoff, the older Spanish fellow speaks.

"Felice tells us you have a pretty impressive haul from that jewelry store last night – you got a crew that help you with that?"

Felice returns to the table and gives me the beer. I take a drink before answering. It tastes bitter; it's actually kinda terrible. "No. I work alone." I say flatly.

"You're a pretty young thing to be working on your own, don't you think?" asks the less cute of the two younger guys.

"No. I don't think," I say, wiping my mouth with the back of my hand. This causes the youngest and cutest one to chuckle again.

"I'll bet," says Melvin looking me up and down. I look at him with the hardest look I can come up with and then shrug my shoulders like I don't care what he thinks.

"It seems to be working out pretty well so far," I say. The table gets silent again and I drink the rest of my beer as fast as I can. "Actually, I don't even know what I'm doing here. I don't need to be grilled by a bunch of nobodies." I walk away while the rest of the table argues and I listen for them over the din of the restaurant. Felice is asking why they're such morons and rambling on about something involving me and decoys, which I don't like the sound of at all. As I walk back into the Nevada night, the cute one follows me.

"Wait up!"

"No," I say, not easing up on my pace.

"Lola, c'mon, hold up." He jogs the rest of the distance between us and I roll my eyes and sigh heavily so he'll know he has inconvenienced me greatly. I slouch my shoulders dramatically and stop.

"What the hell do you want?" I ask. Looking into his pretty eyes though, I suddenly regret throwing the 'hell' in there; he's exceptionally cute.

"Don't take them too seriously, y'know, they just don't love outsiders. I think you should come back in there. Felice thinks you've got some talent."

"And why do you care what Felice says?"

"She's my sister and she's pretty smart too. Been playing the game longer than me. She got me into it actually. She thinks you'd be an asset."

"I don't think so, I'm not too into being a decoy anyway, not my style," I say, looking off into the distance, trying to seem detached. He does a double take.

"How did you hear…" he trails off looking at the restaurant and then back at me.

"Let's just say your sister isn't wrong; I have some talent." I cross my arms over my chest trying to look tough and then change my mind and put them on my hips. "What's your name, anyway?"

"I'm Adrian."

"Alright, see you, Adrian. Good luck."

"Wait," he says.

I stop again. "What already?" I ask, exasperated.

"We won't go back in there, but come get a coffee with me," he says, flashing a lopsided and crazy charming smile at me. This softens me a bit. Nobody has ever asked me to coffee before.

"Alright, but just coffee." It seems like the right thing to say. He smiles the cute crooked smile again and we walk side by side towards a coffee shop a few blocks away. My hand brushes his once and the electric feeling that pulses through me is new too. It is a nice kind of new though, unlike most crap in my life.

Over coffee I decide Adrian is the most attractive person I've ever seen in real life. I myself am not particularly pretty, just kind of normal pretty, maybe. I've come to accept this, though I secretly hope that with age I will become prettier, beautiful even. But even at normal pretty I'm kind of extraordinary to look at. At 16, I'm already almost 5'10" and I have this really long, lithe body and slender legs. I don't have much in the boobs department but the shape of my body is pretty, and I have this wild, curly-ish dark blonde hair that men are always ogling. I have big light blue eyes and a nice mouth, though my teeth are not as straight as I'd like. I'd begged Delia for braces one year, when I realized there could be something done about my teeth, but she'd laughed herself practically into a coma at the idea that I wanted to put metal inside my mouth for a couple years.

Adrian had either put metal in his mouth or just been really really lucky in the genetics department, because, though his smile is a bit lopsided in an adorably cute way, his teeth are perfect, like a movie star's.

We slide into a vinyl booth and order coffee and pie. I don't know why Adrian gets pie, but I get it in the hopes that it will cover up the flavor of the coffee. Once the waitress has left we're just sitting there staring, the silence heavy between us, and I'm beginning to think this was a mistake, despite his movie-star smile and charm.

"So what's your deal, Lola?" he says suddenly, but not unkindly.

"My deal?" I echo lamely.

"Yeah, you got balls of steel or what?" But I have no idea what he's talking about so I wait for more. "I've never seen anyone stand up to Melvin like that. Even Felice is a little bit afraid of him. I once saw a dude piss himself after getting yelled at by Melvin," Adrian says, chuckling lightly. The waitress sets down our coffee and pie and leaves.

"Really? Hmm. I wasn't that impressed," I say, taking a sip of my coffee. "He looks like someone's loser uncle who drank about a thousand six packs too many and likes to touch little kids for fun." I finish. Adrian laughs, nearly losing a full mouthful of coffee back into his cup.

"Balls of steel it is, then," he says, and then adds. "But don't ever say that to his face. Seriously." His face suddenly looks a bit pained. We sit there for another long moment, sizing each other up. He's definitely handsome. I never thought a guy as good looking as Adrian would ever be interested in me, superpowers or no, but he is; I can tell from the way his heart beats. The way his pupils dilate. It feels like hunting, sitting there with him. Like I'm the hunter now, but what about later? I'm worried about falling in love with him. Wouldn't that make me the prey? Regardless, I suppress this strong desire to taste him – to literally just like reach out and lick his cheek – I imagine it would taste bittersweet. People have all different kinds of flavors. Felice tastes almost briny to my senses, while Melvin feels rancid, like something well past its expiration date. There's something else about Adrian, vibes or pheromones or something that he's giving off, something refreshing and new. That's it. New. He feels new. Like a clean sheet of paper, untouched, and full of possibilities. It's tempting as all get out. I'm resisting it, but so far it's kicking my ass, and it's only been like, an hour since I met him. I don't want to fall for this guy. This would be a very inconvenient time to fall in love. I have so much to do and I never put love on the list. I don't know how to insulate myself from it happening. Or deal with it if it actually catches me.

"So Lola," he says. "I gotta ask – how old are you?"

I gulp hard on a bit of cherry. I'm not sure whether to lie. At the last second, I decide not to; I don't know why, "Sixteen. How old are you?"

He smiles broadly. "Seventeen." I can tell we're both relieved and there's a long pause. "I'm sorry I laughed at your name," he finally says.

"Oh, I forgot all about that." I say, and I'm not lying this time either; I did forget. Who could remember something silly like that when you've got Adrian flirting with you? He looks at me and I just know how things are going to go with us. It's almost like I can read his mind, all his plans for us mapped out so clearly in his dark eyes, his smile equal parts playful and sexy. I swallow hard.

It's going to be really hard to keep my head with that smile around all the time.

"So, I guess you better tell me about these people. Your, what do you call them, a crew, team…what?"

"Crew is as good a word as any, I guess. They're mostly good people. Melvin is a dick but he's definitely the brains and connections, and leader by default, I guess, so there's no helping that. Felice and Melvin met up years ago and have been working together ever since. Enrico's an old friend of Melvin's; he's a good guy, solid, y'know? And a little more even-tempered than Melvin. Felice's boyfriend Jorge also works with us. He's a sweetheart, a little dense sometimes, and definitely not super-talented, but he's trustworthy and stable, which is kind of key."

"So, what do you guys do…exactly?"

"Well," he looks around cautiously as if to see if any of the scattered diners are listening, they're not. "I mean, we do the kinda stuff you did the other night. We usually go a little bigger, I mean, in the sense of a bigger take, y'know, since it's got to be split five ways."

"Well, there was plenty of other stuff to take when I took the necklace," I say. "It's just the one thing I had my eye on."

"I kind of love that about you."

"What?" I blush

"Just that you pulled that heist all on your own just 'cause you saw a necklace you wanted. It shows you know what you want. It's good, it's great."

"Um…thanks," I say, my face getting hotter by the minute as I push my plate of cherry pie bits away. Adrian does the same with his plate of blueberry.

"You want more coffee?" he asks, hand half up to motion the waitress. I shake my head, and he changes his gesture to one signaling for the check. On the way out he opens the door for me, which seems old-fashioned and almost innocent. Despite all his excess charm and the villainous occupation, he's a good boy. I can sense it down to the hairs on the back of my neck. We stand for a moment outside and make plans to meet for a late lunch tomorrow. When the conversation lulls he kicks absently at the curb.

"Can I walk you home?" He asks, suddenly seeming shy. I stumble, because I desperately want him to, but I know it's probably a mistake to let him know where I live.

"Oh, no. It's not that far," I stammer.

"I don't mind."

"Let's just say goodbye here for now."

"Okay," he says, leaning into me. I honestly don't know how to react. The everyday me would push him off, probably violently, but I'm finding a gentleness I didn't even know I had. He puts his arm against a lamppost behind me, slightly pinning me and nuzzles my neck. Which is…unexpected. It seems like both an animal thing to do and a sweet thing. And I like it, and him, even more for it.

"Goodnight, Lola," he says into my hair. "See you tomorrow?" he asks, but we both know it's not a question.

"Tomorrow," I say quietly under my breath as he walks away.

I wait until I'm sure he's gone before heading back to my motel. I take a roundabout way home, just in case, but never see anyone tailing me. When I get back to my room I fall onto my bed feeling giddy like a schoolgirl I have never been, never had the chance to be, never thought I would be. I know already that it's probably a mistake to trust him, but I also know that resisting it would be pointless. What's the worst thing that can happen anyway?

A few eggs get broken, right?

I don't know if I've ever thought about the idea of actually being in love before. I mean, like anyone I've had crushes. Regardless of how stupid I thought the idea of "love" sounded, being awesome has not made me immune to it. But after coffee with Adrian I find none of it matters. Hell, after I first saw him and he smiled at me with that crooked smile of his, I knew I was in trouble.

I guess I just don't want to get my heart broken.

Is that even possible?

○

Sharon is becoming a legitimate problem for me. Until recently she's been a thorn in just about everyone's side, but she's provided interesting opportunities for me to do good – returning thrown necklaces and other bits of stolen property, stopping fights before they begin – stupid little stuff that makes people happy and lets me see my mother in my dreams. The dreams, even if they are filled with confusion, violence, and strange warnings I don't understand, are still time with my mother.

Sharon has changed things for me because her bad deeds have forced me to engage with people in a way I never have before. I've been used to people somehow intrinsically understanding to leave me alone, like animals in the wild that know to only hunt the weak or injured. I think I give off something that keeps most people away from me. Like potential adoptive parents. That fact never mattered much because I was always waiting for Jasper to come and get me. Of course when I was twelve, he was 18 and he didn't show, so I gave up on the fantasy. I really had tricked myself at first into believing he would rescue me, but when he didn't, I unpacked my bag again and went back to my regular life. It was foolish to think he would come, considering I blamed myself for the car accident; it was likely he blamed me for it too. But I guess I had hoped that he would come anyway.

When pale and timid Rachael comes to dinner one night with a broken arm I know that Sharon has drawn an invisible line in the sand, and she's daring anyone to step up to it. I begin tailing Rachael everywhere she goes, becoming her self-appointed guardian. I see her injury and chide myself for sitting idly by for too long; it's time to stand up, if not for myself, then for someone else.

So, I wait for my opportunity.

I'm sleeping in my bunk a few days later on the third floor of the dormitory while Rachael reads on hers at the other end of the room when Sharon enters the room all anger and frustration bottled. My senses perk up instantly; it's as if the air in the room tightens all around me, so that I can even feel Sharon's steps and her body weight as it presses into what was once empty space. I'm not sure if she sees me or not, but she goes right for Rachael, regardless, slapping her book out of her hands and across the room. Rachael doesn't even cry out, just draws in a breath, preparing herself for whatever onslaught is to come. Nobody else is in the room with us, and I reach out with my senses to see if I can feel anyone nearby.

We are very alone. Now's my moment.

Sharon slaps Rachael hard enough that she falls backwards off the bed. I move fast, until I'm standing in front of Sharon, her face shocked at the speed at which I've crossed the room. She's holding Rachael's other arm, the one she hasn't broken yet, twisting it backward unnaturally. Rachel is giving off a low-pitched whine that sounds like a trapped animal.

I ball up my right fist and throw my first punch.

It's a good one.

It connects perfectly with Sharon's jaw and she flies back hard enough that when she hits the wall she leaves a little dent in it. She slides down and lands on her butt unceremoniously. Rachael scrambles under the bed like a kicked dog and Sharon looks up at me from the ground, one hand cupping her jaw. It's broken. I look at my fist, shocked at the power there.

"J'am gong ta kl yoj," she says, continuing to hold her broken jaw as if to keep it from falling off. I step back so we're further away from the bed Rachael is hiding under. Sharon lunges and sends an awkward punch toward me, which I catch easily in my hand. I begin squeezing her fist until her hand breaks and the bones turn to powder under the pressure. She screams, but all I can see are Rachael's tiny shoes peeking out from under her bed. Even her feet look terrified. Something snaps in me as I stare at Rachael's terrified feet and I suddenly can't stand someone like Sharon anymore. Her very existence disgusts me.

I push Sharon away from me, hard, intending to be done with her, but she trips on the edge of one of the beds and crashes through a window. I dive after her as she goes through the glass, trying desperately to catch her, but I'm too late. She falls three stories onto the grass below. I watch horrified, paralyzed, my heart in my throat. Sharon's body is twisted badly on the grass below me. I wipe my sweaty hands on my jeans and walk out of the room, Rachael gazing at me from under the bed, her face some strange mix of horror and thanks.

Fortunately for me, Sharon has been such a problem that nobody is inclined to believe her that the mute girl, who has never harmed a soul before, has attacked her unprovoked. For her part Rachael is silent, claiming to have seen nothing. When they find me, nearly a quarter of a mile away, at the other end of the compound, reading peacefully under a tree, not a mark on me, it settles any suspicions that I might be involved no matter what Sharon proclaims.

Sharon's hip, jaw, and shoulder are broken and her right hand is mostly crushed.

Seeing her on the ground all twisted is something I will never forget. And it makes me careful. I decide then and there, watching the ambulance cart her away that it's the last time I will be so careless. I had gone further with Sharon than I had ever intended, hurt her far beyond what was reasonable and it scares me to see my power; to see that I'm maybe not totally in control of it. My emotions had raged when she'd been standing there in front of me. She had seemed disgusting, like an affront to everything I felt inside, and that rage scares me. I don't know if that power exists beyond that rage — can I even tap into it at that level without also tapping into that rage? I'm not sure. It's terrifying.

And so I become more solitary than ever before. If it is possible to be more silent than being mute, I find it.

And I remain incredibly alone.

And I wait patiently for someone to open the front door for me.

●

I meet him the next day for lunch near one of the big casinos, the one with the giant lion face entrance. Inside this one all the cocktail waitresses on the casino floor are dressed like Dorothy, which I think is really lame, but then I see all the guys ogling them and realize they're totally getting off on it. I don't know why I'm surprised by these things. But Adrian never takes his eyes off me, no matter how hot a Dorothy walks by.

We go into some rainforest restaurant. I have no idea what a rainforest has to do with *The Wizard of Oz*, but whatever. We walk through a giant aquarium at the entrance, which looks really cool, but suddenly has me worried he's taking me to some kind of fish place, and I don't really like fish. So I'm nervous all of a sudden, but wondering at the same time why I care what he thinks. It seems to go against all my instincts to care, but there's something about it that also feels natural, like maybe how any girl feels on a date and so I don't know whether to embrace it or shun it, which leaves me only more confused. As we walk by a family eating, I see a hamburger on someone's plate and relax a bit. We sit in a cushy leather booth and the hostess leaves us with menus. It's not three seconds before an overly cheerful voice assaults us.

"Welcome to MGM Grand's Rainforest Adventure! Can I get you something to drink or an app to start?" I feel like the waitress is practically screaming at us in her enthusiasm.

"Uh yeah, I'll have a Pepsi and a water...Lola?"

"Oh, yeah, Pepsi for me too."

"Okay, two Pepsis -- any apps?"

"Yeah, yeah, Lo, how 'bout the appetizer sampler?" I just nod my head okay, my heart skipping beats in my chest, because I love that he's calling me 'Lo'. It sounds so natural, so intimate;

nobody has ever called me 'Lo' before, except Delia, but it sounds totally different when he says it.

When the appetizer sampler comes I eat all the chicken tenders and Adrian eats all the crab and calamari and most of the wontons. The shrill waitress, Kimmy, arrives just as Adrian polishes off the last of the crab and she sets down a giant plate of shrimp pasta, just as she takes away the appetizer plate. The pasta actually looks pretty good even though the shrimps make me wanna squirm. My 'rainforest burger' looks pretty boring in comparison, but it tastes good.

"You really like seafood, huh?" I say between giant bites of my burger.

"Oh man, I totally love it. Ever since I was a kid it's been my favorite food. My mom practically raised Felice and I on fish tacos, y'know? I'm always kind of dying to get out of Vegas; head to some coast where the seafood has gotta be better than the desert, y'know? I heard about this place in Malibu where they literally catch the shit in the morning and whatever they catch is the special for the day because it's so fresh, y'know? I mean, imagine how good seafood that fresh has gotta taste?"

"Yeah, I guess. I don't really like seafood too much."

"Really? Well, I guess that's not that weird, a lot a people don't like seafood. You're totally missing out though."

"Well, to be honest I haven't tried it that much, it's just the idea of it, I don't know, it seems kinda icky."

"You should totally try it then. Here." Adrian stabs a bit of shrimp and winds his fork around some pasta and holds it out to me. I'd had shrimp once before and hated it, but somehow it now seems like the adult thing to do, to try new things. I don't want Adrian to think I'm someone afraid of things. Because I'm not. Also, it seems kind of romantic, so I take the bite and chew. To my surprise, it isn't awful.

"What do you think?"

"It's okay. I like the taste, but it's a little…rubbery maybe?"

"Yeah, shrimp can be that way; it's one of the reasons to get it super-fresh – the better the shrimp, and the better it's cooked the less rubbery it will taste. I'll get some good shrimp one of these days and cook you an awesome meal with it, then you'll totally come over to the dark side with me." I giggle a little bit but think it makes me seem way stupid so I stifle it. A kid at the table next to us starts screaming and I crinkle my nose.

"You don't like kids, huh?" Adrian says without sounding judge-y.

"They're okay, I guess. I do prefer the non-screamy ones."

"Nah, I can tell you don't like them."

"Sure I do, sort of," I stammer. I can't imagine ever wanting to have kids, though, I guess, technically that's not what he's asking me. I know that, like Delia, if I have a daughter one day she'll take my power, probably kill me for it, and I'm just getting used to having it. There's no way I'm going to be willing to part with it anytime soon.

"I grew up with Felice and a whole mess of step-brothers, so I guess I feel pretty used to screaming. Do you have any brothers or sisters?"

"No. It was just me and Delia, I mean, my mom."

"That sounds nice too, I mean the idea of things being calm and quiet sound like bliss. Plus, less sharing."

"My mom and I were never close, 'oil and water,' she used to say."

"Used to?" he pauses. "Did she pass?"

"Yeah. Yeah, she passed."

"Was it recent?"

"Yeah, it was."

"I only ask because, I mean, I'm not trying to be nosy, but you know you're only 16, and obviously on your own, did you just run off?"

"Yeah, it was pretty sudden, her death, I mean, and I don't have any living relatives, so I just hit the road. Figured I'm old enough to take care of myself," I pause, as the conversation is giving him more information than I want to. I try to reverse out of it. "It's working out pretty well so far," I say, smiling at him.

Yeah, it is." We share this long moment of silence before Kimmy breaks in on us again.

"How 'bout some dessert, you two?" Adrian nods at me and so I look at Kimmy.

"Sure. What've you got?" We decide to split a brownie sundae of sorts and when Kimmy finally leaves the table, Adrian changes gears.

"So, I guess I should talk some business," he trails off as if he's unsure it's a good idea.

"Okay, let's hear it," I say, steeling myself up.

"Well, I guess after we left last night Felice talked you up pretty good and convinced them to give you a shot. Kind of like a try out or something. Do you think it's something you're interested in? I mean, I know we didn't make a great first impression."

"Well," I begin, trying to seem professional. "What's in it for me?"

"This time? Probably nothing, probably just earning your place on the team. But the cut is pretty good once you're in. We pull a job every couple months or so, maybe more or less depending on how hot the scene is. It's a nice enough life that I don't have to have a real job so I'm not going to complain."

"If you don't have to work, why does Felice waitress?" I ask, cocking my head to the side.

"Eh, there will never be enough money for Felice. She's pretty cheap, y'know, stingy. I think she also likes the idea of a double life, like waitress by day, master-thief by night or something silly, like the anti-Batman or something."

"But not you?"

"Nah, I'd rather sleep in by day, hang out by night and occasionally hit a big score," he says, smiling and seeming honest.

"So, um, you're more like Catwoman then?" I offer. He laughs.

"Hhn. Yeah, I guess so."

"So, what's the job? The job I've got to do to get in?"

"Well I don't know the specifics, we'll have to bring you in and have Melvin lay it out for you. Some drive he wants."

"Like a flash drive?"

"Yeah, I think so."

"What's on it?"

"I don't know. I'll probably never know. You definitely won't know, at least not this time. That'll be part of the test I'm sure, Lo, how willing you are to take orders."

I look at him warily, "I'm not so good at taking orders," I say. He chuckles.

"Yeah, I noticed. But can you just pretend – just until you get in? Behave yourself like a good girl until you're on the inside? I've got a feeling about you and if I'm right you've got enough talent that you're gonna be able to get away with that mouth of yours eventually, but you gotta get in first. Play the game."

"Yeah, I can play the game," I say, one eyebrow raised.

"I thought so," he says. Kimmy sets the brownie sundae down and leaves hastily. We dig in and are silent for a while. Finally he speaks again. "Is that something that matters to you?"

"Is what something that matters to me?"

"What the job is – what's on the drive, or in the bag, or the box, or whatever."

"Well, I mean it's important I guess, cause I don't want to be taken for a ride, but I don't care, like morally or anything. Is that what you mean?"

"Yeah, I guess I mean morally. Like you don't have issues with that? We've had trouble bringing people in before. Either they want to know too much and Melvin has drama with it, or they get ideas about, oh, I don't know, not liking kind of the 'larger picture' of what they're involved in."

"Like, you mean it could be drugs or something and suddenly I feel bad about putting drugs on the street for innocent kids or whatever?"

"Yeah. Yeah, like that exactly."

"No, I don't have moral issues with it."

"Can I ask why not?"

"Well, why don't you?"

"I asked you first," he teases.

"I don't know. Seems to me that people are responsible for themselves. If someone wants to do drugs, that's their problem. And there's no reason I shouldn't profit from it, I mean someone's going to, right?" I trail off, not sure if my answer is correct. For a moment I've forgotten to be careful what I say and just said what I actually think. I don't know what his reaction will be.

"Exactly!" he bursts out. I smile. It's nice to know that we think some of the same things, even when I'm not trying so hard. "Some people just don't get that," he says. "Some people start to feel bad about things we do, and I'll be honest, I've never seen a good 'break-up' with Melvin. He's a pretty scary guy. So just, y'know, be on your best behavior, stay close to me, don't piss him off too much and you'll be fine."

I smile at him again. "No problem." I'm not thinking it's no problem to 'be good' or to not piss Melvin off, but it's definitely going to be no problem staying close to Adrian. At this point I've already mentally committed myself to staying as close to him as humanly possible, whether I have any interest in his gang or not. But I am interested in his gang. When I used to imagine my 'new life' – before I left home, before I killed Delia – I always kind of imagined myself alone, maybe because that's all I've really known. But now, now I can't imagine anything better than being the awesome talent in a crew of criminals. It kind of sounds like an opportunity for a family I've never had, a non-traditional family that conveniently comes with a hot boyfriend no less. Adrian pays the check and we head back out into the casino.

He holds my hand the whole time.

○

I grow even taller. I'm six feet when I pack my single duffel bag and walk to the front desk to sign out on the morning of my 18th birthday. It's Peg who hands me the pen to sign myself out. She's worked here since I was about nine and as I sign the papers she says "Goodbye, Bonnie" in the funny way I've noticed people who know that you won't or can't answer back always say things.

"Goodbye, Peg," I say simply, handing the pen back to her politely. Her mouth drops open like a fish.

"You? You, you can talk?" she stammers.

I smile at her, pick up my bag, and walk out the front door. Peg stands up and watches me go, mouth agape. I can hear her talking animatedly with other staff even once I'm outside. I hadn't meant to shock them, but it feels kind of nice. I like being underestimated. There's some power in keeping what you can really do to yourself. I'll have to remember it.

Being free of the home is a beautiful thing. I hadn't expected how much I would enjoy being outside those walls and fences, and I promise myself never to go back – there or anywhere else I'm not allowed to just open the door and walk out as I please.

I could have run away years ago, I realize, standing there on the brown grass outside the gates, but it hadn't occurred to me. Despite myself, I seem to have some very clear lines drawn in my head about what I am and am not supposed to do. I'm still not sure where I get these ideas. Sometimes I fantasize that they come from my mother but I was so little when she died that it seems impossible. I still feel she has some connection to it, but when I really look at how the lines feel in my head it's as if they were drawn there when I was being built. When I was growing eyes and teeth and little fingernails, like while my brain was shaping itself, these lines just laid down and took root. I like the lines though; they make me feel more comfortable about some things that I think are still going to come in my life. I breathe in the fresh, free air and look around. I have no idea where to go or how to do anything, but somehow it's all okay. And there's only one thing I want to do, anyway. It's the only thing I've wanted to do for twelve years: find Jasper.

●

It's funny how quickly I become a part of them. I meld into them, folding myself perfectly into the space they have provided. It's nice. There are problems too, but in general, it's nice. It's not like having a parent because mostly I get to make my own rules, but it's a bit like what I imagine having a whole mess of brothers and a sister would be like. They're annoying a lot of the time but it's a comfortable annoying. And it's good to know someone has my back, that someone gives a crap what I'm up to.

And then of course there's Adrian, which is a whole different kind of nice.

I make him wait longer than he's probably ever had to wait for a girl. With that smile, I doubt he usually waits too long. But I'm still worried about getting played, still anxious about what he might take from me when I'm not looking. And if I'm real honest, I'm nervous about having sex for the first time. I can do so much that is seems like it shouldn't be a big deal – but it is – it feels like everything will be different after, like, I will be different after.

And so I hold out as long as I can.

By the time we get to it I'm itching for him in parts of me I never even knew existed. A lot of what helps me wait is my fear. Having never had sex before I don't know what to do, probably like any virgin, but more importantly, as we draw closer to it, I grow more and more concerned that I'll accidentally hurt him. Sometimes I catch myself not knowing my own strength, or not being able to focus it and so I wonder what happens if I finally give in to him and let go. For weeks before we actually do it I have terrible dreams about my fist going right through his abdomen or throat by accident. And then he's bleeding all over me, parts of him in my powerful hands, light going out of his eyes, the word 'why' just hanging on his perfect lips. I wake up nearly in screams, a lot.

It's one of these nightmares that gets us started, actually. We've fallen asleep in my motel bed watching movies and eating Chinese food and I shoot up, breathing hard, the image of my hands soaked with Adrian's blood still stuck to the back of my freaking eyelids. Adrian reaches out for me sleepily.

"What's wrong, baby?"

"Hhhhh," I breathe. He wakes up a little more and puts his hand on my sweaty back. My damp t-shirt makes him alert.

"You okay, Lo?"

"Hhh. Yeah," I say, still trying to catch my breath, making sure to keep my eyes open wide so as not to see the images plastered to them when they close. He pulls me toward him, in spite of my hot, wet skin and rolls me into him like sand filling a shell. Before I even realize it, we're kissing and pieces of clothing are falling away and in moments his skin matches mine in sticky sweetness. He's inside me almost flawlessly, not like I've imagined: awkward and strange, foreign and obvious. There's a pinch of pain, but mostly it's like sticks of butter melting into each other rather than butter being stabbed repeatedly with a knife as I've kind of been picturing. I can't help but feel like it's this way because he's who he is and I'm who I am, that maybe it's more like the butter and knife thing when it's not the right person. It seems like a silly idea, and soon I can't think about anything, even sticks of butter melting into each other.

We lie together after, curled into one another, with no covers on. He's sleeping, breathing softly into my hair in a steady rhythm and for some reason all I can think about is Delia, about what her life had been like when she was my age. I'm wishing hard now that I had asked her things before I killed her. That I'd at least asked who my father is or was, and if she'd loved him the way I love Adrian - hopelessly, desperately, almost violently.

I wonder afterward if that's how it is for every girl, super-powered or otherwise.

Thinking about how much I love Adrian ends up confusing the hell out of me though. I've been me long enough to know that there's something wrong inside. I mean, assuming that bad equals wrong, or that wrong equals bad, or whatever, then am I bad or wrong or both? And most of the time I think I'm honestly okay with that, whatever the answer is. I don't really feel I have a choice about it, like maybe Delia couldn't help it either. That we just are the way we are, deep down in our blood, and no amount of feeling bad about stuff or trying to be different can change it. Like it's a disease that never goes away, like Aveline said in her letter. But I don't understand how love goes along with all the other things I feel most the time. It makes the feelings I have for Adrian seem like an alien inside of me, like I'm an unwelcome creature on a foreign planet. Does the fact that I feel like I'm betraying some ancient part of myself by having tender feelings for him mean something?

Usually I can block all this out, push it from my mind. Except when things are like this, like, happy. It's feeling happy that does it, I guess. Feeling happy is the trigger. It feels wrong inside to be happy.

I think I've got a raw deal, sometimes. Superpowers or not, a person should be allowed to be simply happy, without feeling like they need to strip off their skin.

○

Turning a corner, deep in thought, I don't notice anything, until I see a shadow fall across my path and I almost smack right into her.

Sharon.

Apparently she hasn't forgotten what I'd done to her and has been paying attention to when I'd be released. She looks rough, like the months since she left the home have been hard on her. The hand I crushed is still damaged, permanently disfigured. I suppose I shouldn't be surprised that an orphan's hand wasn't properly repaired. My guilt doubles. Triples. She hides the hand underneath crossed arms when she notices me looking at it. I open my mouth to say I'm sorry but I can see it will mean nothing to her and so I turn away, determined not to get into another physical altercation with her.

"Not so fast!" she almost screams as she reaches out with her left hand and grabs the strap of my duffel bag, pulling me backward. I probably could have dodged her, but my guilt is keeping me pretty contained; I don't want to hurt her again; I've obviously done enough already. Ironically, when I had crushed her hand I'd done it because I naively thought maybe it would keep her from hurting other people. From the look and feel of her now that has backfired horribly. As she pulls me backward toward her by my strap she wraps her right arm around my neck, so that her face is right next to my ear. I am tense and ready to move, but letting her call the shots.

Her knife slides into my side and I feel like I'm just a bundle of nerves strapped together with electrical tape. I yelp and pull away from her. As I pull forward she stabs me in the back repeatedly. Pain and fear shoot through me and the world starts to slip away just as another voice pushes into the alley. My vision is being eaten away at the edges, but I see a pair of huge black boots as I hit the dirt with a thud, the knife still wedged between my shoulder blades.

●

I can tell from the second I come into the room that something is going to happen tonight, probably something bad. There's a tension that I haven't felt since I killed Delia. It feels like an ancient warning system. But since I can't tell what is going to go bad, or when, I decide to just ride it out and try to be extra careful. I wrap my arms around Adrian's waist, burying my face in the crook of his neck, smelling him wrapped up in his old leather jacket. He smiles down at me and kisses my hair.

"Mi niña," he says.

"Hi," I say. At least everything with Adrian seems fine. I catch Melvin watching us and shoot him a nasty look, which he laughs at. I don't know what I'm going to have to do to make that dude shut up and stop laughing, but it isn't going to be pretty. Maybe, when Adrian and I finally get out of here and head for L.A. I'll leave Melvin a parting gift.

I get in the car with the rest of the gang, minus Melvin. Enrico is there, and Felice's boyfriend Jorge of course, and the new guy, Albert. I'm not too wild about Albert being included since I don't know him too well, but I actually trust him more than Melvin, so I guess it doesn't matter much one way or the other. In the SUV Adrian and I sit in the back as usual, making out as we drive to the site. Felice yells at us to 'cut it out' at least three times, which is two times less than she usually does, but we never pay attention anyway. When we get there I hop out and take off my jeans and sweatshirt to reveal my black cat suit, which I have officially begun to call my 'working clothes'. I pull the hood over my hair and adjust it on my face. Adrian steps out after me, all in black, a ski mask rolled up on his head, revealing his face, and a crowbar in his hand. He looks back at Felice, who's driving, as per usual, and Enrico who's looking intently at a glowing laptop perched on his knee. Albert and Jorge lace up their boots, gearing up for their 'decoy bit'. Felice is on the phone with Melvin waiting for a 'go ahead order'. She's holding her finger up, telling us to wait a minute. I look in the distance at the low concrete building and the high surrounding fence. Something still feels off. Felice snaps her phone shut and looks at Adrian.

"We're a go," she says curtly.

Adrian looks at me. "You ready, baby?"

"Actually," I pause, looking around. I still have the creeps; something's wrong. "I don't know."

"What?" he asks, looking around, trying to see what I am seeing, which is of course impossible.

"Something's wrong. I've had a bad feeling all night, and now, well, I've still got it. I think we should bail."

"Seriously?"

"What the hell is going on?" Felice calls from inside the SUV.

"Lola's got a bad feeling. She thinks we should call it off," Adrian says into the darkness of the SUV.

"Oh really? So now Lola's got super-instincts?" Albert laughs. I kinda want to shove Adrian's crowbar up his nose, but Adrian puts a hand on my arm to keep me still.

"I don't know Albert, her judgment has been pretty good so far," he starts.

"Yeah, I'm sure you're not compromised in any way considering you're fucking her." At that I kind of lose it and jump forward into the car, intent on clawing his damn eyes out, but Adrian grabs me by the waist and pulls me back outside with him. I don't really fight it. I hate showing these people what I can do and regardless of my anger, this moment is no exception. Adrian puts his hand up as if to calm me and gets back in the SUV to discuss it with the rest of the group. I hear 'cabron' a couple times and 'cagar' at least once, both of which mean Adrian is pissed. But we lose anyway. We're going ahead with the plan. Of course we are. It's really only Adrian and I with our asses on the line, so, of course they want the score regardless of any thoughts we may have on the subject.

Twenty minutes later we're running for our lives.

We'd gotten what we came for (some stupid box Melvin wanted) and Adrian or I (but it's totally Adrian) tripped an alarm. We're halfway to escaping but Adrian can't keep up with me so I slow my pace and take the heavy box from him in mid-stride to lighten his load, he lost the crowbar ages ago. He still can't keep up and so I slow down even more so that we're at least together.

And then there are dogs.

I hate when there're dogs.

But we're close to the fence, and I'm all 'we're gonna be fine' in my head. Since tripping the alarm though, we're off course, and so where we're coming out the fence is higher than where we originally came over. And since we're not in the right position, the SUV is nowhere to be seen either. I'm looking at the fence and there is just no way Adrian is getting over it, especially not with the dogs on us. So when we hit the fence I send the box flying up over it. It lands in the dust on the other side with a satisfying thud. When Adrian catches up with me he's out of breath and horrified and he tears off his mask, his eyes wide and panicked. I take his face in my hands for just a second.

"Don't worry," I say. He looks at me like I'm insane. "Trust me." I make my hands into a step for him and he looks at me like I'm even more insane. The dogs are getting really close though, so I drop the sweet voice. "Just trust me. Hurry." He points at the razor wire at the top of the fence.

"I'll be cut to shreds, Lola, you're nuts!" he screams.

"Damn it, Adrian, you'll make it. I promise!" I scream back at him. And then I point at the dogs a few yards away. "Would you rather be torn to shreds by those?" Adrian turns and sees how close the dogs are.

"SHIT!" he screams and puts his foot in my hands. I lever him over the fence, and I totally overcompensate with the adrenaline pumping through my veins and he goes flying WAY over the fence. I'm horrified that he'll break his neck on the way down, so instead of being smart and jumping over myself I watch him fly through the air. He crash-lands safely into a mound of dirt and sand just as the SUV pulls up. I'm about to go over myself when one of the dogs jumps my back. The force of it sends me to the ground and it sinks its teeth into my neck. I yank away from it, tearing up my shoulder and leaving a whole layer of flesh in the dog's mouth. I clamp one hand over the gushing wound and hear Adrian cry out, "NO!" as I try to get up. Before I can however I get hit by a second dog, and what feels like a third bites into my back. A fourth joins in and lays into my right calf; I kick that one off with my left foot and it makes a high-pitched yelp as it goes flying in the air. I can hear footsteps and voices in the distance trying to catch up with the dogs and I figure if I can just throw the dogs off and get over the fence and into the car I'll be fine, but then I hear the tires squeal as the car drives away at an accelerated rate. I look up to see if Adrian at least is waiting for me on the other side. Of course, there's nothing.

Nobody.

I'm alone.

I turn, roughly, throwing two of the dogs off me, and the first lunges at me again. I catch the dog by its jaws and pull in opposite directions, breaking the jaw and killing it instantly. I throw the corpse at the two running toward me, hitting one with the body and sending it shooting backward. The other jumps at me and I swing my fist at it mid-jump, connecting beautifully with the face, smashing it to pieces. The third dog that I'd hit with the corpse is heading back my way, albeit a bit more slowly, and the fourth dog has maybe given up, limping away with a broken leg. Dog number three launches itself at me just as I'm about to make a jump for the fence. I pull up short and we circle each other, the dog and I, trying to measure each other up. I lurch forward and it steps back. When my back is toward the fence the dog leaps at me and it leaps high enough that I go under it slightly and set it into the air like a massive, furry, teethy volleyball. It goes over the fence, but just barely, and when it comes down it lands in the razor wire with a howl. I plant my feet and go over the fence myself, and take off running just as the guards open fire. They chase me along the fence line, firing wildly. I keep the pace nice and light for a few seconds until one of them clips me in the arm. I yell back at them. "You need some new fucking dogs! Those other ones are dead!" And then I kick my speed into high gear and leave them in my dust.

I slow my pace a few miles away from the facility and sit down near some weeds to give my body a chance to heal. My neck wound is critical. It takes almost half an hour, but when my neck is in reasonable shape I begin running again and don't stop until I can see the Vegas lights big and bright in the darkness.

It's time to move on. After I kill my old crew, of course.

When I get back to our rendezvous point, the old Spanish restaurant, the car is parked in the back, as per usual. They obviously think I'm dead or they wouldn't have come back here. I go up on the roof, as for maybe the first time ever I am slightly more curious than I am pissed. Actually that's a lie, I'm like royally pissed, but my curiosity gets the better of my anger. There's a skylight in the back room and so I kneel at the edge and watch and listen. There's no talk of me. No remorse, no concern, no animated discussion as to whether we should 'go back for Lola' – nothing. To Adrian's credit, he looks quite miserable, but whether that's because he's left his girlfriend to get eaten alive by dogs or because he's broken his wrist I can't be sure. Mostly they're just dividing up the take as usual, discussing their payday.

I sit back and try to think. I've been discovering, much to my dismay, that I'm not a criminal mastermind or anything. I'm just brute force and my powers in no way include super-intelligence, which kind of pisses me off. I mean, I guess it's possible I'll get smarter with time, but at 16 I'm still clearly just muscle, to myself and to everyone else.

Ah, screw the thinking, I'm made of pure badass action.

I snap the padlock off the skylight pull up the window and drop down through the ceiling. I have deliberately not cleaned myself up, since I look like I've been half-devoured by dogs and figure the sight of me alone will instill some horror. To their credit, nobody faints, though Adrian looks like he might.

"Hello gang. Nice night to be eaten alive by dogs, isn't it?"

"Jesus, Lola," Enrico says

"Dios mio," Jorge breathes while crossing himself. He looks the most frightened, next to Adrian, maybe because he's the most religious. Melvin is the first to say something ridiculous, true to form.

"Well, Lola girl. Thank God you're all right," he says, putting a firm hand on my shoulder, the one not still torn apart by dogs. I shake it off.

"Yeah, no thanks to any of you on that front," I say cutting Adrian a look. He squirms and then curls up like a kitten, incapable of processing any more information. I don't want to kill him but I admit I'm upset he doesn't seem happy, or even relieved, to see me. Silly me to expect a romantic reunion scene. Jorge is the only one that seems to feel any need to explain anything.

"But Lola, we…we saw those dogs attack you, we knew you couldn't survive that, nobody could!"

"Well, surprise surprise, I guess."

Felice steps forward. "How did you survive, Lola?"

"None of your business," I say sharply. They all stand there dumbfounded. I don't even feel much like killing them anymore, now that they look like stupid sheep, but I am taking the loot and moving on, without them. Being left for dead has earned me at least a sweet severance package. I point to the box I've just been nearly killed for. "I'll be taking that."

"Oh really?" Melvin says more than asks.

"Yes. I'm pretty sure I've earned it."

Jorge steps back, not wanting to get caught in whatever is going to happen. Enrico steps forward to try to stop whatever is going to happen and Albert starts bellyaching that there is no way he isn't taking his cut. Just as I'm about to let things get physical (I have this whole idea about leapfrogging over Melvin, grabbing the box and then kind of Spider-man-ing out the skylight with the box in hand) I get hit in the back of the head with something horrible. I stumble but catch myself on a table and pick up a gun lying there innocently. I point it at Felice, who is, no big surprise, standing there with a bloody tire iron in her hand. She raises her hands, dropping the tire iron, which clangs to the ground obnoxiously. My vision swims and Albert makes a move for the gun, but I elbow him in the face, breaking a few bones, knocking him out. "Don't even," I say, my words slurring together slightly. Just as I'm about to put a bullet in Felice I get hit from behind again, and since Adrian's the only one behind me, I know it's him.

I honestly can't believe it – so much for love conquering all.

I fall forward hard, blackness trying to swallow me on all sides. My eyelids flutter trying to beat back the black and I feel Adrian's strong hands rolling me over.

Melvin speaks, bastard that he is. "Good work, kid."

"I...I didn't want to," Adrian says, his voice cracking.

"It was her or me, mi hermano," Felice says.

"You did the right thing," Enrico adds quietly.

I hate all these bastards.

"If those dogs didn't kill her then two blows to the back of the head aren't going to either," Melvin says, his words floating around me like deadly butterflies. "We better make sure she's done."

The last thing I see is Melvin picking up a huge shiny blade. It glints brightly when it catches the light. The thing must be at least nine inches long. He plunges it into my stomach as if he's gutting a fish.

Then everything's black.

○

I wake up tied to a chair, wire cutting into my wrists painfully. The blood's flowing freely and my hands are sticky with it. My vision's blurry but I can see I'm alone. The room I'm in is bare, with only an alarming amount of my blood pooling in the tread of my shoes and spreading across the hardwood beneath me. It's night, but I have no idea how late and the room I'm in is an empty black. There's a bare bulb overhead but the light is off, only a sliver of light under the doorway gives any hint of shapes around me. Pulling on my wrists to see about freeing them is excruciating and so I stop doing it. I can hear arguing in another room.

"I thought you just wanted to hurt her," says a male voice.

"I tried – did you not see me stab her like five times in the back – not to mention once in the kidneys?! The bitch is still alive. I'm telling you – I've been telling you for like, months – there's something wrong with her!"

"Listen, baby, I'm sorry she hurt you, it totally sucks, but this is like kidnapping now, which is messy. I mean I was totally willing to stand by you if you just wanted to get your revenge and be done with it, but this is...well this is a whole other thing. We should get out of it, now."

"Leave if you want, but I'm finishing things with her. However it goes down. She ruined my life and I won't allow her to just walk away and go on with hers like it never happened."

"Whatever. I'm out of it, call me when you're sane again, okay babe?" A door slams shut.

"Jerk." There's a pause and then footsteps come my way, up some stairs and then straight into my room.

I look at her. "I'm sorry I ruined your life, Sharon. If I could take it back I would."

"See, I knew you wouldn't be dead," she spits her words and throws her hands in the air dramatically. "And you're talking now I see…real convenient. I knew that was bullshit all along, you and your stupid mute act."

"It wasn't an act…I just…I was empty."

"Oh wow, and now some of the first words out of your mouth are lame apologies? You should have stuck with the mute thing," she says, leaning against the wall across from me.

"I'm sorry. It's all I can say," I trail off quietly.

"You're only sorry now because you're all helpless and tied to a chair, I don't think you'd be saying those things if I let you out."

"I would, I really would. I've felt terrible about hurting you. I never meant to get so carried away…you just made me so angry."

"HA!" she snorts, stepping forward and shoving her finger in my face. "You sound just like my stepdad blaming my mom and me for when he would hit us – it was OUR fault for making him mad. I'm sure he thought it was our fault when he killed her, too."

"I didn't mean it that way. I mean I was wrong. I don't know what happened. I lost control. I haven't hurt anyone since that day; I promised myself I wouldn't."

"Hmm. Well, I guess we'll see, won't we?" She walks toward me with a hammer in her hand.

This is going to hurt.

Without even blinking, she swings the hammer at my face, shattering my jaw. My face explodes in pain as the vibrations ricochet through my whole body.

"Broken jaw. Hurts, doesn't it?"

My head lolls backward on my neck as if no longer attached and I choke on bones and blood. I try to pull my head up and do so just in time to see her swinging the hammer at me again, this time she hits my pelvis and I feel it splinter inside my body, sending ripples of pain all the way into the strands of my hair. My hands tear free of the makeshift handcuffs instinctively, pulling off most of my skin in the process. I fall forward in the chair. Sharon is already coming at me again with the hammer, aimed for my shoulder, I think. I reach up with one of my bloody skinless hands and grab the head of the hammer mid-swing. "Ennnougggh," I say through my broken jaw. Sharon looks at my horrifying hand, shed entirely of its skin, and crumples against the wall; I think she's fainted.

I watch her for a moment and when she doesn't get up I turn over and free my ankles from the wire, kicking the chair into little wooden shards. I reach up to my jaw, which seems to be knitting itself back together ever so slowly and painfully and look at my hands, which look more like an anatomy chart of muscle groups than someone's hands. I crawl away from the remains of my chair, my hip too shattered to stand, but halfway to the door darkness takes me anyway.

●

I wake up naked in the desert, my head pounding and my skin covered in filmy orange desert dust. It's not quite noon judging by the sun and the already Vegas-level hot and dry all around. I put my hand up to the back of my head, where the ache seems to be emanating from and bring back a gooey sticky mess of partially dried blood. I'm starting to remember how I got here.

"That bitch," I say out loud to the tumbleweeds. Felice had hit me with a tire iron, I remembered that. But I seriously doubt that was enough to put me down long enough to get my butt dumped in the desert, and then I remember the knife. I look at my stomach and see a ragged looking red scar across my abdomen where Melvin's knife must have ended up. So the good news is, I can cross 'tire iron to the back of the head' and 'being gutted with a nine-inch blade' off my list of things that can possibly kill me. The bad news is I am definitely going to have to go back and kill all of them. Adrian too. This is what I get for being nice and wavering on killing them in the first place.

Knife in my stomach. Fucking amateurs!

That said, why did they have to dump me naked? It's going to be a pain getting back into Vegas without any damn clothes. Fortunately my skin seems to handle the crazy hot desert floor pretty well, so I mentally add that to the list of 'things that are awesome about being me' as well and walk toward the highway in the distance.

I'm still too weak for a high-powered run back to the city, but it turns out it's not so hard to get picked up in the desert when you're a naked young girl. Some dude in a pickup truck stops within two minutes.

"Thanks for stopping," I say as I climb in.

He looks me up and down in a long gross gaze. "Sure honey, you okay?"

"Yeah. Totally fine."

"Where are you headed?"

"Vegas. Where else?"

"Too true," he chuckles.

"Hey, you mind letting me borrow one of those shirts you're wearing?"

"Well, sweetheart, you know, I actually have a um...um...skin allergy, whereas my skin can't really be out in the sun, which is why I need the two shirts," he says, his eyes all over me the entire time.

"Your windows are tinted," I say. He smiles at me with a creepy, serial killer-like-grin — I should know, since I'm working on one of those myself.

"That's true," he says simply.

"Okay. Pull over please."

"Huh?"

"Just pull over. I'm not riding all the way back to Vegas with a pervert."

"Pervert? You got me wrong, sweet thing."

"Stop calling me pet names and pull over."

"Well now, I don't really think that's a good idea, darlin'. Who knows who might pick you up next."

"Are you saying you won't let me out?"

"Well, yes. Yes, I guess I am."

"Okay, just so we understand each other, this is your fault, okay?"

"What's my faul-"

"Because I was just like, totally channeling my rage where it belonged, but now you're being disgusting and so I just want you to know you've brought this on yourself." I raise my foot in the air and kick the side of his head through the window, while grabbing the steering wheel with one hand and pulling us off the road. I think his neck broke because it's all wobbly like Jell-O when I pull him back inside the truck. I push his foot off the gas and slow us to a stop on the side of the road. I strip off one of his shirts and put it on before dragging him out of the truck, tossing him over my shoulder, and dumping him behind some dry desert brush. As I do, I notice his feet are shockingly small and so I take his boots as well; they almost fit. I tie his button-down shirt around my waist so I won't have to sit bare-assed on his vinyl seat. On the way back to Vegas, I fantasize about how to kill each and every one of my crew, except Adrian, I keep skipping over Adrian. But Felice is definitely getting some kind of tire-iron-special.

○

It's morning judging by the shafts of soft light spilling into the room through the grimy window. I feel my jaw and find it healed to perfection. A hand gingerly touching my hip tells me it's still a work in progress. Sharon's still passed out on the floorboards nearby. I crawl over to her and take her pulse. It's strong and steady.

I stand up unevenly, broken and still healing, but able to walk. Barely. I'm not sure what to do about Sharon. Hurting her has only made her more of a monster, but I don't know if I know how to do anything but hurt.

All I can do is leave her alone.

I hobble down the stairs and into the street, grabbing my duffel bag on the way out, happy it's early enough that few people are out to see the horror show that I am, my clothes caked in blood, my walk an awkward shuffle.

I make my way to a part of town not far from the orphanage to look for a hideout. It's not a great area and I don't think my rough appearance will be given a second thought. When I find a building that looks sufficiently boarded up and deserted I scale a fire escape and pull a few of the boards off a second floor window before crawling inside. It is blissfully empty, of people, at least, and I curl up in a corner and try to finish healing.

My mind swims with what a disaster I have made of things. On my own and away from the home for less than a day and already I'm a mess. Who was I kidding that I could just do this on my own. And Sharon. I can't even think about her without my heart seizing up in my chest. I've ruined her. I mean, she was on her way to ruin without my help, but her fall out of that window might as well have been me pushing her off a cliff the rest of the way there.

I suddenly lose it; I burst into tears. A wail I wouldn't have though possible escapes from me. I have never felt so alone in my life. Even though I've always felt alone, now there is just this magnifying glass on it, like it's echoing off everything in the entire universe. The sobs just pour out of me, unrelenting in their depth. It's the first time I've cried since I was six.

I'm a monster.

I feel with every fiber of my being that I should be doing something good with my life, that I should be helping people and 'saving the world', but all I have the ability to do is maim, kill, and destroy. It feels so wrong. I'm an abomination. Like I am made wrong – missing some crucial piece of a giant and unsolvable puzzle. I am the Green Lantern without my power ring. I am Captain Marvel without my magic word. There's nothing to guide me.

There is nothing.

Nothing.

I am lost and alone.

I sleep with the honest intention of
                                   never waking
                                                   up.

●

I go after Felice first. There's something about her being a woman and one of my biggest betrayers that pisses me off a little bit extra. Not that I'm the most loyal of individuals myself, but I am feeling pretty justified and superior at this point. Adrian will, of course, be last, even though his betrayal hurts the most. I'm definitely going to have to work myself up to being able to kill Adrian; I still love him. No matter what he's done, I can't seem to help it. I can't turn it off.

The other reason to go after Felice first is simply that I know where she'll be: the diner. I stop at my motel room to change clothes. Not knowing how long I've been out of commission I assume Adrian has given up the location of my room so that they can ransack it for treasure, and they have, the vultures. Fortunately, they've left the things they found to be worthless, like most of my clothes and personal items. I'm not surprised to find my helmet gone and a glance out the window tells me that the bike is gone as well. Felice has surely taken the bike; she's always had her eye on it.

Maybe I can come up with something extra horrible for her.

The room has been torn up, probably to make it look like a robbery (which it is) or a kidnapping (which it sort of is). I curse a couple times and pull on some underwear, jeans, a t-shirt and my beat up Converse. I put the rest of my stuff that isn't destroyed in the only remaining duffel and head out the front door. The bag feels light without my beloved cat suit in it (though maybe that's all in my head). That should be my first question for Felice, although I suspect I'll forget about it by the time we're face to face.

I get back in the pervert's truck with my stuff and the pervert's old clothes and boots. It occurs to me as I drive that he's actually the first person I've killed – well, except Delia. It seems like that should feel weird or strange, killing someone, but instead it feels totally natural, like taking out the trash or something. Actually that's a totally bad analogy since I hate taking out the trash. But it feels almost routine, maybe? Like mundane and ordinary, and instead of wondering why I did it, I wonder why I haven't been doing it more?

A few miles from my hotel, in a dumpster in a McDonald's parking lot, I throw out the cowboy boots. Two miles from there I toss out the shirts in the trash bins behind a closed liquor store. Then I park the car in an empty supermarket parking lot not far from Felice's diner. I leave the doors unlocked and the keys in the ignition, hoping I'll get lucky and someone will take the opportunity to steal it, moving it even further away from me. But it doesn't really matter; I'm about to be a ghost in this town.

On the walk to the diner, I pass an auto repair shop and just casually pick up a dirty tire iron lying around and walk off with it. It feels nice in my hand. Heavy, but almost elegant. I don't think people give tire irons enough credit. On the surface it seems like the choice of a thug or Neanderthal, but really it has a nice feeling to it; it seems like it has more class than using an axe or something. I like it.

At the diner I see my motorcycle parked outside, clear as day, shining in the sun. Bitch. She has some giant brass balls. I almost want to admire her for it, but there should at least be honor among thieves, or something. I go around the back and wait for her in the alley that leads to the dumpsters and is mostly hidden from everything. It won't be long until she comes out for a smoke break, Felice is nothing if not predictable. I lean against a concrete wall and train my eyes on the back door of the diner, the tire iron in my right hand, casually resting behind my right leg.

She emerges, true to form, about eight minutes later, pack of cigarettes in her hand – one already in her mouth and the match struck – as she comes out the back door.

"Hello, Felice."

To her credit, she doesn't jump, but her normal unfazed expression is totally fazed. In fact, her mouth drops open so far that she loses her unlit cigarette, and the match flame continues to burn toward her fingers.

"You're gonna burn yourself," I offer. She looks at the match a second too late and grimaces before dropping it.

"Lola…I…" she stammers. It's good she doesn't have words, I mean – what do you say to someone that you left for dead to be eaten alive by dogs, then hit with a tire iron, then dumped in the desert naked and gutted – as they stand in front of you in an abandoned alley?

"The keys," I say simply, holding out my left hand. She reaches into the pocket of her jeans and takes out her keys. She starts to take my bike key off the ring that houses the other keys of her life. "Don't bother with that. You won't be needing the rest of those…like, ever." She stops, her head still down, her hair falling in her eyes. Her hands shake visibly as she absorbs the impact of my words. She throws the full set of keys over to me. I catch them in my left hand and pocket them without even looking.

"What're you…" she starts.

I smile at her coolly. "Oh, let's not ask silly questions now. I think I just told you what I'm going to do to you Felice. I'm going to kill you. And you know what? You totally deserve it. I'll be honest, when I killed my mother, I felt this twinge – not a twinge of guilt or regret or anything, you understand – but a twinge that I was supposed to be feeling something and that it was missing in me. I suspect I'll feel that twinge again when I kill Adrian later today, but right now? I gotta say, I'm not feeling any freaking twinge." With that I let the tire iron slide out from behind my leg. "Recognize this?" Her eyes widen, the whites shining brightly from her face and she finally panics and tries to get back into the diner but I'm on her before she can even turn the knob, pressing her against the door with my body-weight and breathing in her ear, "Let's not get anyone else involved, okay?" With that I snap the handle off the back door.

"What are you?" she breathes.

"Mmmm. I don't really know what I am, Felice. It's an interesting question, but one I'm afraid we don't have time for today," I say, totally overloading on over-the-top cartoon villain dialogue. A well-placed blow to the knee knocks her to the ground and she yelps almost quietly, but the next one might not be so quiet, so I have to work fast. I beat her until she looks like little bits of broken bones in a bag of flesh instead of a person. She was dead after the second hit, the rest of them were just for me. Afterward, I pick up her body and drop it in the dumpster where it belongs. There's blood on the ground, but I don't care, and I've actually remained surprisingly clean, which is nice.

When I'm finished, I head to the restaurant, where they'll probably all be hanging out like morons, easy pickings, the whole lot of them. When I peek through the skylight though, I'm relieved to find that Adrian isn't there. I hope he's not coming at all. Without drama I drop through the skylight and land in the middle of the room, much like last time.

I look around, happy at the shocked faces, though Melvin looks more pissed than surprised.

"Déjà vu, huh?" I say to the room arms outstretched.

"What the hell?!" Enrico says.

"This is impossible!" Albert chimes in.

"Hmm," I say. "Lets make it extra déjà vu-y…" I point to the safe in the back of the room. "I'll be taking that."

They all look at the safe, Jorge as white as a sheet and ready to not only give up any treasure, but also willing to proclaim me either Jesus resurrected or the devil incarnate, I'm not sure which. And does it really matter? Albert and Enrico are similarly ready to give me anything in order to make me leave but Melvin, as always, needs more convincing. I look at him hard. "Please say 'over my dead body' – I'm just dying for someone to say that," I smile. Melvin grins thinly back at me and pulls out a gun. I admit, I'm a little afraid of the gun. Having never been shot I'm not sure what will happen, and if I'm knocked out again, Christ knows what they'll do to me and who knows if I can recover from their shenanigans a third time. Can I re-grow a head? Melvin shoots at me and I move fast enough that the bullet barely grazes my arm, like a tickle. He continues shooting and I continue moving, and as a result he shoots Jorge in the head. At this Albert and Enrico fully panic and the noise gets ratcheted up a couple notches. I grab Albert and use him as a human shield to approach Melvin, who mercilessly shoots Albert twice in the chest. When I'm close enough that I'm confident I can beat the bullet, I move faster than ever before and snatch the gun from Melvin's hand, taking his trigger finger with me in the process. He howls like mad and sinks to his knees. Albert is crying at my feet with two critical wounds and I shoot him in the head just to shut him up. Melvin looks surprised; I don't know why. Enrico has his hands up in the corner of the room.

"Lola, please, please don't. This was not my idea…this was never my-"

My eyes on Melvin the whole time, I level the gun at Enrico and shoot him without even looking. I hear Enrico hit the wall wetly and then crumple to the ground insignificantly. Melvin finally looks something remotely resembling frightened. He's lying down now on his back, holding his now four-fingered hand like a baby. He's right next to the safe. I walk over and stand above him. "Tsk, tsk," I say. He looks up at me, still not with respect, but with something closer than he ever has before. I straddle him and just above me his shirt is turning black with blood from the finger I tore off. I poke him in the head with his own severed finger.

"The combination, please," I say. He looks at me with hate and impotent rage and I throw the finger over my shoulder and press the gun into his mouth, his teeth clack against the barrel loudly. "The combination," I repeat, harder. He shakes his head and I roll my eyes. He's so difficult. If he wasn't such a jerk maybe I'd respect his stubbornness. "No?" I say. "Oh, you know what? I don't even need it, watch this." I break the handle off the safe with my bare hand. Unfortunately, the door does not fall open as I had hoped, and Melvin, who still has a freaking gun in his mouth, actually has the balls to smile. What does it take to impress this man? I rear my fist back and plunge it through the wall of the safe, which works beautifully, even though my hand is a bloody mess when I draw it back. His face finally registers some understanding and he looks genuinely scared, if only for a moment. I pull on some of the sharp metal until I'm in the safe, staring at all Melvin's fortune, and the bulk of mine, which he has obviously appropriated for himself. After I'm sure Melvin has registered my awesomeness on the level he should have all along, I pull the trigger.

He still seems surprised, and pissed, even in death.

I grab a big black canvas bag from one of the desk drawers and fill it with everything from the safe. I am a rich rich girl, and rightly so. As I finish up, Adrian walks in the door.

Of course.

○

I feel better. I feel new. Like I have been slumbering in a cocoon and am now emerging strong. Reborn. My clothes look the opposite of new however, stiff and caked in dark blood. I unzip my bag and pull out some of the few items of clothing I own and change, testing my muscles as I stretch, my mind racing about what I should do next.

I've had doubts about finding Jasper ever since he didn't come for me six years ago, but when I left the home I was sure it was the right thing to do. But now, with things having immediately gone so horribly wrong, I'm conflicted. When you hold onto something so tightly for twelve years though, I guess it's hard to let it go. Maybe impossible. He's still all I want in this whole world. And if he doesn't want me around, he'll have to tell me himself.

The public library has a few computer terminals with free Internet access and after cleaning myself up a bit in the bathroom, I wait my turn patiently for an available machine, hoping the name Jasper Braverman is still as unusual as it seemed when we were kids. After a few minutes, I've learned only that either there is no Jasper

Braverman in our hometown or he's unlisted. I expand my search, trying Philadelphia first. Jasper loved the Sixers when we were kids, and as a result, Philly, so it seems like a good place to start. There are three J. Bravermans with addresses listed in Philadelphia and all three have phone numbers attached. The library is closing soon, so I write everything down and head to the train yard, stopping at the only working pay-phone I see to try the numbers. If none of these work I'll have to go back tomorrow and try again. Keep trying until I find him.

I have to psych myself up to make the call, and can only finally do it when I convince myself that I'm going to hang up when someone answers, or at least pretend not to be me. The first number goes directly to voicemail with a woman's voice, she's called Jen. The second is a disconnected number and I hold my breath as the third number clicks over to voicemail. I recognize his voice even before he says his name and my breath catches between my chest and freedom.

You've reached Jasper Braverman. I'm away from my phone, please leave a message at the beep.

I hang up.

It's amazing.

I can hear that same twelve-year-old brother I so looked up to, but now he sounds more like my father, all gravely but kind. I'd forgotten he had sounded that way and there's a little strangled sound in my throat for a moment as I remember. I waste all my change calling back to listen to his voice and hanging up just before the beep. And his voice alone is enough to have my heart beating triple time as I wait for a train headed to Philly. Finally, in the depths of night I'm able to jump on one passing through in the right direction.

Trying to sleep in the car, I can't help but fantasize about meeting Jasper for the first time again. My mind races. He's 24. Will I recognize him as I recognized his voice? Will he recognize me? Does he still blame me for the accident? Did he ever? Will he forgive me?

●

I can't read Adrian's face. It's a bunch of percentages of things like surprise, fear, love, and hate, but it doesn't add up to a hundred percent and no one emotion seems to be winning.

"Lola?" he says, holding his arm and staring at me. I can't believe he can't smell the blood. It's all I can smell.

"Adrian," I say, dropping my head, resigned but unhappy about it. I realize now I've been playing mental roulette in my head 'if he doesn't show up, I let him go. If he shows he's gotta die,' that kinda thing. He still doesn't appear to see the carnage around him, and there's still no romantic reunion to celebrate the fact that I'm not dead. What the hell does a girl have to do to get a movie style happy-ish ending?

I'm not prepared to die a third time for it.

Adrian sees the gun in my hand and finally notices the chaos of the room. You wouldn't think it would take long to process four dead bodies in a room, but I like to think his happiness to see me makes him a little extra slow, heaven knows he wasn't that quick to begin with.

"What…what have you done?"

"What have I done? What have I done?! You've got to be kidding me. You people left me for dead once and then killed me again before dumping me in the desert and stealing all my shit, I'm pretty sure I'm on the high moral ground here. This is practically self-defense at this point, and if it's not then it's at least like, justifiable homicide." I watch him taking stock of the room, and his relief is obvious when he doesn't see Felice's body among the carnage. "Don't get your hopes up Adrian – I did her first," I say, my voice hard and flat. His face falls.

"Lola, are you going to kill me too?" His eyes have that puppy dog look that I'd first fallen for, but I raise the gun and point it at him anyway.

"I'll make it fast, okay?" I offer softly. He starts to cry a little bit, which actually annoys me, but I can't deny that my hand is shaking, which has never happened before, not since getting my powers, and really not even when I killed Delia. He closes his eyes.

"Okay," he says, his voice trying to hide a tremble, his cheeks wet. That kinda kills me, that he says that. It's much better than trying to appeal to me with a last ditch 'I love you, Lola' (though that would have been nice to hear, truth be told). I can't help but admire the fact that he isn't begging, isn't stooping, isn't trying to play me. At the last second, I turn the gun and shoot him in the meaty bit of his thigh, instead of between the eyes. I'm out the skylight with my bag of loot before he's had a chance to scream.

If anyone were to ask me if I cried into my helmet as I was leaving Vegas I would have said no, but I did. Adrian broke my heart and I'm surprised that it had been so easy for him to do. Just because I am the way I am, and I am as strong as I am, I guess doesn't mean I'm totally invulnerable. I like to think it also means that maybe I'm not as bad as I always think I am inside. If I can care about Adrian, enough to make his betrayal something worth crying over, then maybe I'm not as broken as I thought. I don't know how I feel about that.

So I just ride the motorcycle faster and try to leave all of it in my dust. I'll be in Los Angeles in a few hours and all of this nonsense will be behind me. Perhaps that's the only way to get rid of these feelings, to ride away from them, to leave them with the carnage – I certainly don't know what to do with them if I hold onto them.

I don't make it to L.A., not even close actually. I stop 90 miles outside of Vegas, in this shitty little town called Baker, which is famous for this giant kind of run-down-looking thermometer. Apparently, it's the largest in the world, or the U.S., or something. It's super-unimpressive and I blow right past it and into the nearest convenience store. My hands had been shaking on the road and I'm telling myself it's from hunger. Anything so long as it's not me feeling bad about the slaughter I left in my wake back in Vegas. I'm trying to not let it get to me, but it's really the first time that I've just bathed in blood. And my hands are shaking.

So what.

After using the surprisingly clean bathroom at a 76 station I grab a diet coke and stalk the aisles for junk food. I barely look at what I'm grabbing, just picking up handfuls of the most brightly-colored packages until my arms are nearly full. At the register I drop the armload on the counter, save for one package of cupcakes, which I rip open with my teeth while still balancing the diet coke in my other hand. The cashier has her back partly to me and her feet up on a stool, a cell phone glued to her ear. She's snapping her gum and talking at the same time, which should be impossible, but apparently isn't. I'm not really in a hurry and my eyes are still hungry so I run my hands across more shiny packages of sugar and eavesdrop.

"No! I'm telling you it was SO gross…Yeah, a spike through his thing…YES! I swear Julie…"

My ears perk up and I lean over to look at her, eyebrows raised.

"Well no…I didn't get a picture. They made us turn our cell phones off, duh, otherwise it would be like all over YouTube and crap. But I have the flyer…no, of course it doesn't show that, but it shows… other stuff…" she gets quiet, listening to her friend. I stand at the counter, drumming my fingers impatiently on the Formica, while I lick cupcake off my hand. The girl pretends not to notice me, so I throw a Skor bar at her. It hits her right in her bleached blonde head and she sits up.

"Hey!" she says, looking pissed and rubbing the back of her head with her free hand, though it couldn't have possibly hurt.

"Yeah. HEY. Can I buy this crap or what?"

"Uh, yeah, can you hold on a freakin' second?"

"Yeah, um, I've already been holding."

She sighs dramatically and rolls her eyes, making her instantly at least three times less attractive.

"Jule – I gotta go. Yeah, I'll call you back," she stands, the flyer still in her hand and she starts ringing me up, hitting the keys extra hard, I suppose so I will know how extra annoyed she is. She's probably my age, but I feel a lot older.

"What were you talking about…Molly?" I ask, reading her nametag.

"Um. Like none of your business."

"What is this?" I ask, snatching the flyer from her hand with lightning speed.

"Hey!" she shouts for the second time. She's shocked, but also maybe a little scared and it quiets her down considerably. I'm always surprised by which people have good instincts and which don't. I wouldn't have pegged peroxide-brained Molly as even knowing what instinct is, but she's feeling like prey very suddenly; it comes off of her in waves that I can almost taste. It's the kind of thing that can save a person's life, maybe. I look away from Molly and her large prey eyes and examine the flyer. It's for a carnival sideshow and front and center is a man tattooed head to toe and pierced dozens of times. But that's not what really catches my eye. There are over-the-top stage names for all sorts of freaks, and on the bottom left it says, 'Strongest Woman Alive!' I look back at Molly.

"Where was this?"

"Uh. Phoenix. I was in Phoenix this weekend to see my brother…the address is um…at the bottom," she trails off and looks away. I stare at the words 'Strongest Woman Alive' like they're written in my own personal language, one that nobody else can understand. Molly shifts her weight uneasily. "Your total is $19.01."

I drop a twenty on the counter. It's crumpled from my palm. I hadn't realized I'd been squeezing it. "I'm taking this," I say, holding up the flyer, and grabbing my plastic bag of treats. She opens her mouth as if to protest but must think better of it because she only, casts her eyes to her shoes silently.

Back on the road again, I'd hoped the words from the flyer would fade away, but if anything they burn brighter in my brain.

Just outside of Barstow, I see the sign for the I-40 headed for Needles, which is the direction I would need to go for Phoenix. Without hesitating I take the exit. It's going to take me in the opposite direction of Los Angeles, but there's nothing specific driving me to L.A. anyway, and since reading those three words I pretty much can't think of anything more important than being in a room with the 'strongest woman alive.'

Should be interesting.

O

It's still early when I find myself standing outside his house, across the street, under the shade of a big tree. When he emerges from the front door the sight of him hits me like being doused with ice water. He looks just like our father. Tall and broad shouldered but slim with dark, thick, almost unruly hair. He has a strong, handsome jaw line and skin much more olive than mine, which is pale and pinkish. I want to run up to him, embrace him, escape with him, and never have to talk about what has happened to us. But I resist. I've long ago forgiven him for not coming to rescue me, but my sin seems much greater than his; it always has.

I tail him from a safe distance, my exceptional sight making me particularly good at it. We walk for nearly fifteen blocks, until he comes upon a big elementary school with a small, mostly asphalt yard. Kids are hustling into the building as a long, loud bell rings out and as Jasper draws closer he breaks into a jog. I cross the grounds filled with swings, a jungle gym, and basketball hoops, heading for a bank of windows on the ground floor. The second to last window has an overflowing rowdy bunch of kids – maybe second graders – and Jasper bursts through the door smiling and out of breath. Some of the kids shout his name and I can't help but smile at the sound of it. He has a hell of a time calming them down and getting them all in their chairs, but it all seems in good fun. I watch as they take turns coming up to the front of the class and talking about the most important person in their lives. Some of them have drawn pictures or brought props like photos and toys to represent their person. It's mostly a hilarious parade of pets and parents with a couple of best friends and uncles thrown in until a kid named Noah, serious but with a mischievous glint in his eye, comes to the front of the class. I can tell from Jasper's expression that Noah is one of his favorites. He's smiling even before Noah starts.

"My favorite person is my new baby sister, cause she's going to be my best friend an' slave 'til I get a baby brother, which will be much better," Noah says with pride, holding up a pair of pink baby booties. Jasper starts to laugh and then covers his mouth and coughs, while several of the Noah's male classmates nod solemnly in agreement.

"Does your sister have a name, Noah?"

"Yeah, it's Emma, but I call her E-dawg."

"I'm sure your mom loves that," Jasper says with a smile. Noah nods confidently.

"Ya, she likes it," Noah pauses, arms crossed, "You got any brothers or sisters, Mr. J?"

Jasper corrects Noah's language, "You mean do I have any brothers or sisters."

"Ya, ya," Noah says waving his hand dismissively, "Do ya?" I'm holding my breath in anticipation of Jasper's answer.

"No," Jasper says simply and with a smile, "No brothers or sisters for Mr. J," he says ushering Noah back to his seat with his pink booties proudly in hand.

This information hits me like a bullet. Like a million bullets. It's not even like there is sadness in his face. He said it as simply as if I had long ago been wiped away, or worse, never existed. I pull back from the window and stumble over my own feet across the yard, eventually falling into a swing far too small for me. My sneakers drag clumsily across the black tar, tears falling onto my jeans in desperate little plops.

Clearly, he hasn't forgiven me.

I'm not sure how long I wallow, but a small clear voice rouses me from it. "Your hair is pretty," it says, and I look up to find a tiny girl in a quilted orange jacket far too warm for early June staring at me. I wipe my eyes, embarrassed.

"Thanks," I say, smiling a little.

"Are you sad?" she asks, pulling herself up into the swing next to me, her little pointed toes barely grazing the ground. "Did someone kill your turtle? 'Cause my brother killed my turtle and even though he sayed it was an accident I still cried lots."

I try not to smile. "I'm sorry about your turtle. What was his name?"

"His name was Gregory," she says, deadly serious. I try not to smile again.

"That's a very good name for a turtle."

"Ya," she nods in agreement.

"What's your name?" I ask.

"Nu-uh, you gotta tell me yours first, or else you're a stranger and I ain't 'sposed ta talk ta you," she says.

"I'm Bonnie."

"I never heard that name before," she says thinking hard. "I'm Celia," she adds, putting out her tiny hand for a proper handshake. I take it gingerly and we have a little silent shake together.

"What are you doing out here, Celia?" I ask, looking around, wondering about her parents.

"I got to go to the dentist," she says, sticking out her tongue in disgust.

"Where's your mom?"

"Inside. She tol' me to sit still on the steps."

"Well, this isn't the steps," I say tentatively.

"Jeez! They're right there," she says, gesturing at the steps thirty feet away.

"Okay, okay," I say, raising my hands in defeat.

"What are YOU doing out here?" she asks with a challenge.

"Just saying goodbye to someone," I say.

"Who?"

"My brother," I say, and Celia turns up her nose at the word.

"Hmmm. Just be glad you don't have no turtle," she says under her breath. This time I can't help smiling and have to stifle a laugh. Just then Celia's mother emerges from the building.

"Celia!" she yells a little too loudly and Celia pops off the swing.

"See ya Bonnie," she says running toward the front steps.

"See ya Celia," I echo back.

Halfway to her mother, she turns around, not unlike a pumpkin in her puffy orange coat. "I still like your hair a real lot!" she shouts.

I smile and shout back, "I like yours too."

Long after Celia and her mother have left, I pick up my duffel and leave the yard. There's nothing for me here. He's obviously moved on. I don't want to hurt him any more than I already have.

It's back to the train yard for me.

I wait all afternoon for something headed west and take the first one that even suggests that direction. I'm going to start over somewhere else. Maybe even be someone new.

●

I wake up in my crappy Phoenix motel room, the gross comforter on the pretty much gross floor, the white sheets in knots around me and candy wrappers strewn across the bed like opened presents. I've slept a long time, maybe even into the late afternoon. I'd shed my blood caked clothing like a second skin the night before and I stare at them now wondering what I should do with them. I suppose a dumpster somewhere will do. I hop across the dark carpet and into the bathroom, hoping a hot shower will loosen up my muscles after the long bike ride. I don't really hurt but my body feels more stiff than normal. The shower is glorious.

Later, my hair in a fluffy white towel, I dig through my bag looking for new jeans and a t-shirt and cuss at the bag when I remember that I never managed to get my cat suit back from whoever had it, whoever stripped it off me in the desert. I kick at the bed in frustration. Before fully committing to my t-shirt and jeans I go digging through the bag of loot from Melvin's safe. Inside his bag there's a separate, smaller plastic bag, which has a bunch of the stuff he stole from my room including my first stolen necklace and miraculously, at the bottom, my cat suit, folded nicely. I pull it out and try to shake it free of wrinkles. It's a mess, covered in old blood and there's a huge tear where my abdomen is supposed to go. There's also a rip in the calf, a bunch along the shoulder and neck, and tons on the back, I guess, from where the dogs attacked me. I don't know what the hell Melvin could have wanted with a cheap nylon cat suit covered in blood but the potential creepiness gives me a slight chill and makes me gladder than ever that I put a bullet in him.

I fold the suit back up, happy to have it, regardless of its condition and pull on jeans and a black t-shirt. The cat suit would be better, but this will do. It never occurred to me until I saw the flyer with those words 'strongest woman alive' that there might be others like me, but now that I've thought about it, I can't get it out of my mind.

The show is in a massive run-down warehouse, but I can tell it just from the size of the crowd and the shitty signage that it doesn't come close to filling the space. It truly is just a sideshow of freaks, and not really a circus or carnival or fair or whatever they call them. I pay at the window of a makeshift booth and walk in among aimless sheep all headed toward a main stage. I try to follow some posters that go in the opposite direction, but a wiry punk-looking kid not much older than me stops me and kind of ushers me back the other way. I point toward the other posters and the smaller stage I'm heading to at the other end of the warehouse.

"Miss, the main stage is behind you. The show will be starting in a few minutes."

"I'm not interested in the tattooed dude. I came to see the strongwoman."

"Sorry then, doll, but she's not on tonight."

"Why not?"

"She only does the weekend show. The bigger show that includes all the acts. This is Monday, only the big names go on tonight, she's not on until Friday."

"You've gotta be kidding me." I pull out the flyer from my back pocket. "It doesn't say that on here," I complain, thrusting it at him.

"Yeah, it does. See here at the bottom. 'Not all acts available at all shows'."

"But it doesn't say which damn acts," I say. He shrugs his shoulders like it is the least of many problems in his life, a 'sorry' that he doesn't mean at all. I think about punching him in the face. But I take a couple deep breaths and decide not to; he's not what I'm here for. I start to walk away and then turn back. "What's her name?"

"Whose name?"

I roll my eyes. "The strongwoman."

"Lena. Her name's Lena."

"Thanks," I walk away and think about heading out, still having no interest in pierced and tattooed freaks that, at best, have a high tolerance for pain, until I see a woman in a white corset top and pristine white leather pants leaning up against a wall talking to a guy with a giant head. She's extremely fit, with the biggest arms I've ever seen on a woman in real life. I look at the flyer. Same short dark hair with a single curl on her pale forehead, same broad shoulders and narrow hips. Same thin lipped smile and dark eyes. I take a seat in the back, close to her and her big-headed friend. When the lights go down and the music starts pounding, the bass echoing up through my metal seat and, colored lights dance across the stage, I hear her speak to her friend.

"Ugh. I can't watch this show another time today. I'm going to go out for a smoke." Her friend nods and I watch her duck out a side exit. I wait a few moments and follow her out. She's walking through the parking lot to a field, cigarette already lit. Once she gets to the open field it's dark enough that the burn from her cigarette is the brightest thing around. When I'm close enough that I know I'll startle her I call out.

"Hey, Lena," I say. I'm surprised she doesn't jump. She just turns around coolly.

"Yeah?" But her eyes narrow as if she had expected to recognize me and now doesn't. "Who's that?" she asks, squinting a little bit.

"I'm Lola."

"I know you?"

"No."

"Then what are you doing out here? Audience and fans aren't supposed to be out here, this area is private…restricted."

"Sorry. I just wanted to talk to you."

"Yeah? What about?"

"Well, I guess I just wanted to know how you got into this – how'd you become a strongwoman?" I ask, trying to sound young and naïve. She snorts a laugh.

"College drop-out. Broke up with my boyfriend. Lifted weights. Got lost. Needed to pay the bills. It's a real skyrocket of a career. Don't tell me you're interested."

"Sorta," I say. She squints at me again, eyeing the slender bones in my wrists.

"Gotta say kid, it doesn't really look like you've got it in you. Maybe pick something a little more up your alley. You ever even lifted weights?"

"No. But I'm pretty strong."

"Sure. I'm sure you are." She flicks the cigarette into the dirt, stamping it out with her white boot. I don't know why she's wearing all white, it seems weird.

"How strong are you?" I ask, innocently as I can.

"I don't know…I mean, how do I even answer that question? Faster than a speeding bullet? More powerful than a locomotive?" she laughs again. "Hard question to answer."

"Ballpark it," I say, too sharply, regretting it almost immediately as I can see it trigger an alarm somewhere in her, as if everything in her has suddenly tensed up.

"Nah. I've gotta get back in. Can't have you giving away all my secrets anyway," she starts to walk back to the auditorium and I grab her arm hard as she passes me.

"Ballpark it," I say again even harder.

"What the hell? Get your hands off me," she says, smacking my hand off her with surprising force.

"Nice," I say, nodding.

"What the hell is wrong with you?" she asks, sneering and rubbing her arm where I'd grabbed her.

"Let's arm-wrestle," I say, smiling in the dark, revealing all my shining, slightly crooked, teeth.

"Why the hell would I do that? Get away from me before I call the cops."

"Why does the strongest woman alive need the cops?"

"Don't be a moron. Get out of here now."

"No. Let's arm-wrestle."

"I'm not arm-wrestling you, kid. Get the hell out of here, NOW," she turns to walk away and I draw back my fist and punch her in her lower back, hard. Not hard enough to cripple her, even if she is just a normal person, but hard enough that she'll take me seriously. She falls to the ground on her knees, her skintight leather pants instantly covered in mud and dead grass. Her hand goes to her back.

"Jeezus. What's wrong with you?"

"I said, let's arm-wrestle."

"And I said no."

"Let me put it another way," I breathe, leaning down near her ear. "We arm-wrestle and you win, I'll let you live."

"And if I don't arm wrestle you?" she asks, sounding unsure for the first time.

"Then I don't," I hold out my hand to her, offering to help her up. She looks at me like I'm insane, which is fair, I suppose. For a second I think she's not going to take my hand, but then I see something click in her eyes and she reaches out to take it. When she does, she pulls as hard as she can, trying to pull me down onto the ground with her, but I see it coming and anchor myself. I don't move when she pulls and the effort yanks her shoulder out of joint. She cries out in pain.

"Gonna be harder to arm-wrestle now," I say, clucking my tongue against the roof of my mouth with disappointment. She kicks at my legs, trying to sweep them out from under me. I think briefly about dodging her leg, but at the last second decide to take the kick, see what she's got. I steel myself for the impact and I feel her shin break against mine. She screams again. I worry for a moment that someone's going to hear her, but I can still feel the pumping bass through the ground and even 'oohs and ahhs' above the music as the performance continues. Lena lies on the ground, pathetic and bleeding. I kneel down next to her in the mud, glad I'm just in jeans and not my precious cat suit.

"I just wanted to see how strong you were. See if you were anything real, anything I should be worried about." I survey her broken parts. "Clearly, I didn't need to be concerned." Underneath the pain, there's some relief in her eyes; something I've said makes her think I'm not going to kill her. I almost feel bad for leading her astray and I frown a bit. "I do have to kill you though, can't have people like you walking around knowing there's someone like me. Besides," I say, my voice becoming a bit of a growl, "I find the idea of you disgusting. Almost like you're a total affront to my existence. Yeah, you shouldn't be pretending to be something you're not...not without expecting the real thing to come and challenge you least ways." I lean on my knee. She closes her eyes, probably feeling sorry for herself, and I can taste the fear rippling off her body. It's like a salty metallic wave that fills my senses. It's delicious. And I want to swallow it whole. "I would like to know though, just out of curiosity, if you don't mind, how much can you bench press?" I ask. Lena's eyes stay closed.

"360 is my best."

"Hmm. Is it just me, or is that not much?"

"It's good. It's very good. It's more than most men can..." she trails off.

"But, it's not even like a record, is it?"

"No."

"So what I want to know," I say pulling out the flyer from my pocket and holding it in front of her face. "Is where do you get off calling yourself the 'strongest woman alive'?"

"I...I don't know," she stammers. "What is it you want?"

I stand up, put my hands on my hips, and look around the field. "Hmmm. Y'know Lena, that's a hell of a question. I mean, in the broader scope of things, I'm thinking world domination of some kind, but tonight, tonight what I was looking for was someone with power. And I really didn't find it, did I?"

"Just let me go, okay? I'm not going to tell anyone about you." She props herself up a little.

"Sure, sure, no problem." I lean down and put my hands on the side of her face, as if to tell her a precious secret and then I twist her neck sharply to the right. She lies there, filthy in her formerly pristine white clothing, staring up blankly at where the stars should be. I feel revolted and scammed. I walk back toward the auditorium muttering to myself, "360 pounds." Although, the truth is, I have no idea how much I can bench-press. It's certainly more than 360, though. It's gotta be. Maybe one day I'll have to find out.

On my way back to the auditorium I see some trailers for the traveling show and have an idea. There are six trailers, one with 'Manager' written on the door. I head over to that one and break in. The lock is cheap and snaps off in my hand. Once inside, I ransack the place looking for a schedule of performances. In one drawer I find exactly what I'm hoping for: a calendar showing other performances throughout the country and a list of other traveling shows, where they'll be and when. I guess so they can avoid being in the same areas at the same time. It even has a map. It's all I need to find any other women pretending to be strongwomen. It's worth checking out. They might not all be as fake as Lena. In fact, there's a show east of here a few hundred miles with a strongwoman. Yeah, maybe "Joan – The World's Strongest Woman" will actually have something legit to offer.

○

I ride the rails trying to forget about Jasper. About Rachael and Sharon. My mother and father. And I focus on the idea of starting over until it's the only thing I can see.

It sounds clean. It feels clean.

The idea of being someone else, maybe in a whole new city, with an entirely new name. With those things, can I also somehow have a new past?

I'm not sure how long I've been on the train but at least one night has passed.

On the third night, sleeping in an abandoned car that's not going anywhere, totally unsure of where this new me should go, I have a different dream of my mother. Though they're generally all black crows and strange portents I don't understand, this one is really just a vivid memory of her the year she died, played back in a bright Technicolor dream. It's one of the last memories I have of her, though I'd long ago forgotten it until now. She's strong and vibrant here, seeming more like the mother I remember, not like some mythical creature constantly trying to warn me of imagined future danger. And more than just seeming like my mother, she seems like a woman; a girl even.

Just a girl finding her way, like me.

In the dream we're at a carnival, the tinny familiar music soft in my ears. She's left me with my brother and my father so we can go on rides and eat sweets, but I've given them the slip and followed her through the crowds like a miniature spy, afraid to let her out of my sight, afraid she'll disappear if I let her. That was always my fear, even then, that she was going to disappear on me.

I watch her from under cover of a clump of rowdy teenagers as she buys a sideshow ticket and slips inside. Though the sights inside are probably alternately fascinating and horrifying to a child of five or six, I'm not paying attention to any of it, because all I can see is the look on my mother's face. Most people walking through the show gasp in horror, or laugh and point fingers, but my mother's face is serene; a contemplative, compassionate slate of kindness and solidarity that I can't understand, like she's in her own personal church. What is she seeing in the distorted reflections of these people that I cannot? When I emerge from the sideshow I can't for the life of me remember seeing anything inside except her face.

When I wake, the tinny carnival music is still heavy in my ears. I can't shake it and, for a moment, worry I've trapped myself in some half-dream, half-waking state. After a few long moments however, I realize that the music is real, and that it is, in fact, the music that must have brought on the dream and not the other way around. I pull my duffel bag together and hop off the train car and into a dark, empty field. I turn around, trying to feel where the sound is coming from.

It's behind me.

I climb up the ladder on the outside of the car and pull myself onto the roof. As I do, I see the bright colored lights of a traveling carnival illuminating the horizon. I smile, excited for the first time in a long while.

People are streaming into the front gates. It looks like admission is free, which is good because I don't have extra money to spend on carnivals. I don't know if my sense of what is right would allow me to sneak in, and I suddenly know I have to go in. I jog across the field with my bag slung over my shoulder and wander

in casually, mesmerized by the lights, my eyes peeled for anything
that looks like a sideshow. I see conjoined twins manning a corn
dog/hot dog kiosk and wonder if everyone here will be as
interesting as the girls running the food stands. Toward the back of
the carnival, on the right, past most of the rides and across from the
funhouse, I finally see it: a real live sideshow. I'm honestly shocked
that they still exist – it seems like something from olden days, but
beautifully painted posters line the walls up to the entrance not
unlike the way it looked when I followed my mother in so many
years ago. The first poster reads '*Casanova - The Most Handsome
Sword Swallower To Ever Walk The Earth!*' It's followed by a newer
looking poster of '*Mona & Nona – The Singing Siamese Twins – Joined
At The Hip With Perfect Natural Pitch!*' which is weird because the
women look nothing like the conjoined twins I saw at the corn dog
kiosk. Next to the twins is an ominous poster for '*The Fabulous Mr.
& Mrs. Ink!*' and an image of an intertwined couple that appear to
be covered entirely in tattoos and nothing else, Next is the '*The
Maddrox Family of Miracle Midgets!*' which is mostly broad smiles
plastered on tiny faces, bodies clad in bright spandex. But the
poster next to the Maddrox Family stops me in my tracks. A poster
for '*JOAN – THE WORLD'S STRONGEST WOMAN!*' and
suddenly I am oblivious to everything else around me. Underneath
the bright red text is a fairly realistic rendering of an enormous,
beautiful woman with dark hair and long limbs lifting a huge barbell
above her head. I take the next few steps toward the poster with
my arm outstretched and trace the slightly fading red words with
my finger, surprised how important they feel to me.

I'd never thought of this before; that there could be
someone else like me out there. That instead of getting lost and
becoming someone else I should instead be looking for others like
me, to find where I really come from and what I really am. It all
seems so clear staring at Joan's poster. Seeing her looking back at
me through the canvas I can't believe how much I want there to be
someone like me; how much I've been yearning for it without
realizing it. Tears pool up in my eyes at the thought of the
loneliness falling off of me in sheets as I confess all my secrets to
someone who can understand.

I buy my five-dollar ticket, a painful price for my meager
remaining funds, and walk through the doorway. Inside, I hear
what must be Mona and Nona's lovely singing pour from one tent

and the 'oohs and ahhs' of people watching the Maddrox Family, and a few girls emerging from Mr. and Mrs. Ink's tent with disgusted looks on their faces. "I can't believe they are totally naked. So gross!"

But I have my eyes on only one prize so I ignore all of this and push through to Joan's tent, located at the very end of the sideshow. When I get there, it's empty, people not having made it to the end yet. I carefully pick out what I deem to be the perfect seat, right in the middle, third row, and wait for the small, tiered benches to fill. Props cover the stage: a huge barbell, a giant tree trunk, a massive boulder, a medicine ball, a partial hull of a rusted car with two front seats still intact, and in the background, a massive scale.

Within ten minutes the tent is filled to capacity and there is a strange buzzing inside me that I've never felt before, like a giant butterfly is beating its wings furiously in the cage of my chest – equal parts terror and excitement, nauseous but exhilarated. I'm not sure what's happening to me, but I'm trying to chalk it up to anticipation, even while my body screams out something different. My vision blurs and the room spins. I clutch at the edge of my wooden seat until my palms bleed as I try to keep myself upright. My heart is hammering and my throat is dry, I'm not sure if I'll faint or fly. This is the moment.

I realize, as the curtains part, that I'm expecting to see my mother.

●

I stride through the front gates of 'Joan's' carnival, with an eye out for the sideshow. I have to admit, this carnival looks like a winner – there are all sorts of freaks walking around, including actual Siamese twins running the hot dog and corn dog kiosk. If real, honest-to-god, though powerless freaks are running food stands, what might they have lurking in the actual sideshow? I'm getting giddy with anticipation, and buy a corn dog from the prettier of the Siamese with a wallet I lift off a young couple in love.

I see the sideshow in the distance and make my way there while devouring my corn dog and observing the freaks all around me with an annoyed eye. I'm beginning to understand that 'freak' is definitely the right word. People with deformities, and even crazier, people who deform themselves on purpose, and people who pretend to be things they aren't. Ironically, I've realized that I at least have more respect for the real freaks, since maybe they don't have as many options. But what of these people who turn themselves into freaks on purpose? I can't figure that out at all. I suppose a person could argue that I turned myself into a freak when I killed my mother, but I'd like to see anyone turn down my power. And also, it totally called to me. Long before I even knew what it was I could feel it calling to me, like those Sirens that killed that Othello guy...or whatever that story was. No. I'm not like these people. I'm unique in the world. I'm more and more sure of that every day.

But when I walk into Joan's tent it's like someone hits me with a sledgehammer.

Something is here for real.

It's not like with Lena.

I can taste it.

Real power.

I grab onto some benches nearby and take a seat near the edge of the tent before I almost faint. The feeling is so powerful it's like the air is water pressing on me from all sides, like I'm a submarine about to be crushed by ocean depths. Some guy next to me offers me a napkin and asks if I'm okay, but it sounds like he's underwater and a thousand miles away.

"Fine. Leave me 'lone," is all I manage. He doesn't like that and scoots farther away, which is my preference anyway. I put my head between my legs and breathe in some deep breaths trying to get my bearings. What if whoever is here causing me to feel this way is feeling this too? What if I can't stand up, let alone fight, if they reveal themselves?

What have I done?

PART II:

and here we test our powers

•

I mostly watch the show through my hands. I can only assume Joan is the one causing all this pain and conflict in my body since she's the star with the purported power, but I feel so freaking sick I can't bring myself to do anything but stare at the ground through my hands. The best I can do is an occasional glance at Joan, who seems completely unaffected by my presence.

Through the snippets and stolen glances her show looks like bullshit but that doesn't mean she is. Maybe she spends half her time hiding out, just like me, pretending she is less than she is. I have to admit, if she's faking it's a pretty good cover – hiding out in plain sight and all that. It makes sense in a backwards way.

There's an unnaturally bright light somewhere in the tent but I'm too disoriented to be able to tell if it's just part of the show or something more troubling.

I feel vulnerable in a way I haven't since before I killed Delia. All weak and kitteny, like I couldn't even take a punch, let alone throw one.

It's horrible.

o

She is, of course, not my mother.

This is also not the Joan from the poster I have fallen in love with; this woman is only about five foot seven, and though you can see that she was once a great beauty, her face is now streaked with lines and sagging skin caked in too much stage makeup. She wears a complicated costume that covers most of her body and makes it difficult to tell where one part of her begins and another ends. She also looks very unhappy. She's smiling, of course, but it looks like the forced smile of a professional showman. Her eyes actually look unbelievably lonely. In fact, it's her eyes that convince me she might be the real thing – seeing my own loneliness reflected back at me so strongly.

My hands tighten on the bench as things inside me continue to roll and screech, and I worry about snapping the bench in half and sending all the people next to me careening to the ground, so I put my hands in my lap. I ball them into tight fists, my nails cutting into my flesh, and trickles of blood seeping out between the cracks of my fingers and onto my jeans. What is happening to me? Is Joan causing it? It's been building ever since people started filling the stands and if it keeps going I feel like something is going to explode from inside me. As I try to keep my focus on Joan my muscles feel like they're humming hard inside my limbs, like a car on a starting line, ready to leap forward. The world around me is spongy and unreal. I feel like poking the man sitting next to me, to see if he is made of flesh, or of water that will ripple and collapse away from me. There's a fire in my gut that is both pleasure and pain, and it threatens to tear open like a cut tension wire, snapping the world around it into glass shards. The feeling is almost enough to solidify my belief in Joan before she does anything and despite her outward appearance.

The show itself is predictable at best, with Joan playing to the crowd more than doing anything too fantastic. She lifts and moves heavy things. I hear occasional gasps from the crowd – as if they didn't expect to actually be impressed. My physical situation is becoming so bad that I can barely look at her. There's a bright, unnatural light coming from somewhere that isn't Joan, but I'm afraid to look for it. What if it turns me to ash? Right now I couldn't even run from it, let alone fight it. How do you fight powerful mystery light, anyway? I look up to see Joan lifting a large car frame with people in it for a brief moment. There's a smattering of surprised applause before half a dozen men step in to take it from her. Joan takes a bow and exits quickly and efficiently and it's as if she was never there. I half-fall, half-run from my seat and duck out the side-exit, both in panic to escape and in crushing fear that she'll disappear. As I move from the tent, and Joan moves from me, the feeling subsides slightly, enough so that I can at least stand erect and stop cutting into my palms with my clenched fists. I'm hesitant to get closer to her when I see her enter a trailer in the distance, for fear of feeling all those things again, but I'll also never be able to forget those feelings and I need to know where they're coming from, what they're about.

And most of all, I'm desperate to see if she sees anything in me.

•

As the show ends, I sit still, waiting for my bearings to return to me and, sure enough, as the tent empties out, I begin to feel more like my badass self again. I wait until I'm alone in the tent – the lights still on, the dusty floor quiet all around me, empty wooden benches my only company – before I try to move. When I stumble off the bench and make for an exit it's in the opposite direction of Joan.

The deeper into the carnival I go, and the further from Joan's tent, the better I feel. It's strange, when I think about the feeling now I realize it hadn't exactly made me feel weak, but it had definitely been like touching something powerful, something I wasn't so sure I was stronger than.

I take a slow walk around the carnival, attempting to shake off the last tendrils of the strange feeling.

Trying to remember what a total badass I am.

○

It starts to rain as I move toward the trailer I saw Joan enter and when I get there I realize that I've been holding my breath the whole time. I release it in one massive exhale and rap, as lightly as possible, on her door. I feel like I've been waiting my whole life for this moment.

There's no answer so I rap harder.

A croaking "come" is all I hear in response. It's certainly not the voice of my mother I realize I've still been hoping for. I hesitate, there in the rain, wanting so desperately for something important to happen once we're face to face.

Wanting someone like me. Someone to talk to. Someone to understand everything.

I turn the handle and push through the door into the darkness. It seems incredibly overwhelming, that darkness, but my eyes adjust and I manage to not trip over the multitude of things that litter the floor. I keep my head down, out of fear or respect; I'm not sure which. A light near the back clicks on and illuminates the space in a pale yellow glow.

"Uh, who are you?" she asks, not unkindly, but confused, her voice coarse. I keep my eyes trained on my shoes as I stand there like an idiot delivery boy waiting for a tip that's never coming. I reach for my voice but it just cracks. I look up and see the room is covered in posters of Joan. They begin to the left of me and go all the way around the room, seemingly in order of appearance, as the first one is of Joan very young, maybe 16 at most. The poster proclaims her "JOAN ~ THE AMAZON QUEEN". She is rendered beautifully, barely clothed, long dark hair flowing freely down her back. She is lifting a car in the image, but she looks more like supermodel than a strongwoman. She's stunning. As my eyes flick around the room I see her beauty declining as age and abuse take hold and her body becomes more and more disfigured, until the last poster, the current poster. The poster I had first seen, a poster in which she is still beautiful, but now, in comparison to the others, seems like a sad testament to time. I look toward the back of the trailer trying to separate her from her silhouette in the doorway.

"Can I help you?" she prods.

"I...I..." I stammer like a schoolgirl with a crush. "I just really wanted to meet you," I say. She laughs, a kind, almost wise. laugh.

"Why on earth would you want to do that kid?"

"I just thought..." I trail off, feeling stupid. I just thought maybe we were related? That sounds so dumb. She's going to think I'm an idiot. Suddenly she moves from the doorway into the main room and I almost fall backward in shock. Up close, with no trick lighting, costumes, and makeup, she is nothing like the poster version of herself. Her skin is pockmarked, her body rough, darkly hairy, and strangely-muscled. Her hair has mostly fallen out and she's holding a long brown wig in her hands. I try to hide my surprise but she sees it anyway.

"They don't put that part on the poster," she says, nodding her head at the inaccurate image, "Or if we can help it, on the stage," she adds. She then looks at the "Amazon Queen" poster opposite the current version. "You know the worst thing? I could lift that car frame back then, I could even do a couple reps with it – I mean with the drugs I could – and I was still so beautiful. But now? Hmmmph. Age, life, and too many drugs, and I look like this and I can't even lift that car anymore. Not the metal one least ways, just the fake one we use now."

"Drugs?" I'm dumbfounded.

"How else you think I did it, kid? Steroids. I don't know of another way…of course if I knew then, what I would have to look at every day, how I'd feel, maybe I'd have thought twice," she eases herself onto an old sofa. "'Course I was such a glory hound back then…" she stares at the ravishing but faded image of herself. "Maybe it wouldn't have made a difference."

My whole world crumbles. This woman is not related to me, doesn't understand me, and can't tell me the secrets of me. She isn't a closeted superhero; she's just a girl in a carnival sideshow who has turned into an old woman in a carnival sideshow. She must see my dejected look.

"Did I disappoint you, kid?" she asks.

I shake my head.

"But I wasn't what you were expecting?"

I shake my head no again.

"Sorry about that. But it's probably just as well for you to learn that now, I guess. Most of the world isn't what a body would expect," she says wisely, fidgeting with a dark wig in her hands.

I look at her. "Thanks for talking to me,"

"Sure," she says, and then adds dryly. "Anything for a fan."

"Take care, Joan," I say, turning to leave.

She calls out to me as I put my hand on the door. "Hey, what's your name?"

I turn to her. "Anna," I say. It's the name I've been thinking I'd use for my 'all-new life' but it sounds wrong when I say it aloud and Joan looks at me, one eyebrow raised in question. "No, no, that's not my name," I whisper. "My name is Bonnie Braverman," I say, squaring my shoulders at the sound of it. She presses her lips together and squints her eye a little bit as if she's imagining up a poster for me.

"That's a real good carnival name, Bonnie. You could make good use of that name."

"Yeah," I say. "But, maybe not here."

She nods in agreement. "Yeah, maybe not here. I don't think this is the place for you."

"I think you're right," I say. "Goodbye, Joan."

As I shut the door behind me, I hear Joan say goodbye to me as well. Outside the trailer, I am suddenly as dizzy as I had been in Joan's tent while she performed. The powerful nausea comes at me full force in a wave and I run to the edge of the field nearby to throw up. I crawl into the tall grass and heave, for what feels like minutes, into the damp dirt. It exhausts me, and when there's nothing left to throw up I lie back on the crunchy grass and stare up at the sky. My muscles are humming and everything feels tight and loose at the same time, like I might come unstuck from time, the universe, something. The green and yellow strands of grass sways above and around me in the breeze, occasionally cutting into my view of the black-blue sky and handfuls of stars. I don't know what's causing these intense physical symptoms, but it can't be Joan. I felt nothing standing there with her. I try to think about the people I'd seen in the tent at her show, but I'd been so focused on Joan, and so disoriented that I can't recall much else.

I suddenly feel a little afraid about what might be watching me, what might be looking for me. Despite my mother's cryptic dream warnings, I've always felt so invisible and so protected because of what I can do and so it's particularly unsettling to suddenly wonder if I'm being hunted. I crawl under a break in the chain-link fence and then deeper and deeper into the open meadow surrounding the carnival, trying to escape the feeling.

●

I find the right trailer by playing a giant game of hot and cold with myself. Veering one direction and feeling better and then veering the other and feeling the world become a Tilt O' Whirl on crack. It's hard to fight my natural impulse to feel better and avoid puking my guts up, but eventually I'm about fifty feet behind a pretty lonely-looking trailer, practically on my knees with the pain in my gut, knowing that, despite the sorry looks of me, I must have hit the goddamn goldmine.

I half-stumble half-crawl to the trailer and when I knock, a woman inside says, "Yeah honey, you forget something?" I glance around wondering who she might be talking to, but don't see anyone nearby. Once inside, I see Joan, and the look on her face when I walk in is priceless, and if the feeling of sickness hadn't been fading, instead of increasing, I would have thought she was who I was looking for based on that look.

Her trailer is dark except for some warm light coming from a backroom. There are posters covering the walls, most of her in younger, hotter days. It's almost sad. She'd been pretty smokin' when she first started out, and maybe just a little older than me, but she isn't much to look at now, that's for sure. She's all old and ruined now, and standing there, maybe twelve feet away from me, filling up a doorway in an old bathrobe. The scene reminds me of Delia. In fact, despite their obvious physical differences Joan does remind me of my mother, in all the pathetic ways.

And I find myself angry with her. Angry that she isn't my mother and angry that she reminds me of her in the first place, but I can't decide which is worse. I can taste her fear and desperation even though I haven't done anything yet. Tasting her fear is making my stomach growl and I didn't realize until now that I'd been hungering for fear like hers. It's been days since I feasted on Lena, you know, like metaphorically feasted...I didn't actually eat her or anything...gross.

I wonder if I should feel bad for Joan instead of mad at her.

I wonder again if there's something broken inside me and think of Adrian, for just a moment. I slide my finger along a dusty, fake wood tabletop. "Hello Joan."

"Who are you?" she asks, trying to sound strong. I appreciate her attempt, it's quite frankly more fun when they don't mew like injured kittens.

"Lola. Lola LeFever," I say. She laughs a little under her breath. "What's so funny?" I ask, my voice hard and flat.

"You're just a kid. I can see now that you're just a kid, but that's a good name I suppose...if you're in a circus."

"It's a good name no matter where you are," I say.

"No, really only if you work for the circus...or maybe if you live in a comic book, I guess."

"What does that mean?" I demand. Angry that this worthless, deformed woman is enjoying herself at my expense.

"Lola LeFever? It's ridiculous..." she trails off, chuckling to herself.

"Listen grandma, I'm not here to talk about my name. I'm here to freaking kill you - so you might want to try to take this – and me – a little more seriously."

"Oh, I see. Lola LeFever is going to kill me? Please. You sound like a mediocre porn star...at best."

"You're gonna take that back," I say, my voice hardening. She laughs again. I'm getting real sick of her laughing. "Y'know this is why killers shouldn't talk to their victims. Often enough, I've found my victims don't understand how serious the conversation is until it's much too late. I keep trying to help you understand how serious it is, but you're ignoring me."

That gets her. She's still trying to be tough, but I can see a change in her eyes – the acceptance of what she had first felt when I came in. I make a move toward her and she takes half a step backward. Once she does that it's all over, and she knows it. I can see it spread from her eyes into her whole face, like disease. The fear ratchets up in the room until it's almost solid, like I can touch it and squeeze the life out of it, just like everything else.

"You know, I came here because I thought you might be something special – something like me – but I can see now you're worthless, just like the rest," I say. She takes another step back from me, but she's got nowhere to go. I move across the room at neck-breaking speed, and we're eye to eye faster than she can blink. She breathes in like she's going to say something but I'm tired of hearing her talk. She's never going to say anything again.

I plunge my fist straight through her chest. I feel her heart beating in my hand, for just a moment, before it's permanently still.

Her body falls away from me and hits the floor with a defeated thud. I jump away from it, leaving a bloody handprint on the wall in the process. I wash my hands in the tiny kitchenette sink and dry them on a ruffled yellow towel, tossing it at the body wedged in the hallway on my way out the door.

I step outside feeling sated and full. I break the knob off the front door, hopefully putting a little distance between me and the discovery of the body.

My instinct is to leave immediately, but I can't resist a few more passes around the grounds in the hopes of tracking down whatever was giving off the power I had wrongly attributed to Joan.

I pace the carnival, reaching out with all I've got, trying to locate that horrible feeling from before. It's bizarre but as sick as it had made me feel, it had also been strangely intoxicating. In a way, I can't wait to get another taste, as much so that I can devour that raw untapped power, as for the chance to kill it and make sure there's nothing standing in my way on my path to awesome world domination.

But if I'm totally honest, part of me is relieved not to find it. I'm not sure I'm stronger than it is. Whatever it is. Once I finally get ushered out of the carnival near closing time, I hop on my bike and head west. At first I'm headed for Los Angeles, as I've been planning all along, but when I see the sign for Reno, I change my mind and head back home instead. I never wanted to go back there, but I've got questions now, questions that I suddenly feel very sure I can get answers to in that stupid old trailer.

I'm pretty happy now that I didn't burn it down.

○

I must have passed out in the field, because I find myself about a mile from the carnival in the morning, all alone and feeling almost myself again. The colored lights in the distance are flat and dark, no longer twinkling. I stand up, unsure, like a baby deer, and when I don't fall over I decide that I should get as far away from this place as possible. It doesn't have what I'm looking for anyway, and with the memory of my entire being telling me to run, I'm not even sure I have a choice.

And so I run, as fast as I can, truly letting loose for the first time in my life. And it turns out I can run very very fast.

When I find the train tracks again I jump the first empty car I find headed east. At some point   maybe in my conversation with Joan – maybe before, or maybe just now – running away from whatever was at that show, I've decided that I should go to New York. Manhattan sounds like the kind of place a superhero should go. The kind of place where there's a lot of good to be done, and also the kind of place where someone like me can both do good and also maybe slip into the shadows and blend in.

●

I'm lying in my old bed from the days I lived with Delia in this god-forsaken trailer, in the middle of nowhere, staring at the curved ceiling. The bed, the room, the trailer, all feel so small. It seems like a hundred years since I lived here and it hasn't even been one. I feel so old for sixteen. Like a million things have happened to me since I left, most of them crappy. I wonder if that's how it was for Delia too. She died so young. She couldn't have been older than 40, but she seemed older than that to me, she always did, even when I was little, but she must have been young back then.

Maybe it's in our DNA. Live hard and fast – and short.

I head to Delia's room to find what I came for – evidence of someone like me. I guess that whatever or whoever I felt at Joan's show must have had the same idea as me – that maybe something like us would go there. But did it feel me as I felt it? And if it did, was the feeling as intoxicating and horrifying as it was for me?

So yeah, despite never wanting to come back to Nevada, and most especially not to this old trailer, I'm here trying to detective my way through all this crap. Not my strength. Of all the times I've been annoyed not to have the stereotypical supervillain brain, this one is the most frustrating. But half an hour into tearing Delia's room apart I do find something: a small wooden trunk, buried underneath cheap suitcases and tacky clothing in her junky closet. I drag the trunk out into the room. It's locked and I see no key so I just smash an old metal jewelry box against the lock until it breaks open. Inside, there's no treasure or jewelry or ancient tomes, in fact, it's practically empty, just a stack of old letters tied with a pink ribbon sitting in the bottom of the chest. The pink ribbon strikes me as odd; Delia didn't seem like a pink kind of person. I tear the ribbon off and flip through the stack. There's sixty or seventy letters, all addressed to Delia, and all from someone named Scarlett Braverman. They're pristinely preserved and in chronological order, the oldest at the bottom. Seeing them, the whole thing seems so unlike Delia that I wonder again what else I've missed in my mother. The thought, as always, is unpleasant and so I push it away. I slide out the first letter from its envelope; it's fairly short, on thin white paper, the writing a pretty and compact cursive.

March 6th
Dear Delia:
Thanks for trying this out with me. I know we've had our battles, but I feel strongly that if we're going to stay out of each other's way as we've agreed to try, then it's best we at least stay in touch. So you can know where I am and I can know where you are. Also (and I'm sure you'll hate like hell my saying this) but I like talking to you. I know things are difficult for you, and I know it's not really the same for me, but I also feel like you understand me more than anyone on earth might, whether we like it or not. In a strange way we are sisters, and if we can find a way to make this idea of mine work…communicating rather than fighting each other, maybe we will, hell, I

don't know…maybe we can live some version of normal that doesn't eat us up inside quite so much. I know it's a revolutionary idea, maybe even a stupid one, certainly one our mothers, and especially our grandmothers would not approve of, but we're not our damn mothers, right?

How is your Lola? I can't pretend that she is not the primary reason that you agreed to this, and for that I'm thankful, even if on some level I have to view her as the enemy. Please write back soon so that I will know you've not changed your mind.

Scarlett

I hold the letter out in front of me for a full minute. "What the fuck?!" I say to the empty room. I skip a dozen or so letters and pick another one, same return address, somewhere in Pennsylvania.

September 3rd
Dear Delia:

I'm glad to hear that you and Lola are well. If she's as headstrong as you say, she sounds like she's going to be a lot like your mother Aveline, or maybe even Hedy. Crap, if she's like Hedy, the whole damn world is in trouble, yeah? My Bonnie is so much like my mother Jean, so quiet and serious, and strong in a way I never was, and she looks so much like pictures I saw of my grandmother Audra it still shocks me sometimes, the sight of her. I hope you are well. Your last letter sounded…fraught. Anything I can do?
S

This time I ball the letter up and throw it across the room. "WHAT THE FUCK!?!" I kick a hole in the wall and toss the furniture around the room until it no longer resembles a bedroom. This woman Scarlett knows more about my life and my family than I do. I'd heard Delia speak about her dead mother Aveline, usually in a drunken stupor, rambling incoherently, and of course I had that one short letter from Aveline to my mother…but who the hell is Hedy? Once I calm down I find the stack of letters again, pinned under the broken bed frame and I flip to the last letter. The tone is decidedly different.

June 29th
Delia:

Can you feel it coming for me? I didn't think I'd be so afraid. But it has edged closer to me all day. I can feel it in the air crackling around me. It's funny, I would have thought I wouldn't be afraid, knowing it was coming all this time, and feeling so weak in so many different ways since Bonnie came, but I'm still surprised by it. I find myself lost in thought imagining what it will be. It's too gruesome though and when I catch myself I have to push it out of my mind. I wonder, are you frustrated with me? Perhaps even angry? We agreed to this whole insane plan because I convinced us both that we could be with our daughters longer, that we would have longer to teach them, a chance to give them something different than the short time we had with our mothers, and yet here Bonnie is only six and my time is up regardless of our plans. The mysteries of this life we lead will never cease to amaze and frustrate me. I often wish for a roadmap. I never know enough. I'm counting on you though, counting on you to be good, once I'm gone. You made that promise, and I will hold you to it, even in death. In some way you have become my friend over these years, the only person who truly understands me, and I'm grateful for it.

May your daughter grow strong, but be rational, as I know that you are.

Scarlett

This is the last of the letters. I'm filled with impotent rage. This woman Scarlett knew my mother in a way I never did, and never will. I can't decide if I'm angrier with Delia for keeping herself from me, or myself for killing her before I could understand the larger picture that obviously lives here. I tear the rest of the trailer apart, half-in-rage, half-hoping to find more information. I throw the trunk and as it collides with the wall it splinters into pieces. Through the shattered bits something pokes out from part of the broken lid. I wade through the crap strewn about the floor and pick the top up. There's a yellowed newspaper article wedged inside a false wall in the lid. I break it in half carefully and remove the paper. It's a news article, but the date is torn off.

Possible Earthquake Seizes Malibu Canyon, Significant Artifact Discovered in Aftermath

Late Friday evening, residents of Malibu, Calabasas and adjacent Los Angeles neighborhoods awoke to what appeared to be an earthquake around two am. Scientists have been unable to pinpoint what Los Angeles fault line may have caused the quake, as there appeared to be several points of impact, and some experts have even gone so far as to say that it may not have been an earthquake at all.

Nearby residents however, disagree. "I nearly fell out of my bed when I felt the impact. And three mirrors in the house broke, along with two windows in the front room," says Trish McCoy of Calabasas. "I don't care what the experts say, I've been living in LA long enough to know what a quake feels like and *that* was a quake."

Commuter Jeff Grimes agrees. "I was driving home from my friend's place in Malibu and the entire mountain nearly came down on me – and then the road ahead of me crumbled when a huge mass of something crashed into it and tumbled down the side."

Road crews have been working non-stop since early Saturday in an attempt to repair the road, which has been completely destroyed in at least one area (fig.1) while a mass of boulders and rocks litter other parts of the road and will require significant clean up. Authorities expect Malibu Canyon to be open to traffic by the end of the week at the earliest, leaving many drivers to find alternate routes to their jobs and homes.

Upon searching the area authorities found a strange stone artifact on the ground near the center of impact. According to UCLA historian Dr. Jason Gahres, the artifact is Celtic in nature and not native to this area (fig. 2). The artifact unearthed in the disturbance will be temporarily on loan to LACMA while the authorities wait on confirmation of its origin.

Authorities are not willing to comment, at this time, as to whether the damage in Malibu Canyon and the surrounding areas was in fact caused by an earthquake or a natural disaster of some other kind.

Next to the article is a black and white photograph of the damage done to the road, which looks like a giant bullet (or maybe two) were launched into it from space; as well as a faded photo of the artifact mentioned in the article. The stone in the photo is kind of crude and clunky, and bizarrely large, like the size of my palm, maybe. There's a small piece broken, a corner of one of three interlocking circles. The three open circles make up the outside edges and are joined in the center by a solid circle that has an intricate carving of a crow. The carving is the only non-crude thing about the whole design. It looks to me like it was supposed to be a necklace of some kind. Big and bulky and totally not my style, but weirdly impressive all the same. The longer I stare at the photo, the more I'm drawn to it. My eyes linger over the shapes and I feel a strange humming in my chest. Almost as if the symbol is calling out to me. This is important; it feels powerful.

It feels as if it belongs to me.

And I want it.

I get on my bike and head back toward L.A. That was the original plan, and it's a good place to start looking for this stone since that's where it was when my mother tucked this information away.

○

It's mid-June and I've been in the city for about two weeks, long enough to have found a crappy job I'm terrible at in a busy coffee shop in midtown Manhattan. They tried putting me on the register, but I was pathologically quiet with the customers. They moved me to the barista position within the hour.

Coffee doesn't need to be talked back to, I guess.

I'm still not great at it, probably in part because I've never acquired a taste for coffee, myself. I prefer hot chocolate, which kind of makes me feel like a kid, which is weird because, in all other ways I feel like Old Man River compared to my co-workers. They're a combination of high school seniors, college students, and a few post-grad, tattooed artsy types, and though I'm older than only the two high school seniors – and not by much – I still feel ancient in comparison. Their conversations are all filled with talk of classes and parties, dating and clothes, music and movies. Stuff I mostly know nothing about. My thoughts look nothing like theirs. I fantasize about befriending them so that I can know about those things too, but it seems impossible. It seems more likely that I could fly than make friends. So, instead, I'm consumed by thoughts of guilt. I haven't saved one person since arriving in the city.

So much for me being Superman.

Hell, forget being Superman, I can't even pay the rent on my crappy little motel-room-with-kitchenette with what I'm making here. Apparently, I don't have the skills to be Superman or Clark Kent.

I think I need a second crappy job.

Two part-time jobs and a lousy motel room is not exactly the star reporter gig and dudes in distress rescues I was imagining – okay glamorizing – in my head as I rode here on train cars like a hobo. If the superpower part of me would just fully kick in – tell me what to do – where to do it – maybe then I wouldn't mind so much that I'm making coffees and taking out the trash while my co-workers plan backpacking trips around Europe for when their classes end.

But I know no secret password, and so I go to sleep every night hoping that something will change, or that my body will evolve, or that I'll just figure something out.

And then, all of a sudden, it does and I do.

On a Sunday that's full of gloom instead of sun, I go out walking and eventually take a train out to Montauk. I've never been, and for some reason it seems like a good idea. Mostly, I like the way the word looks on the sign and sounds in my mouth.

It's kind of deserted and surprisingly cold when I get there, despite the time of year. Only a few souls wander around aimlessly in the sand and clouds, lost, like me. It seems lonely, which seems right. At dusk, I start back unsure when the last train is.

There are other people on the platform waiting, but they're scattered. We're all like puzzle pieces that belong in different boxes; pieces that will always remain separate and ill-fitting. I keep my distance. But out of nowhere I feel a slight burn in my chest. I don't know what it is, where it's coming from, or why, and it's followed only by the sound of running, the far away rhythm of shoes slapping pavement, and fast. I close my eyes and concentrate. It's getting closer and louder. There's yelling too. I can't make out the words, not because they are faint but because they are layered in with so many other sounds. I feel him far behind me – the shift of the air, the slight vibration of the concrete below me as he gets closer.

I turn away and close my eyes as the sound and feel comes nearer, imagining him in my mind, getting the picture of him without actually seeing him. He's big and moving too fast. Something is clutched to his chest. I realize suddenly that underneath the burning in my chest, I'm afraid. My hand is shaking and so I clench it to make it stop. It does, but the rattle moves into my teeth and then spreads throughout my body, fear infecting me like a disease. I almost walk away, but the warmth in my chest roots me to the ground as the pounding of the feet thunders closer and closer to me.

I step just slightly to the side, out of his path, away from the trench of the train tracks. The feet get so close and still pay no attention to me. I cock my arm back and as the feet start to pass me I throw my fist toward their space, connecting with the back and side of the jaw that belongs to the feet, sending all of him flying forward at incredible speed. When he finally hits the ground, some twenty feet away, he actually slides across the pavement on his stomach a little bit, like a penguin skimming across the ice after catapulting out of ocean depths. He's still breathing when I step away into the slowly darkening shadows, and then away from the scene entirely.

I circle back around later to find a handful of cops and a crowd of bystanders being kept at bay. A woman is wailing that he is the man that robbed her and attacked her friend. The cops are doing the things that cops do. I slink away like a criminal and wait for the train where it's less crowded. I feel both desperate and euphoric, both insane and completely lucid, afraid and yet more fearless than ever.

I wonder when I'll feel the burning in my chest again. I wonder how long I'll have to wait for it to tell me what to do.

Not long.
The following Tuesday, when I'm walking home from the coffee shop, I stop in the middle of the sidewalk. The burning is happening in my chest again, like what I felt before but a hundred times more intense. It reminds me a little bit of what happened at Joan's, but it's different. A million New Yorkers try to run me over, oblivious to my stopping, but I stand strong. A woman hits the pavement hard when she bumps into my shoulder and it doesn't give. I reach down to help her up as a stream of cuss words come out of her pretty mouth. She seems to soften a little when she notices my hand held out to her. She takes it, but we both stumble and fall as I am suddenly hit with a new wave of fire rushing across my chest. I lay my open palm against my heart in shock and surprise as the woman and I both go down together. She gets back

up, cussing even more than the first time, but softens for a second time when she sees me on my hands and knees breathing so hard it must look like my bones are trying to shed my skin. She crawls over toward me, shouting occasional obscenities up at the people that continue to trample us unaware. She puts a hand on my shoulder.

"Hey…are you okay?"

I look at her. She has big clear green eyes. She reminds me of someone. I think she's the first person I've really looked in the eye since Joan. It must be as intense for her as it is for me, because she breathes in a little bit and draws back. Her hand flutters away from my shoulder. I nod at her and hold up a hand suggesting she keep her distance. She scoots away from me, through the onslaught of feet until her back is up against the stone of a building. I put my hand to my burning chest, as if it can do something there, other than helplessly hold in what feels like an explosion about to come out through my chest like a bomb. I look at her again and she's watching me – this strange expression on her face – as my body is again racked with heaving breaths. This time I throw up.

That gives me a wide berth in the foot traffic department.

After throwing up I feel a little better, even though the burning in my chest continues. I close my eyes and crouch into a catcher's position on the sidewalk and suddenly have my bearings back – almost as quickly as they left me. Everything clears like the auto focus on a camera, the burning continues, but now it's like it's talking to me instead of ravaging me.

I stand up as people continue to walk around me, annoyed at the obstacle I am to them. I look over their heads, left and right, until a razor beam focus points where I should go, a small less crowded side street. My palms are sweaty and my mind is racing, but I don't know if I could stop even if I wanted to. I run across the street and into a small bodega on a hidden corner. Just as I walk in, a man pulls a gun on the clerk at the counter. There's no moment to be afraid this time because before I even know what's happening and in perfect synch with the simple act of walking into the store, I swing my fist at the gunman. He never even sees me, although I'm not aware I'm moving any faster than normal. In one fluid movement, as his body crashes into a display eight feet away, I have the gun in my other hand. How I managed to get it from him is a blur, but feels like a perfectly executed math equation. And with its conclusion, the burning in my chest ceases as startlingly as it began. The clerk is saying something to me that I can't hear. I put the gun on the counter and walk out the door. The woman from the busy street is the first and only thing I see when I come out of the store. She's still sitting there, her back against a building, her view a direct line of sight into the store. Her green eyes are wide. She looks a lot like Alice from the home. I stare at her and she stares at me. I smile a little bit at the same time she does. And then I start running.

I know what I'm supposed to do now.

I don't know why I didn't have this sixth sense or whatever it is all along, but part of me thinks maybe it means I'm growing up, evolving into a real superhero. Like maybe the world knew I couldn't handle it before, but now, now I'm finally becoming me and the world knows it – or maybe I'm just learning to listen to myself.

Either way, it's the first time I've felt happy in a very long time.

●

I find myself incredibly bored in Los Angeles and with no brilliant idea about how to find my stone. I have visions of storming the LAPD, but have no idea which location, or if I'd be able to get in and out without getting captured. I still fear the idea of getting captured by the government – of being strapped down and experimented on. Sure, I'm well-nigh invincible but that doesn't mean I can't be taken captive – and live for what, like, forever? Spend forever being experimented on? I think not. I've seen the movies. I figure the farther I stay away from government agencies the better my chances are.

So instead I just try to lose myself in the little things for a while. I do all the things I'd been imagining. I go to the beach. And it's cool, beautiful too, but I don't feel much looking at the waves. I'd expected to be moved. To feel small in comparison to something so epic. But I don't feel small, I feel only confusion. I have to admit that I'm a bit lost and for the millionth time, I'm forced to consider that maybe killing Delia was a mistake – not that killing her was a mistake – but that I should have waited until I got some answers first.

The other thing that's annoying about the ocean is that it reminds me of Adrian. That's super-annoying, actually. I've been thinking about him a lot. Wondering if he's angry with me. I mean, surely he is – I killed his sister, and brutally at that – but I do believe he loved me, and I did spare his life. So, maybe, he's also a little bit grateful. Maybe he's missing me. Or maybe he's already replaced me with some cute dumb bitch that won't be so much trouble. You know, girls that won't shoot him in the leg and wouldn't have killed his sister. Whatever. Not my fault. He betrayed me first. I would have done anything for him, until that moment.

Still, him missing me seems like too much to hope for.

And I'm not sure why I care. It's not like he's in my life anymore, but I catch myself hoping for it in spite of myself.

When I get tired of the innocent little things – like sitting on the beach – I return to crime. I rob a jewelry store, a convenience store, and an Apple store because I decide I need a laptop and an iPod. I steal like twelve laptops and throw them all in the Los Angeles River (which is more like a crappy concrete canal) except one that I keep. I do the same with the iPods and iPads – keeping a sleek silver iPod and none of the iPads. I steal a shiny car from a dealership at four a.m. one Saturday night, but crash it into the Los Angeles river the next night after realizing I prefer my bike.

I've gotten used to my lame motel rooms, but frequently consider what my other options might be. I don't know anything about buying a house, or renting one, or what might be involved if someone needs my name.

I don't even know my social security number – or if I have one.

I dream foreign things. Up until now, dreams were infrequent at best, but ever since I read about the stone – ever since I felt whatever it was I felt at Joan's carnival – the dreams are different. In one, I'm commanding an epic battlefield of men engaged in bloody battle. I fly above them becoming fat on their kills. Sometimes, I turn into a crow, sometimes I turn into three. In another dream, I'm a slithering snake swimming through a river tinged with blood and emerge from it a cackling old woman. In another I run through forests, low to the ground and hunting something – it's men. I'm hunting men. When I catch them, I tear them to pieces with my wolf jaws and then roll around in their blood, covering my fur with it and howling at the moon while strange women, all who remind me of Delia but are not Delia, watch from the trees, their pale eyes reflecting the moon sharply like mirrors. When I'm done I take to the air, my black crow feathers light on the breeze. Sometimes I think I see Delia – sometimes I know I do – but she never speaks to me. If I wasn't so bored, I'd say I'm going crazy, but since it's the most interesting thing that's happened in weeks I just shrug it off.

I chase boredom away one day by driving up the coast through Malibu. I turn onto an abandoned drive and follow a road toward the ocean. A remote house far off the road and overlooking the beach sits there sadly, proudly. It reminds me of me. I watch it for a week before breaking in. It looks like people haven't been here in months and there are no immediate neighbors, no mail comes, no paper. When I get inside I also find no telephone, electricity, or cable – it sucks about the cable. The water works though, and the gas must be on because I can get hot water in the bathroom. There's an inch of dust on most everything.

I move in with my three duffel bags the following day. I park my motorcycle in some bushes near the south side of the house and I keep my stuff all in one place near the big sliding doors so that if anyone shows up suddenly I can climb down the rocky ridge with my bags in an instant. I figure I can hear someone coming if they even pull into the drive off of the main road. It happens a couple times, people lost or exploring, but they always turn around before getting too close. It's a pretty sweet pad. The house is set awesomely above the beach, with a huge stone deck and pool overlooking the ocean. It's been chilly out, but I don't really get cold, and so I sleep most nights in the hammock or on one of the chaises on the patio, preferring the sounds of the ocean and the sky to the false quiet of the house and the overly decorated, dusty rooms.

The pool is empty and, after a few days staring at it, I fill it up with a hose I find in a side yard. It takes nearly a day to fill it up. That'll be a big water bill – glad I won't be here when it shows. I'm sure I'm not doing it right, that people don't usually fill pools with hoses, but I don't care. It looks great and I catch myself staring at the water for whole hours without looking away. I find chlorine in the garage and guess at how much to add. I get pretty close I think because it smells a bit but doesn't sting my eyes when I get in, although maybe my eyes are immune. Guess I'll never know, unless

I have a pool party with some non-super-powered folks. Yeah, that'll happen.

I don't actually know how to swim, but I figure it's high time I figure it out and I'm not about to sign up at the local Y for some baby swim lessons.

As I wade in a sudden bit of fear overtakes me. It's a good motivator though and so I go all the way in, fast and hard. It's not pretty at first (I look like some kind of half-drowned rat doing a half-assed dog paddle) but I like how the water feels and in a couple days I'm not so bad. After that I start swimming every day. Both because I like it and because I'm bored out of my goddamn mind. I suppose it's also because I'm avoiding the fact that I have no idea what to do next.

After two days of swimming laps I decide to try the ocean. I hide my bag in the yard and climb down the rocks, scratching the hell out of myself, but the cuts are healed by the time I reach the bottom and stick a toe in the ocean. It's colder than I expected. I wonder briefly about drowning – if it could actually kill me, if it would be painful way to die. I can't decide if it seems horrifying or peaceful. I swim out in strong powerful strokes and am shocked when I look back and can barely see the beach. It's getting dark and the moon is already faintly in the sky. I lie on my back and float effortlessly. I should feel energized and powerful, invulnerable and potent, but all I feel is lost. I'm afraid of people after everything that happened in Vegas, and I don't like feeling afraid, it pisses me off. But I don't have a handle yet on what I should do about it. Every freaking person I've ever known or trusted has betrayed me. Not to mention, most of them were idiots and they still managed to kill me and leave me for dead, twice. What if someone not so stupid gets their hands on me? And why can't I come up with a plan of any sort to get my stone? Turns out I'm a pussy, and one with a puny brain to boot. I think back to my early, naïve, days where I thought I could take over the whole world as easy as snapping my fingers. I'm not even coming close to world-takeover, and it's 'cause I'm afraid of everything I don't know and maybe I'm stupid. For someone so powerful I sure feel afraid a lot of the time.

I swim back to shore in the dark.

My first attempt is not really pre-meditated, and I don't call it a suicide attempt, though others probably would. I call it "testing my limits." After scaling the rocky cliff back up to the deck of the house I look back down on the beach – the glistening tips of waves lapping the shore – and I jump.

It must be three hundred feet to the ground, but the rocks don't fall straight down and I make no attempt to launch myself out from the edge, so my limbs catch on every sharp, jutting rock as I plummet toward the sandy beach. The pain is excruciating – I break several bones, and land badly on my hip and arm, on a large flat stone. My hip feels shattered and when I reach down with my undamaged arm I can feel the hipbone under my skin, smashed into sharp shards. Further up my torso my skin has broken apart and ribs are poking out, white bone under red blood in the moonlight.

I start laughing.

○

When I try to take out enough money for my next week at the motel, the machine spits out my debit card almost angrily and I realize I've seriously got to get a second job.

I walk around the city wracking my brain for something I could do and maybe be good at, or at least something I'd be better at than endless half-caff-double-whip-no-foam BS.

The only thing I can think of that I might be a natural with are books, so I go to the New York Public Library in the hopes that something there will click for me. I bound up the massive stone stairs, past the regal lions perched out front and plunge myself into the building, the feel of it immediately welcoming, certainly more so than my coffee shop. It smells old. Maybe the library and I can be ancient together. Maybe I can feel less out of synch with the whole world here – at home with the books. I approach the first person I see with a nametag and try to stop myself from being too excited about this new idea.

"Where can I find out about job opportunities?" I say brightly. The girl sniffs and juts her chin toward a desk with several women moving around behind it. At the desk, a girl my age looks up.

"Can I help you?" She asks with a slightly forced smile. I nod, ignoring the fake smile.

"I was wondering if you had any job openings?"

"We do have a Page opening…is that what you're looking for?"

"I don't know," I say, shrugging. "What's a Page?"

"They work with the librarians here – assisting them – re-shelving books…you know, doing whatever they need."

"Sounds great. I love books so, yes, anything with the books," I say. She smiles benevolently and hands me a clean application and a pen. I've only written my name when she asks what school I'm attending.

"I'm not in school," I say, and it stings a little as it slides out.

"Oh,' she says, her voice dropping in register. Something's wrong and the hairs on my arm stand up. Things are about to go sideways. "I'm sorry, I'm afraid you have to be enrolled in a school program of some kind to be eligible to be a Page."

"Oh," I say. It stings more now. "Are there, are there any other jobs that I don't have to be in school for?"

She looks down at a sheet of paper for a moment. "Um…there's a custodial position…" she offers tentatively.

"Oh," I say again. She smiles up at me, and then, as if uncomfortable with the entire situation, walks to the other end of the long counter to answer a ringing phone. I guess it's really the first time in my life that I've flat out been told I can't have something because of who I am. I mean, it's been implied all the time, I guess, but never really said out loud. It sucks. I guess wanting something is risky. I slide the paper away and turn to go when an older woman whose smile reminds me a little bit of my mother's speaks up.

"Bonnie?"

"Yes?" She's read my name off of my application. Her nametag says 'Tamme.'

"I'm really sorry about that, sweetie," she says. "I've never really agreed with that rule. But you know, if you're interested, we do sometimes have unpaid internships where school enrollment is not a prerequisite. It might be a good way to get your foot in the door. Quite frankly, they prefer you to be in school as an intern as well, but I could pull a few strings…"

"Oh." I look at my feet; she's being so nice. "That's really kind of you, but I need the extra money, and my free time is kind of…spoken for," I say, thinking of my crime-fighting nights that don't pay anything but certainly take up a lot of time.

"I understand," she says politely, then adds, "You might want to try a bookstore then."

"Thanks, that's a really good idea," I say, feeling slightly better.

"Hold on a second," she says, raising a finger and then typing into her computer. After a minute the printer behind her whirs and buzzes. She picks up the print out and hands it to me. It lists over a dozen bookstores in the city. She takes out a pen and writes her name, phone number and address on the edge of the sheet. I look up at her, questions in my eyes. "Use my name if you need a reference," she adds.

"But…you don't even know me…" I say. She nods beatifically.

"I can tell you're a good one. Besides, everyone in this city needs help once in a while."

It's funny when she says it because I suddenly see how true it is and wonder if this is a karmic reward for the little good I've done. It's probably not a good thing to think about, getting rewarded for doing good, it's probably the opposite of how a superhero should think, but I'm so grateful for the help I'm not going to question it.

I go to seven bookstores before someone will even consider giving me an application. It's all stony faces and dusty books until the seventh shop. Finally, I get a smile and an application, but still no openings. It's only on shop number nine, a big store downtown full of row after row of new and used books, that I get both an application and a nod from the girl at the register that they're actually looking for someone. I take the application and fill it out at a packed coffee shop around the corner. When I come back twenty minutes later a young guy is on the register and gestures me over to a customer service window when I show him the application.

"Hi," I say tentatively to the guy standing at the window.

"Jamie?" he asks, somewhat annoyed. I'm glad I'm not Jamie.

"Um, No. Bonnie," I say and hold the application out warily. He glances across it, eyes darting from line to line.

"It's your lucky day Bonnie, this Jamie is forty minutes late. You want to have your interview now?"

"Uh, sure," I say, glancing at my jeans and t-shirt.

"I'm Tim," he says, extending his hand. I shake it, trying to apply just the right amount of pressure, worried I'm failing, worrying about everything. But when his first question tumbles out, I know something is finally going right.

"What's your favorite book, Bonnie?" He asks. My mind suddenly clears; this is a question I can answer.

"The Loneliness Of The Long Distance Runner," I say.

"That's an interesting choice…" he says, looking at me as if he's sizing me up.

"Um, thanks?" I half-ask, not sure if he's complimenting me or deciding to send me packing.

"Come on into the office and let's do this right," he says smiling. I follow him back and we talk for nearly half an hour – mostly about books, which is the only thing I'm sure I could talk about for thirty minutes – and when we're done – I have the job. I start on Tuesday. My smile is enormous and probably ridiculous, but it feels good to know maybe I'm not some incompetent teenager that's going to get thrown out of her rundown motel room or, you know, starve to death or something insane.

I'm waiting for a train downtown, still high from getting the bookstore job hours ago when it finally happens again. I'm so blissful and sated that I almost miss the fire feeling creeping into my chest. I catch the last tendrils of it as it drifts away from me, and look up, anxiously trying to identify where it's originating. An empty train screeches through the station, never stopping, blowing strands of hair into my face in its wake. It's long after the day's rush and my platform is almost empty. All that remains is a girl with an iPod sitting on a bench far away, a man with a suitcase exiting through a turnstile, and a kid with a hoodie furiously clicking away on his phone.

On the platform across the tracks there are only three people, all of them on their own, seeming sleepy-eyed and dreamy, moving almost in slow motion. Except for the rumbling of the tunnels, all is quiet. I've just started to wonder if my senses have gotten things wrong, when a man on the platform across from me enters the station and jumps the turnstile. He runs full tilt toward one of the tunnels. He has a dark gun in his hand – it looks like a shadow, a deadly shadow. He moves like the devil is chasing him but I see nobody in pursuit. I step forward, narrowing my eyes, watching closely and intending to cross the tracks, but a train enters and buzzes through the station – all light and air and rattling glass. Through the windows of the train passing by I'm able to make out the gunman pushing a young man as he disappears into the tunnel. I gasp audibly as the young man falls onto the tracks. He doesn't get up and nobody appears to have seen him fall but me.

None of this would be the end of the world except that a new train is entering the station and it's headed right for him. My mind races and my heart clenches at the thought of not getting there in time.

The moment the train on my tracks passes I dart across the massive gap, leaping over the rails between us. I heave him back onto the platform just as the oncoming train breathes a whooshing hot whisper on the back of my neck. I sit silently for a minute, entangled with the stranger, his head somehow lying peacefully in my lap as if he's napping. He's young, only a couple years older than me, maybe, and handsome. His glasses have partially fallen off his face and I adjust them, wishing he'd open his eyes so I could find out what color they are. I catch myself tenderly brushing a dark curl of hair from his brow.

And for the first time in my whole life I really think about love.

What it might be like to be in love.

In love with a boy like this.

My heart flutters around like trapped birds in a cage and my skin flushes hot, thinking things I've never thought before. I'm tempted to fish out his wallet so I can know his name. So I can put a name to this sudden new dream of mine. But I resist. His eyes blink open and closed a few times before they settle on open and I draw in a sharp breath. They're dark brown with tiny flecks of green. They're beautiful. But it's not just that they're beautiful, it's that they're also soft and kind. So many people feel all hard angled edges and cynicism to me. But mostly what I see in his eyes is gentleness. It's intoxicating and horribly unique.

"Wha – what happened?" he asks.

"You got pushed onto the tracks," I say, savoring the sound of his rough voice, hoping he'll speak to me again.

"Am I okay?" he asks. I chuckle.

"I think so," I say. "You look okay," I add helpfully, shrugging a bit. He smiles broadly despite the obvious confusion I see in his eyes.

"Good," he says authoritatively, nodding slightly, but the confusion overtakes him and he stumbles on his words again. "Who...who're you?" he asks, one eyebrow slightly cocked. He smells like the woods. I don't know how that's possible in the city, and worse, in this dank subway tunnel, but it's true. He smells woodsy and fresh. He smells like life. The urge to take credit for saving him is powerful. I want it so much I can taste it on my tongue, as if saving him will help me know him better, or him to know me. I resist again.

"I'm nobody," I say. His eyes focus on me for one second before glossing over.

"You're pretty..." he says, and then passes out. It's the first time anyone has ever called me pretty before. It's embarrassing how happy it makes me. I shake him lightly, worrying he has a concussion and should be awake. I stand up, lifting him, my arms under his shoulders and the backs of his knees, intending to take him to the hospital, but just as I step forward I see a bystander pointing my way and police rushing through and over the turnstiles. I set him down carefully and dash into the dark tunnels behind me. The irony that it's the same path the gunman took is not lost on me. There's some shouting and some pursuit, but I speed through the tunnels until I can't hear them anymore, trying to forget the whole thing.

Especially trying to forget the stranger's face.

In some ways I think his face is the most dangerous thing I've ever encountered.

●

In the morning all my limbs are mended, my skin sealed back up, and though I'm covered in dried blood, I feel fresh as a daisy. I add another item to my list of "awesome stuff about being me" and scale the wall toward my patio.

Later I take my bike down to Venice Beach in an attempt to chase the boredom away and walk up and down the boardwalk watching all the freaks for a couple hours. There's a crowd outside a bookstore and I linger, wondering what's going on. But it's just some silly book signing for a psychologist named Dr. Elizabeth Grant. I'm about to take off in the other direction when I see the title of her book, "Gods Among Us". It strikes a nerve.

I pick it up and skim pages of it while people filter in and out, gushing and blushing, as she signs copies. The pages aren't as intriguing as the title had led me to believe. In a few minutes, the crowd has dispersed and she's sitting at a desk alone with copies of her book. She's making notes in a small leather-bound book.

I walk up to her as casually as I can. "Do you still practice, or whatever?"

"Excuse me?" she asks politely, looking up and taking off her glasses.

"Do you still practice or do you just write about the shit now?"

"I mostly write. I take on a few patients, but mostly as case studies," she pauses. "Would you like me to sign that for you?" I look down at the book in my hand.

"Uh, sure," I hand it to her across the table.

"Whom should I make it out to?"

"Lola."

"Lola. That's a name with a lot of history," she says. It's the first time anyone has even appeared to take my name seriously. I immediately decide not to tell her the 'LeFever' part, but I still can't help making a snide remark.

"So I hear."

"Nothing wrong with a name with history," she says, smiling and holding the book back out to me. Her voice is silky and tastes like chocolate to my ears. I realize I haven't spoken to a single soul since Joan.

"I wouldn't know much about that, I guess."

"Which...history, or your name?"

"Both, I guess. I dropped out of school and I'm not a big reader," I say. She has a way of asking questions that makes me want to answer them, or maybe I'm just desperate for someone to talk to, anyone – bullshit therapist or not.

"When did you drop out?"

"Recently."

"Was there a particular reason that you left school?" I pause before answering her. I'm not sure whether to lie or not. In that moment hanging between us, I decide to tell her the truth, to always tell her the truth, regardless of whether she'll believe me and regardless of whether this conversation lasts two minutes or two years.

"I killed my mother," I say, looking at her directly, but she has a good poker face. She absorbs the information easily and I can't tell whether she believes me or not. Even if she does believe me, she probably thinks I mean it like, metaphorically, or some crap. "And I thought it was best to leave town after that."

"And you've been on the road…on your own ever since?" I'm impressed that she doesn't press on the mother thing, like 'why did you kill her' or 'how do you feel about that', even though I think I kind of want her to ask me anyway.

"Yeah. I hooked up with some people in Las Vegas, but it didn't end well and I've been on my own since then, yeah." She opens her mouth to speak again, but a group of middle-aged women each holding a copy of her book step up to the table and chatter at her excitedly. She smiles coolly and takes out her pen. I head toward the door but she calls out to me. I walk back and she hands me a piece of paper.

"Here. It was nice meeting you."

"Sure." I walk outside into the sunshine and open up the paper, her office business card is inside and the note says 'I'm interested in speaking with you more about your life, if you're willing – anytime. Elizabeth'. I crumple both the card and note and shove them in my pocket.

Her instincts are both really good and really bad. She feels a story in me and she's right, but she's also playing with a serious fire she's not gonna be capable of dealing with.

Should be fun.

○

All weekend I'm distracted thinking about the boy on the subway platform. His face pops up in my mind all the time and I catch myself fantasizing about a normal life with him. Something more than I've got now – my crappy job (er, jobs) and crappy motel room. A boyfriend, a job, an apartment, maybe a pet, or at least a plant. It all sounds so deliciously decadent, but also innocent and simple.

The preoccupation isn't good for my work. I screwed up at least a dozen drinks over the last two days and my manager has been watching me the way I suspect someone that's about to fire someone does. I smile broadly, trying my best to charm him out of the idea. It's not my strength, charm.

But the distraction has been even more problematic for my nighttime work.

I arrive, nearly too late, on the scene of a man getting jumped in Central Park and am almost criminally absentminded when a man tries to rape a woman on a surprisingly crowded subway car. I'm frustrated and silently cursing myself on my way home, but simultaneously wondering if there's any way to both be me and to have a new life, to have the boy. I feel like that day, on the subway platform, has pulled back some second skin I didn't realize I had. And now I'm obsessed with making that other girl lurking inside me a reality. I try to keep my eye on the ball. On my way to my bookstore job I think of everything I can that isn't the boy. I can't afford to screw this up.

I'm slightly better at my bookstore job than I am at my barista job, but I'm still better behind the scenes in the quiet with the books than I am with the people and the registers. My bookstore boss seems to understand this better than my barista boss does and so I feel a little better about the whole thing. I have a few co-workers, mostly students, some nice and friendly, some not so nice.

Standing behind the textbook counter one afternoon stacking books on my cart and listening to Erica, one of the "not so nice", sigh above me, I smell the boy from the train. I spin around, both anxious to see him and worried he'll actually be there. It seems impossible. In this city of millions, it's impossible…isn't it? But his scent is burned into my brain from that night. I've spent whole days imagining his handsome shape, almost like he's a cardboard cut-out I can pin all my other dreams to…I don't think I could forget his signature if I tried – the sound and smell of him, the feel, and even taste – it's all uniquely him. And there he is. Standing large as life halfway down an aisle, not twenty feet from me, and coming this way.

It's him.

It's unmistakably him.

I turn suddenly and move to duck down behind the counter in a panic, but I knock down a stack of books in the process. Erica mutters "klutz" under her breath and I ignore her, because now he's seen me too. He pauses suddenly, mid-stride, and he's cocked his head slightly, a spark of recognition in his eyes, and for a second I don't know what to do. And then I just bolt, like a deer, through the door, dropping a handful of books. From the safety of the backroom I hear Erica sigh and mumble more rude things. I lean against the wall and listen. I can hear them talking through the thick wood door.

"Uh, hey," he says, almost awkwardly, but in that same dark toned voice from the other night.

"Hi," she says. She knows him, familiarity is obvious in her tone.

"Do you know that girl?" he asks.

"Um, who?" she asks, her voice seeming all sing song-y. I don't know why she sounds like that. She doesn't sound that way when she talks to me.

"The redhead that just dashed out of here."

"Oh. She's new. I don't know her name…something with a B…or maybe a P…why?" Whatever! She totally knows my name!

"No reason. She just looked familiar to me." There's a long pause and I feel like I can almost hear him thinking, but he just says, "Well, never mind. Thanks."

"Clark, wait!" Erica calls out, her voice high and false. Clark. His name is Clark.

"Yeah?"

"So…um…like what classes are you taking this semester…you haven't come in for any books lately."

"Oh…I'm not taking any classes right now, so…no new books yet."

"Oh," she pauses awkwardly and then starts again with a saccharine sound in her voice, almost a low animal purr. I can't decide if I'm angry or jealous – I definitely don't know how to make my voice purr. Then again, I just ran out of the room rather than talk to him, so what's it matter if my voice could purr. "Well then, what brings you in?" she asks, but it's all leading and sexy, and I can hear the smile on her face.

"I was just in the neighborhood, y'know, browsing," he says, oblivious to the sexy voice.

"And did you find anything…worthwhile?" she asks. I feel like vomiting, I can imagine her twirling her hair.

"No," he says, and there's a finality to it that shocks the purr right out of her.

"Oh," she says, her voice falling. He backtracks slightly, I hope just out of kindness.

"Um…I mean, no books for me today," he says casually.

Her voice brightens, but just slightly. "Oh, yeah, sure. Well, come back soon," she says. I clench my fists.

"Okay…yeah, sure," he says, and then from a further distance, "See ya." His footsteps carry him swiftly away. I can't help but smile. He doesn't like her. Even though she's pretty and normal and everything he should probably want. I breathe out and close my eyes. I don't know why I care so much, but it's suddenly all I can think about, superpowers or no, my whole brain is filled with thoughts of Clark. And some strange hopefulness about his interest in me – even though I'm afraid he'll figure out where he's seen me before.

The next time I run into Clark there's no escaping because we end up in the same aisle, me with an armload of textbooks. I see him and my face must do something between lighting up and panicking, but it feels horribly strange and I turn frantically on my heel to flee but realize there's no way out, unless I want to plunge through the solid concrete wall, which I could maybe do, and which seems almost reasonable right now.

"Hi," he says, as if it's the most natural thing in the world to say. I wouldn't know as the world has entirely dropped away from me and I can't feel my feet or the fingers that are surely attached to my hands, let alone the pile of books I hope stay in said non-existent fingers. I've forgotten what language is, all that exists are those warm brown eyes with glittering green flecks that look so deep into me I feel like one of us is sure to drown. He's pausing a long time, probably waiting for me to say something, but since I've forgotten what language is and can't remember if I have a tongue, I can't come up with anything. "Um, I'm Clark," he says thrusting out his hand. I blink at his hand a second and then drop all the books on the floor and take it gently, trying to be the graceful

Bonnie and not the Hulk Bonnie. His eyes are big and his mouth is smiling at the pile of books and his hand is big and warm and a little bit soft, but rough around the edges. I shake it calmly, as if my whole world isn't exploding with delight. He's paused again, but I'm still without words. I rack my brain for what I'm supposed to say.

"Bonnie," I finally manage.

"Bonnie," he says, as if seriously considering my name, which is nice. We're still shaking hands, which is probably weird, but there's no way in hell I'm going to be the first to let go. "Do, I…have we met before?" he asks, his head cocked slightly to the side. I see that same spark of recognition as he tries again to place me.

"No?" I say, but it comes out as if I'm asking him. He laughs. It's a big, beautiful laugh that I want to swallow me whole. He's quiet again, for a long moment, almost like he's studying me, and then he looks at the books all over the floor and our feet and he chuckles a little.

"Lemmehelpyou," he says, and it comes out all as one word, which is adorable. He's nervous too, which makes me feel slightly better and almost glad I opted to NOT break through a wall to escape. We bend down at the same time and narrowly miss butting heads. We fumble about, stacking the books on the small cart and drinking each other in without ever looking at one another. Our hands touch once and I recoil like I've touched lightning. When we finally come back up, we barely miss heads again. He stares at me for a minute and his smile makes my kneecaps feel like soup. I'm not entirely sure how I'm still upright.

"I know this is like ridiculously weird and sudden, but…would you like to go out with me sometime?" he asks.

"Tonight," I say. He laughs again.

"Okay. Yes. Yes, tonight, definitely. When do you get off?"

"Six," I say.

"Okay, six, yes, six. I'll meet you here?"

I suddenly think of Erica and her knife-y eyes.

"Outside," I say.

"Okay," he says, his smile never diminishing. Everything feels like it's in slow-motion, like I'm underwater. As if what he might say next is caught up in a wave that I'm waiting to crash, and then it does, but not because he speaks, but because Erica darts into the aisle behind Clark, and shatters the moment as if it had no more power than a faint dream.

"Clark! There you are!" she shouts into the quiet of our aisle and takes Clark's arm, pulling him out of my orbit, "I found that book you were looking for…C'mon," and with that, she yanks him away from me. Just as he's disappearing, he looks back and smiles this massive bright smile and mouths the word SIX, somehow still grinning. I think I smile back, but my insides feel all oatmeal-y, and my face feels like the sun, so I can't be sure. When he's gone the world seems smaller somehow. How is it possible to feel this way when I said only four words to him? My whole world is suddenly bathed in color, and I feel alive in places I didn't know existed.

It's wonderful.

It's scary.

Half an hour later, when Erica pins me down in the backroom while clocking out, I feel less oatmeal-y and warm.

"I don't know what you think you're doing," she says, as if it's part of another conversation we've already been having. I look around to see if there's anyone else she could possibly be talking to, but we appear to be alone.

"Um…?" is all I get out before she begins hissing at me again.

"I have been flirting with that guy for like eight months and he's finally starting to come around, so you better just back off," she says, her nostrils flaring, her eyes flashing.

"Um…I didn't do anything?" I offer up, more as a question than anything else.

"Oh please," she says, rolling her eyes so hard I imagine they're going to spring out of her head. The funny thing is, until just now I'd thought Erica was really pretty. She's got this beautiful hair like sun, long darkly tanned limbs, and sparkly hazel eyes and perfect teeth, but she suddenly looks like a monster.

"Um. What did I do?" I ask. At this she stalks away and points her finger at me before leaving the room.

"Stay the hell away from him." The door slams behind her and another voice pops up from behind a desk piled with books and a computer.

"Ugh. What a bitch." I lean over the desk and see another girl – slender, with huge dark eyes and a tiny silver nose ring, her name tag says Liesel – lying on the floor on her side, behind the desk, reading Tropic of Cancer. She doesn't even look up at me, but just continues reading and points a finger in my direction. "Don't listen to her. I've seen that dude. Totally cute. You should go for it."

I look down and blush. I don't think I know how to "go for it" anyway, but I guess I'll find out soon enough.

But I didn't think this whole "date" thing through, because I don't have anything to change into – not that I have anything worth wearing anyway, and I look a mess, and what was I thinking?! At 6:05 I'm waiting outside the store, leaning against the warm stone wall, after I'd tried desperately, five minutes earlier in the store bathroom, to make myself presentable. Running a comb through my long red hair and applying some sheer lip-gloss and a coat of mascara. I'm lucky to have pretty good skin, which doesn't need a lot of make-up, which is mainly fortunate because I don't know the first thing about make-up and am not very interested in it either. I'd looked at my jeans and t-shirt and suddenly wished the bookstore had a strict dress code, so I'd have worn something different, which feels like a totally alien thought in my head. Until this moment, I don't think I'd ever thought about my clothes as anything other than something to cover up nakedness, and now I look like a freaking waitress or…bookstore clerk, I guess, for my first date ever. When I look up from examining my nails for dirt, Clark is coming toward me.

It's 6:06 and I know my life is changing.

He offers me his hand and flashes his charming smile and I'm so excited and afraid of what might be happening.

"Hi," I say shyly, trying not to smile so big, trying to keep my voice from trembling. There's something about him. He's not like every other boy. He looks almost shiny to me, everyone else dull and faded in comparison.

"Hi," he says back. He touches my arm lightly and I can't remember anyone ever having touched my arm in that exact spot before. It feels nice. It feels important. "Let's go, then?"

"Yes please," I breathe. I imagine somewhere in the world Erica is cussing at me under her breath, but I try not to be too smug about it. I feel free and happy, maybe. It's hard to know what happy is if you're not sure if you've felt it before, but I remember my mother's eyes and hair, my father's smile, and our yellow kitchen. Yes, this is definitely happiness, I remember it.

We go to a little Ethiopian place nearby where we sit, legs crossed, on deep wine colored pillows, staring across a low table at one another. It's dark and light and loud and quiet all at the same time, and looking at him sucking down water – after the too hot whatever it was that he just ate – I know I love him already. But even I know you don't tell a boy you love him after spending an hour with him.

"I only started interning there because it's what you're 'supposed to do,'" he says, talking about the big corporate law firm he's working for this summer, "Well, that and I wanted to impress my dad, prove myself to him," he confesses after the plates have been cleared. "Silly, right?" he half asks, blushing deeply.

"No." I pause, trying to picture my mother's face. "I think I can understand that. So, is he proud?" I ask. Clark sucks in a breath and blows it out dramatically.

"Jury's still out," he says, smiling. I laugh at the lame joke and cover my mouth to hide it. "Yeah, I think he's probably just proud of me for being his son, you know? He doesn't actually care much for the city and there's not much to be proud about in what I'm actually doing," he admits.

"Why not?"

"Well, I mean, I do well in school, and I got accepted to a good law school, but the internship, it's nothing much. It's basically doing everything nobody else wants to: a lot of paper shuffling and low level grunt work. It's a great learning experience, but I don't like some the firm's big corporate clients. I'd rather do more pro bono work, I guess, or maybe be an ADA or something less soulless. Maybe environmental law," he trails off.

"Is that what your father does?" I ask.

"Yeah, he runs a small practice in Maine, specializes in environmental law. He seems to sleep easy, which I've come to see the value in," he says chuckling lightly.

"What about your mother?"

"She died when I was nine," he says simply.

"Oh, I'm sorry," I say, feeling like I've shot him in the chest, and that as a freaking orphan I should have known better.

"It's okay, it was a long time ago," he says, taking a sip of his water. I don't ask the next question because I know I wouldn't want anyone to ask me, but like anyone who has lost someone, he knows the question, knows it's laying there unasked between us. "It was a car accident," he says, putting down his glass. I breathe in slowly wondering if maybe a little bit of our twin pain is part of what draws me to him so powerfully.

"Mine too," I say quietly. He looks up at me, surprised.

"Your mother died in a car accident." He says quietly.

"Both of my parents," I say. "When I was six." It feels almost a relief to say it out loud. In twelve years I haven't actually said it to anyone.

"Oh, Bonnie, I'm sorry,"

"It's okay," I say, swallowing my forced smile. "Like you said, it was a long time ago." There's a long, serious pause between us and he suddenly lifts his glass to toast and I raise mine, unsure what we're toasting to.

"Car accidents," he says lightly. "Making kids miserable since just about ever." He smiles clinking his glass against mine. I'm serious for a second, looking at him, studying him, and then we both burst out laughing. I'm laughing so hard I'm crying and people are staring. It feels good to laugh about it. It's one of those clichés – if you don't laugh you'll cry. I never realized how true it was before, but I guess that's why they're called clichés. It feels glorious to make light of the tragedy we've been carrying around on our backs and I catch my breath and raise my glass again.

"I'll do you one better," I say and he smiles and prepares himself for another black toast, "Orphanages – splitting up families since inception," I say clinking my glass to his and drinking deeply. We both laugh again at the absurdity of it all, and we stop and touch our sides simultaneously.

"Ouch," Clark winces, and then looks at me more seriously. "Orphanage huh? That must have been rough."

"Yeah, my brother, Jasper, and I were split up, sent to group homes. There wasn't any family that could take care of us. I think that was the hardest thing actually. I mean, my parents were dead and I was devastated, but here was this person that was alive and loved me as desperately as I loved him and yet we couldn't be together." My words come tumbling out in a rush, surprisingly raw. I can't help but wonder, who is this amazing person I suddenly feel like talking to. With him I feel like stringing whole sentences together into paragraphs. Bonnie Braverman, the once-mute girl, talking in whole soliloquies.

Sitting across from Clark, I feel that if I can just be with him, I will never have to worry about anything ever again. Something about him makes me feel normal, makes me just like everyone else in the restaurant, the city, the world.

After dinner he walks me home. I don't want him to, mostly because I don't want him to see where I live. I don't have a gift for taking care of myself the way other people seem to – buying towels, or changing dirty sheets, or cooking food and putting leftovers in cute little Tupperware containers for later. It doesn't come naturally to me and it has never seemed important, until now. Until now, when Clark risks seeing my badly-furnished motel room (which I have painted entirely yellow) and my not even passable homemaking skills. Now, it seems important. I wish more than anything that I could take him back to some cute little East Village apartment, maybe complete with a nice roommate and they can chat while I make tea. As we get closer to my neighborhood he asks me the question I've been dreading, the question that might ruin what even I, virgin dater, think was a pretty great first date.

"So I have to ask…how old are you?" he asks, looking at me sideways a bit.

"Does it matter?" I ask, trying to be light.

"I hope not," he says, clearly nervous.

"I'm 18, but I'll be 19 soon…okay not soon, but in…May. How old are you?"

"Twenty," he says, clearly relieved.

"That's not so bad," I say, equally relieved. "You're really young to be so far along in school…you must be really smart," I say.

"I do okay," he says good-naturedly. And I suddenly feel like an idiot. What would he want with me? I'm just some kid, some girl that has no parents, grew up in an orphanage, and has a crappy public school education and no SAT scores to speak of, let alone some impressive Ivy League education, fancy law school acceptance letters, and swanky internships. Superpowers don't seem like they give me any advantage, all of a sudden. In fact, they seem like only a disadvantage. Like something that might threaten him or scare him, like something that could even put him in danger.

My mood darkens quickly. He notices and elbows me lightly in the arm.

"What's wrong?"

"Um. Nothing."

"C'mon, what happened…you got all sullen."

"Well, I just…you must be really smart and you're getting this great education, and someday soon you're going to have a serious, really grown up job…you are soooo not going to be interested in me. I'm just like totally mediocre in comparison…me and my stupid non-career jobs."

"I don't think you're mediocre at all," he says quietly. "In fact, I think you're the most interesting person I've ever met."

I look up, happy, but confused. "Why?"

"I don't know really…" he starts and I can't help laughing because it sounds really bad. "No, I mean…" he laughs. "Sorry that sounded terrible, I just…there's just something about you. You're different than anyone else I've ever met. It's kind of intoxicating, actually," he says. I smile to myself more than him now. It's nice that he can see that there is something different about me, even if it's a secret. We turn the corner and we're close to my crappy motel so I suggest we part.

"No, let me walk you all the way," he protests, looking around gallantly.

"It's okay, my place is really close, and I've been here for awhile. The people here know me, I'll be fine." He looks around again.

"You're sure?" he asks. I nod.

"I'm sure," I say.

"When can I see you again?" he asks.

"Tomorrow?" I venture optimistically. He laughs.

"I'll come by the bookstore. When do you get off?"

"Six."

"Six it is then," he says, and stands there awkwardly for a minute. There are no more questions to ask, but neither of us wants to leave. I'm so nervous my toes are sweating. I have no idea what I'm supposed to do now. It was easy just talking with him – about books and movies, about his life and mine. He made me forget that I didn't know what to do. But now I can only think about what comes next and that I don't know what it is. I try not to look directly in his eyes, it's like looking directly at the sun –

burning, intense – and when he looks back at me it's like he can see back into me, maybe even too deep. But I can't help it, I look and he looks back. I lean forward and brush his cheek awkwardly with my lips, before turning and running away like a little girl – shy and embarrassed and very much feeling eight instead of 18.

"Bye!" I shout as I run. He says bye too, though quietly, and any girl without superpowers wouldn't have been able to hear it. I'm glad I can though, because I can tell by the corners of it that it was all caught up in a smile. His skin tastes somehow both salty and sweet and I can taste it all the way home.

In the morning everything still retains its bright, lovely color.

And I look like an idiot.

I smile all morning like I can't turn it off. I had no idea I have so many teeth. I shower, very aware of my body. I open my closet, very aware of the lack of options hanging there. I walk down the street, very aware of every red strand of hair brushing against my cheek. I feel almost like a grown-up and so I buy and drink a strong, dark coffee, very aware of how it feels in my mouth. I still don't really like it, but maybe I could learn to?

Even though he's not coming until six I listen for him all day as I bounce around the bookstore. He has a distinctive sound that I know I'll recognize. It's unique, like everything else about him. He weighs about 190 pounds and is strong, but walks carefully, almost quietly, like an athlete that's forgotten he's no longer on the field. It makes him easy to hear, easy to distinguish from other people. There's also the deepness of his laugh, which I think I could pick out from a mile. Time will tell, I suppose. After an agonizing day where suddenly books I once loved seem dull and lifeless, I hear him, his feet coming past the registers and past customer service. He bounds up the stairs and, after turning a corner, sees me in the Science Fiction aisle. Everything else in the world seems like it's on pause, just waiting for him. And then he steps up to me, and it's like everything starts again. I breathe him in, soaking up everything about him.

"Hi," I say in my most casual voice, which is really my most practiced voice, because I'm not sure what casual should sound like and I've been practicing really hard.

"Hi," he echoes, though his 'Hi' sounds better than mine. "So, um, Sunday, my roommates are having a party for 4th of July. They bought a grill from some guy on another floor and managed to wedge it onto our tiny patio. I mean, you have to stand inside to use it but they're really excited about this whole idea of a 4th of July barbeque in the apartment. I'm sure we'll probably get arrested or something but um...man, I'm rambling...I'm sorry."

"It's okay."

"So, um...will you come?" he finally asks. I smile, every tooth in my mouth acts like it wants to be seen.

"Yes," I say and feel myself blushing as he breaks into a relieved smile.

"Okay, great!" he says and then reaches into his back pocket and pulls out something wrapped simply in brown craft paper. "Here," he says, thrusting it at me. I hold the package lightly, confused to be getting a present. Nobody has ever given me a present before, well, not since after I went to the home. I shake my head in amazement and open the flap gently. I pull the book out of the wrapping carefully and quickly see that it's a first edition of The Loneliness of the Long Distance Runner. My mouth drops open and I turn the book over, examining it. It's beautiful. He reaches over and opens it to a page in the back. It says 'Clark Spencer. 55 Greene Street #2D. 6:30 p.m., July 4th'

"You...you bought a first edition of my favorite book so that you could write your address in it?"

"Yeah. The woman who sold it to me almost had a heart attack."

"Um, there's probably like, scrap pieces of paper up by the register..."

"Yeah, but you'd never remember that. Then maybe someday that piece of paper would get thrown away and one day we'd even forget the first illegal 4th of July apartment barbeque we went to. This way, we'll always remember it," he says. I look at him, stunned.

"I don't think I could ever forget something like that."

"Well, I wanted to give it to you anyway," he says, shrugging and smiling. I narrow my eyes playfully.

"What if I hadn't said yes?" I ask. His eyes get all big and innocent.

"Well then, I'd still have given you the book, but you'd have to look at my name and address for eternity and wonder what you missed," he says. It's far too charming an answer for the likes of me and so I default to stumbling idiocy.

"I don't know what to say," I mumble, blushing and holding the book carefully, tracing the old edges with my finger, trying not to realize that other than my mother's bracelet it's easily the most priceless thing I've ever owned. It's also the first gift I've been given in twelve years.

"Just say you'll be there at six-thirty," he says, all boyish charm and hopes.

"I'll be there at six-thirty."

"Good," he says resolutely and then smiles for just a second before walking away. On the stairs he looks back at me and smiles again, but it's less boyish now, more handsome, more serious. More a portent of things to come. And suddenly I'm really nervous.

I have no idea what I'm doing.

The first date happened so fast I almost didn't have time to think about it, but now, this second one is two days away and those days stretch out before me as impossibly long and full of nothing but waiting and worry.

I go into the backroom to re-load my cart and put my gift in my locker. Liesel is on the floor, as I've come to expect, but she's moved on from Tropic of Cancer to Metamorphoses.

"Hey," I say.

"Hey," she says and then adds nonchalantly, "Watch your back, I just saw Erica and she's like…on a tear."

"About?"

"Yeah, she knows you went out with that Clark guy…or are going out with him again, or something…she's freaking."

"Wow. I mean, how does she even know that?"

"Who knows? Books here have ears so far as I can tell," she says shrugging.

"What should I do?" I ask before I even realize I'm asking a near stranger. But Liesel considers it seriously enough to even put her book down for a minute, which I've never seen her do before.

"I think, I'd punch her in the face. Not a slap, but like, a full on punch - BAM!" she says, doing a little punch with her small fist. I try not to laugh.

"Um, I can't do that," I say, wishing I could. She screws up her mouth.

"Yeah, you're right. Too much. But the whole thing is just so catty and stupid. So cliché and unimaginative, you know? Like fighting over a dude? Really? Seems ridiculous."

"Ridiculous," I repeat hollowly, still not sure how to handle it.

"Just ignore her, I guess," she says, "I suspect being ignored drives someone like Erica bonkers."

"But I don't want to drive her bonkers," I say.

"Oh. Well. Then I'm out," she says shrugging and going back to her book. And at just that moment Erica comes flying through the door.

"You have GOT to be kidding me," she screeches, "He asked you out again?! YOU?!" her face is flushed and when she says 'you' she gestures at me like I'm some kind of horrifying object. She looks like she's been crying.

"I'm sorry." I offer as genuinely as I can, shrugging my shoulders and lifting my hands up helplessly, but even I know it comes out sounding confused.

"Unbelievable!" she screams. And I don't know if it's just my super hearing or what but it feels loud enough to shatter glass, or at least bother Liesel, when nothing else seems to.

"Oh. My. God." Liesel says, popping up from behind the desk. It startles Erica, momentarily, from whatever tirade she's about to launch into. "Leave her alone already, Erica. She didn't do anything. Dude likes her. She likes him, happy ever after and all that crap. Just move on already. If you keep acting like you lost something you actually wanted people are going to realize that you're not the most beautiful person to ever operate a cash register. Do you really want that?!"

Erica stands there with her mouth hanging open and then shuts it, turns on her heel and walks out of the room.

"Wow," I say, dumbfounded. "Thanks."

"No problem," Liesel says lying back down behind the desk with her book. "Calling 'em like I see 'em is like my one gift in this world...my superpower if you will. But I so rarely get to use it for good instead of evil, so I should thank you," she says.

I smile, to myself, since Liesel has already checked back into one of her fictional worlds, and load the cart up with books, wondering if this is how people make friends…and enemies.

●

It's only a few days before I show up at Dr. Elizabeth Grant's office with no appointment. I suspect it surprises me far more than it will her. I'm not sure if I'm here out of mind-numbing boredom or because I haven't quite been able to get her out of my mind. Her receptionist, or assistant, or whatever she is tries to throw me out at first but thinks better of it after a minute and lets me sit in the waiting room. Elizabeth comes out in less than five minutes, talking to the assistant, practically before she even opens the door. "Jan, can you type up these notes, I've got to get out of here if I'm going to-" She stops mid-sentence as if sensing someone in the room and looks up. "Lola," she says, breaking into a small smile. The assistant sighs.

"Yeah, there's someone named Lola here to see you, but she doesn't have an appointment," she says with a snotty edge to her voice.

"Hi Doc," I say with a little half-wave.

"It's so nice to see you, Lola. Why don't you come in?"

"She isn't on the calendar," Jan says, repeating herself, obviously irritated. "And if you don't leave now, you're going to be late for the conference."

"I know Jan. It's fine. Why don't you head over to the conference, make apologies for my lateness. I'll close up and get there as soon as I can, okay?" Jan nods her head like it's decidedly not okay. Elizabeth ushers me into her office. It's modern, with clean lines and perfectly placed books and objects. It looks like she does – deliberately assembled, but not unappealing. There's artwork on her walls and I wonder briefly if she picked it because she likes the way it looks, or because it's supposed to mean something, or just because it goes with the room. She motions me to a coffee-colored leather couch and I plunk down, not sure what the hell I'm going to say to her.

"So, Lola. I'm glad you decided to come by. Can I ask what made you decide to?" She sits in a matching coffee-colored leather chair opposite me and crosses her legs smoothly. I remember my decision to not lie to her.

"Curiosity, I guess."

"Curiosity? About what?"

"About my name. You said it has a history…and a lot of people have made fun of my name, so I thought maybe you could tell me what's up with that."

"Well, the name Lola has taken on a kind of seductress connotation, or perhaps more accurately that of a young girl that is sexually precocious, thanks to Nabokov's *Lolita*, published in the 1950s." She pauses, I guess waiting for a question or acknowledgement from me, when I offer none, she continues. "Lola was one of the nicknames for Lolita in the book, and Lolita is a well-known diminutive form of Lola. So I suppose when people meet a pretty young girl like yourself and hear that your name is Lola, they have an association with the history and, well, that book and the subsequent pop culture connotations of your name."

"Is that it? I thought maybe there'd be more to it."

"Well, it's also the title of a brilliant song by The Kinks, written in the 1970s," she offers, smiling.

"Hmmph."

"You're disappointed?"

"I don't know."

"There's also a song called Whatever Lola Wants, written for a musical in the 1950s, which has been remade innumerable times…my personal favorite is by Sarah Vaughan," Elizabeth says, smiling. I'm not interested in any of this, though I already know I'll be downloading it all to my stolen iPod when I get a chance. She must see my mind wandering because she switches tactics. "The actual meaning of the name Lola is interesting, but I doubt most people know it, so it's unlikely they're reacting to that," she says.

"What's the actual meaning?"

"Sorrows."

Something about that word hits me like a brick thrown at my chest.

"Really? Sorrows."

"Yes. Does that mean something to you?"

"Nah. No. I doubt my mom knew any of this stuff, she wasn't a big reader or anything, but 'sorrows'…I can see her naming me sorrow."

"Why do you think your mother would name you 'sorrows'?"

"She just probably knew what I was up against. It fits. Honestly? I kind of like my name better now. It makes a lot more sense...and at least I know what people are snickering about. So, thanks." I stand up to leave.

"Would you like to talk again sometime, Lola? You seem like maybe you have a lot on your mind," Elizabeth says without getting up from the chair. She seems overly anxious despite herself; she doesn't want me escaping into the night. I pause with my hand on the door, I'm about to say 'no' if only as a big 'F you' to her, but suddenly I feel like there's a lot I want to say.

"Do you know what the name 'Bonnie' means?"

"Well, I know it means pretty...but there may be other meanings," she starts.

"How do you know so much about this?" I ask.

"Just a hobby of mine. I can find out the other meanings for you easily enough...if you can wait just a minute," she says. I shrug my shoulders; her desperation is showing.

"Sure." I lean against the closed door and Elizabeth goes to her desk and clicks the mouse to her laptop, types a few things in and looks up at me.

"You know, it may not mean anything. Sometimes, there are no really concrete meanings...and sometimes they're archaic and strange...Lola has a pretty direct meaning, but they're not always so direct."

"Like how?" I ask.

"Well, for example, my name, Elizabeth means 'God is my oath'...or 'God is an oath', or sometimes 'consecrated to God'"

"Yeah, I have no idea what that means," I say. She laughs.

"Me either, really," she says, typing in a few more words and reading the screen for a moment before looking up at me. "Well, it looks like 'Bonnie' is either English or Scottish in origin and means pretty, or French in origin and means good and pure of heart," she says, reading from her screen. The word 'good' hits me like another brick in the chest. Of course her name means 'good' and mine means 'sorrows'. Of course.

"Thanks," I mutter and turn to walk out again.

"You know Lola, there is another meaning for your name, it's much less common, but some list your name as meaning 'strong woman' – maybe your mother knew about that, too." I pause, hand on the door, unsure what to say.

"Maybe," I say, turning the knob, intending to leave, but at the last second I hesitate in the doorway. "Thanks Liz."

She seems to bristle ever so slightly but recovers almost instantly. "Anytime," she says casually. I can tell she wants to ask me to come back, but she's smart, she doesn't push.

"See ya around." I take off out the door, glad that Jan isn't there to do any more of her scowling. I'd like to say I won't be back, but I know I will be. I have a thousand questions and a few new ideas.

o

The day of the party, I change my outfit about 83 times, which is especially impressive because I only have a few pieces of clothing. I finally end up in jeans, my beat-up Chucks, and an old Wonder Woman t-shirt I found in a second hand shop. It's also the first outfit I tried on. It's hot out, so I pull my hair back into a ponytail. I look so mundanely average I can't imagine what Clark sees in me. It looks like I could be going on a date, I guess. It also looks like I could be going to work, or to do my laundry, or any other totally ridiculous non-important thing. I double-check the address in the back of my book, even though I'd memorized it the first time I'd looked at it, and head out the door.

At Clark's apartment, the music is already very loud and I suddenly regret my super hearing. I can feel the bass in my spine, and I'm not even inside yet. A very tall guy with broad basketball player shoulders and a shaved head opens the door. He has a huge mouth with glittering white teeth and smooth, dark skin. Before I can think what to say, he thrusts out his hand.

"You must be Bonnie...I'm Ryan," I take his hand and we shake and he steps his massive frame aside so I can get in the door.

"Hi," I say. Once inside, Ryan motions to a small group of people, never taking his eyes off me.

"Jake! C'mere!" I look at Ryan confused and in a moment a blonde guy, maybe five foot seven, looking laid back and happy and like he just got back from a beach somewhere is standing with us. "This is Bonnie," Ryan says pointing his beer at me. Jake looks me up and down, which should probably seem creepy, but there's something innocent about it.

"Hey Bonnie, good to meet you, I'm Jake, Clark's other roommate," he says taking my hand.

"Um…hey," I say, and look at them both like I have no idea what to say next, because I don't. After a second Jake laughs a little.

"Sorry, it's just Clark like…never dates. Or almost never. So we're just like, super curious about you."

"But I get it," Ryan chimes in, "I totally get it."

"Yeah," Jake agrees.

"Get what?" I ask.

"You. I get why he's so into you. You're like…" Ryan trails off and Jake interrupts him as if they're sharing the same brain.

"Totally."

"Totally like what?" I say, feeling more lost by the minute, and quite sure I don't need to be around for the conversation to even be taking place.

"Um…you, you're just like, I don't know…I can see why he likes you."

"Yeah," Ryan agrees this time.

"Um. Thanks?" I say, still lost and unsure. Just then I see Clark. He rushes over and elbows them both out of the way.

"Oh god. Leave her alone," he says. Jake and Ryan laugh good-naturedly. He looks at me, his eyebrows knitted comically. "Did they say anything horrible?"

"Um, I don't think they said…anything," I say honestly.

"Man, we didn't do anything," Jake protests.

"Yeah, we just said we get it is all," Ryan adds.

"Get what?" Clark asks suspiciously, his eyes narrowing.

"Why you dig her," Jake says, his smile somehow even bigger than before.

"Oh my god," Clark says rolling his eyes and ushering me away. Jake and Ryan are calling out to us "Don't go!" but Clark pushes me into a room off a hallway and closes the door as if we've escaped zombies. "Sorry about that," he says very seriously, but I'm just trying not to laugh.

"It's fine. I'm not even sure what's happening."

"They're just…whatever, they're good guys for the most part, but they're just like…I don't know, like a bunch of gossipy teenagers or something, I can't trust them around anyone."

"They seem nice…but weird," I add, raising an eyebrow.

"Definitely," he says, "To both."

I sit down before I realize we're in his bedroom and then wish I hadn't. Bedroom is way above my preparedness level. He sits next to me on the bed, but not close. And it's suddenly very still and quiet as the music in the living room changes over. "Nice room," I say, looking around causally. He looks around too, as if trying to see it through my eyes.

"Thanks," he says, and we sit in silence for what feels like whole minutes and then the music blasts again and I hear a squeal of laughter and then more people arriving.

"Okay. Are you ready to go back out there?" he asks.

"I smell hot dogs," I say, as if that's an answer. He smiles and I try to recover, "I mean, can I have a hot dog?"

"Yes, definitely."

"Okay then, I'm ready," I say as if hot dogs are the thing that will keep me sane out there. And he takes my hand and leads me back out into the bright noise.

I eat four hot dogs from the illegal patio slash grill situation and meet dozens of people, none of whom I can remember moments later. Jake and Ryan continue to be charming and weird, usually at the same time, and it's all so incredibly nice and normal that I'm sad I can't take it, but after an hour and a half, the noise is getting to me. This much noise and this many people, in such a confined space, it's just too much. I have a headache the size of a small state from all the sensory overload. I don't know what a party feels like to someone with normal senses, but to me, with everything heightened, it seems like 100 parties, all at once, all jammed into my head. I'm about to tell Clark that I have to go. In fact, I've been searching for the right words for nearly twenty minutes, the words that will make it clear that it has nothing to do with him, just with my super-senses being totally overloaded – without, of course, saying anything like that – when he reaches for my hand and whispers warmly in my ear.

"Let's get out of here." I nod and follow him out into the hallway and then into the city. We don't say anything as he pulls me along the darkening streets. After several blocks he stops at a big building. "I want to show you something," he says and opens the front door with a key. At the elevator he has to use a code inside. When we step off we're outside again, in a lush dark garden on the roof of the building. Clark leads me forward a few steps and then releases my hand and goes to a nearby wall. I'm standing on cool grass, some blades of it reaching up into my jeans. Suddenly the garden is illuminated by tiny strings of white lights. It's a secret magical feeling place.

"Where are we?" I breathe.

"It's great, isn't it?"

"Beautiful," I say. "I didn't know something like this could exist…in the city like this."

"Sure. Rooftop decks, one of the greatest things about the city, if you ask me. They're a bit too rare, but maybe that's what makes them so magical."

"Whose is this?"

"It belongs to my family," he says, and there's something in his voice, like he's ashamed to admit it, or embarrassed. How you could be embarrassed by something so beautiful is beyond me.

"Where are they?" I ask. It seems empty and silent.

"Well my dad hates the city, so he's never here. He keeps the place for my mother's family, I guess. In case they want to visit. But they never come. They wanted me to live here while I was going to school. But it seemed…wrong. How could I have a normal life…something like what everyone else at school has if I was living here, right?"

"So, you're like really rich or something?"

"My family is, not me. But I guess, I mean I get to take advantage of it all the time…I should just get used to it. Makes me seem like a jerk if I pretend I'm not, right?" He says, shoving his hands in his pockets, looking down at his feet. I shrug.

"I don't think you're a jerk," I say. And as he looks back up, there's a huge pop and the sky explodes in color.

"Oh my god," I say, watching the sky turn brilliant shades of red and then gold.

"Oh, yeah," Clark says, looking at the fireworks, "That's why I brought you up here. Amazing, right?" I just nod, unable to take my eyes off the bursting colors. He kneels down and motions to me.

"Come down here. It's the best view. I discovered it when I was a kid." He lies down in the grass and I lie down next to him, the grass bending under my weight, cool blades of it poking my back where my skin is slightly exposed. The sky grows bright again, this time in blues and greens then silvery yellows. Pink, purple, orange, and blue again. More red. It's hypnotic and the most magnificent thing I've ever seen. I turn to him as the sky goes electric blue around us.

"Thank you," I say. He turns to me, propping himself up on his elbow.

"You're welcome," he says. He leans forward and he's closer than he's ever been before. I can almost taste him, his skin, his breath, his soul almost. I close my eyes and try to savor the moment, one that won't ever happen again. But suddenly, just as his lips touch mine, I hear a piercing scream. I yank my head back, nailing him in the lip with my chin.

"Ow," he says touching his lip. I look at him, horrified. I want to make it better, undo what I've done, but the woman is still screaming and it's all I can hear.

"Oh my god," I say, covering my mouth and sitting up. "Are you okay? I'm so sorry…"

"Yeah, I'm fine, are you okay?" he asks.

"Uh-huh. Yes. Fine. But um, I have to go," I say, scrambling to get up.

"Right now?" he asks, stunned.

"Yes!" I call, already at the elevator and pushing the button.

"Bonnie!" he yells after me, his voice a mix of confusion and concern.

"I'm sorry!" I yell as the elevator doors close behind me. And I am sorry. I've just ruined my first kiss and maybe now I'll never even get it. He'll probably never want to kiss me again. Man, I'm never going to have nice things. By the time I burst out the front door onto the street the woman's screams are muffled. I'm worried I won't be able to find her, but I run south, and strain my ears for more. I hear her twice more, and it's just enough to pinpoint her. I come crashing into a black alleyway and see two men shapes looming over a woman. I stand there for just a minute and one looks at me warily while the other smiles as if he's getting a two for one special.

"Get her," he whispers to the wary one, but it sounds like a booming command in my ears. He rushes me, despite his wariness, and he's big and fast. When he's an arm-length away I ball up my fist and throw it at his face. I connect and the sound of his cheek shattering is surprising bliss. He cries out and holds his cheek like a baby. His friend is cussing in the background. Broken Cheek comes at me again, less wary and more pissed. He lunges and manages to grab a bit of my shirt as I spring backward. We fall to the ground ungracefully. I hear the other one coming closer but I can't see him with Broken Cheek on top of me. I smack him in the same cheek as before and he wails and bucks up enough that I'm able to get my feet between our bodies. I launch him off of me, and hopefully into the lower stratosphere. His friend is on me before Broken Cheek even lands, thirty feet away in a moaning heap. The friend has a blade and he stabs at me with it. I move just enough that it misses my midsection and breaks his wrist when it connects with the concrete beneath me. He recovers quickly though and I'm barely able to get up before he's coming back at me. I hear the sound of feet running for the other end of the alley and hope it's the woman, escaping. The knife comes at me again with his other uninjured hand and I juke backwards and swat hard at his wrist. The knife pops free and clatters across the ground, sliding to a stop under a dumpster, nicely out of reach. He yells out in frustration and runs at me, but I grab the edges of his shirt and use his own momentum to send him flying at the wall. He hits it head-first with a dull wet thud. I stand in the alley quietly, waiting to see if either will get up for more, but they're done.

I'm about to exit the way I came in when I see the woman again, with two policemen in tow. She's pointing at the three of us and saying something garbled. A policeman says 'freeze,' and I do, for just a second, before turning and running full tilt for the opening at the other end of the alleyway. One of them chases me half-heartedly, but I'm already gone.

A few blocks from the scene I start my walk home, lost in conflicting thoughts of Clark's mouth and beating up rapists in an alleyway. It was less than twenty minutes ago that I was there with Clark in his magical rooftop garden but somehow it feels like a lifetime ago. It's dawning on me now more than ever before that getting to have Clark and still being me is nearly impossible, something I'll never quite manage. Without even realizing it, however, I find I've wandered back to Clark's building instead of home, perhaps some part of me deciding to fight the idea that I can't have both things, can't be both things. Drowning in some toxic mixture of euphoria, regret, excitement, and resistance, I almost don't see him until I'm right in front of him as he closes the door to the building I'd run out of such a short time ago.

"Bonnie?" He looks me up and down. I must be a mess – the kind of unsexy mess you become after rolling around on New York City streets – but I don't care. I don't say anything, I just step toward him. Our bodies fit together, some parts touching lightly, others pressing tightly. I brush his lips lightly with mine, unsure of everything, except what I want. He tastes alive and beautiful, and a little like vanilla. We part for just a second, his eyes searching mine, and then he puts his hand on my neck, his thumb brushing my cheek, my jawbone. He pulls me in closer and kisses me deeply.

It's the kind of kiss worthy of fireworks, the kind of kiss that makes superheroes weak in the knees.

●

I wait almost six weeks before I go back to see Liz. I've decided to call her Liz because I'd seen her bristle ever so slightly at the nickname when I used it last time.

This time when Jan sees me, after a look of surprise and maybe disdain crosses her face for a split second, she simply nods and pushes a little button on her desk that I assume alerts Liz to a patient waiting. Liz appears in less than a minute, a surprise in her smile when she sees me pacing the small room.

"Lola. How nice to see you," she says, stepping aside in her doorway, one hand out gesturing me inside.

"Uh, sure. You too." Everything is the same as last time. I sit on her leather couch. She sits across from me and crosses her legs, heels digging in to the rug and the sound of her nylons brushing together as she adjusts herself.

"I'm glad you came back…" she begins, dragging her sentence out and waiting for me to reply. I just nod and give her a conceding half smile. "What made you come back, if you don't mind my asking?"

"I don't know. Mostly I think I just wanted someone to talk to."

"That's fair. A lot of people see therapists for that reason. What would you like to talk about?"

"It's just I'm pretty new to L.A., I don't have any friends here," I pause, realizing that while this is true, it's also kind of a lie as it implies I have friends elsewhere, which I don't. "Actually though, I don't have any friends anywhere."

"Do you have trouble making friends?"

"Yeah. I'm not that interested in trying to make any new ones…considering what happened with the last ones."

"Do you want to talk about that?" she asks. I pause, making sure my answer is honest and realize that right now I honestly don't want to and so I tell her so.

"No."

"Okay." There's a pause in the room, which becomes a long silence. It doesn't make me uncomfortable and while it doesn't seem to make Liz uncomfortable either, I think she's going to break before I do. She does. But maybe she didn't know it was a contest.

"Do you want to talk about your mother?"

"I suppose," I say.

"Were you and your mother close?"

"No. I mean, there was totally a time when I was very young that I wanted to be just like her…she was like a god to me and I just bathed in her presence, but she was very checked out, even then. There were times I saw her make an effort, but not many, and usually she couldn't focus on the effort long enough for it to pay off. She was a drunk. I'm pretty sure she was a drug addict too. She was out of it almost nonstop, I'd say since the time I was six or seven."

"That must have been very difficult."

"I wouldn't use that word."

"What word would you use?"

"I'd say…disappointing. I was always pretty good at taking care of myself, ever since I can remember at least, but it was disappointing to have to, I guess. I expected more of her. Especially as I got older and realized what she could have been, who she should have been."

"Who should she have been?"

"Well, for starters, a good mother, among other things."

"Are you angry with her?"

"I was. No, I still am. Yeah, I'm angry with her."

"Why?"

"For a lot of stuff. Being a crap mother, not telling me stuff she should have told me…" I pause, considering my next statement carefully.

"Can you finish that thought…you seem like you were going to say something else."

"Yeah, I just, I think her dying was overdue, but I wish I'd asked some questions before she bit it."

"What kind of questions?"

"Y'know, like who my father was, or where he was. I mean I could be Immaculate Conception or some shit, for all I know."

"Do you wish you knew your father?"

"Not really, I just wish I had the information. Y'know I was just a stupid kid when she died, I didn't know anything about my family or where I came from, or even much about her."

"You know, you're still a kid, Lola, I don't think you should be so hard on yourself."

"Trust me Liz, I'm no kid, regardless of how I may look to you."

"How do you mean?"

"I've just been through a lot."

"Do you see that as your fault?"

"Um, no, actually. Y'know, I thought it was at first, because I did bad stuff and I kind of knew it was wrong when I was doing it…but the more I've lived with myself, the more I've realized I don't really have a choice about it."

"We all have choices, Lola."

"Sure, sure. I make choices, everyday I make choices, but ultimately, my destiny is being guided by something else, something that, in the end, I don't think I get to say one goddamn thing about."

"Are you talking about God?" Liz furrows her brow at me.

"No. Well, I mean I guess I could be. It doesn't feel like God though. It's just a feeling. A feeling that I'm different and that I'm supposed to be doing something with it…and that I don't have much choice about it."

"What are you supposed to be doing?"

"Jesus, if I knew that I wouldn't be here, Liz. I know I'm supposed to be doing something, but there's just nothing to point me in the right direction. I'm hoping you and your big brain can help me with that part."

"I'm not sure I'm following you, Lola," Liz pulls her glasses down a bit and peers at me over them, as if seeing me with her naked eye will somehow clear up her confusion.

"It's like…it's like I'm a missile with a nuclear warhead…just waiting to go off…but there's nobody to point me at anything. And I'm just this weapon built for destruction, you know…but I don't have the brain that can point me to a target. I'm just the weapon, and without the additional information, the codes or location or whatever, well I just sit on the ground impotent. I mean you might as well hang dirty laundry on me."

"Lola, I'm afraid I'm even more confused now…"

"It's like, at least if I was a heat-seeking missile I'd have a chance, you know, because at least I'd be heat-seeking. Sure, I'd probably still need a little help, but I'd be better off than before at least."

"Lola…"

"Follow the analogy, Liz…or metaphor…or whatever! I'm a weapon primed for destruction, but I needed to get some crucial details from Delia, and now it's too freaking late, and so I'm running around bumping into shit without any clue about what the hell I'm supposed to be doing."

"Okay, okay, I see what you mean." Liz raises her hands up a little bit palms down, making a gesture intended to calm me. It doesn't work. I'm annoyed.

"Jeez," I get up and head for the door, pissed that I had to explain it to her in tiny baby bites. I mean, I'm pretty impressed with my analogy, especially considering my tenth grade education, but the fact that she can't follow me is frustrating.

"Lola, where are you going?"

"I gotta go."

"Okay, will you be coming back?"

"I don't know. Probably." I walk out the door, slamming it a little too hard, and cutting Jan a withering look.

o

It happens so fast with us. Not like I had briefly tried to imagine, awkward dates and first kisses, and ages before anyone really felt anything real. Instead, he becomes my whole world instantly. And though it's strange and surreal and maybe not how it's supposed to go, all I can think is how lucky I've been to find him. I wonder if everyone gets this lucky, but maybe just once, and maybe sometimes, it doesn't last.

I hope it lasts; already, I can't remember what my life was like before him.

And today, I had this great idea that I should cook dinner for Clark at his apartment, as if me doing that will solidify, in my own mind, that I'm good enough for him, that I can take care of him and be a great girlfriend, that we can have a totally normal life.

Worst. Idea. Ever.

I don't know what I was thinking. Not only can I not cook, but I don't even know how to grocery shop. I've been wandering around this grocery store for 45 minutes already, with a scribbled list in hand for some recipes I found in a cookbook at the bookstore. I have exactly two things in my basket, toilet paper and Cheetos, neither of which are on the list and the latter of which I broke into ten minutes ago and have been nervously gnawing on ever since. I've got Cheeto dust on my jeans and now on all three bundles of asparagus that I've been staring at for six solid minutes.

And, I have no earthly idea how to pick good asparagus.

I wish my powers were good for things like picking out asparagus. Is there a way to divine where the asparagus came from? Why are some of them thick and some thin, and over there, there's white ones. How will they taste? Do they all taste different? Which are the freshest? Oh my god, this is the hardest thing I've ever done.

A woman accidentally elbows me as she reaches for her own bundle of asparagus. "Sorry," I mumble edging myself out of the way a little and eyeing the ones she picks up. How does she know?! I give up and put all three bundles in the basket with my Cheetos and toilet paper.

There are like a thousand more things on the list. We're going to be eating at midnight.

As I'm poring over about a hundred different kinds of cheese in a dairy case the burning hits my chest. I haven't felt the burning since that night on the street, that 4th of July, just before my first kiss with Clark. I don't know why I haven't been sensing anything. Selfishly, I didn't want to question it, but now, now that it's here, it's like being hit by a truck. I look up and that razor focus that tells me where to go and what to do yanks me toward the back of the store. I can smell the fire already.

Somewhere along the way I drop my basket and any ideas I harbor of being some great girlfriend that cooks dinner.

As if a fire wasn't enough, I can feel something else is wrong. Something deeper and more dangerous. As I push toward the swinging produce doors I realize that the fire alarms aren't going off and just as I think it, the power in the store cuts out entirely and dim emergency lights click on. Some people just look up from their shopping with a cocked eyebrow, more annoyance that concern as they wait for everything to revert to normal, but others panic instantly and run toward the front doors. Before I make it to the produce doors the fire pushes through them, claiming a whole section of refrigerated meats. People are running toward the front of the store now like a crazy, spooked herd of animals. Somewhere toward the front there's a huge, unnatural clanging sound of metal slamming against something and so I pick an aisle with a view to the storefront and see that the metal security gates are, for some reason, closed, trapping everyone inside. Crap.

The fire surges into an aisle right in front of me, and because I have terrible luck, it's the paper section and the fire eats the whole row like it's made of kindling, burning a path straight to the front of the store, and dangerously close to the shoppers. Their screaming triples in volume to match the heat. I don't blame them for screaming; it's pretty damn scary in here.

Near the back but on the side of the store I see an emergency exit, which I'm surprised nobody has thought of and I move toward it. A young man in a business suit beats me to it and is trying the door. He pushes against it with everything his body has and nothing happens. I run the rest of the way. It feels like in slow motion, and I pull him away from the door, tearing his expensive jacket in the process. I think he is going to be angry with me, some stupid girl pulling him off of the door, but instead his face is filled only with fear, and tears, and the understanding that this is it. This is his moment. I lay a strong hand on his chest.

"It's all going to be okay," I say. He believes me so much for a moment that I think even I believe me. He steps back and now I hit the door with everything I have. Nothing. It doesn't move an inch. There's a dent in it where my fist has landed, but it's no closer to opening. I consider punching a hole in the door and tearing into it until there's enough room for people to crawl out, but the fire is advancing toward the door's location quickly and I don't think there's time for this to be a feasible exit strategy. The guy that cuts the deli meats and cheeses is running past us toward the front and I stop him, a hand on his forearm

"What's wrong with this door?" I ask. He looks around frantically.

"The delivery guys, they park their trucks there; it's probably blocked," he says, tearing his arm away and heading toward the crowd piling up against the glass at the front of the store.

"Of course they do," I say to myself. Even if I could get a hole in this door, if there are trucks parked there that people have to crawl over or under. we'll never get everyone out in time. I look at the boy and we duck as heavy smoke rolls above us. Our faces are slick with sweat and flushed red, the heat is getting to us both. I suddenly wonder what will happen to me if I burn to death. Will I even die? Will I just keep burning and not die? I've rescued people from fires before, but I've never been trapped in one. The thought of dying repeatedly while these people burn alongside me is horrifying and shocks me back to reality.

"C'mon," I say to the boy. "Back to the front." He follows me dutifully, maybe because he saw what I did to the door or maybe just because he doesn't know what else to do. On the way I grab an armful of dishtowels and motion for the boy to do the same. I wrap one of the larger ones around my face, as much to hide myself as to cover my mouth from the smoke. I hear sirens in the distance, but they're too far off to make a difference. We are all going to die in here – well, maybe not me – that's still up for discussion, but everyone else if I can't get them out in the next few minutes. The smoke is causing people to faint left and right. If they're lucky, they get caught by a stranger, if they're not, they hit the linoleum with a thud. While we're making our way to the front of the store, the cookie and cereal aisle goes up in flames. People, at least forty, cluster at one side of the front of the store, behind a row of sodas and bottled waters. Half of them have fainted, the other half look ready to go at any moment. I touch the boy on his shoulder and point. He runs into a group and huddles up, passing out dishtowels and I give the ones I'm holding to the group on the other side. More than half of the store is engulfed in flames, and the wall of glass is moments away from becoming merely a wall of fire. I move as far away from the flames as I can risk. I reach a hand out to the glass or whatever the hell it is that is keeping us in, some kind of re-enforced ridiculousness better suited for a prison than a grocery store in Manhattan.

"Be careful, it's hot!" Someone screams out. Sure enough, it is hot to the touch, and getting hotter by the second. I put my right palm against it and press hard. It burns me, but I can feel a little give there in the glass. Someone yells out and someone else faints as they listen to the skin on my palm sizzle. I turn around to face the crowd, making sure most of my face is still covered.

"Okay. I'm getting us out of here. Everyone get on the floor." I blink as everyone obeys. I'm shocked that anyone is listening. A few people mumble things, but they all fall in line. The young healthy ones help the too young and the too old onto the floor. I look at the flames advancing behind me and to the left, creeping across the glass like magic. I'm afraid. I'm afraid of being burned alive, and just living through it, but I'm even more afraid of listening to all these people die in here with me as I live through burning to death. It's too gruesome. We have to get out now.

I look at my hand. It's better, not fully healed, but better. This is good. Maybe that means I can take the heat long enough to push through and free us. I put my hands on the glass. It's hotter now than moments ago, and the flesh on my hands sizzles immediately. I press against the wall. It bends under me a little, but maybe because it is so hot now, it just folds a bit, it has even more flexibility than ever before, and it is going to take so much more to break it.

I scream as I feel my flesh melting down off my hands and onto the glass. People around me scream with me. Maybe because they can see what's happening to my hands, or maybe because they're afraid I'm not going to be able to get them out, or maybe because they're burning too. The last thought surges within me and

I press harder, give more. I feel it go. First just a little, and then all the way. The glass bends away and breaks, and I dig deeper and press with everything I have until I feel a huge chunk of it fall away onto the concrete outside. I am so pleased for the second before the fire hits my back that I don't have time to notice the flesh is completely burned off both my hands. I think I'm on fire as I yank apart the security gate and fall forward into the street. I start to shake off the fire like a dog shakes off a soapy bath. As the flames leave me I'm hit with water from a hose. Not a fire hose, but a garden hose. A hardware store owner, very pleased with himself, has doused me. I turn back to the wall. The back draft has come and gone, the fire surging back into the store, thick black smoke rolls around the street and inside the building and even onlookers are tearing up and coughing. I tear back some of the sharper glass, plastic, and metal with my destroyed hands, making the space larger and people start pouring out while the flesh on my back begins the painful process of knitting itself back together. The whole time I keep the now soaked towel draped around my face in the hopes that between that and the black smoke the cell phones I can already hear snapping away won't get anything useable of me.

I see the boy helping to carry out an older woman and we nod to each other respectfully before I make my escape. A few people look at me in the crowd as I run away, and a few even call out, but none try to stop me. Perhaps it's respect; perhaps it's understanding or gratitude. Whatever it is, I'm grateful for it. I look at the flesh on my hands as it grows back, covering the bone and muscle ever so slowly. It's painful and gruesome to look at, but I know they're healing. And I know that everything is as it should be, that is until I remember Clark and my 'grand perfect girlfriend dinner plans.' A dozen blocks from his apartment I buy new jeans and a t-shirt and change into them inside a Taco Bell bathroom after washing myself down as best I can with the sink, paper towels, and an overly aggressive hand dryer. The flesh on my hands is new and pink, and crazy sensitive, but I don't have time for sensitive. I ditch the smoky clothes in the bathroom trashcan and, three blocks from his apartment, pick up a pizza.

When I come in, Clark looks at his watch and then looks at the pizza box in confusion. I shrug my shoulders.

"I changed my mind," I say, smiling and then add, "I'll cook for you next week." But I know it's unlikely to ever happen again, and maybe he knows too. Fitting these two lives together is too hard. Something is going to have to give. I saved almost 50 people from a burning supermarket – it's a great thing to have done – and I'm beaming on the inside, but I'm full of lies and deception when I'm with Clark, and I can't bear it, the feeling of that wedge of my lies between us. I don't see how the two parts of me can live together in harmony, not without being a crappy girlfriend, or letting lots of people die. I think I have to stop. Either being with Clark, or being what I am. How can I make that decision? I mean, for anyone truly good inside, it wouldn't even be a question for. What does that say about me? Clearly saving people is more important. But I've gone my whole life barely knowing what happiness feels like and now that I have it, I don't know if I can give it up. It's too hard. I feel split in two, choosing between impossible things.

As Clark and I literally clink together our glasses for a toast at our favorite restaurant to celebrate our two-month anniversary, I feel the burn in my chest with an intensity that I haven't felt since the fire at the grocery store a few weeks ago. I look up at Clark and push it down deep into myself, taking a bite of his scallop dish and smiling as if nothing is wrong.

By the time dessert comes, the feeling has disappeared, and over flourless chocolate cake and the last drops of the champagne we're both too young to have bought legally, I breathe out a relieved sigh, I had a nice anniversary dinner, not diving out of the restaurant or making lame excuses, and the world hasn't ended. I can have both things. It's totally possible. I can make this work.

But on the walk home, two blocks away from the restaurant we run into ambulances and police cruisers in the street, all bright syncopating red and blue lights in the darkness. And I watch as they wheel nine bodies out of a liquor store with sheets over their faces, blood seeping darkly through the clean white.

"Oh man," Clark says, pausing, eyes wide at the horrifying scene. Everything runs out of me like a river and I crumple onto the dirty sidewalk. Clark stops short midsentence and reaches out to me. "Baby, are you okay?" He bends down toward me.

"I have to sit down," I say, my voice all breath and hardly any sound. I'm shaking and sweating, my cheeks flushed, my eyes full of tears.

"What's happening?"

"I just felt dizzy all of a sudden." Lies multiplying every time I speak.

"I think we should take you to a hospital," he begins and reaches his hand out to hail a cab.

"No," I say, my voice like a blade. "I'll be fine." I stand up. I can't risk him taking me to a hospital. Who knows what they'd find, and I'd only end up putting more lies between us.

"Are you sure? You look pale, and your hands are trembling," he says, touching my hands gingerly. I will them to still.

"I'm sure," I say, forcing a smile across my teeth. "It must be the champagne...I've never had champagne before, maybe I had too much," I say. Which, if alcohol affected me normally, would probably be true. So it's almost not a lie. He still seems unsure, but can feel the resolve in my tone.

"All right," he says, and takes my hand.

That night, alone in my stupid motel room I try not to cry. All those people dead because of me. This is the kind of thing that haunts a person their whole lives. How can I ever let go of it?

I can feel things peeling away at the edges.

My guilt about everything is the only thing anchoring me to anything. I'm going to have to make a choice. I can feel it coming as surely as the storm my mother has been warning me about since that first dream I had after that rainy night on the roof. Is this what she meant? Is this the storm that is going to destroy everything in my life...is the storm just me and what I am?

●

I set my hand on fire just to see what it feels like. It's pretty horrible and I almost regret doing it, except I watch the skin knit itself back together like magic and I can't help but be impressed with myself. The pain is excruciating but I can add 'dying by fire' to my list of "things that are awesome about being me" list. I also mentally add it to a new list I've started called "Things I Might Be Able To Survive, But That Would Be Decidedly Unpleasant." After my rough couple days learning to swim I've already put drowning on the list.

For the hundredth time I look at the gun I acquired from Melvin's safe after killing him and wonder for the hundredth time whether I should give it a try.

I'm honestly not sure I'm ready for the gun. I already know my body will heal a simple gunshot wound since Melvin grazed me in our little battle, but I wonder if I can survive something more intense. Surely a bullet to the head will put me down, maybe permanently, can a body heal if there's no brain to heal it?

In the end, I decide to shoot myself in the leg. I screw on the silencer and go out to the patio, sitting near the edge so that the blood can roll down into the rocks. Clenching my eyes shut and aiming the gun at the meaty part of my leg (about where I shot Adrian), I pull the trigger.

The pain is like needles of fire and for a minute I think I'm going to pass out. I push through the dizziness and taste blood where I've bit my tongue accidentally. I stare at the wound, willing it to hurt less, and to my utter shock, it slowly does.

I concentrate on the wound with everything I've got and watch it slowly pull itself back together, the flesh recombining and pushing the bullet out of the wound. The bullet lands with a clink on the rocks and my skin continues to stitch itself back until there's nothing there but a little raised scar. In a few minutes my leg is good as new.

And this is why I do crazy shit like shoot myself in the leg – look at the awesome things you can learn.

I go downtown to the big police station on First Street and loiter outside for ten minutes before I gear up the courage to go in. I've got this idea that maybe it could be where my stone is, like in some evidence archive or something. Inside, it's a combination of chaos and calm. Tons of policemen that look nearly as bored as if they might be working at the DMV, unfazed by the commotion all around them. The noise is deafening, even if you're not cursed with super hearing. It's pretty easy to be unnoticed among the colorful clientele out here, but not in other rooms. In other rooms I can see from here it looks like just cops. Maybe if I knew where to look I could try my best impression of a stray hurricane-like wind and get there. But I don't know where to begin. Where do you keep decades-old evidence? The basement? The attic? A box? A filing cabinet? A plastic bag in a tray? How big would the room have to be, how much stuff must there have been over the years. What if they destroy stuff after a certain point? Burn it all up in an incinerator, or just send it to the dump? If it is in a room somewhere, how many cops are between me and whatever room it's in. Is there a sign in sheet or a locked door? For that matter, how many Police Stations are in L.A.? I came to the big one, but who says that's the right one?

The movies don't cover this part.

I walk out fifteen minutes later, kicking at the sidewalk grooves in frustration and cursing my puny brain, yet again.

I'm never gonna find my damn stone.

○

It turns out I'm selfish and horrible.

Because I haven't left Clark. In fact we're more inseparable than ever, and I just keep my head down, as if I can sense nothing. Pretending that I don't see things that are happening. Pretending I'm just like everyone else. Pretending I didn't let nine people die so that I could have a "perfect" dinner with Clark. Pretending I haven't let how ever many other people die since then. I haven't saved the day or even chased a scream in weeks.

I'm the worst person on earth.

And ironically, being the worst person on earth isn't even going to be the thing that makes Clark leave me, because he's finally insisted on seeing my motel room, and when he does he's going to realize I'm a complete freak and leave me anyway.

My hand shakes as I put the key in the lock and I turn to him with a pleading look.

"Let's not do this," I start. "Let's go to the movies…let's go to the beach…or Ooh! Coney Island!" I say, making my eyes wide with false excitement and clapping a little. Clark laughs and takes the key from me.

"Enough. We're seeing this crappy motel room of yours, you've tricked me enough times with that Coney Island bit. I'm starting to think you have abducted children in here." He turns the key and swings the door open wide, shielding his eyes in mock horror. "If there's anything horrible going on in here, stop it right now!" he yells to the room and I smile despite my teeth chattering in fear. Clark opens his eyes and his mouth drops open. "Jeezus

Bonnie…" He walks into the room and looks everything up and down, eyes wide. I shuffle my feet in the hallway, kicking at the doorjamb, afraid to see my own room through his eyes. He starts laughing. "Baby, this is hilarious. It looks like an art installation." I look up, hopeful, and see him touching a light fixture covered in yellow paint. Seeing the room with him in it doesn't look as scary as I thought, because he thinks it's funny, not insane, and so everything has somehow been miraculously saved. He's saved me from myself once again. I'd painted the entire thing a pale yellow, from linoleum bathroom floor to bedside tables. It's all the color of buttered toast and the paint cans are still sitting in the closet all sealed up and waiting for a second coat.

"You think so?" I ask, stepping inside timidly.

"It's awesome." He reaches out and pulls me into him, staring at the ceiling. "It feels like living in a stick of butter. I feel like I should move in with you and we can be, I don't know, people in some kind of bizarre, fucked-up fairy tale. The Buttertons of Butterdom. I love it, we're sleeping here tonight," he declares. I balk.

"We don't have to."

"No, we totally are. I've never stayed over with you, all these months. We're doin' it." He pauses suddenly, reconsidering his words. "I mean…staying over, we're staying here…unless, I mean, unless you don't want me to…which is, you know, totally fine…" His words are all over the place, like he's twelve. I want to giggle, but it all feels very serious suddenly. We've kind of avoided the sex question all this time. There's been lots of kissing and touching, and even sleepovers, but it's all been kind of innocent, chaste even. And I like that, mostly 'cause I don't know what the hell I'm doing, but more and more…well, more and more I think about it – when I'm with him, when I'm not with him, all the time, in fact. And now, it just feels different all of a sudden. He's being awkward and shy and I feel anything but.

"No, I want you to stay," I say. And I do, I want him to stay more than I can articulate clearly to anyone, even myself, really. He's been so nice about it, it never really occurred to me that I was really making him wait, but I realize now, looking at him, really looking at him, that it must have been a great effort for him to wait for me and be so casual about it. Now that I'm paying attention, it's so obvious. His lust for me is seeping out of him like an animal in heat, which sounds bad, but I don't mean it that way; I mean it like it seems natural. Like all of a sudden it seems like something I don't have to be afraid of. Not with Clark, at least. Clark, who has been like something out of a black and white movie – an old-fashioned gentleman from a time when men laid their jackets over puddles. I love him so much, it seems like it can't be contained inside my puny human ribcage. It seems bigger than everything.

And like that, the decision is made.

Without ceremony, I take off my t-shirt and smile at him. He's surprised, and even steps back a bit.

"Are you sure?"

"Yeah," I say. "Totally."

He smiles and takes his shirt off too. He acts tough, like he's just going to stand there all handsome and shirtless, but then he melts, which is so him, and folds me into him. Inside his embrace is the safest I've ever felt, save maybe being in my mother's kitchen so long ago, but it's a different kind of safe, and maybe just because I'm a different kind of girl now, I prefer it. It almost makes me feel like I don't even need to be a superhero. I can't imagine all arms feel this way; Clark's are magical. But maybe it's like that for anyone in love. He kisses me softly, more gently than he ever has before, like he's giving me a chance to change my mind. But I don't want to change my mind. And when I open my eyes, he's looking back at me. He smiles in the middle of our kiss, which is one of my favorite things about kissing him, and I know I've made the right decision. When we fall into the bed a few minutes later, I'm very glad the sheets are the one thing I didn't paint.

Later, lying together like spoons in drawers, he starts asking me questions. They're a little dangerous, but they're covered in kindness and love so I'm not quite so afraid of them anymore. "Is there any reason for the color yellow?" he asks, and then quickly adds. "Don't get me wrong, I think it's an inspired choice, but it's...odd."

"My mother. I, you know I don't remember her much, but I do remember, well, I think it was our kitchen. It was painted yellow. The memories, the images, makes me feel safe and happy...warm," I say. He's quiet for some long moments and I can feel him craning his neck, looking around the room a little, exploring it beyond the yellow.

"Is that why you don't have any…stuff? Because of your mom and dad, and the home and the way you were raised?" he asks gently.

"I guess," I say. "I never really thought about it much." There's another long silence and then he's kissing me on my shoulder.

"Well, I love it. It's – I don't know how to say this – but it doesn't really surprise me. You're different from anybody I've ever met, and so, of course you live in a crazy-looking all yellow room." I smile because I know he means it and we fall asleep in my butter room closer than we've ever been. I wonder if it's the closest we'll ever be. Is there something closer than this? He's so worthy of the things I'm giving up to be with him.

In the morning, after seeing a rat in the motel hallway the size of a housecat, Clark changes his mind and asks me to move in with him. My mind reels with possibilities.

The walls bend and shift, reeling along with me.

My carefully constructed house of cards slides around precariously and begins to swallow me whole in its deconstruction.

How can this request be both everything I secretly want – a picture perfect normal life with Clark and a day job (okay, two) and paying bills and having plants and maybe even a pet – and yet simultaneously feel so scary and wrong? Like something I'm nowhere near ready for. Less than six months ago, I was homeless and lost. How can I be ready to have all this and not screw it up? But I can see on Clark's face it's an offer that isn't casually made – and that it won't last forever. Turning it down may mean it never comes to me again. In fact, his face looks not unlike an open door, one that could close at any minute. I feel the two MEs pulling in opposite directions, the one that's all superhero and secrets running for the hills screaming, and the one that craves a perfect little life with him reaching out and trying to bolt itself to the floor next to him. I can almost imagine both lives actually existing – and being amazing – I can't imagine them co-existing. Does every girl feel this way, superhero or otherwise? Two lives and two worlds pulling us in neat pieces? What you want versus what you're built for, forever at odds? Maybe I'm no different than any other girl on earth. Maybe the decision is always this hard, this full of compromise and fear.

I'm taking too long.

The door closes.

I can see it in his face.

"No...you think it's too soon," he says softly. I don't say anything. "Yeah, no, you're right...too soon," he says and stuffs his hands in his pockets and looks away from me. I go to him and link my arms through the crooks of his, pressing myself against him and leaning my head on his shoulder.

"I'm sorry," I whisper. "I'm not ready...I'm scared."

"It's okay," he says, kissing my hair, the top of my head. "I'll ask you again."

"You promise?"

"Yes," he says. I'm not sure I believe him, but it's nice for him to promise just the same. "You still have to move though," he says, lightly but seriously into my hair.

"Okay," I say, never taking my head off his shoulder.

●

When I show up at Liz's office again, Jan is just putting on her coat and headed out the door.

"Hello Lola," she says coolly.

"Jan," I nod.

"She's actually on her way out as well," Jan begins.

"Why don't you tell her I'm here...we'll see what she says," I challenge, sitting on the couch, leaning back assuredly, one arm slung across the sofa back. Jan drops her head down slightly.

"Yeah. Hold on," She goes into Liz's office, after knocking politely twice with her knuckle on the frosted glass part of the door. She comes out in less than a minute.

"She'll see you now."

"Great. Thanks," I say, not meaning any of it. There's something about Jan that really annoys the hell out of me.

"Have a good night," she says, grabbing her bag and heading out the door.

"Mmm-hmm." I walk into Liz's office. She stands up from her desk to greet me, and we both sit in our designated seats.

"Hello Lola, I wasn't sure you'd be back."

"Well, lucky for you, I still don't have anyone to talk to, so you're the big winner." I raise up my hands a little and shake them like she's won a sarcastic prize of some sort. She laughs a small laugh.

"I do feel a bit like a winner, Lola. You're a very interesting girl. I thought a lot about our last conversation."

"Yeah, about that, that was my fault. I gave you like too much information without giving you all of it and then expected you to get the whole picture."

"Well, that's very generous of you, I'll admit I do feel like I'm missing some pretty big pieces to your life. I'd like you to explain them to me so that I can understand…if you don't mind."

"Whatever."

"But first, it would be good if we could come up with a schedule so that I can be sure I have ample time to speak with you. Also, while I don't require payment for patients that I consider as case studies, I do have to get your permission to use you as a case study."

"What does that mean?"

"Well, in your situation it means that I may use some of what we discuss in here, with your anonymity intact, of course, in my next book."

"Fine."

"Really? Well, that's great, hold on one second." Liz goes to her computer and within a few clicks and types sends something to a tiny printer under her desk. She brings over two sheets of paper and a pen. She hands them to me and I sign and date both. She takes one back and I shove the other in my pocket. She glances at her copy briefly before putting it down on the desk.

"LeFever?" she says, reading my name on the page. I feel muscles in my arms and abdomen clench unexpectedly.

"Yeah?" There's an edge in my voice that I haven't intended.

"That's a very unusual name."

"Do you know what it means?"

"No, I don't. It's probably of French origin, maybe an English or New England version of the original French." She says. My back is still stiff like I'm expecting to be shot. She looks at me, "Do you know what it means?" she asks.

"No, I always just assumed." I trail off.

"Assumed what?"

"I don't know, that it meant disease, you know, fever. And in French, I knew it was French, I only took one semester, but I learned enough to know that LE is 'the', so I thought you know, 'the fever', like maybe, 'the disease'," I say. Liz laughs carefully, trying not to make me feel stupid, which is not working, but I'm feeling too hot and sweaty for some reason to care much about her laughter right now.

"I'm sure it doesn't mean that, Lola. It's a little too literal. I mean, sure there are literal names out there – someone named 'Weaver' probably came from a line of actual weavers if you go back far enough – but it's unlikely that's what your name means. Here, do you want me to look?" My eyes flick to the computer and she must read 'yes' somewhere on my face because she goes to it and taps her little keys and moves her little mouse. She looks up at me.

"See, it means 'ironworker', or maybe 'smith'."

"Wait...smith...wouldn't that person just be named like, 'Smith'...I mean, that's an actual name."

Liz comes back to her chair, smiling again. "I told you, not an exact science...also, I'm no expert, just someone who likes names and has a passing interest in their meanings," she says. There's a long pause as she watches me, "Are you relieved?"

"Relieved about what?" I look back at her a little too hard and feel like I'm giving away all the feelings I have about my last name.

"About the name's meaning. I mean, you seemed a little concerned about what it meant."

"I guess it's good to know that's not what it means, but it's meant that to me for so long...I don't know that I'll ever not believe it," I say. I'm being too honest. I feel like she's pulling back my skin and looking at my insides, at the truth on my insides covered by the lies of my outsides.

"I gotta go," I say abruptly.

"Lola, I'd like to stay with this...you seem emotional about this and we should talk about it."

"I gotta go," I say again and put my hand on the door.

"Okay...but we didn't pick a day or time for you to come back."

"Uh. Fridays at six."

"Okay. I can make that work. I'll see you next Friday then?" I'm out the door before I can answer her.

I'm not sure I'll ever be back. I don't like how this sharing is starting to feel.

○

On my break at work, I use the computer to look online for apartments. Everything is insanely expensive, so I quickly change my search to looking for apartment shares and rented rooms. I've written down about a dozen names and phone numbers – all for places that either sound terrible, or are so far away from everything I know that they might as well be in another state – when Liesel comes in for her usual mid-day lying-on-the-floor-reading break (she's moved on to Frankenstein). She barely even glances at me as she settles in, but when I've given up my search and am heading back out she pipes up. "Looking for a new place to live?"

"How did you-" I start, eyebrow raised, "Oh yeah, the books have ears," I say gesturing to everything around us with a wagging index finger.

"Yup. I know everything," she says, winking. I smile back at her. I like her. She's so direct. I wish I could be more like that.

"Yeah," I say.

"Might be, I have the perfect thing," she says, laying her book down on her chest.

"Yeah?"

"Yeah. My brother, Ben, and I are looking for a roommate for our spare bedroom. We've got a great second floor walk-up in Chelsea. If you don't think it would be too weird to work together and live together?" she says.

"No," I say, jumping at the chance. "I mean, we barely see each other at work anyway," I add helpfully. She nods.

"Yeah, that's what I thought too. Plus, I like you. You seem…solid," she says looking me up and down.

"Solid?" I ask, not sure what she means.

"You know, honest, together. Also, you're not a jerk," she adds. I laugh.

"Thanks."

"Plus, if you live with Ben and me, it will be like living in a cartoon or something," she says, a twinkle in her eyes. I raise an eyebrow.

"How so?"

"Well, you're like Amazon tall," she says, "And Ben and I are both super short…it'll be funny." I realize as she says it I've never seen her standing up, she's always lying down, and sometimes just appears out of nowhere like Batman. And as if she's reading my mind, she stands. "See?"

And indeed I do, even with her wrapped afro that easily adds six inches to her height I'm a good eight or nine inches taller than she is. I look down at her and nod.

"You're right. We look like characters cast for some absurd comedy," I say.

"Totally," she says, plunking down again, "So, come by today. You get off at six?" I nod silently. "Come today after work and I'll show you the place. Decide then." I nod. It's all happening so fast.

"Okay. Thanks," I say. Liesel tears a piece of paper off a pad on the desk and scribbles an address and hands it to me. "I'll see you at like six-thirty then," I say, examining the address and then putting it in my pocket.

"Perfect," she says and lies back down with her book.

At 6:28 p.m., standing outside Liesel's address, I know I've hit the jackpot. The building is beautiful and in a really nice neighborhood and close to anything a body could want. How she can afford to live here – even if she had ten roommates – on our bookstore salary eludes me. I go up one flight of stairs and knock softly. Liesel opens the door and she looks somehow the same but different. She seems more open and less guarded. Still direct and unafraid to speak her mind, but also softer. She's also wearing fluffy giraffe print slippers, which immediately makes her twice as adorable.

"Woo," she says, taking my hand as if we're meeting for the first time. "You look even more awesome tall here than at the bookstore. I guess it's the context," she says, gesturing to the space around us. I smile.

"Yeah, I guess."

"Sorry," she says, pulling back a bit. "Is that rude? I hate when strangers comment on how small I am, maybe you hate it too. I guess I just always wanted to be tall, I forget that maybe it's not awesome all the time." She gestures me inside and I walk into the light filled living room.

"It's okay," I say. "Probably advantages and disadvantages just like being short." Liesel smiles effortlessly, showing off a mouthful of gleaming white, slightly imperfect teeth.

"You're right," she says nodding, strangely serious, really thinking it out. "You can reach all the high shelves, but you could never fit in the cupboard under the kitchen sink." I look at her, one eyebrow raised, a smile pulling at the corners of my mouth.

"Why would-"

"You never know!" she says throwing her hands up enthusiastically. My smile grows full and I laugh. There's something wonderful about this girl. She's all open and honest, like the crap that most people seem to cover themselves with has all been stripped away. She's laid bare in a way I find totally appealing. She's like looking at a song. A true one. I have this feeling deep inside myself that I'm going to know her my whole life, that she's going to be vitally important to me, that I can trust her. She looks back at me from a hallway to the right of the living room and gestures at me emphatically. "Come see the room!" I follow her dutifully, knowing I would take it even if it was gray and sad and shaped like a coffin. Anything to be in this girl's soothing, warm presence. But the room, like her, is bright and open. It's full of pretty modern furniture mixed with some old pieces that look like genuine antiques. The combination creates a strange blend of old and new that's oddly comforting. There's a painting on the wall that looks like 'real' art, not that I would know the difference anyway. The room itself is surprisingly large for a New York City bedroom. There's a double bed against one wall, a dresser and a desk with a chair on another. In the corner, near two matching windows is an upholstered reading chair. As charming as it all is, I'm mostly interested in the windows. There are two, of reasonable size, and in a stroke of luck, one of them opens onto a fire escape. Even better, they face the quiet alley side of the apartment, not the more exposed street side. I turn to Liesel.

"It's lovely," I say. She looks around, pleased.

"Yeah, I've always liked this room. Quiet, good light."

"Have you lived here long?" I ask.

Her face clouds slightly, just for a moment before she recovers her brightness. "Me? No. It used to belong to my grandmother once upon a time. Ben has been living here since our folks died a few years ago. I uh...I've just been here a few weeks." It seems like there's an ocean of story in her pauses, but I don't want to be nosy, so I let it go. We step back into the hallway and she points toward the end. "My room's there and Ben's is at the end. We share the big bathroom at the end of the hallway." She gestures to a door across from us. "This smaller bathroom here would be yours." She props it open and small is indeed the word for it. I could probably touch each wall with a fingertip if I fully extended my arms, but it has a shower, a toilet, and a pedestal sink and mirror, all meticulously clean, it's perfect. We walk back out into the living room. "And of course you would share the rest of the space with us – kitchen, living room, and a small dining room," she says, gesturing to the rest of the apartment, which, in traditional Manhattan style, you can see all of from our single vantage point. Still, it's a massive upgrade from where I've been living, in every way possible. Liesel and I stand there together quietly, looking at the rooms and then she turns and looks up at me, "So...you want it?" she asks gamely.

"Well...yeah, definitely...is it that simple?" I ask.

"Pretty much," she says, crossing her arms and then looking up at me, a funny knowing look in her eyes. "I have a good feeling about you. I like you, have since I first met you."

I nod happily, I like her too. "What about your brother...Ben...won't he want to meet me first?"

"Nah," she says, pffting her lips slightly and waving her hand dismissively. I laugh.

"You sure?"

"Yeah. I'm the boss of him," she says teasingly, her voice full of warmth and humor. "He's a good big brother, he lets me have what I want. Besides, he knows I'm always right about these things."

"These things?" I ask, confused.

"Things you should trust your gut on," she says as if it's the most simple truth around. I smile. I like her more every time she opens her mouth. "So, move in tomorrow...sometime after noon?" she half asks, half commands.

"Yes," I say definitively and shake her hand again, trying to find just the right amount of pressure. I don't want to scare her away now with crazy hulk strength. I have this feeling she's going to be my best friend, and I'm shocked by how badly I want that.

Just as we're finishing our handshake, Ben comes tumbling through the door, carrying an impossible armload of groceries. Liesel springs up to help him and I follow. Liesel takes a bag from him and I take four and as I do so he looks up at me.

"Um…hey?" he says.

Liesel, already on her way to the kitchen with the bag, shouts back. "Ben, Bonnie; Bonnie, Ben."

I smile, trying not to be too much of an intruder. "Hi Ben."

"Hi," he says. "I'd offer to shake…but neither of us have the hands for it."

He has the same warm presence as his sister. Soft and sweet, but clever. I follow him into the kitchen and help them unpack their groceries as Liesel chats us up.

"So, I told Bonnie she could have the extra bedroom. She's gonna move in tomorrow," she says and Ben nods, as if he doesn't mind and isn't surprised. Liesel hands me a jar of jam and elbows Ben, "Watch this. Hey Bonnie can you put that up in that top cupboard?" I reach up easily and set the jar on the otherwise bare shelf.

"Oh, brilliant!" Ben says, genuinely delighted.

"We're terrible people," Liesel says. "We're totally using you for your height."

Ben raises his hand and wiggles his fingers as if showing it off. "But if you ever need someone with itty bitty bones to reach into a tiny space to retrieve something you've dropped…we're your people!"

"Deal," I say, feeling at home with them already and wondering if this is, more than what friendship feels like, what family feels like.

●

I pick him because he looks a little bit like Adrian.

His eyes especially remind me of Adrian. His hair is a little too long, but it's close. His name is Stan. We're at some stupid rave club and he's dense and pretty, which if I had planned this, is exactly what I would have had in mind. I pick him up without speaking a word, which I have to say, even I'm impressed by. I grab him by the lapels of his jacket and kiss him hard. When I release him, he's full of bumbling words. I keep a hold on his jacket and drag him out of the club with me. He's shouting to his friends things like "I guess she likes me!" and "I'll see you guys later." Putting all kinds of innuendo into words that don't have any business having innuendo. I'm hoping he knows how to shut up for more than two minutes so I can get this over with. He'll only be the second person I've ever slept with, if I can manage this, and I don't want anyone to suspect I'm nervous about it, but I am. I'd thought, after Adrian, maybe I'd just never do it again, that maybe that was my one and only chance at love, and with love, sex. Maybe nobody gets a second shot at love, but maybe especially a girl like me. All the same, I didn't expect to take anyone home, but when I suddenly saw a bit of Adrian in Stan I couldn't seem to help myself. So, it's me and Stan, The Innuendo Idiot, together trying to wipe away the memory of Adrian.

When we get out onto the street he stumbles forward into me and I push him off a bit.

"Do you have a car?" I ask.

"No, I came with my friend, Mark."

"Okay, we'll take my bike."

"You have a motorcycle?"

"Yeah." I start walking to where my bike is parked and Stan follows a few paces behind and I hear him whisper "Hot" and I consider calling the whole thing off.

"What's your name?" he asks.

"Lola."

"Oh, that's hot," he says, intending me to hear it this time. I roll my eyes, hoping he'll stop talking. It's harder to imagine he's Adrian when he keeps saying stupid crap like that. A few car-lengths away from where my bike is parked there are a whole bunch more that say 'Hells Angels' on them. I grab one of the Hells Angels helmets and give it to Stan.

"Put this on," I say. He holds it in front of him like it's made of poison.

"You're stealing this? From Hells Angels? You can't steal from Hells Angels man…they'll like hunt us down and kill us…literally." I sigh, grab him again, and kiss him, pushing my tongue down his throat, letting my fingers linger across the front of his jeans. It feels unnatural to do it. I have to force it. I don't really want to do anything with him. In fact, I feel, with every fiber of my being, like flinging him away from me. But I've gotten it into my head now that being with someone else may be the only way to get over Adrian, the only way to make Adrian my past instead of my everything. I don't know why he still has that power over me, but he does, and I need to kill it and move on.

"Put. It. On." I say. This time he does. I'm not worried about Stan's safety, of course, but I am worried about getting stopped by cops. I have plans of getting over Adrian, not a bloodbath in the streets of Hollywood. Although both sound tempting, truth be told. Stealing a helmet so that I don't get pulled over makes perfect sense to me.

"Where do you live?" I ask.

"Can't we go to your place?" he says, eyeing the Hells Angels bikes and clearly uncomfortable in the helmet.

"No. My place is no good," I say. I don't add, 'because I don't want to have to clean up after myself if things go south'. Stan's nervousness about the proximity of the Hells Angels bikes makes him cave and he gives me his address. I put my own helmet on and we head off. Stan keeps trying to grope me as we ride, and I think about breaking one of his fingers to get him to cut it out, but I figure, no matter how many times I shove my tongue down his throat, that will probably send him running. I smack his hand away when we get off the bike and he nurses it like an injured puppy, but leaves me alone until we get inside. He lives in a lame studio apartment, and probably drives a BMW. Everybody in L.A. has a great car – it's like a rule or something. There's an old, dingy futon on the far wall and a bathroom in the back. The place barely has furniture, mostly things substituting for other things; a milk crate operating as a stool to sit on, a concrete block as a side table. I wrinkle up my nose and look at Stan.

"What do you do for a living?"

"I'm an actor," he starts. "Starbucks," he finishes. I nod, the picture becoming clear.

"What kind of car do you have?"

"A Lexus."

"Of course you do," I look away so he can't see me roll my eyes.

"You want a drink?" he asks, hovering by the fridge insecurely.

"No. Come here," I say. He obeys. "Turn off the light," I say when he gets to me. He looks more like Adrian in the dark. If I can pretend he's Adrian maybe I can just get through this. Quick and painless and onto the next. He reaches for the wall and hits the light switch, while I pull the futon into a flat position.

"You just get right to it, huh?" he says, watching me with the futon.

"Pretty much," I say, pushing him down onto the mattress. He falls roughly. I straddle him and tear his shirt off. Stan looks at the fabric a little strangely, laying in my hands in shreds.

"Hey-"

"Shhh," I say and begin kissing him again. He shuts up pretty easily. I close my eyes and get both of our pants off with a little help from him. Underneath me he no longer feels like Adrian, even with my eyes clenched shut. His hips are too wide, his shoulders too narrow, his skin not as smooth, and when I peek, he's far too pale in the streetlight glow from outside. I suddenly feel nauseous. It overtakes me and the room spins. Stan fusses below me.

"What's wrong, baby?"

I swing my leg over him and slide off his body, perching myself on the edge of the futon, my head between my legs. Stan reaches out, part-comfort, part-impatience, pulling some hair back from my face. I smack him away.

"Hey!" he says, massaging his hand. "You're the one who's been driving this ship, babe." His words cut hard. They're a reminder that I was in charge and am now also the one chickening out. I think about trying again with Innuendo Idiot Stan but the room rolls and I nearly lose my last meal at the thought of it. The scent of him in the room, the remaining taste of him in my mouth suddenly seem abhorrent. "So, is this gonna happen or not?" he sighs. My fists clench at the thick mattress and something snaps in me. I look at him sideways, my eyes narrow slits.

"Depends what you mean by 'this'," I say, and pounce on him, wrapping my hands around his throat before he even knows what's happened.

It's fast and once he's dead, I feel surprisingly sated. I climb off of him and go to the filthy bathroom and splash cold water on my face.

Walking away from the scene I'm not sure if I've killed him because it's who I am and because I can, or because I don't have a choice, or because I'm afraid and embarrassed that I wasn't able to sleep with him. I shake my head and try to forget all of it while driving home, trying to pretend that my muscles aren't humming higher and harder than ever. It's like a drug, like the best fucking drug on Earth.

○

I pack up my things the following day at noon. It takes roughly three minutes.

I don't want to seem overly anxious, but I head out anyway, taking my duffel bag, suitcase, and a frying pan I've never used before. I don't know why I bought it. It just seemed like a thing that normal people would buy, I guess. By 12:30, I'm standing outside my new apartment building, excited and nervous, feeling like this is a whole new chapter of my life, sure that things are changing.

And I'm right.

Because just at that moment, standing on the sidewalk, looking down the alley, I see a woman do a back flip off the second floor fire escape. In fact, I'm pretty sure it's the fire escape out my new window. She dives off of it as if it's nothing. Her muscles glint in the afternoon sun and her mane of raven colored hair is too ethereal and black at the same time to seem real. I'm standing there, just off the alley way, with my bags and frying pan, my mouth hanging open awestruck as she hits the ground, soft as a cat, and takes off out the other side of the alleyway in a light run. I'm in such shock for a moment it doesn't occur to me to chase her down. And when I snap out of it, she's gone. Like I imagined her in the first place.

When Liesel opens the door for me with her wide grin, I should open with something normal like "Hi." But instead I go for insane with, "I'm pretty sure I just saw some girl do a back flip off my fire escape…is that a normal thing?" Liesel blinks, takes in a breath and I think maybe she's contemplating lying, but then she sighs heavily and moves to the side to let me in.

"That's just Bryce," she says. "She's…a friend…sort of an ex-girlfriend…kinda," Liesel says chewing on her lip a bit and then screwing her mouth up. "She stays over every once in a while."

"She have something against the front door?" I joke, hyper-aware that I'm planning to use the fire escape in a similar way, maybe even for similar reasons. Liesel sighs a little and takes my frying pan from me as she closes the door.

"Bryce is…unusual. Yeah, let's go with unusual," she pauses. "Not that unusual is bad of course."

I set my bags down and raise my hands. "No judgment here," I say. "Mostly just curiosity." Liesel takes the frying pan to the kitchen and sets it down. She seems heavy with thought, and when she looks back at me I think she's going to say something major but a look of confusion crosses over her face.

"Is that all you brought?" she asks. I look down at my duffle and suitcase.

"Yeah," I blush. "I travel light." Liesel's expression is still heavy and I look back at her concerned.

"Is everything okay?"

Liesel nods and chews her lip anxiously. She gestures me to the living room couch. "Maybe you better sit down before you unpack, Bonnie."

Uh-oh, I knew this was too good to be true. My mind races, realizing how attached I've become to the idea of living here in the last 18 hours.

"What's wrong?"

"Nothing. I just…" she pauses a little and fidgets on the couch. "Ben said I shouldn't say anything to you about this…that I should wait until we knew you better, but I just…I don't think it's fair to keep it from you. I'm a really direct person…I find anything but honesty clouds things…" She trails off and then begins again. "So I'm just going to tell you something, and if you want to leave afterwards, no hard feelings, okay?" she looks up at me sweetly and I just nod my head. She pops her giraffe print slippers off and curls her tiny feet under her on the couch and chews her lip again, clearly agonizing on how to start the sentence. In the end she goes for blunt, which isn't surprising, I suppose.

"So, I just got out of a mental institute about three months ago," she says and I admit it surprises me, though not necessarily in a bad way. "There's…there's nothing really wrong with me…" she says getting quiet for a long time before starting again. "I mean, I'm not dangerous or anything," and then under her breath she says, "I don't think…or…not anymore." The stress of this is taking its toll, her eyes are softening sadly and her lip is quivering a little. I've never met someone that I've felt was less likely to be dangerous in my entire life, and I have good instincts about these things, so I just take her hand until she looks up at me.

"What happened?" I ask. She looks me in the eyes and it's powerful, like I can see all the way inside her, and maybe she can see inside me in the same way.

"A couple years ago, after our parents died, I crashed a car into a house and hurt some people really bad," she says, her voice barely a whisper. I blink at her stupidly. "That's what I was put away for," she says, resting her elbow on her knee and her cheek on her palm. "I was there for a year. I just got out when I turned 18. I was on a suicide watch, and under strict observation. But I'm not crazy. I mean, not any more than anyone else is I don't think," she says seriously.

"Okay," I say, kind of honored that she felt she could tell me all of this. She blinks at me with giant dark eyes and I know we could leave it there, but it seems like there's more, I feel almost like she wants me to ask, like she's not sure how to tell the rest unless I ask. "Who got hurt in your accident?"

"It wasn't an accident," she says, clearing her throat. "I did it on purpose." It comes out not matter-of-factly or casually but with a purity that shows me, yet again, that truth is important to her.

"Why?" I shouldn't pry, but I can't help it. She seems like an enigma to me. Clever and bright, maybe even wise beyond her years, and willing to share it all. I want to feast on it, as if it can teach me so much that I haven't figured out about myself yet.

"I was trying to kill myself," she says, picking at the edge of her t-shirt. I don't know what to say then, and I think maybe I should just say nothing. She keeps going when I don't and I feel I made the right decision. "I just blamed myself for my parents' deaths…for the accident that killed them and I…well honesty? I was really mad. There was…I can't really describe it…a rawness inside me that I just couldn't explain to anyone, or contain, or control. Does that make sense?"

"You have no idea," I breathe. She looks at me quizzically. "My parents died in a car accident when I was little...and I've always blamed myself." I confess, and it does feel like a confession as I've never said it out loud before, just said it over and over to myself, letting it fester and grow powerful inside me. She breathes in sharply and we seem to understand each other more than ever before. Liesel slides off the couch and fetches a picture frame from a bookshelf nearby. She comes back to me and puts it in my hand. It's her family, warm and smiling. "These are your parents?" I ask.

"Yes."

"You look like your mother," I say, another thing that unites us.

"Everywhere but the height and the booty," she says laughing. It's true, they both have beautiful almond shaped faces and dark velvety skin, big dark eyes, and the same wild black curly hair tied up in a bright scarf and poking up and out, but Liesel is thin and delicate while her mother is soft and round, tall and broad, with a smile that looks like it could devour sadness whole. The smiles are especially the same. In the photo Liesel's mother and a small, wiry, pale professor type – complete with elbow patches on his jacket – are clasping at each other with what I can only describe as pure love. Her brother Ben looks more like her father, the same light skin and sandy brown hair, sweet in the eyes. Apparently none of the family got her mother's height. "It always kind of bothered me that I don't look like him at all," she says, as if reading my mind. "My father, I mean. It's wonderful, of course, to see her looking back at me in the mirror, but I miss him too, and he's not there," she says, taking back the picture and staring at them. It pains me to hear her say what I have felt so many times myself.

"Maybe that's why your brother looks like him so much then, so you can both always see your parents in each other," I say, surprised at the insight. She smiles widely, as if I've given her some great gift.

"I'd never thought about it that way before," she says, pausing. "That's nice." She says it more to herself than to me. "I'm really lucky to have him. Do you have any siblings?"

"I have an older brother too, Jasper, but we're...estranged," I say and the word comes out like I strangled it somewhere in my throat.

"I'm sorry," Liesel says, looking down and clearly feeling bad for making me feel bad, which is nice, but not necessary.

"I have to ask," I start, unsure if it's a good idea. "How does a car accident equal mental institute? You seem really...um...sane..." I trail off. She looks at me, her gaze piercing but somehow not sharp.

"Well, as near as I can tell the world doesn't know crap about crap. It seems to me that people are most comfortable when things can be put in boxes. It made people comfortable to put me in a box and say I was crazy...that the only reason I would do what I did was because I was crazy. If you ask me, I did the sanest thing in the world. It may have been wrong, but it wasn't crazy."

"How do you mean?" I ask.

"I got a lot of crap from people at school, you know, we lived in a small college town, interracial parents...Ben got it too, but he was always better at making friends than I was, and at some point I just started being over it...and I acted out like any jerk kid probably would," she pauses.

"You don't seem like a troublemaker."

"Well, I was. And there was this one girl, Mindy Williams. The day of the accident...I mean the thing that caused the accident...I'd gotten into a fight with Mindy – a bad one – punches and hair pulling – the whole nine. And my parents had been called to the office about it. They got in the car accident on the way to the school. So, I found out they died while sitting in a stupid plastic chair next to insufferable Mindy Williams. And I blamed myself, I did, and I wanted to die for it, but I blamed her too..."

"You crashed into Mindy Williams' house?" I say, putting it together.

"Yeah. And she wasn't even home. But her mother and father and little brother all got really badly hurt. It was wrong, but I don't see how it was crazy. But for most people, they have to believe I'm sick, that there's something wrong with me, otherwise I guess they figure, the world is full of people crashing cars into people's houses. They have to believe that they can put someone like me away and give me counseling and therapy and drugs and make me not be like that. Otherwise, how will they sleep at night? Y'know?"

She makes a lot of sense. It's like she's jacked into some kind of powerful truth and it just comes spilling from her mouth with no filter. I feel like I would buy anything she was selling on late night TV. I like it. I wonder if it has to do with everything she's been through. Maybe tragedy makes the most interesting people, or, at least, the most interesting to me.

"You seem a lot older than 18," I say.

"Well, yeah, maybe, but don't you feel that way too? I mean, losing your parents forces you to grow up fast, don't you think?" she pauses. "Like, if I had it my way I'd still be an inconsequential troublemaker looking forward to college and causing my parents all kinds of annoying grief." There's a wistfulness in her last sentence that I understand. She's right about growing up fast when bad things happen. It's what I've been feeling ever since moving to New York and trying to be a 'grown up' – decadently mourning a childhood I never had. I think everything on my plate has made me feel old and wise despite my reservations and concerns. I've been on such a conflicted path, so unable to commit to anything. First I hurt Sharon and tried to deny the power I knew I had. Then I pinned all my hopes on finding Jasper, only to realize he'd given up on me long ago. And then all I wanted to be was lost, but I found Joan and she inspired me to embrace what I really am. But when I tried to fulfill my destiny as a superhero I was kind of a massive failure. And then I fell in love and became a selfish happy jerk. Now I live in some kind of insane limbo, in love and in denial, dancing between the two. Does that make me flighty? Or just constantly evolving? I'm not sure, but I hope it's the latter.

I decide to let myself evolve once more.

"You're right," I say to Liesel evenly, locking eyes with her. "People should be honest with each other, so I should probably tell you…I'm a superhero."

Liesel's expression is blank for a moment and then with a twinkle in her eye she simply says, "I knew I was right about you."

Over the next few weeks, I kill six more boys. And when I say 'kill' I mean try to have sex with and fail – and then end up killing them. Every time. Their names are Ed, Allen, Randall, Jim, Theo, and Darius. They all remind me of Adrian in some way or another. Ed had a soft, gentle way about him that was like Adrian; Allen's hands were similar to Adrian's, as was what he did with them; Randall was the exact same height and weight; Jim had the same laugh; Theo had the same charming, lopsided smile and perfect bright teeth; and Darius ate more seafood in one sitting than I would have believed possible.

I'd love to say I felt empty after killing them, that I was wracked with guilt, but honestly, the only thing I felt for sure after all of them, was hungry for more. Well, okay I also felt frustrated and confused that I still couldn't bury my memories of Adrian, but mostly hungry. Adrian betrayed me, totally sold me out, maybe even tried to kill me, and yet still he plagues me. Mostly because I miss him. I loved him and trusted him and he was my only friend, and that's harder to replace than it looks, I guess. These little boys I've been killing certainly don't come close.

It's that frustration that drives me to Liz's office again. I walk in without knocking and Liz catches a gasp in her throat.

"Sorry to startle you," I say. Liz puts her glasses on.

"Are you?"

"Am I what?"

"Sorry to startle me." She sits in her chair. I look at her and think about the question. She's right, I'm not sorry at all. I'm pushing on her and testing her limits just as I've been testing my own. I like Liz, I realize. She's annoying in many ways, but mostly, I like her, even if she doesn't believe I killed my mother. It's clear she doesn't and never has, but I think maybe today I'll make it clear to her.

"No. You're right. I'm not actually sorry."

"Thank you."

"For?"

"For being honest with me. That's all I'm really asking of you here, Lola. I'd appreciate it if you could honor that."

"I really have," I say, meaning it. "I don't appreciate being called a liar, Liz."

"I didn't say you were a liar, Lola, but I do think you haven't been completely honest with me."

"I really have," I repeat. She raises her right eyebrow skeptically. "I haven't lied to you once," I say seriously. She seems confused and she flips back and forth through pages in her notebook. Then she looks up at me, her mouth open as if she's about to object, but when she looks me in the eye I know she can see it's true.

"I believe you, Lola."

"Good. You should," I smile a little. "I feel almost like we should start from the beginning now," I say. She looks at her notes a bit dumbfounded and speaks almost under her breath.

"Yeah."

"So. I killed my mother," I begin.

"Why?" is all Liz can manage. I don't think she's blinked for a full two minutes and her voice sounds much breathier than before, like now she's afraid of my answers instead of thinking she's telegraphing and charting them.

"Well, she was a shitty mother, Liz, but the real reason isn't because she ignored and hated me, it's because she had power, real power – not some kind of hippie flower power bullshit – and I just knew that if I killed her I'd get it."

"And?"

"And I've got it," I say, smiling wide like the cat that has the canary.

"When you say you've got power, what does that mean, exactly?" Liz asks, putting the metal tip of her pen against her teeth. I consider, for a moment, how I can spend hours explaining it to her, trying to convince her, and decide it's too much effort. So instead I look around the room for something to break. I stand up and walk to her bookcase. I pull out a copy of her book from the shelf. It's thick, maybe four hundred pages. I put my hands on the top of the book, and tear, with minimal effort in opposite directions. The book tears neatly in two and Liz's pen hits the hardwood floor with a little plink.

"Oh my god."

"Yeah, so I mean it, like, quite literally," I say, tossing the two book halves onto the desk. Liz is still sitting there, minus her pen, mouth hanging open.

"You wanna see something else?" She doesn't move. I look around the office for something impressive. I want to break her laptop in half, but I figure she'll freak out if I do that, so I decide to go with something less controversial. There's a huge gorgeous looking four-drawer filing cabinet in the corner, it looks more like art than office furniture. I grab it and lift it a foot off the ground. There's a slight ring of dust around the indent in the rug and the fibers underneath are tamped down from years of punishment. "You really need to clean under here," I say matter-of-factly, before setting it down gently. If Liz had another pen to drop she would have dropped it.

"That...that cabinet is filled with files...it must weigh five hundred pounds!"

"More like four fifty," I say, dusting off my hands from all my hard work and walking back to the couch.

"You want me to do anything else?" Liz's eyes dart back and forth between the cabinet and the torn book. I decide to do one more trick. I sit on the couch and cross my legs. When she finally looks me in the eye I lift my hand from my lap and grab the fingers of my left hand with the palm of my right and in one quick movement snap them all backward, never flinching. It hurt like hell, but she doesn't need to know that. Liz cringes, dipping her head slightly into her raised shoulder. A small sound like a kicked animal escapes her as she looks away, her eyes closing instinctively.

"Lola," she whispers. I leave my left hand up, so that when she looks at me again she can see all the fingers hanging backwards off my hand.

"Don't worry, Liz, it'll heal. Fast too," I say. She looks back at me and sees the broken fingers. She shudders visibly and closes her eyes again. For the first time she looks like she wishes she were anywhere but here. And for the first time I'm feeling quite comfortable here.

"How did you kill your mother?" she whispers.

"I poisoned her and drove her off a cliff. When she hit the ground there was an explosion, maybe, I didn't really pay attention. I knew when she was dead because I felt her power pour into me as she died." It's the first time I've said it out loud like that. It sounds both badass and sad. Liz opens her eyes and I can see that she's really seeing me for the first time. I lay my hand on my lap, waiting patiently for the fingers to rebuild themselves.

"And," she clears her throat. "How many other people have you killed?" I calculate in my head.

"Fourteen," I say. She clears her throat again. When her voice comes out it is a pale imitation of its former self, squeaky and unsure.

"Fourteen?" She closes her eyes for a long moment and the squeaky voice continues, "Who?"

"Well after my mother – she was the first – I killed this guy Melvin and most of a crew I was working with in Vegas."

"Why did you kill them?"

"He and the whole crew, including my then-boyfriend Adrian, betrayed me and left me for dead on a job, and then when I didn't die." I hold up my still broken but healing fingers, as if to illustrate my point. "I showed up and they tried to kill me themselves...even dumped me in the desert and left me there. But I got all better and so I went back and killed them all."

"How many?"

"Melvin, Enrico, and Felice. Melvin actually killed Albert and Jorge himself sorta by accident."

"What about your boyfriend...Adrian...? You didn't mention him." I pause, realizing I've left him out and I don't know if it's deliberate or not.

"No. I didn't kill him. I shot him in the leg." She sits up a little straighter.

"Why didn't you kill Adrian?"

"I don't know. I was going to. I was," I say and I'm not sure if I'm trying to convince her, or me.

"But what happened?"

"I don't know. I've thought about it a lot...I'm not sure. I mean, I loved him, but I thought I'd be able to do it...but when the time came, I don't know...at the last second I pulled the gun, hit him in the leg."

"Well, I think that probably...means something."

"Yeah? I'd love for you to tell me what."

"Well I don't...I don't know. Did you feel remorse for any of these other killings? Your mother?"

"No. Most of them deserved it as far as I'm concerned."

"Who didn't deserve it?" I don't expect this question and it throws me a bit. She latches on and pushes harder. "Who didn't deserve it, Lola?"

"I mean, I don't know, they could have been really crappy people in life, so I can't say if they deserved it or not..." I trail off and look around almost guiltily.

"Did they do anything specific to you?"

"No, some of them did nothing to me."

"Who were they?

"Well there were a bunch of men I killed recently, but then there was also this woman called Lena and another woman called Joan."

"And who were the men...do you know their names?"

"Stan, Ed, Allen, Randall, Jim, Theo, and Darius," I say. Liz scratches some notes on her pad.

"You said this was recent, did these men live around here?"

"Los Angeles? I guess, I found them all here."

"How long has this been happening?"

"Over the past couple weeks."

"A couple wee-" she's shocked but regains her composure. "When was the last one?"

"Last night." There's a long silence while Liz tries to think of a question whose answer will horrify her less. Her eyes drift over to the newspaper on her desk, the headline below the fold says **FOURTH MALE VICTIM FOUND, NO SUSPECTS**. I smile sweetly as her eyes return to my face.

"Did you know these men?"

"No. I picked them out and..." I trail off. I don't want to admit that I didn't manage to have sex with any of them, it makes me feel like a failure, like an inexperienced failure. "...And I killed them."

"Was there any reason you picked out these men, specifically?"

Damnit. She's got me.

"Yes."

"Okay...can you elaborate?"

"They all...they all reminded me of Adrian a little bit."

"Interesting," she says. I hate when she says 'interesting'.

"Why?" I ask.

"Why do you think you'd be interested in killing men who remind you of Adrian?"

"Because I didn't kill him originally?"

"Could be. Does that sound right to you?"

"Well…"

"What?"

"Well, I mean, I guess that could be true like subconsciously or whatever…but um, more consciously I picked them with the intention of sleeping with them."

"And I take it you weren't successful in that?" she asks, looking up over her glasses. I glare at her.

"No."

"Why not?"

I sigh. "I don't fucking know."

"Okay, let's go back a bit – why were you 'trying' to have sex in the first place?"

"What do you mean?"

"Well, you make it sound like an unpleasant task – something to be crossed off a list."

"That's how it feels," I say quietly.

"Why?" Liz pushes

"Because I'm trying to forget him," I snap.

"You'd be surprised how normal that is Lola," she says almost kindly, but then hardens. "But not the killing. That's not normal, and it's got to stop." There's a long pause. "So you didn't actually sleep with any of these men?"

"No," I say, my cheeks flushing with shame.

"It's nothing to be embarrassed about, Lola."

"I don't want to talk about this anymore," I say, crossing my arms sullenly. We sit quietly for a few moments and she switches gears.

"What about the women…who were they? How did you know them?"

"They were carnival freaks…women who travel with sideshows and stuff…they were 'strongwomen'," I say curling my fingers in little air quotes on strongwomen.

"They were strongwomen?" she repeats the question, she sounds stunned.

"Yeah, I mean, they weren't really, they were just buff regular bitches, but they called themselves strong women, you know, 'World's Strongest Woman' blah blah blah."

"Why did you kill them?"

"I was looking for something like me."

"And they weren't…like you?"

"Not even close."

"And how did you feel about that…?"

"Disappointed. Pissed. Frustrated. Mostly offended."

"Why did you have to kill them though, I mean they posed no threat to you if they didn't have any power."

"Why not?"

"Why not what?"

"Why not kill them? Just as good as leaving them alive."

"See Lola, it's horrifying to me that you'd say that. I mean, that kind of talk makes you…not only a serial killer, but also, probably a sociopath…but it doesn't really match with what you said about Adrian. How you could have regret, or love someone, and also have a complete disregard for human life…it's a strange kind of compartmentalizing…" she trails off, staring at me. She's still afraid of me, but the doctor in her, or scientist, or whatever, is still curious. I shrug my shoulders.

"I don't know. I mean, it's why I'm here, I guess. I thought you could tell me what the deal is."

"Do you think of Adrian now?"

"All the time." It comes out faster than I mean to say it and it surprises us both.

"You still love him?"

"I guess I do."

"Interesting," she muses.

"I hate that answer."

"Well Lola, this is all very complicated. You're very complicated. I'm going to have to think, and you're going to have to think too."

"All I do is think about it," I snap. I'm annoyed. Why the hell would I be wasting my time with her if I could figure out what's broken about me on my own?

"Is this what you meant before…when you said you wished you'd asked more questions of Delia before you killed her?"

"Yeah."

"You mean because you think she could have explained some of what you're going through…that she might have experienced it herself?"

"Yeah."

"Do you think she ever loved anyone before?" The question hits me like a bullet.

"I – I don't know. I haven't thought about it much."

"What about your father?"

"I told you, I don't know who he is, or was. He wasn't around. I never even asked. I thought you were taking notes…Jeezus," I say, crossing my arms, pissed that I have to repeat myself.

"What else would you have asked Delia?"

"I don't know. Why we are, how we are, WHAT we are. If there's a way to change it or make it different. Why there's apparently another girl out there like me she never bothered to warn me about."

"There's another girl like you?"

"I guess. I think I felt her at one of the carnivals. I went back home and found some old letters of my mother's – apparently her name is Bonnie." There's a beat and then Liz remembers.

"Oh. The pretty, the good…"

"Yeah," I say, sulking.

"Where is Bonnie now?"

"I have no clue. I don't know how to find her."

"Well, why do you think she was at the carnival?"

"I don't know…I used to think it was just a coincidence…"

"And now?" Liz presses.

"And now," I press my fingers to my temples and clench my eyes shut. "Now I guess I just think she was looking for something like her too. So she wouldn't be alone."

"Is that why you think about her? Because you'd like to not be so alone too? Because it might be nice to know there's someone else out there like you?"

"Nice?" My head snaps up at the suggestion and I narrow my eyes at Liz. "I don't want to feel all nice with her. I don't want to…cuddle."

"Well, then, why do you want to find her?" she asks. I look at Liz, my head cocked. After all this time talking with her, she continues to miss the big picture. Even if this girl is like me, she's not someone that can help me be less alone in the world. Bonnie is one thing and one thing only: a threat to me.

"To kill her, of course."

O

After outing myself to Liesel and then to Ben – because as I've quickly learned with the two of them, trusting one of them is trusting them both, they keep nothing from one another – things in my life shift again. I suppose it would be silly to assume things would stay the same after a declaration like that, but saying it out loud somehow makes it more true, more powerful. And I can't deny myself…what I am…or at least what I know I should be doing, anymore.

And there's wonderful beauty in that. Accepting myself and what I can do and be. But there's horror in it too. Because I don't ignore the screams anymore. I go after everything I reasonably can. Over the next few weeks I do amazing things – I stop twelve rapists, twenty-six muggings, five convenience store robberies, two car accidents, and rescue two kittens from trees. Actually, it turned out to be the same kitten twice, but who's counting?

I feel euphoric most of the time, almost high off of my good deeds like they're drugs I've long been addicted to. The rest of my life is in chaos though. Things are coming apart, and fast. I almost get fired, from both my jobs, and then I do get fired from my barista job, although it's hard to care too much about that since I hated it anyway. I leave Clark suddenly and in mid-sentence more times than I can count. I break dates and when I do show up I'm painfully late or ditch out early. Twice he's found strange holes in my clothes and when I can't explain any of it – the absences, the holes, the sudden departures – we have terrible fights. He's starting to not trust me and it feels horrible, in part because he's right, he shouldn't trust me. I'm lying to him. But I don't know how to explain anything, and even if I could would he even believe me? And if I could convince him, would he stay with me? Would he tell me to stop? Is there any chance things could just be the same between us? Is it dangerous for him if I'm a superhero? I feel somewhere deep inside like it is dangerous for him.

I stay over at his apartment one night, after a decadent evening of movies and popcorn, as I try to make up with him after a particularly bad fight, but at three in the morning I feel a tug of nausea and I slide out of his bed and creep across the floor. I grab my jeans from a chair and my shoes that I left by the front door.

I'm in the apartment hallway with my shoes in one hand and my key to his apartment in the other before I realize what I'm doing. Clark, sleeping in the quiet apartment behind me, silently, beautifully, and blissfully unaware. Once on the street I run as fast as I can, and it is like I'm speed incarnate, headed toward a fire in an apartment on the Upper East Side. I'll be damned if I'm going to read about another family burned alive when I could have helped. Even if it does jeopardize the only happiness I've ever had.

I beat all the fire trucks.

A lot of people are on the street watching, both casual spectators and those who have managed to get out already and so I duck into the alleyway. The fire is really going. It must have started on a low floor because the bottom half is engulfed in flames, and swiftly swallowing the rest. Unfortunately, as a result, the fire escapes look rather useless. I scale the building next door and once on the roof I'm able to easily jump to the roof of the building on fire. The fire door is locked from this side, but I'm able to wrench it open. I'm not sure why anyone trying to get out isn't already up here as this part of the stairwell looks clear and the buildings are close enough that the jump between the two is easy enough, superhero or not. There's only maybe two high floors not covered in flames. If there was anyone below floor four they're beyond my help now. I try to concentrate on the screaming, and beneath that the heavy breathing and panic, to find survivors in the chaos. When I break down the first door on the fourth floor I see why they're not on the roof. They're just children. Two of them. Boys, maybe five and six years old, faces slick with tears, sitting frozen in fear on their couch with teddy bears in their hands as if waiting for a superhero to rescue them. They both recoil at the sight of me, probably breaking down the door was not my wisest move, especially since the hallway looks a bit like hell - literally. They both erupt into glass- shattering wails, and I scoop them up, wishing I didn't have super hearing. One of them pounds on me with his little fists but the other one just passes out. I bound up the two flights to the roof and burst out the door. I jump them across one roof and then another.

"Stay here okay? I'll be back." I say to the conscious one. He nods and pats his brother's hair. I bound back across the buildings and back down to the fourth floor. The flames are coming even faster now, and I break down the door. I don't have the kind of time I'd like to explore the apartment. If I'm going to have a chance with anyone on the fifth floor I have to be fast. It seems empty and so I move on. The first apartment on the fifth floor is also empty. But in the apartment across the hall I find a huge football player of a man passed out cold from what looks like two six packs and a fifth of Jack. I check the rest of the apartment and once I'm sure it's empty I go back into the bedroom and heft the linebacker across my shoulders. I'm on the roof and making for the building next door and we'd be golden, except the dude wakes up as I'm making a run for the jump to the next roof. Just as my feet leave the edge he thrashes hard like a fish caught on a line.

We fall.

In tandem, like two rocks tied together, and all I can see in my mind is us both hitting the ground and him never getting up again. I reach out instinctively with my hand as we fall and manage to snag the edge of the roof. At the same time I reach blindly for him and catch him by the waist of his jeans, the unexpected weight pulls my arm out of joint and I cry out. He does too, clearly suffering despite the save. Hopefully he'll forgive me the temporary pain. He's still confused and thrashing though, and now in pain, and I don't have much choice but to launch him over my head and onto the roof above us. He hits with a thud and I wince, hoping his new injuries are less than what I'm saving him from. I scramble up the side of the building and find him writhing on the roof, hands in his crotch, moaning. I slam my shoulder against the ground and jam it back into joint with a yelp. I pull the linebacker to his feet and we stumble toward the next building. At the gap he stops hard and pulls back, flailing his arms madly, chattering something incoherent about heights. I look around, hoping nobody is watching, well, nobody except the boys, which can't really be helped, and clock him as gently as possible across his square jaw, catching him as he goes down. The two boys watch me with eyes wide and mouths open. The good news is they seem more shocked than scared now. I lift the gentle giant over my shoulders again and make the small jump to the roof. The boys continue to stare.

"C'mon boys," I say lightly. "Let's get off this roof." I gesture to the back of the building. They nod their heads in amazement and we make our way down the fire escape very slowly, pausing roughly ever ninety seconds to give the one named Richie time to think about his next steps. Once safely on the ground, I take them around the corner to where the fire engines now are, parked and wailing in the street. People outside the building are crying and wringing their hands, and news vans are arriving. I can't chance being seen. Richie sees his mother and makes a run for it. Sam is about to join him but I grab his little hand. "Sam, I have to go, but I'm going to put this man down right here and I need you to tell one of the firemen to come help him, okay?" I say. Sam nods solemnly.

"Thanks for helping us, lady."

"Sure," I say, smiling and feeling ridiculously warm inside. I'm about to dash off when he pulls on my hand.

"Are you Superman or something?"

"Something like that," I say.

"I thought so," he nods sagely. I smile again and escape into the shadows. A moment later, he goes running into the crowd for his mother and a fireman. I watch from the sidelines as he diligently brings a fireman over to the linebacker. My heart is swelling with happiness. It's almost as good as being in love.

I sneak into bed less than an hour before sunrise. Clark rolls over into me, his warmth mixing with mine and I feel a tear between us. A tear between this perfect thing I have with him, and the perfect thing I was doing an hour ago. I know that I can't have them both. There's going to be a moment when I have to choose.

In the morning, eating cereal with Clark, Jake, and Ryan I see both Sam and Richie on the news and almost lose my Cheerios right back up into my bowl.

"Superman saved us!" Richie yells at the TV, pointing to his Superman pajamas.

Sam shakes his head solemnly. "Uh-uh," he says. "Not Superman, it was a girl…it was…Wonder Woman, but her hair was different."

Richie pushes him. "Was not Wonder Woman! Wonder Woman wears a swimsuit, she didn't have on no swimsuit!"

Sam pokes at Richie's Superman logo. "Well, she didn't have a cape neither!" he says, certain that that proves his case. The reporter laughs and the cameraman pulls back on the shot, focusing on the reporter while Sam and Richie jostle one another in the background.

"Those kids are awesome," Ryan says, stuffing cereal in his mouth. Jake nods his head vigorously in agreement and I'm just sitting there, my mouth hanging open, petrified about what might come next.

The reporter smiles brightly through the TV. "Well you heard it here first Paul, Superman, or Wonder Woman, definitely saved these boys and another tenant from a burning building last night," she says, touching her ear as she listens to the in studio newscaster. The television goes to a split screen and the newscaster asks some follow up questions and I continue to hold my breath.

"No information on the identity of this Superman though, Lane?"

"Unfortunately no Paul. Our only witnesses are Sam and Richie here as the other gentlemen in question was passed out cold and has no recollection of the event. But whoever it was, they surely saved three lives as firefighters claim that, due to the nature of the fire and quickness with which is spread and the location, it's unlikely they would have been able to get to the tenants on the upper floors in time…back to you, Paul," the reporter adds with a toothy smile. Clark gets up and puts a hand on my shoulder lightly. I jump what feels like three feet in the air.

"Whoa. You okay?" he asks. I nod and swallow a bit of Cherrios lodged in my throat.

"Mmmhmm," I say and force a smile.

"You ready to go?" he asks and motions to the door.

"Oh, yeah," I say, startled, "The park. Yes. Ready!" I grab my jacket and we head out the door together, Clark shouting goodbyes to Jake and Ryan who make teasing kissing sounds at us as we leave. The sight of my two worlds colliding is unsettling to say the least. I should seriously consider investing in a mask.

And I resolve never to stay over at Clark's place again. It's too dangerous. Too complicated.

A few weeks later, after a late brunch, we're walking back to Clark's apartment when we're suddenly overrun by kittens in the street. I think I'm dreaming at first, that I've stumbled into another world and everything seems like it's on pause, then Clark looks at his feet and lifts one to narrowly avoid a rogue kitty.

"What the hell?!" he says turning around and watching three or four kitties run around the sidewalk and dash into the street. Taxis screech to a halt. Horns start and the noise of the city crashes in on me.

"You see them too?" I breathe desperately. He looks at me, one eyebrow cocked.

"Of course I see them – they're everywhere!" he says and then, "C'mon, We've got to help round them up." We spend the next half hour chasing kitties around the street, gathering them up and returning them to the owner. They belong to some woman in the park adopting them out to people as part of some kind of pet rescue. The last kitty, a particularly clever one, will just not be caught. It takes both Clark and I, and finally me, cheating, quietly using my super speed, to catch her. The adoption woman lets us take her home as a thank you, after properly grilling us on how the kitten will be cared for. We don't argue in front of the woman about whose place the kitty is actually going to be living in, but since I don't know how Liesel and Ben feel about kittens, I suspect Clark will win that fight. I wrap her up in my arms and nuzzle her. She scratches my face. I don't think I've ever had a pet before, I'm very excited about it.

She's mostly white with little black shoes, and a very distinctive black eye, like another kitty has punched her in the face. She looks like she loves to fight; she's a good match for me I think. When Clark asks what we should name her I immediately deem her "Joan – World's Strongest Kitty".

The burning in my chest overtakes me with a vengeance while holding Joan and leaning into Clark on the subway ride home that day. I sit up very straight. Clark asks me what's wrong. I shake my head, nothing. The fire runs across my chest and through my veins with renewed intensity. This one is bad. Really bad. I look around frantically, trying to figure out the source. I'm listening to everything all at once and I feel the familiar razor focus inside me. For a second I think I will just try to ignore it. That since Clark is with me it's too complicated. That if I try hard enough I can just forget that anything is happening, but I remember those bodies being brought out of the liquor store, bloody and silent, and Clark's smiling face across from me at dinner as I ignored a massacre I could have stopped. The consequences are too great. It's too selfish to keep holding on to Clark, I can't ask others to keep paying such a heavy price for my inaction. Besides, Clark is on this train too, what if whatever it is gets him too? And thinking about it like that seals it. I know with certainty that I'll never be able to block it out again. I will always have to act, because it could always be Clark. And everyone is Clark to someone else. If the fire wasn't so insistent I think maybe that realization would have broken me right then. Instead, I close my eyes and focus. Instead, I do exactly what I know how to do. What I was built to do.

Clark sits forward, concerned. "Bonnie," he brushes some hair away from my face. "What's wrong...you look flushed." I push his hand away from me with my free hand.

"Be quiet. I'm listening," I say. He looks pale, his eyes searching around the train for what I am listening for.

"Bonnie, you're scaring me..."

"Be quiet," I say calmly, thrusting Joan at him. "Hold her, please." Clark takes the kitten, who now seems alarmed as well, mewing angrily. With Joan safely in Clark's hands, I stand up. Clark tries to stand up too. I push him back down. Hard. Things are different now. I hold him there, my hand flat against his chest, looking around the train and beyond to the other cars. "Please stay here," I say to him, a little bit coldly.

"Baby, you're scaring the hell out of me. What's wrong?" I look at him for the first time since I felt the bad sound and I don't know what it is he sees in my eyes but he understands how serious I am and stops resisting against my hand, stops trying to stand up with me. I suppose this is the moment when he realizes that our problems are not over, and that he maybe had no idea what he was dealing with all this time.

"Please, just do this for me," I beg. He nods and pets Joan on the head to silence her mewing. I walk toward the back of the train through to the next car, and then the next, and the next. Sure enough, three cars back, there's a bad man and a bad sound coming off of him, the likes of which I haven't felt in a long while.

I try to sit back down, to do nothing, to be like every other scared little kitten on that train praying that bad things will just go away. But it's not possible, it's not who I am, it's not who I can be, it's not who I'm supposed to be, and no number of days playing house can make me be someone else. I wish it could, but it's just not in the stars.

The man with the bad sound has an absurdly large bloody knife and there's a young boy on the ground, maybe twelve years old. The boy is still breathing, but it's shallow and ragged, he's been stuck deep with that knife. His dark blood is running down the grooves in the floor of the train, faster with every turn and rumble of the tracks. Some people are aware of the blood and slinking away from it like it's a poison that will get them too. Others are letting it slide under their shoes and gel in their pant legs. There's a girl too. A little girl, three years old, maybe four, her throat already slightly pink behind the knife of this man. They look like brother and sister. Her eyes are red from crying. There are another three-dozen people in this car alternately shuddering and screaming at this scene, trying to gauge their own escapes. I make my move forward and people are immediately caught up in it, yelling at me in hushed tones. "Girl, don't go over there!" "Don't you see that boy got a knife!" "Stupid girl – sit down! You're going to get us all killed!"

I crouch down to touch the boy's blood sliding down the floor. The man with the knife looks at me. He pushes the girl at me hard, and she stumbles across the floor, sliding in her brother's blood. I catch her with one hand and pass her off to a woman trembling in her seat behind me. Before the man can reach the back door of the subway to move to another car I'm there. But he sees my reflection in the glass and turns before I can get a hand on him. He hits me hard and I go down. The blood on the floor helps take me down, and the fact that I'm also overly concerned about landing on the boy and crushing him doesn't help. The man kicks me in the stomach while I'm down. And while gasping on the floor for breath he tries to bring the knife down into my chest, but I raise my right arm at the last second, blocking his downward stroke. In the same motion I grab his forearm with my blocking hand and pull him into me so he'll share the disadvantage of the slippery blood. He does slip and I'm able to use that second to get up. Once standing, I clench my right hand. It's strong. I can feel it. One is all I will need.

But I want more than one. It's because of people like him that I can't have Clark and a kitten and a job and a normal life.

I hit him and his head flies backwards like he's been hit by a train. He blinks, shocked, and shakes his head. I look at him and realize something is wrong with his eyes. He's on something, he is feeling no pain and not going down easy. I hit him again.
Again.
Again.
Again.

I hit him until he doesn't get up. And then I turn around. Someone has dragged the little boy away from us and two people are trying to resuscitate him. Everyone else is staring at me, holding their collective breath. I stand on one side of the train, arms at my sides, fists clenched, breathing heavily, while everyone else huddles on the other side of the train staring, as afraid of me now, as they had been of him. I can't see straight, I feel a little dizzy, but the burning is gone, and in a way I feel the best I've felt in ages. Everything will be okay. A tall man to my right speaks up.

"Uh, Miss...uh...your arm." I look at him almost in slow motion and then look down at my right arm. The man's knife is buried to the hilt in my forearm, the tip sticking out the other side. It looks strange sticking out of my arm like that. I cock my head, looking at it, then grab it with my left hand and pull it out. It makes this strange "shtuck" sound as it comes out of my bone and someone in the back throws up, while a woman screams, and someone else faints. It clatters loudly to the floor.

"Thanks," I say to the man. No sooner have the words left my throat, do I hear the soft mewing of Joan.

No.

No.

NO.

I look up, my vision clearing a little and see at the very back, by the door, Clark standing there with Joan in his arms. His face is a lonely, blank slate that I cannot understand. I look down at myself, covered in blood. The blood of the boy, the man, and myself, all mixing together into one. The train comes to a lurching halt. Nobody moves. The doors open and I step over the body and out onto the platform. A woman there screams when she sees me. I start running. Nobody comes after me.

●

A bell rings on the door of a dry cleaner's shop in Venice and as I walk through a tiny dark-haired woman pops out from behind a rack of plastic covered clothing, endless shiny sheets of it glinting in the afternoon sun.

"Yes, can I help you?"

"Yeah," I say, pushing my hair out of my eyes and pulling my old cat suit out of the duffel bag and laying it on the counter. I'd rinsed it in the sink like a thousand times, until the water ran clear, getting all the blood out of it but it's still all torn up from the knife and bullet wounds, not to mention dog bites. "Do you think you can repair this?" I ask, politely, but not sweetly. The woman looks at the cheap, dark fabric and puts on the glasses hanging from a chain around her neck. They fall down to the edge of her nose instantly.

"I can fix it, but you'll be able to see all the repairs...it will never be like new, never the same again," she says, looking up at me to see if I'm interested anyway.

"That's okay," I say. "Neither am I." It sounds more foreboding than I mean and when she looks at me, I cut it with a smile. She cocks her head.

"You know, the fabric is not that expensive...it might be cheaper just to buy a new one," she suggests with a light shrug. I take my sunglasses from off my head and put them back on.

"Yeah, I know. This has...sentimental value," I say. She nods her head politely.

"Can it be ready on Thursday?" I ask.

"Yes. Thursday anytime after one o'clock. Okay?"

"Sounds good."

The woman runs her hands over the fabric, counting up all the little cuts and tears from the dogs as well as the abdomen slice and then writes up a little slip and gives me the pink copy. I smile again and thank her for her time.

I'll get the suit back on Thursday, and Friday I'll see Liz for the last time.

O

I run all night. All over the city. It pours rain on me everywhere I go, and it feels right. Which is to say it feels sufficiently depressing and epic. I can't decide if the universe is judging (and punishing) me, or trying to cleanse me for rebirth.

Somehow both seem right. As the sun starts to come up I realize that no matter what I decide to do, I have to at least say goodbye, I can't leave it the way it was on the train. So I head back Clark's apartment in the rain, my hands stuffed in my jacket pockets. The rain has washed away the blood from my face and my clothes, but I can't get my hands clean for some reason. By the time I get downtown and near his apartment, I've discarded my shoes. The rain has soaked them so thoroughly that they had started to fall apart somewhere in Central Park.

I put the key in the lock and instantly know he's sleeping in his favorite chair with the lights on. I can hear his low rhythmic breathing much closer than if he'd been in the bedroom, and the apartment door is warmer to the touch of my hand than it would be if all the lights had been turned off at a reasonable hour. I open the door slowly as Joan mews quietly at the crack. She skitters back away from me when my clothing starts sprinkling water on her. I just look at Clark for a while and can't move. His face, is both calm and somehow also furrowed as if he's concerned for me even in sleep. The cordless phone and his mobile are clenched in his hands, his laptop open at his feet on the floor. When I finally move again, quietly, to get a towel from the closet to clean up the puddle I've left on the hardwood floor, a board creaks and he jumps sky high. Disoriented, he looks at me; I'm sure I'm quite a sight, but as soon as the veil of sleep leaves him he rushes toward me and embraces me, harder than he ever has before. It lasts a long time and when he releases me it's only to touch my face.

"Are you okay?" he searches my eyes for some explanation.

"I am," is all I can say. He lowers his hands to mine and holds them. This makes me nervous. He looks down at them and steps back, they're still stained with blood. This seems to make him think twice about everything he's been thinking over the past hours. In the deluge of questions that I can see forming behind his eyes, my wellbeing is slipping into the background.

"Bonnie. What's going on?" he asks loudly. I glance toward Jake's and Ryan's rooms at the other end of the apartment. He shakes his head lightly. "They're not here. They're away," he says, clearly wanting to move on with his inquiry. I remove my hands from his and walk to the hall closet to get the towel. He follows me. Joan tails behind us both, concerned. I try to dry off my hair a little bit and take another towel into the hall for the puddle. "Stop,

Bonnie. Don't worry about that now...please...you're freezing and soaking. Let's get you out of those clothes." I stand up from the puddle and take off my jeans. "Where are your shoes?!" He cries out, pointing at my bare feet. I shrug my shoulders, like a kid.

"I don't know."

He purses his lips together, trying not to comment, and takes the wet jeans from me. We walk into the kitchen and he puts my jeans in the sink. I take off my jacket and hand it to him as well. When I do he grabs my arm.

"Bonnie!" he cries out, incredulous. I look at him and he searches my face. "What the hell is happening?! I saw you take that knife out of your arm. This cannot be all there is! There's...there's no wound...what...what is going on?!" he turns my arm over and back again obsessing over the flawless skin. I look at him, very sad, seeing how this is all going to go, wishing that it could be different.

"It wasn't so bad as it looked," I say lamely. He hardens.

"I saw it, Bonnie. I saw it all. That knife was coming out the other side of your arm. How is it possible that there's nothing? I've been imagining you all this time at some hospital getting yourself stitched up, even though I've called every hospital in New York and found nothing. Now I see...not only do you look like you've been swimming in the East River for the last twelve hours, but you barely have a scratch on you. You have to tell me what the fuck is happening, and you have to do it now!" Clark forces me into facing him, and his eyes are such a strange look of anger and fear and love and revulsion that I can't bear to say anything. I wrench my arm away from him and take off my shirt, tossing it into the sink with the rest of my clothes. I walk to his bedroom in my wet bra and underwear, Clark and Joan on my heels. I strip off my underwear and pull new, dry clothes from my drawer. "I deserve an answer, Bonnie," he says between clenched teeth, full of so much emotion, so many different ones he doesn't seem to know which one to settle on. We've come so far in the five minutes since I walked through the door, back when there was only concern for me. I go into the bathroom and lock the door behind me. I can tell from Clark's breathing that he's leaning on the door. Joan has managed to slip in with me and is trying to jump up onto the lip of the tub and is falling repeatedly onto her kitten butt, destroying in a series of little experiments, the theory that cats land on their feet. I turn on the water as hot as I can get it, and start scrubbing my hands with the bar of soap. I scrub until they are as clean and sterile as a surgeon's hands, until there's just a little nub of soap left, and then I scrub until that nub is gone too.

The glass above the sink is all fogged up from the water. I write some words in the fogged up mirror and then erase them. I turn off the water and look at Joan, who has managed in my washing frenzy, to succeed in her mission to the lip of the tub, and then fallen into the tub and been unable to climb out. I pick her up and set her back on the tile. She cocks her head at me briefly before attempting the jump to the lip of the tub all over again. I open the door to the bathroom and look at Clark sitting quietly on the bed, hands on his knees. I sit down next to him, my raw hands in my lap.

"I can't explain anything...I'm sorry...and you wouldn't even believe me if I could explain it," I say. Clark reaches for my hand, but stops short, as if remembering where they have been, what they have done. "Did he die?" I ask softly.

"The kid will be okay," he says, unable to look away from my hands.

"I meant the man, did the man die?" I look at him, but he still can't take his eyes off my hands. I clench them in embarrassment.

"They don't know yet...I mean, he's in a coma...Bonnie...you have to tell me something...otherwise...I mean, what can I possibly think?"

"I don't know what you'll think," I say. "But there is no explanation I can give you that's going to help." My mind reels, I don't know how to start the sentence that might clear things up for him, since it's not even clear to me. I'm a superhero baby, but I'm a bad one because I hurt people sometimes and I don't know what I'm doing. And who knows if I might get you hurt too, my brother wants nothing to do with me, and what I am maybe killed my parents. Yeah, that will clear everything up for him.

"Bonnie...baby, we have to get you some help," he says finally, desperately. And as he says the word help I feel the weight of all the world falling in on me, because this is it. This is the moment when I lose it all. This is when the world gets to take away the only thing I've ever found to love. And it seems so unfair to punish me in this way. My eyes start to get blurry and before I know it there are tears pouring out of me. I don't know if I can do it now that it's the time to make the break. Leaving him is too much price to pay. It can't really be the price I am being asked for. I brush a handful of tears away and steel my voice.

"There is no help."

"There's always help. There are people who can help you…doctors…or treatment…therapy…pills…something…there has to be, we can fix it," he says it softly, wanting it to be true, believing that it must be. I stand up.

"Trust me Clark. There's nothing. There's nothing to be fixed," I say, almost angry at him, for maybe the first time, for suggesting that I need fixing. I walk to the front door and pick up the towel. I toss it into the sink with the ruined clothes. There's an extra pair of my sneakers in the hall closet and I put them on. By the time Clark comes out of the bedroom, head hung low, I have my hand on the doorknob. He looks panicked, but like he knows as well as I do that he's helpless in this moment.

"Where are you going? Please don't, Bonnie," he picks up Joan, who is now in full kitty wail.

"It's better for me if you get rid of those clothes that I came here in, but I understand if you don't," I say.

"Is that it? Is that all you can say?" his eyes are so transparent with pain and loss that it physically hurts to look at him.

"There aren't words…," I start. "There just aren't even close to words in any language for me to tell you…for me to explain…what you mean to me…see? I can't even come up with words to explain that there aren't words." I turn the knob and walk out the door, closing it on my life and everything I have ever wanted and cursing the entire world and everything that has ever taken breath or born a thought. There's no room for people like me, and yet, here I am.

And where do I go? Where on Earth does a person go when she realizes there's no place for her? You can't possibly try to fit in, because if you do, if you manage to carve out some beautiful niche of happiness for yourself, then one day it will be taken from you as surely and truly as the sun rises each morning.

Going home feels wrong. Even though I love Liesel with all I've got, and Ben too, and I know they'd comfort me, I don't want to be comforted. And Clark might come for me there. I don't think I could leave him a second time. I was barely strong enough to do it the first time. I go to Penn Station. Not with the intention of running away so much as escaping.

I need time.

I need space.

I need quiet.

I look at the boards for the farthest quietest place I can get to tonight. At 2:00 in the morning there's a train going to Rockport, Maine and something sounds…right about that. I buy a ticket, a painful $92.00 and call Liesel. She puts up a fight, but in the end tells me she loves me and to come back soon. I promise I will. She promises to be kind to Clark if he shows up, not that she could be anything but. She also agrees to talk to Tim at the bookstore, to let him know that I've had a family emergency, maybe with luck I won't be fired when I get back. I wait for six hours in an uncomfortable seat in the lonely station. When my train is finally called I get on and curl up in the seat and fall asleep. Exhausted and painfully sad. It takes more than ten hours and includes a stop in Boston and one in Portland. At the Portland stop I actually almost get off the train, but resist. Something is bubbling about inside me, all anticipation and nerves and it's hard to stay in my seat. Halfway between Portland and Rockport it's all I can do not to jump off the speeding train. My brain wants me to move so badly. But I gut it out, and the intensity lessens as I get closer to Rockport. When I finally exit in Rockport, something about the place feels right, even though I don't know what that means. But not as right as whatever I felt an hour behind me. Something is picking at my senses, pulling me to it, perking me up and tugging on me from the outside to the in. On a main street filled with sweet houses and shops, and quiet as a tomb, I turn southwest, the way I'd come, and start walking. I do something I can only describe as following my nose. Drawn forward as if there's a fishing line tied to someplace deep inside me and someone, or some thing, at the other end is reeling me in. I hitch a ride with a trucker and go half an hour southwest along the coast, following the tug of the line, which gets stronger and tighter with every mile. I get out when he makes a right that takes us inland and the tug lessens. I walk a good four miles southwest again, following the imaginary line, when someone else picks me up. We go another half hour along the coast in that direction, but whatever magical marker I'm being drawn to, we must pass it. The intensity is like a fist inside my chest and then it's like it just unclenches. When I get out of the car, the nice driver, a man in his 50s with a big head of salt and pepper hair, seems concerned.

"You sure you know where you're going Miss? There's not much out there," he says, worry heavy in his voice as he looks past me to the quickly darkening road I'm headed toward.

I smile back at him and without thinking say, "It's okay, I'm from here."

●

Cops are staked out all over the place.

I have no idea how long they've been there, but none of them actually notice me when I casually walk by on a separate block and then scale the back of a building across the street from Liz's office building. I don't know why the hell they bother to come so early if they don't even know what to watch for, or how. I don't know why cops think they're so clever. It's just like in the movies and on crappy TV shows where they think they're blending in and they're just the most obvious damn things in the room. I mean, who are they kidding with those white earpieces with cords tucked into their jackets? I can see those things from a mile away, even without my freaking super-vision. They're shuffling newspapers and sitting in cars, waiting for buses but never getting on, sweeping the street like curious janitors, and they even have a girl that looks about my age on rollerblades and with an iPod that's probably not an iPod, plugged into her ears. She actually might have fooled me, but since she rollerblades constantly around the building and back again, over and over, on a loop, she's as easy to make as the rest of them. There are also two cops in the empty office next to Liz's, and one pretending to be a patient in the waiting area that I get a look at a few times when Liz opens the door to her office. The ones in the office next to Liz's look out the window constantly with binoculars, but never once, in four hours, bother to look my way.

Morons.

I harbor brief fantasies about a policeman massacre. Maybe in the papers they would call it the Policeman's Ball of Blood...or Massacre in Venice? I could kill them all and just kind of bathe in their blood. It would be quite a sight. It would certainly solidify my reputation, assuming Liz has told them about all my victims, assuming they have confirmed the names and details. They must have, or there wouldn't be thirty cops here. But part of me still fears cops, or if not cops then at least the government at large. It's ironic that my inability to be killed – as my little tests continue to prove – has actually made me fear the government more, not less. Visions of being strapped to a table and experimented on have only grown in my imagination. My tests are fine – those are on my terms, but someone else's tests? No way. It's a fear strong enough to keep my fantasies of a policeman massacre as just that, a fantasy. At least, for now.

And so, I wait. As the time for my appointment approaches, Liz grows considerably more tense and obvious. She paces and sweats through her silk lavender blouse, which I can see even from across the street. I feel the fabric of my newly patched up cat suit clinging to my body, the repairs obvious and sitting on the surface of the shiny material like fat, black eels. I rub my fingers over these scars, scars that should match scars on my body, but of course don't since my body is all magical and shit. I think I like the suit even better now. Now it's like a history of my life.

Once six comes and goes, the policemen start to get more and more restless, less and less sure that Liz isn't just a crazy bitch who made the whole thing up. By seven most of them have left, leaving behind only a small contingent of officers. I yawn. By eight-thirty the rest have left except two camped out in the office next to hers, dozing off in chairs, feet propped up on desks and the one in her waiting room. Liz is packing up her office and ready to go home.

I get across the street and onto the nineteenth floor. I take the stairs so nobody will hear the elevator ding. On Liz's floor, I walk past her door and to the empty office next door with the cops resting and bored inside. It doesn't occur to me until now that this might actually take finesse, that I've never killed a couple cops before and that I've got to do it quickly so that Liz doesn't panic and escape. I'm not so worried that she'll actually get away, but I do want to surprise her, and I do want our confrontation to happen in her office, where it should. There's a table with a plant at the end of the hallway and I grab it. It's one of those nice heavy terra cotta ones. Perfect. I open the door smoothly, as if I mean them no harm. One is asleep and snoring, but the other looks up and must recognize me from Liz's description. He gets out only, "It's he-" before the plant hits him in the face with a crash. I have to get the other one before he fully wakes up, so I slide behind him before he's able to get his feet off the desk, and I snap his neck, so he doesn't have time to shout anything. I check the pulse on plant face – he's gone too. Nice. Nice and quiet. I'm even impressed with myself and my little plant idea. I'm not exactly the king of ideas so I'm pleased how things have worked out. There are two sets of handcuffs and some keys on the table and I pocket everything. You never know. Just then the door opens and the third cop falls backward, scrambling to get away. I spring at him like a freaking jungle cat and snap his neck the same as the other one. I drag him inside and close the door to the room casually.

I get to Liz's door just as she turns to switch out the lights.
"Hi Doc, let's go back inside," I say darkly.

○

I've been walking south and slightly west for awhile now, probably four or five miles, and the sun has set and it's dark and quiet and I feel a kind of peace I haven't felt in...well, I can't remember how long. There aren't a lot of people out here. I see an occasional car, some lights off the road that suggest some houses dotted along near the water's edge. Mostly what I hear is water, and wind, and animal sounds. It's such a relief. I've gotten so used to being around people, and in such a large city that I've forgotten what bliss it is to be just away. How deeply quiet it is in comparison.

But there are pangs too. The pang of guilt. Sure I can't feel any danger out here, but it doesn't mean horrible things aren't happening to people outside my immediate radius. Would it be selfish and horrible of me to live here forever in peace and quiet. My own Fortress of Solitude? And more than that, no amount of peace and quiet is worth being utterly alone. I miss Clark like someone has torn my heart from my chest and replaced it with sawdust. I miss Liesel and Ben, their laughter, their warmth.

With an old, gravely driveway to my left, the fist in my chest is as tightly clenched as it has ever been, and as I pass the driveway, it lessens just slightly. So I back up a few steps and turn down the drive. I can't wait any longer and so I begin to run, but as the driveway turns, the feeling wants to pull me into the trees. I follow it, veering off the gravel and into the soft earth, pushing branches from my path and stumbling my way through. I break through the trees, nearly falling down onto a rocky beach and as I do, the tightness in my chest, the taut fishing line feels like it explodes, evaporating and leaving me with a strange and settled warmth in my chest. Ahead of me, bathed in a pale, partial moon is the ocean, and out a small distance from the shore, a small island. I brush myself off and walk across the rocks to the edge of the water. The way the island is situated it's creating a slight cove, so that the water behind it that hits the shore at my feet feels more like a lake than an ocean with tiny almost imperceptible ripples. More serious waves lap at the shore of the island itself. The island hums at me, but I'm not sure what it's humming. It's almost as if it's sitting on a nuclear reactor. Power, strength, mystery, and maybe even something dark and frightening seethe from it. It's hard to pinpoint which thing I feel most intensely. I look up and down the beach, I'm surprised to see a lonely blue cottage, which must belong to the gravely driveway I veered from. Most surprising however, is that I remember it. Set back from the water a bit and up slightly on a small bluff. It is exactly as I remember, though I didn't know there was anything to remember until just now. It's tired looking, worn down and abandoned, but it resonates something in me. Love and happiness I think. I walk toward it, faint memories exploding in my brain gently, if that's possible. The wooden porch is old and slightly warped, nobody has cared for it in many years, and I get a nasty splinter from the railing. As I look up to the door, I see there is something carved on it. I kneel down and trace the rough edge. The carving has deteriorated pretty severely, rotting away and bleeding into itself, but it's the image of a bird, I think, and three conjoined circles. Touching it creates a faint hum in the tips of my fingers. I peek through the dirty windows and feel more memories bubbling up about the dark spaces inside.

I turn to look at the island from the porch and as I do, I have a sudden flash of memory, much clearer than the others. An image of Jasper, maybe ten years old, helping me swim to the shore, and my mother already there, walking out of the trees to greet us on the beach.

I walk toward the water and stare at the island. It's thick with trees, but surrounded by a sand and rock beach on this side. I can't tell how big it is, but the foliage is dense enough that even I can't see through to the other side. I look around to make sure nobody is watching me and realize how remote the house is. I see only a few lit windows dotting up and down the beach. I strip off my t-shirt and sneakers. I pull off my jeans and leave them all in a little pile on an ancient wooden beach chair that looks ready to crumble. I wade into the water. It's bitingly cold, but nothing my body can't handle. I swim to the island and the entire time it's like some crazy déjà vu is taking place. I feel somehow myself and ancient and also six years old all at once. At the shore I look back toward the cottage and realize I have definitely seen it from this perspective before. In fact, my strongest memory of the cottage is from this exact angle. I look behind me into the trees. What was I doing here at six years old? I follow the tug on my insides deeper into the woods. The moon is not full and it's faint, but bright enough with my vision to guide me through the woods, though a bank of clouds is making things more complicated. I push through trees and bushes for nearly ten minutes before I stumble into a clearing and as soon as I do the clouds vanish and the moon shines much more brightly down onto me. It's a not a particularly large space, no more than a dozen feet wide, with trees rising up dramatically on all sides. As I step out of the woods and into the clearing I hit stone, not soft ground. The second my foot touches the stone I know I've hit whatever has been pulling on me since, well, I'm not entirely sure when it started, but it might have started as far back as Penn Station, otherwise why would I have bought the ticket to Rockport in the first place? The energy I'm feeling is like a pulsating beat that reverberates through my entire body. I get on my hands and knees and sweep the nettles and dead brush off the ground. As I do it I can feel the grooves in the stone, and without even looking I know they're the same as the carving in the cottage's front door. Once the stone is cleared off, I step back and take it all in. It's a huge piece of rock, something, more than ten feet across and intricately carved with the same three intertwined circles and bird image. I kneel down and spread my fingers out across the stone. It's so powerful, but I can't access it. It feels important; it feels pulsing with something, but it's like I'm missing a key, or a password, or something. It feels locked. It drew me here, I know it did. But now that I'm here it's almost like it's singing to me that I'm not ready.

But what will make me ready?

I lie down on the stone, arms out, for what must be an hour, hoping something will come to me, but all that comes to me is the cold from the rock seeping into my skin, then deeper, into my stone-like bones. I finally give up and head back through the brush to the shore. My bare flesh is prickled with cold and cut up from walking through the trees. I wade into the water and look toward the cottage and see a woman standing on the porch.

It's my mother.

●

Liz shakes visibly when she answers me. "Lola, you're really late." She looks at her watch, as if she doesn't know exactly what time it is already. "I'm sorry, but it's just way too late, I can't stay, I have somewhere I have to be." She can't look me in the eye and her voice is thick with fear. I lean against the doorjamb, almost touching her, close, like we're intimate friends.

"I'm gonna have to insist, Liz," I say. She bristles and tries to be firm.

"Insist on what, Lola? You're hardly in a place to insist anything. This is not a negotiation. Your appointment was for six. It is now," she pauses to check her watch again, "Nearly nine. I've been lenient in the past about you being late, but this is too late, and I have other commitments."

"You're wrong, Liz."

"Wrong about what? I most certainly have somewhere to go."

"You're wrong about me not being in a place to insist anything. I think we both know exactly what place I'm in. So get back inside the goddamn office," I say, pushing the door open wider and smiling a mouth full of shiny teeth. She shudders slightly but slides back inside the door. When we get inside the waiting room Liz takes out her mobile phone and holds up her finger as if to tell me to give her a moment.

"I need to make a call, tell them I'm running late." I smack the phone out of her hand and it goes flying across the room and smashes the glass of a black and white photograph over the reception desk, landing on the floor in splinters. Liz draws back her injured hand.

"No calls," I say matter-of-factly. She backs up towards her office door and she turns the knob when her hand lands on it, without taking her eyes off me, though she can't seem to bring herself to look at my face. Surely she's noticed the cat suit by now, it can't be comforting. Once in her office, she reaches for the light.

"No lights," I say, placing my hand firmly on hers until she relents and abandons the switch. There's enough light coming in from her windows for us to see each other clearly, and I don't want anyone possibly peeking in from outside. Liz moves to sit in her regular chair. "The couch," I say, pointing her to it. She reorients herself and sits on the very edge of the couch, perched like a bird about to take flight. I sit comfortably in her big leather chair. I cross my legs doing my best impression of her. I almost wish I was wearing a skirt so that I could make the same swishing sound that Liz does when she crosses her legs. I like that sound. The cat suit makes an interesting sound, but it's not the same.

"So, how was your week?" I ask gamely. Liz laughs awkwardly, a brief hope surging in her that this is not going to be horrible. I can see the idea light up behind her eyes and take flight. Sometimes, I do like to get their hopes up.

"Um, it was fine, Lola, how was yours?"

"Fine. Fine. Thanks for asking." I smile at her but it doesn't seem to reassure her. "So, Liz, I gotta tell you, I got here a little early today and I noticed that there were about thirty cops waiting for me."

"Cops? Lola, I just...I have no idea what you're talking about." I look at her hard and she crumbles.

"You need help Lola, you need real help. You can't go around killing people and hurting yourself, I had to turn you in, I didn't have a choice."

"You know...that sounds really familiar." I pause and put a finger to my chin as if trying to puzzle something out. "As a matter of fact, wasn't it you that told me that we all make our own choices?"

Liz stammers, "Y-Yes, but-"

"No but. You brought yourself here. You wanted to write another bestseller. Your instincts told you – rightly so – that there was something unique about me, something dangerous, but you wanted your bestseller and you were happy to use me for that purpose and so here we are. You decided to engage with me, you decided all of this, and now you've decided to betray me and I don't think for one moment you're stupid enough to believe you're going to get away with it." She's still shaking, trembling under her blouse so that it shivers constantly, but her response is insightful and surprises me.

"Is this why you picked Friday at six for your appointment? You were always going to kill me, and if you kill me on a Friday night-"

"-Then it takes them longer to find your body," I finish for her.

"Then, then, really none of it was up to me. It didn't matter what I did, you were always going to kill me." She seems to think she's come up with some brilliant counter argument.

I sigh dramatically. "No Liz, it's just that I know people. They suck. They always betray you. I knew you would betray me, it was only a matter of time, and I knew that once you betrayed me I would kill you. And so here we are. Your choices." I put my pointer fingers into a little meditative steeple position that I've seen her do before. It seems fitting. Liz breaks down in front of me. She's a shuddering, crying mess, practically ruining her pretty silk blouse, but it was going to be ruined in a few minutes anyway, so I don't suppose it matters. I take her notepad out of the top drawer and put it in the wastebasket. I take the laptop and smash it into tiny shards with my fist. It's possible some techie somewhere can still salvage something from it, but she's already given the police all her notes and surely they've got my fingerprints, so I'm not sure how much any of it matters anymore. Maybe I'm doing it more to scare her. She runs, but before she can even get to the door I grab her by the back of her neck and throw her up against the wall. It knocks her out and she lies in a little silk and high heels heap on the expensive rug. I use a lighter in one of her drawers to set fire to her notebook and toss it into the wastebasket. I've known how I was going to kill Liz since the first day that I came to visit her in her office, but it just occurs to me now, for the first time ever, standing over her, while smoke slowly fills the room, that she's more useful to me alive.

Instead of putting out the fire I kick over the trashcan and spread the fire across the floor. The sprinklers pop on almost instantly. It's actually great they come on, because I'm feeling a bit dirty and they feel like a nice cleansing rain. I pick Liz up and sling her over my shoulder, her hip jabbing me in the ear. We're both pretty soaked when we hit the hallway, and I head toward the stairs and go up two flights to the roof.

The sirens are screaming in the street, only a block or so away. I look up at the sky. I've been thinking for a while now that I should probably be able to fly; I don't know why not – I can do almost everything else I've ever thought of.

So I close my eyes and concentrate. The sirens are distracting, and Liz is starting to moan a little bit. I set her down carefully and force all of the world away from me and focus. I push down on everything inside of me and then just let it explode up and through me. I shoot into the air so fast it feels like I've been shot out of a cannon. I slow down and levitate for a moment, trying to just appreciate the awesomeness of it, looking down on the city and the people-ants below me, as I should have been doing all along. This officially goes on the top of the 'list of things that are awesome about being me'. I touch back down on the roof and pick Liz up, cradling her like Superman rescuing Lois Lane from a burning building. Though in Superman's case, I don't suppose he started the fire. I lift off the ground and point myself northwest, headed for the house in Malibu with my newest asset, the brains of my new operation.

O

"MOM!" I scream, my voice tearing at the sky. I dive into the water and swim frantically, pulling myself through the cold, dark sheets with every ounce of power I have. It's all I can do to keep my head down so I can swim faster, at each stroke I want to look up and make sure she hasn't disappeared. When my feet hit the rocky bottom, I scramble up the bank, pulling my wet hair from my eyes to see if she's there, sure she'll be gone. But she's not. She's still there. Wavering and flickering like a candle, but there. Indisputably there.

I run to the house, the rocks tearing up my feet. At the porch I pull up short, afraid I'll barrel right through her. She turns to me, ethereal and beautiful, her red hair glowing about her like a halo.

"You're not ready, darling," she says as I rush to catch my breath.

"What, Mom, what does that mean?" there are so many things I want to say, so many questions I want to ask, but they've all turned into an impenetrable ball of wire in my head and I can't sort them out.

"It's my fault. I should have seen it. Found a better way to warn you. It's coming for you and you're not ready," she shakes her head sadly, and she flickers more, becoming almost watery.

"Then, then what can I do to be ready? What's coming?" I ask. These aren't the questions I had thought of asking all these years, but they're what come out regardless. I move forward to touch her even though it's clear there's nothing to touch. She shudders back a bit.

"The power. Your dreams. The dreams you used to have, of the storm? It's coming, you don't have much time left."

"So help me," I say.

"Oh darling, I can't," she says and shakes her head. "You have to get there your own way."

I smash at the porch with my fist, breaking a board into splinters. "Then why are you even here?!" I shout, surprised at the anger in my voice.

"I wanted to see you," she says simply. And when I look up, to apologize, to tell her that I wanted to see her too, that I'm glad she came, even if it's in the same riddles and nonsense that has always followed her – she's gone. As if she was never there. As if I've been ranting at an empty porch.

I sit in my wet underwear on the steps, shivering until I'm dry, and then I put my clothes back on and curl up on the porch to sleep, hoping she'll come back, even if only in my dreams.

But somehow I know she won't.

In the morning I begin the walk back to the road, and then the slow trek back to my life. By late evening I'm back in Manhattan and the world is a cacophony of noises, both good and bad.

As I walk back home the good is quickly overwhelmed by the bad. I feel the fire powerfully in my chest and I follow it. It's a strange one this time, feeling more like a slow burn, rather than a flash. I'm not sure what that means, but it's got me curious. I begin running. The further east I get the fewer people I see until finally I'm down by empty docks I've never seen before. The fire feeling is coming from a warehouse on one of the docks, abandoned and quiet, except if you could assign a picture to the feeling I get when I look at it, it would look like a building engulfed in fire, to an almost cartoonish degree. Flames licking at the sky, smoke pouring into the world in great billowing clouds. But in reality it's silent and unmoving and I wonder if my super-senses have finally gotten something wrong. Just as I'm about to turn around there's a sharp clap of metal and a shout from inside. I rush to the doors and fling them open.

Inside, I can make out a dark-haired woman throwing an impressive right hook at a man twice her size. I blink as he takes the punch and rolls backward. She spins on her heel to address another man coming at her from behind and kicks him, catching him hard in the gut and doubling him over. I have no idea what's going on, but it's at least six against one, and one of the six has just picked up a heavy wrench from a tool bench and all of that makes it easy to decide who to help. I dive into the fray just as the man with the wrench brings it down toward the back of the woman's head. I leap between them and block his downward motion with my forearms crossed in front of me. He blinks twice as if I'm a mirage he dreamed up. His face contorts and he starts cussing. I uncross my arms, pushing out as I do, and flinging him away from us. He goes tumbling end over end with the force, dropping the wrench in the process. We stay that way, she and I, with our backs facing one another and waiting for the next wave. I'm not even sure if she knows I'm here, but there's something comforting for me in knowing she's there, in hearing her grunts and punches that sound just like mine. It seems like we fight forever, knocking them down and then waiting for them to come back around, but it's probably less than ten minutes. Finally, they stop coming and it's just us — our hearts pounding loudly, our breath ragged — standing in the middle of the mostly dark, mostly empty warehouse, a pile of men, broken and bleeding, coughing and wheezing, and no longer interested in getting up, surrounding us. I turn to her, not sure what to say after such a strange event and see, through the slats of moonlight, that it's the girl from the fire escape window. The girl that used to live in my room at Liesel's. Bryce. Liesel said her name was Bryce. I squint my eyes at her a bit and say her name as a question. "Bryce?" She cocks her head at me slightly, confused, a smile tugging at the corners of her mouth.

"Do we know each other?" she asks. I break into a broad smile.

"It seems like maybe we should," I say. She breaks into a similar smile and takes a look at the jumble of men, a few of them struggling to get to their feet and failing.

"I'll say," she agrees. After a minute of looking at the men she turns back to me. "So, what's your name?"

"Bonnie," I say, reaching out my hand. She takes it and we shake.

"You've got a great right hook," she says.

I arch my eyebrow. "No better than yours."

"Thanks," she nods appreciatively and then adds, "C'mon, let's go."

I look uncertainly back at the pile of men. "Do we need to-"

"Eh, just leave them," she says casually waving them away.

"Um, what did they...?" I'm suddenly afraid they've done nothing wrong and I just beat up a bunch of innocent bystanders. But as I try to finish the sentence she opens a door near the warehouse exit to reveal a room filled with hot stuff. Full purses, jewelry, leather coats, watches, anything that could be grabbed off a person and run off with is there, piled high on a long table and spilling over and off of it onto the ground. Must be hundreds, maybe thousands of stolen items.

"Not exactly the Elephant and Castle Gang, but still, quite a haul," she says, letting the door fall shut on the piles of stolen stuff. I raise an eyebrow at her. The Elephant and Castle gang, a group of smash and grab artists in London that began as far back as the 18th century is not exactly run-of-the-mill reading material. Bryce either had a first-class education, the likes of which I can barely comprehend, or she reads as much as I do.

"Should we?" I'm about to suggest we call the cops, or tie them up, or both, but before I can finish the sentence I hear sirens in the distance.

"I called it in before I showed, they should be here any minute," she says, her grin wide and pleased. "But we should get out of here; I don't like questions."

We slip out the big warehouse doors and head up the dock and toward the city, just as the first cop car pulls into the area. As we walk, calmly and deliberately, careful not to rush, I examine Bryce, though I try to keep from being obvious. She's almost as tall as me, about 5'11" and has long lean limbs and curves. She's wearing all black and no jewelry except a small silver key linked through a thin silver chain around her neck. Her skin is a little on the pale side, and her hair is such a dark black that in the light it almost has a Superman-ish blue tint to it. It falls in long waves down her back, nearly to her waist, it's so long. Her eyes are big and blue, clear and sharp, and her mouth is wide and pretty. Mostly, I'm struck by how unbelievably beautiful she is. Really. Seriously, intoxicatingly beautiful. The kind of beautiful that you would turn to gaze at if it passed you on the street, just so you could look at it a little bit longer. She looks like a movie star or a model, although her right cross and the twinkle in her eye makes me think of her more as a rock star.

She seems powerful.

She seems…like me.

And looking at her – wondering about her, recalling how great it felt to fight alongside her – I immediately feel less alone. Like that silly girl I was standing in Joan's trailer all those months ago, wasn't so silly after all. That, of course, there's something else like me out there in the world, and I'm looking right at it.

I'm standing right beside it.

And the world feels very right.

Bryce and I end up in an all-night diner on the Lower East Side, Bryce drinks coffee and eats three different kinds of pie - blueberry, cherry, and rhubarb - each on their own plates – switching between them at random, while I sip hot chocolate and chew on an egg sandwich, mesmerized by everything about her.

Bryce looks up from one of her slices. "I can't believe you know Liesel and Ben," she says chuckling. "It's such a strange and very small world in a way, isn't it?"

I nod, swallowing a bit of my sandwich. I'm not sure what I can ask, what I should ask. What would I bristle at her asking me? I mean, despite how close I feel to her after the fight in the warehouse, we're really just strangers. I don't know what the rules are or should be, but I can't deny how connected I feel to her. So, I just ask her the thing that's reverberating loudest in my brain.

"So, what do you want to do, Bryce?" I ask, putting the sandwich down.

She looks up from her blueberry pie, her doe eyes somehow innocent and also serious as graves. "I want to save the world."

"Okay," I answer back, nodding earnestly, returning to my sandwich, my faith in life restored.

We're the same. We want the same thing, and suddenly, together, I know we can do anything. We part ways that evening with plans to meet up the following night at my place.

I'm grateful for the distraction because every moment I'm not throwing punches, I'm thinking of Clark, of the empty, dull ache inside, where things used to be filled with him. I miss his face and his hands. His voice and his eyes. Everything about him, even the irritating things, now seem like great losses to me. I accidentally (but totally on purpose) walk by his apartment on the way home, and only by some superhuman miracle am I able to resist knocking on his door and throwing myself at his feet begging him to take me back.

●

I wake up to the sound of my name, and it's been a long time since that's happened. It's annoying but also somehow comforting.

"Lola. Lola, wake up," she sounds more irritated than frightened, which is not really what I was going for, but whatever. I open one eye, the bright California sun is already high in the sky and pouring through the doors and windows.

"What time is it?" I ask, rubbing my neck and cracking my shoulders from the long night's sleep in the awkward chair. Liz glances at her slender silver watch.

"Nearly one," she says.

"Wow. I must have been really exhausted," I say, yawning and stretching. I look around, remembering the previous night. Returning to the beach house and cuffing a still knocked out Liz to the intricate ironwork of a giant metal and concrete table that weighs at least 500 pounds. I remember thinking that it looked a little bit like a sacrificial slab, which I have to admit, gave me ideas, but I resisted. Why kidnap her only to kill her? Liz glances at the half full water bottle by my side.

"Can I have some of that?" she says, reaching out her free hand.

"Sure," I say, tossing it to her. The cap is loose though and as it tumbles toward her it drenches her blouse and hair. She sputters and looks up at me like a drowned cat. I'm already laughing.

"Thanks a lot," she says dryly. I cover my mouth.

"Sorry," I say. Then I notice her bruised hand, probably from my smack last night, "And sorry about your hand."

Liz looks down at the shirt and then her bruised hand cuffed to the table, then back to me and around the room. "Where are we?" she asks.

"My house. Nice, huh?"

"Actually," she lifts her head to take in the room again and then levels her gaze at me, "The view is spectacular, but otherwise it's rather tacky."

"Oh really? Apparently you've grown some balls in the last fourteen hours, huh?" I smile at her and lean back in my chair.

"Well, you're obviously not going to kill me, I take it you've got something else in mind. I assume I have to be alive for that something else," she says, lifting her chin in the air defiantly.

"Sure, sure, but what condition you're in, while still being alive, is pretty much up to you," I say. I see her shudder but she tries to hide it.

"Fine. What do you want from me?"

"You're so smart, you figure it out," I say, standing up. "I'm going to get some breakfast. I'll be back in a few minutes. You can scream and someone will maybe even hear you, but I'll definitely hear you," I say, tapping on my ear. "And I guarantee you that I'll get back here in time to take care of you, before any 'help' arrives. Ladies' choice," I say, shrugging. She doesn't make a sound as I head out to the patio and take off like a shot.

I'm back with two bags full of Taco Bell and 2 diet cokes within fifteen minutes. I hold up the bags and walk into the main room where Liz is sitting patiently, her blouse almost dry.

"You didn't ever mention that you could fly," she begins.

"Oh, it's new," I say. Liz looks at me skeptically, one eyebrow raised. "Seriously," I say. "I've only known how to do it for about fourteen hours." I sit down in front of Liz with my legs crossed. "I wasn't sure what you liked to eat, so I got a little bit of everything."

"I can assure you it wouldn't be Taco Bell," she says with a superior sniff of her nose.

"Well, it's what I felt like, so it's what you get," I say. She doesn't respond and so I take out a plain taco and hand it to her. She begrudgingly opens the package and takes a dainty bite.

"So, Lola, are you going to share this great plan with me, or what?" she asks finally.

"Actually," I say, between mouthfuls of burrito. "That's the great thing about all this – You're going to be my big plan."

"What do you mean?"

"Well, I've been hating the fact that I'm not so bright, that for all my power I'm really just glorified muscle. Ever since I hit into these superpowers I kept hoping I'd become some great criminal mastermind, but it's just not in me. I haven't really like, taken the bull by the horns, or whatever, with many situations, mostly because I'm not really sure what to do and that leads to a couple things: one, a lot of missed opportunity; and two, in the case of what happened to me in Vegas – I liked working with a crew, but I didn't really like working under a 'boss'. I have the power, I should be the boss, but I could never quite figure out how to get it done." I pause and tap the side of my head. "That pesky lack of brains again," I say offering a half-smile. Liz looks at me like I'm nuts. "Anyway, I got to thinking the other night that surely not all criminals are masterminds, and I thought about some of the mob guys I've seen in movies, they don't seem too smart. But they're really good at crime. So, what do they have that I don't have?"

"What?" Liz asks flatly, reaching out for another taco.

"They've got a network. They've got people working for them, and some of those people are smart. So that's what you'll be. My brains. And with you working beside me, we'll get this thing started right." I take the lid off a container of nachos and start digging in.

"What is this 'thing,' then?" she asks, totally placating me, which is annoying, but I've prepared myself for her taking a while to get used to the idea.

"I dunno yet exactly," I say, reaching into the small pocket in the cat suit and pulling out the article that I found in Delia's trailer. "But we're going to start here."

"What's that?" Liz asks, reaching out for the thin paper. I bat her hand away.

"Don't touch it, you'll get taco on it," I say protectively. I lay the newsprint on the cool marble floor, smoothing it out so she can read it. "Before I'm going to do anything huge I need to eliminate my competition. Bonnie's the one thing that might be able to stop me, so I'm going to kill her, you know, as we discussed in therapy. And I think this thing will give me the edge I need to get that done." I point to the faded picture of the stone.

"What is that...some kind of Celtic symbol or something?"

"I dunno. I need to find it. And you're going to help me."

Liz throws her last taco wrapper toward the trash bag. "I still don't know why you need me?"

"I need you so I can find this thing," I say, exasperated, questioning how good her brains really are.

"But the article says it's at LACMA," she says, equally exasperated.

"Huh?"

"The museum," Liz picks up the article. "The article says it's going to the museum."

"You think it's still there? This article is like, really old," I say.

"Well, yes, but that's where I'd start at least," she explains.

"You don't think the cops took it back?"

"Maybe, but I'd start at LACMA – The LAPD probably let them keep it on loan – unless its country of origin requested its return."

"Country of origin?"

"Well, it doesn't look American or Native American to me, maybe Celtic."

"So, maybe it's what, in like Ireland or something?"

"Maybe, but start at LACMA."

"Okay. Fine. What's LACMA?" I ask. Liz rolls her eyes dramatically.

"It's the Los Angeles County Museum of Art," she says.

"You don't have to be a bitch about it," I mutter and after a long pause add, "So then what's the best plan for breaking into the museum?"

"I think you're over-thinking it, Lola – you have superpowers – why don't you just buy a ticket and take it during business hours."

"You think?" I ask skeptically.

"The correct answer is usually the most obvious one."

"Hmph. That sounds too easy."

"I guess we'll see," she says, shrugging her shoulders and taking a sip of her soda.

"You wouldn't be trying to get me caught, would you?"

"No. I figure that just means more people caught in your crossfire. Not to mention, what happens to me then?"

"Good point," I say, "I'll go first thing in the morning." There's a long silence as Liz stares at old tacos and chews on her lip. "I hooked the TV up to a generator…you wanna watch a movie?" I ask.

"Depends on what you have, I guess," she says, looking back at me, resigned, but I like to imagine slightly less miserable than before.

o

Strangely, Liesel is not wild about my newfound friendship with Bryce. And Ben, even less so.

"Just be careful," Liesel says cautiously, avoiding my eyes. I look at her, genuinely confused. I know she wants only the best for me, so I don't doubt her concern, but I can't understand it.

"What?" I ask looking from Liesel to Ben and back again. They're both avoiding my eyes. "What?" I say again. "What am I missing?" I sit down at the kitchen table with them, careful not to break their tiny furniture, which fits them perfectly but makes me look like I'm playing in a doll's house.

"It's just-" Ben starts but Liesel hisses at him.

"Ben. Shut up. You can't say anything. It's private. It's not our place," Liesel says, looking back at her hands.

"But Liesel," he says and talks about me like I'm not there. "She could get hurt. We have an obligation, I think."

Liesel gnaws on her lip, clearly stressed. I'm dying of curiosity, but I don't want to put Liesel in a bad position.

"It's okay. I don't need to know. Whatever it is, it's okay. I can take care of myself," I say looking at them both. Ben tries to talk again and Liesel cuts him a withering look and he raises his hands in defeat. Liesel looks at me.

"I...we can't tell you. But promise me you'll ask her how we met, okay?" I lay my hand on hers.

"I promise," I say and push Ben lightly on the shoulder as I get up. "Stop worrying. You're both freaking me out," I say. I go to my bedroom to get a jacket and hear them whispering loudly at one another in the kitchen. They never argue, so this must be serious.

When Bryce shows, the tension only ratchets up more. Liesel comes to give Bryce a hug, but Ben keeps a polite distance. I put on my jacket and we head out, worried glances from both Ben and Liesel following us down the stairs and into the street.

"They seemed extra tense," Bryce says casually.

"Yeah, I think they're not crazy about us hanging out...you have any idea why?" I say, trying to keep things honest and open, upfront but not confrontational.

"Oh, yeah, probably because Ben thinks I'm nuts. I was in the mental institute with Liesel. And I didn't get released, I escaped," she says all casually, as if she just happened to mention that today was Tuesday.

"Oh," I say, stunned. "So, are they like looking for you or something?" Bryce shrugs her shoulders as if she couldn't care less.

"I don't know. Sometimes they do, sometimes they don't."

"Sometimes?"

"Mmm? Oh, yeah, I've been back in a few times. They don't like it so much when you escape." she says. "Liesel tried to help me when she got out – it got a bit more complicated when Liesel and I dated, for about two seconds. I adore her but it wasn't serious – Ben didn't approve, then or now. He insisted I move out. He wasn't wrong; they could get in trouble for having me there."

I nod again, absorbing it all. It's not that shocking really, like Liesel said, people love to put people in boxes. I'm sure if I'd been more honest and trusting in my life I'd have ended up in a mental institution too. I'm sure 'I'm a superhero' doesn't go over well with doctors. Hell, it's a big part of why I left Clark. That he'd think I'm insane, that he thought there was something wrong with me, that he thought there was something that had to be 'fixed.'

But I'm not worried about it with Bryce, maybe I should be, but I just can't. There's something special about her, I can feel it in my bones, and I feel good with her, I feel right. And I need it, I realize, need her. I think I've been needing her for a long time actually.

By four in the morning we've chased off a would-be rapist, stopped six muggings, and returned a lost dog. We both surge with pleasure at our tiny miracles. Bryce and I are perfectly synchronized almost as if we can read each other's minds and it makes me deliriously happy. Trudging back to the apartment, exhausted from our evening of superheroing, we come across something much more dangerous. I stop in the middle of the street, the burning fills my chest powerfully. Bryce looks around cautiously, reading my signals as if we share a primal link.

"Where?" she breathes. I point to a small corner store, warm yellow light pouring into the dark of the city. We walk without speaking into the store and immediately separate.

I'm looking at about nine different kinds of Doritos when a guy bursts into the bodega and pulls a gun. Bryce is on the other side feigning a great interest in batteries and when the gun comes out she starts the waterworks immediately.

"Hands in the air!" the gunman screams at the clerk. Two men not far from Bryce stare at him as if they've stepped into some strange nightmare. The clerk's hands are up, the color, long-drained from his face, and the gunman spins wildly on the rest of us, although I don't think he can see me. The two bystanders hit the ground in unison, nearly knocking themselves out with the speed. And this is when Bryce makes her move. Eyes full of tears and clutching at herself hysterically she moves toward him.

"Oh my god!" she wails. "Please...please don't hurt me." The gunman swings frantically back in her direction; nearly smacking her in the face with his gun she's so close. But one look at her, all distraught and beautiful and he softens. It's a visible effect, the gun lowering and then pulling away completely as he bends his arm and leaves it resting lightly on his shoulder, the gun by his ear, his body language mostly relaxed. I'm behind him now but I can imagine his expression, I've seen it before when men get an eyeful of Bryce. The beginnings of a smile, one that eventually breaks widely across the face into something less innocent the longer it lingers.

"Honey, it's gonna be fine, just get on the floor, real slow…" As he talks, Bryce carefully begins to crouch down as if to obey. I sidle up behind him and in a flash of movement, snatch the gun from his hand, breaking his wrist. He cries out, but before he can turn to face me, Bryce springs to her feet and throws a perfect right cross that sends him flying into a display of hostess treats. Bryce has a beautiful right cross – much prettier than mine. It's happened so fast that neither of the bystanders have even looked up and the clerk's mouth has only dropped open wider. I set the gun on the counter and Bryce and I smile at the clerk like idiot children expecting a cookie. He relaxes instantly. And instead of saying anything (or giving us a cookie) he hands Bryce a wad of small bills for our trouble. We nod our thanks, smiles still plastered on our faces, and leave without a word. As we near the end of the block I can hear him chattering on the phone to the police while he yells obscenities at the unconscious gunman on the floor of his store. Bryce and I buy gelato at an all night deli in the tiny bit of Little Italy at the edge of Chinatown and lick our spoons as we walk home, content with our place in the world.

"Next time, do you want to be the decoy?" Bryce asks between bites. I glance sideways at her.

"I don't think I've got the um…necessary assets," I say.

Bryce laughs genially. "Sure you do. It's all about the performance anyway."

"I don't really think I'd be good at that part either," I say.

"Suit yourself," she shrugs. "You know, I heard these two guys in the park today talking about something going down tomorrow night. I think we should check it out," she says.

"Okay," I say.

"Should we call it a night?"

"Yeah, but let's do a last pass through a few of the alleys on our way," I say.

"Yes." She says, her eyes glinting in the streetlights. She tosses her spoon and dish in a trashcan and rubs her hands on her jeans, "Ready when you are." I toss my dish out as well and we start jogging towards Chelsea. It feels good. Running was always a time when I was alone, and there's nothing wrong with that, I guess, but it's nice not to have to be alone. It's nice to know that

Bryce gets me and I get her, and that we're linked by something unique and powerful. Despite missing Clark, I feel content. Maybe not always happy like I was, but content. And maybe that's all a person has a right to hope for.

●

I buy a short, dark wig and a ridiculous pink jacket in a tacky store on the way to LACMA. I put both on after parking my bike on a side street about a mile from the museum. I shoot into the air and hover for a moment, making a mental note of the location before taking off for the museum. A few blocks away I set down and adjust the wind-blown wig. After just a few steps I feel a tug. Like a fish on a line.

I follow the feeling straight to the museum, the pull getting stronger with every step. There's a small line just inside the door. I wait in it and even pay the suggested fee. I figure if I'm going incognito, I better go all the way. Once inside, I don't have to check the drawing in my pocket because I literally feel the stone calling to me. And suddenly I'm standing in front of it. It looks just like the faded photo, except, in person it looks like it's glowing, but only for me. To anyone else it's probably just a hunk of unremarkable rock from some other country. I'm not sure what the carving means. It's definitely a crow, or something, but given my dream about being a crow that feels right. There's a small plaque to the side that says **ON LOAN FROM THE LAPD**. I snicker quietly to myself, "Ah, Liz, I love that big, beautiful brain of yours." The article in my pocket is also in the display case with my stone. MINE. It feels like mine already.

I feel more strongly than ever before that it belongs to me. It wants to be in my hand almost as much as my hand is itching to possess it. I look around and see two cameras, one at either end of the hallway. I wait for a group of kids and a tour guide to turn the corner and slam my fist through the reinforced glass. The alarms sound instantly, but I'm already halfway to the exit, my wig and jacket ditched in a trashcan. I'm just a blonde blur stealing through the front doors before they can lock it all down. I'm going so fast as I tear into the street that I take flight by accident, breaking into the sky at unbelievable speed, "Holy crap," I say looking down at the city, sonic booms echoing in my wake. I look at my stone, "Hello Gorgeous, welcome home." I clutch the newfound power tightly and turn towards Malibu, forgetting all about my bike.

Back at the house, Liz is glaring at me behind her gag. I pull it off her mouth and unlock one of her hands, "What?"

"Was it really necessary to gag me?" she asks, indignant and massaging her jaw.

"Probably," I say, shrugging.

"Did you get it?" Liz asks.

"Yup," I say proudly, holding it out to her so she can bask in its glory. "I did it, just like you said actually." I pause and then add, "Good work."

"So, what is it?" she asks reaching out her hand for it. I ignore her.

"Um, I don't know, but it's mine. Like, deep down I know it belongs to me."

"Can I see it?" she asks, exasperated.

"Alright," I say, eyeing her skeptically. Liz palms it, turns it over, then hands it back to me, unimpressed.

"Just looks like an old piece of carved stone to me," she says, shrugging.

"Yeah, well, shows what you know. It suped up my powers something fierce," I say, feeling the ridges of the stone. Liz sighs, disinterested and looks around the room.

"Can I go home now?" she asks.

I try not to laugh in her face, but it escapes anyway. "Um, no."

"What do you mean? I thought you wanted that thing. Now you've got it. What do you need me for?"

"You're the brains of the operation, Liz, I can't make it all work without you."

"What operation, Lola? It's just you and me."

"For now," I say, pleased with the beginnings of my plans for world domination.

"Lola. I want to go home. You must let me go," Liz says very seriously.

"Sorry, Liz. I need you. I've already explained this to you, I'm not that smart, and I'm pretty sure you need to be smart to do crime, I mean to do real crime, you know? Crime that makes a difference, and now I've got you, so you'll be like, my right-hand man."

"I'm your right-hand man?" Liz asks with an expression I can't quite read.

"Yup. And maybe my BFF too, we'll see. All we need are some good minions and I figure we'll be pretty much on our way. Once we have some minions, we figure out – by which I mean you figure out – how to find Bonnie and then I'll kill her. With her out of the way we'll really be able to get started."

"And by 'get started' you mean?"

"Well, I haven't decided for sure yet, but I think 'Lola – King of Los Angeles' has a sweet ring to it." I stand there, waiting for her to be impressed, but she's looking at me like I've lost it. I decide to let it slide. "What do you want for dinner? I'm thinking Chinese," I say, walking out of the room.

After gorging ourselves on Chinese food, I cuff Liz to the headboard in one of the bedrooms so she'll quit whining about aches and pains and her wrinkled linen skirt. As right-hand men go, she's a bit of a prima donna. I go into another bedroom and change into my cat suit and then walk into Liz's room to show it off to her. She's seen it before, when I was kidnapping her, but I don't really think she was paying sufficient attention.

"What is that?" she half-sneers with her nose practically in the air.

"My old cat suit," I say, feeling the history of the fabric.

"You actually wear that thing out of the house? On a day that isn't Halloween?"

"What would you suggest I wear, Liz? I'm a freaking super-villain. Jeans and a t-shirt just doesn't have quite the same impact."

"Don't you have like hundreds of thousands of dollars Lola, you couldn't at least upgrade? What is that even made of, nylon, or," she sniffs again. "Acrylic?"

"I don't know what it's made of Liz," I groan. "It's got, you know, personal significance to me," I say, walking out of the room.

"Nothing personal is that important," she says under her breath as I leave the room.

"I CAN HEEEEAARR YOU," I shout back at her from the bedroom. I hear her sniff again defiantly.

With Liz safely put away for the night, I go out to the patio with my new toy. There is no doubt I feel more powerful with it in my possession, but I want to know the specifics. So far, I'm only sure that the stone is somehow connected to me and makes me a bit stronger and faster – but does it have limitations?

I hold the stone in my left hand and swing my right first at the south stone wall, which practically explodes on impact. I look at my clenched fist and a smile spreads wide across my face. "Nice." I place the stone on a deck chair nearby and immediately I feel the power ebb slightly away from me. I can still feel the power radiating from it, but it doesn't hum inside me in the same way. I take aim at an intact part of the wall with the same abandon as before. I pull my arm from the two-foot hole in the wall. Still impressive, but notably less than with the stone. I pick it up again. "So it's got to be on me," I say to myself, clutching it tightly. "What else can you do?" I whisper to my stone. I sit on the patio, legs crossed, and grip it tightly with my hand, closing my eyes and concentrating. After a few minutes it's almost like the stone is vibrating in my hand. I dig deeper, and as I push I feel the stone actually pulling power out of me. I feel unsure and almost break the connection, not loving the feeling of losing power, but something compels me on. A moment later a sharp snap sounds and it's as if some kind of internal radar turns on inside my head and a blinking light starts beating, like a bright heartbeat. I push harder and the light comes closer, or I draw closer to it, I can't tell which. The light beats, beats, beats, hypnotically and almost in synch with my own heart. I'm practically on top of the light when I look around and see I'm standing in a huge park. But just under the surface of the park I can see my patio and pool, like the park is only a filmy photograph projected on a wall. Like seeing a dream while awake. I see a sign that says Fifth Avenue and as I turn a jogger runs straight through me. Everything looks wavy but I see a green sign that says CENTRAL PARK nearer to the street. "New York," I say to myself, looking around. I pull back a little and it's almost like I'm floating above the city now, and I can see the edges of river beyond the island, and there's the bright heartbeat again – lighting up the lower half of Central Park and moving very slowly down and to the left. "Omigod," I say out loud, yanking myself out of it all and back to my patio. "It's her. I can freaking find Bonnie with this." A huge grin nearly breaks my face in half. I'm exhausted but elated and I lie on the cool patio slowly recovering the energy that the stone drew from me to locate her.

By this time tomorrow I'll have my hands around Bonnie's neck.

o

We camp out that night in the park, waiting for Bryce's information to make good. And sure enough, around four in the morning, six men break into the Central Park Boathouse. I'm a little nervous because we're rarely so outnumbered and I'm pretty sure at least two of them have guns, but Bryce seems unfazed, as usual. We scrunch back into the shadows and whisper together before running along the deck, jockeying for better positions. Bryce barely makes a sound but I can tell from her quickened breathing that she's as jacked in as I am. We separate, Bryce staying by the doors near the moonlit lake, and me making for the darkness of the garden. I break the handle off a door near and slide inside. The men are mostly arguing, but I'm not listening to what they're saying. I don't need to.

Sitting there, listening only to myself, ignoring the words of these men and waiting for Bryce's signal I realize that I never listen to anything anybody actually says, which is maybe why I don't have much interest in speaking. Instead I listen to what they tell me. I hear all the sounds a person never even knows they make. How a person walks, breathes, when they pause, the speed of their heartbeat — all these things tell me more than any number of sentences they could assemble to describe something to me. I peek around the corner and see Bryce in silhouette as she walks through the same door the men came through.

"Hi!" she says brightly to the room, as if it's the most natural thing in the world. If I weren't so nervous about the odds I would have had to stifle a laugh. The reaction of the men is so typical. The first guy to see Bryce offers a long low whistle and another chuckles. A third looks at his buddies.

"Look at this! A supermodel lost in the park at four in the morning. What are you doing here, sweetheart?" he asks, stepping dangerously close to her.

"Hi!" she says again equally as brightly. One of the men smartens up.

"You think, is there something wrong with her?" he poses.

"Nothing we can't take advantage of," number six says, lust pulsing off him like an animal. He'll be my first, I decide right then. As number one reaches out to touch Bryce's cheek, I slide into the room and take number six from behind, covering his mouth and lifting him out of the room in a sleeper hold. He's out so fast that I'm able to get back into position behind number two before anyone wises up. I tap number two on the shoulder and throw a punch that flattens him, he hits the ground, unconscious. The other four snap around and see me standing there, their partner at my feet and Bryce capitalizes on their surprise, throwing a beaut of an uppercut to number one who goes flying backward into a stack of chairs. By the time number one has landed I'm all over three, four, and five delivering rib-breaking kicks to each of them. It's over almost before it's begun. Bryce and I standing there in the moonlight, five thugs unconscious and spread out all around us. Bryce shrugs her shoulders.

"I thought they'd put up more of a fight," she says. I nod in agreement. She peers over at the one she knocked out. "I think mine had a glass jaw," she adds. I chuckle.

"You want to look in the box or me?" I ask.

"Go ahead," she says, dragging the first one outside onto the deck. She checks him for any weapons as I open the box. It's a bomb. Fortunately not set. My heart flutters at the scariness of it, but then swells with pride at what we have accomplished. Who knows how many lives we saved tonight? Bryce pokes her head in.

"What is it?"

"A bomb," I say.

"Omigod. It's not set is it?"

"No," I say.

"Thank goodness. I don't know about you but I was totally absent on bomb-defusal day at superhero school," she says, ducking back out and dragging another thug with her. I chuckle again. We check the rest of the thugs for weapons and load up whatever we find carefully on the table next to the box. We drag the rest of the thugs outside and tie them all up to the wrought iron fencing. If Bryce missed bomb-defusing day, she definitely didn't miss tying knots day. Bryce writes a note to go with the bomb: *DEFUSED BOMB INSIDE. PLEASE CALL POLICE AND HANDLE WITH CARE*, which she puts on top of the box lid. She writes a second note and pins it to the front of gagged thug number one's chest. *THESE ARE CRIMINALS CAUGHT BY YOUR FRIENDLY NEIGHBORHOOD SUPERHEROES. PS. THIS STUPID ONE DEFINITELY HAS A GLASS JAW.*

We return to the park and decide to stay the rest of the night, to ensure that nothing goes wrong tomorrow at the boathouse; it's nearly dawn anyway. We both fall asleep, hands under our heads, staring up at the blackish-bluish sky. I feel good. And I can tell Bryce does too, because her lips are turned up at the corners a little, even when she sleeps.

●

In the morning I wake Liz up with coffee and an Egg McMuffin. She's slow and stiff.

"Hurry up," I grumble, unlocking the cuffs so she can use the bathroom. She rubs her wrist.

"What's the hurry?" she asks, shuffling into the bathroom.

"I found Bonnie," I say, between bites of one of my three egg and cheese on biscuit sandwiches. There's a long silence and then a toilet flush and a spray of water. Liz emerges drying her hands on a tiny pink towel.

"You found her?" she asks, looking at me already clad in my black cat suit and boots.

"Yup. The stone helped me." I pause and look at her pointedly. "I told you it was special. Anyway, she's in New York City. Having the stone is like having her tagged like a goddamn endangered species – it's freaking awesome. She was somewhere in Central Park yesterday, it couldn't pinpoint her exactly, but I figure I can get close enough," I say, biting into my next biscuit sandwich. Liz sits on the edge of the bed and unwraps her sandwich. Her face is an impassive mask.

"What are you going to do?"

"Kill her," I say simply between chews. Liz swallows dryly and nods in my direction.

"Three sandwiches?" she asks.

"Eh," I shrug, "It takes a lot of energy to be super-powered." I unwrap my last sandwich and dig in. Liz chuckles slightly in spite of herself. I search the bag for another orange juice and hand Liz the morning paper, which I stole from someone's yard. She takes it from me and looks at the stuff above the fold and then flips it over while sipping her coffee. After a minute though she freezes, her cup to her lips.

"What?" I ask, staring at her mask of a face, a look I don't understand frozen on it. She doesn't answer me, but finally hands me the paper. Under the fold is an article – though it looks more like an ad – offering a $100,000 reward for details about missing Dr. Elizabeth Grant, details that might lead to her recovery. I lightly punch her in the arm. "Hey! Look at that, you're famous. Well, I guess you already were sorta famous, but this is famous-er. Your book sales will probably like, triple." She's painfully silent. "What's wrong?" I prod, nudging her again, staring at the paper and trying to piece together what exactly is upsetting her.

"Did you see who's offering the reward," she says finally, quietly. I scan the text and read aloud.

"'*Offered by William G. Silverman and Silverman Publishing*'," I say and then shrug. "Yeah, so what?"

"That's my publisher," she says. And I wait, trying to be patient for her to say more. "You think you're alone, Lola? Try being fifty-two and having the only person care that you've been kidnapped by, no offense, a serial killer, be your publisher, and not because he's your best friend, but because you're worth millions."

"Well maybe he's just the only one who can afford to offer a reward," I suggest. She smiles lightly.

"That's nice of you to say, but the reality is there is really nobody else. A few colleagues, an ex-husband in Seattle – we don't speak – my parents passed years ago. No siblings. No children. It's funny. It never bothered me until now. I really thought my life was pretty full, it looks pretty empty now," she says, tossing the paper away from her.

"Well, look at it this way, now that you need a friend, you could have one. Yours truly," I say. Liz smiles weakly again. "What do they call that?" I ask.

"Irony," Liz says. "Or maybe poetic justice." We finish eating and drinking in silence and then I nod her over to the bed again and take out the cuffs but Liz stands up and smoothes her skirt.

"I would like to be handcuffed in the living room please so that I may watch television," she says primly.

"Okay, whatever you say, my queen," I mock. I follow Liz out to the living room and cuff her to a big stone end table so she can sit on the couch. When I bring the gag she whimpers a little.

"What?" I ask.

"Is the gag really necessary, Lola?"

"Afraid so," I say.

"But Lola," she starts as I lock her up. "What if you can't kill her? What if she kills you? If something goes wrong you're signing my death warrant too, are you really okay with that?" she pleads. I put the gag on her.

"I guess you better pray I emerge victorious then," I say nonchalantly. Liz leans forward, adjusting herself and as she does so, a heavy silver chain slips out of her blouse. It glints in the sunlight and I get an idea. I unclasp the lock. "I'm gonna borrow this, okay?" I say. Liz's eyes narrow as she watches me link the thick chain through one of the open circle gaps in my stone. I slip the new necklace over my head; it will do for now, at least. I walk out of the room calling out. "Don't worry, I won't be long," Liz's muffled protests follow me into the hall.

I sit on the patio with the stone around my neck, verifying Bonnie's location, which still looks to be somewhere in Central Park. "What is she doing, living there? Weird." I meditate – or do the closest thing to what I think meditation is – for another brutal half hour, until I feel my strength returned to full power. Once I have it all back I shoot into the stratosphere like a freaking rock star. I can't wait to see the look on Bonnie's face.

Somewhere over Manhattan I start to feel a bit nauseous. Like I did in Joan's tent. I decide to set down in a big wooded area, afraid that the feelings will overpower me again and I'll just fall out of the sky. The blinking light that is Bonnie is somewhere just below me anyway. The feeling on the ground is a lot stronger for me than it was in the air, so I know I'm close to her. But I find, strangely, I'm not as sick as I was last time. I feel all the same things I felt before, but they are not as incapacitating. I chalk this up to the amplified power of the stone, and play my little game of hot and cold, trying to locate her exactly, which is a little more difficult, but a lot less painful, now that the symptoms are less intense. I realize that though I'm tired after my flight, I'm already getting used to it. Less than ten minutes after setting down I feel almost at full strength.

I'm about to add it to the list of 'things that are awesome about being me', but I find I'm growing tired of the idea.

The game of hot and cold gets boring, and seeing all the innocent civilians around biking and jogging I get a better idea. If Scarlett's letters to Delia are any hint, and Bonnie is the goody-goody I suspect she is, she'll come running.

I step back into the woods a bit and push a tree straight onto the bike path. A biker doesn't stop in time and does a header into the pavement, screeching as he goes down. Several people come running and I step further back into the shadows of the trees and push on another one until it falls into the crowd. They try to scatter but I push two more trees onto the path and even before they finish falling the park is filled with screaming and crying. Babies.

o

When employees began arriving at the boathouse in the morning we had surveyed the commotion from a peaceful bit of grass nearby. Everything appeared to go well. Nobody got hurt, a bomb squad came and took away the bomb, and all six of our thugs were led away in handcuffs. It was such a good feeling that we decided to stay in the park, rather than go home to sleep. Bryce jogged over to a kiosk and bought us both a hot dog and a pretzel each and we shared a soda while watching people jog and lounge and generally be happy. It was nice to see the park like this and know that we'd helped make it this way, that because of us, it wasn't all flames and explosions and screaming people.

But our joy is short-lived as by midday I hear an incredible chaos somewhere nearby. Bryce hears it too and we go running in that direction. But as we close in I start feeling dizzy and veer off the grass and past the path and plunk down on the soft dirt in a group of trees. I put my head between my knees and try to concentrate. Bryce comes up behind me.

"You okay?" she asks, concerned. I wave my hand at her trying to signal that I'll be fine, but before I can even finish the motion I start to feel more sick, the same visceral sick that I'd felt outside Joan's trailer. I hold up my hands in front of my face and they rattle like dry leaves in winter. "Bonnie, you are seriously freaking me out," Bryce says, bending down toward me. "What should I do?" My heart hammers in my chest and the nausea takes over. I pivot to my knees and my stomach knots up trying to crawl into my throat. I vomit into a pile of dirt and wait for it to pass. Surely it will pass. Bryce leans down and pulls my hair back from my face gently. I throw up again. The feeling is not going away, in fact it's intensifying. We sit together for whole minutes and then all of a sudden, my vision clears. The nausea passes. I should feel all better, but a dread I'd never felt before has overtaken me. Thick clouds are rolling over the park, cloaking everything in a night like darkness. People begin to pack up, feeling the pressure of a storm coming. Looking out onto the lawn I see a girl, about my age, standing on the green grass with tendrils of bright light leaking out of her. Lines of light seep out her limbs, snake across the lawn, and spread like disease across the park. She's standing there like something out of a dream. Like the storm my mother's been warning me about.

And there it is.

Because I look back at Bryce and for the first time I realize she's as human as anyone else. Exceptional maybe, but human and normal and not like me. Not like this girl leaking her bright poison all over the lawn is like me. Bryce is just Bryce. It's so easy to see now, I don't know how I missed it, except that I wanted it too much. I had friends in Liesel and Ben, and a lover in Clark, but all this time I've still been looking for a sister, and who but Bryce could have passed for that? And looking at this girl that looks like some twisted version of me, it's almost comforting to know that, in a way, I was right all along, that there is something else like me out there. But it's not Bryce, and I'm a naïve fool, because I should have realized that if there was another half of me out there, then, of course, it would be something closer to the opposite of me, not something the same as me. And a split second after realizing that, I realize what that means.

It means she's come to kill me.

I look up at Bryce. "Run," I breathe. She looks back at me, confusion all over her face.

"What?"

"Run!" I shout, pushing her away from me and then running through the trees and trying to draw this girl away from her, away from everyone. But I feel like fainting and lean against a tree to keep myself upright.

●

In less than a minute my stomach lurches hard with nausea and I know she's here.

Across the path, stumbling forward from a stand of trees, a shock of red hair, face pinched in pain, holding her stomach, one palm leaning on a trunk, holding herself up, is a girl. It's her. I know it's her as surely as I knew the stone was mine. And there's white light pouring out of her. Just seeping from her as if she's a nuclear reactor with a crack, leaking her insides all over the world like ropes of electricity. It looks kind of disgusting.

Also, though I've never been able to read anyone's thoughts before, I realize that I can read hers as clearly as if I'm sitting inside her brain with a flashlight. Like they're lit up on a huge neon billboard beside a desert highway. I can read every thought she has. Mostly she's afraid.

This is going to be even easier than I thought.

Just as I smile, she looks up and locks eyes with me. Dark blue and piercing. It's like looking in a backwards mirror.

And she knows. I know, she knows.

I clench my fists and fly at her like a bullet.

Hitting her feels like running into a freaking mountain and my shoulder comes out of joint with the impact. We bust through at least three trees before I crash us roughly into the mud, narrowly missing a stone wall. She's thrown from me and I'm up before she is, moving to her side in one motion as I yank my shoulder back into joint. I'm standing above her as she opens her eyes. The impact didn't even knock her out. I'm impressed. Also, slightly nervous for about the first time since I killed Delia. I may be an absolute badass, but maybe she is too?

It's starting to rain heavily. Thunder and lightning crackling all around us.

I think maybe we're causing it. How awesome is that?

I swing my leg back and try to kick her in the stomach with a momentum that will send her flying up into the sky, at least above the treetops. But she reaches out at the last second as my leg comes forward and catches my foot in her hands. I'm so shocked I don't notice that she's got another move, twisting my foot sharply to the left and pulling me down onto the ground in a painful snap of my leg.

She's broken my goddamn leg.

I kick her in the face with my other leg and she goes flying backward into the stone wall, leaving a giant human-shaped dent in it as she falls to the dirt. She's still not unconscious though, which is what I was hoping for, and she shakes her head, stunned and surprised at the impact, but already getting up. I can't believe it.

I focus all my energy on my shin, willing the bones to heal. They obey me just as the gunshot wound in my leg did the first time I tried to speed up my healing. She sees this and can't hide her amazement. I take it to mean she can't do this, or at least hasn't figured out how to yet. And then I poke around inside her head. She's terrified. She knows even less about whatever we are than I do it seems. She can't heal at will, she can't fly, and I can tell she can't read my mind or she'd be trying to hide her obvious fear from me.

This is awesome.

She stands up, she's taller than I am, broader too, her bones larger and stronger-looking. It doesn't matter, I learned long ago not to judge a person on their looks. All I need to do is break her damn neck and this will all be over.

O

Thankfully, she's knocked me well clear of Bryce with the impact of her first hit. But I must get us farther away, not just from Bryce, but from everyone. Fortunately the rain is sending park-goers away in droves, but there are still a few lingering under trees and umbrellas, hoping to wait it out. I can't have innocent people being collateral damage. I hope that Bryce will see how serious this is and just leave. It's not like her though, she's too proud and loyal. But I hope for it anyway, even as I see her running toward us, a horrified look on her face as she sees the destruction we've already caused. I will myself to move and run to Bryce at a speed I've never even tried before, intent on scooping her up and running away with her. Somewhere safe. But the stranger gets there first. She elbows me in the face and at that speed it's like running into a building and it breaks my nose. There's blood and rain in my eyes and when I look up again it's to see Bryce throwing a punch at the stranger. It's a good punch – Bryce's solid right cross that always connects – but the girl moves so fast it looks like Bryce is on pause. Before Bryce even finishes her swing, the girl has swung back at her and I watch her go flying off into the trees nearly twenty feet. I'm half-surprised the blow didn't just disintegrate Bryce on impact, but the girl obviously knows what I've missed all along, that Bryce is just human and she doesn't have to waste any extra strength taking her out.

Even before Bryce hits the ground the girl has turned her focus back to me. 'HEAL!!!!!' I scream inside my head with everything I have and it actually seems to work a little bit. The blood that's clouding my vision clears and I scramble away from her intent on just running way, hoping she'll chase me. But she's too fast and she plows into me from behind, I go tumbling forward and scrape part of my face off on some slick, sharp rocks.

I'm still intent on running, to see if I can get the girl to follow me, when Bryce crawls out of the trees. She's cussing and pulling wet leaves and branches out of her hair, and if I wasn't so frightened I'd laugh. Her jaw is broken, but she's otherwise okay. The girl rolls her eyes dramatically.

"Not you again," she says and there's a coldness there, a casualness that frightens me worse than anything that's happened so far. She's on Bryce before I can even shake the fear. I'm running toward them with everything I've got, but the girl lifts Bryce up over her head like a wrestler and slams her down across her knee, breaking Bryce's back – nearly breaking her in half.

At first, I think Bryce is screaming, but then I realize it's me, because Bryce is already dead. I skid to a halt next to Bryce's broken body, the light always in her eyes before, now just gone.

Gone.

And it happened so fast.

Just like the accident when I was six.

Everyone alive and fine and laughing.

And then everyone dead but me.

The girl has stepped back, at first I think out of some kind of bizarre respect, but then she clucks her tongue. "Friend of yours?" she asks innocently. I look up at this strange girl, bathed in rain, flashes of lightning going off in the sky above her. Her head is cocked to the side quizzically, almost like an animal, an animal that understands nothing.

"Yes," I choke, my whole world breaking.

"Too bad," she starts, pausing dramatically. "For her, I mean. She should've learned to pick better friends, rather than ones like you with giant targets on their backs," She finishes glibly, very pleased with herself. I swallow hard on my sobs.

"Who are you?" I ask, surprised by the steel in my voice, my hands clutching fists of Bryce's dense, wet, beautiful hair.

"Lola," she says matter-of-factly. I look up at her again and see for the first time that she's wearing a strange stone necklace. It looks broken and is unnaturally large for a necklace. I want it. I don't know why. But it's calling to me, somewhere deep inside of me. It's mine. Lola takes notice.

"You like it, huh?" she asks, lifting it up and admiring it. "Well, you can't have it," she says and kicks me in the stomach sending me crashing through more trees.

When I land I decide that my best bet is still just to run. But she's on me before I can even take off. My only chance is to get away from her for a second and then get her to follow me. She's walking up to me, stepping over fallen trees, and I'm on my hands and knees, breathing hard, half-dying, half-feigning. When she's standing over me, I pop up throwing all my weight behind my punch. It's the first time in my life I haven't pulled a punch, and I'm hoping it will end her, break her in two. But I know it's a futile hope, she's so much stronger than me. It does send her flying backwards impressively though, and before she lands I break out of the woods as fast as I can, running at a speed I didn't even know I was capable of. I don't see her behind me, or feel her, though the nausea has passed and I'm not sure it's alerting me to her anymore. If anything, being around her now makes me feel a little bit super charged; not actually stronger, but just hyper aware of everything.

<Bonnie. Where do you think you're going?>

I buck fiercely, like a startled horse, and nearly knock a
stand of trees over in my confusion. She just spoke to me inside
my own head. And if she can talk inside my head, it's a good bet
she can read my mind too. I try to hide my thoughts from her, but
have no idea how to do it and so I go back to concentrating on the
road in front of me. I'm already running faster than I've ever run
before.

I must run five, maybe six miles darting through streets and
traffic and pedestrians like a blur of wind before she actually
physically catches up with me. We're at the far end of the island,
near Fort Tryon Park when I hear her in my head again.

<Bonnnnnnieeeeeeee>

I look around wildly, not letting up my pace, unsure where
she is, trying not to panic at the odd sensation of someone who is
trying to kill me talking into my brain.

<Bonnnnnnnnniieeeee> she says again. This time I crane my
neck hard to the right and catch a blurry glimpse of her flying not
three feet behind my right shoulder, low to the ground and fast.
Really fast. She'll overtake me in seconds.

I cut hard to the left toward Fort Tryon Park when I see it
ahead, and she crashes forward – not anticipating the turn – into a
huge streetlight and two trees. Her impact sends the streetlight and
trees crashing toward the street. She stands up on the sidewalk and
brushes herself off casually and I see that everything's falling toward
a passenger bus. I change direction, maintaining my speed and
jump straight at the falling light and trees, knocking them
awkwardly past the bus and safely onto the street behind it. I crash
to the ground on the other side of the bus, rolling to try to absorb
the impact. The bus continues past us both, braking to a halt a few
dozen yards down the street, and I hear people on the bus
screaming and crying, mostly in what sounds like fear and relief.
Kneeling in the street, catching my breath, and trying to get my
bearings, I see her blonde head looking back and forth between the
streetlight and trees, the bus, and me, as if trying to assemble a giant
puzzle. Her light blue eyes narrow and her mouth curls up into a
sinister smile. A sound like a child's laugh escapes from her throat
and I realize that though I couldn't have done anything differently,
I've made a horrible mistake. She lifts off the ground effortlessly
and flies over to the bus, and then, her eyes locked on mine the
whole time, she plunges her hand through one of the glass

windows, grabs a passenger by the neck and hurls him out of the bus and up into the air. She does it over and over again until there are at least half a dozen passengers in the air falling towards the street.

●

I grab the first neck I find and fling it cavalierly into the air. I do it again and again and again. I'm not sure how many times. When I look up I see Bonnie running and jumping into the air, catching people like little carnival prizes and setting them down as gently as possible onto the street. I'm laughing so hard my cheeks hurt. But before I can reach for another passenger, she's launched herself at me and forced us back over another stone wall and into another park. Her shoulder in my gut knocks the wind out of me momentarily. When I open my eyes we're both on the ground catching our breath. It's funny to realize that my endurance is kind of crap since I never have to make this much effort. I'm about to reach out and break her stupid arm when she swings her right fist at me and the punch sends me into the stone wall. I find myself partially-imbedded in the stone and with a broken jaw. I take a minute to focus my energy on healing my jaw, which proves to be a mistake, as she's in front of me before I can extricate myself from the wall.

"Who are you?" she asks coldly. I decide not to answer her questions while stuck in a wall and instead try to kick her away. She jumps backward, narrowly avoiding my kick. I lift myself out of the rock, but as I step forward she's in my face again. She reaches out and grabs me by the neck, lifting me off the ground. This is totally insulting. I'm pissed, and annoyed to admit that though I'm sure I'm stronger and faster than she is, she's still giving me a run for my money. I claw at her fingers, digging into the bone. She doesn't flinch.

"Why would you do that?" she asks, true confusion and horror in her voice. I assume she's talking about throwing the passengers around. My jaw is almost healed, I think I can probably speak, but I talk into her head anyway as it scares the shit out of her.

<Why not, Bonnie?>

"Why are you doing this?" she asks again, tightening her grip on my throat. And just then I see her eye catch on the stone around my neck again. I recognize the look in her eye; it looks like how I felt when I first found it. She thinks it belongs to her the same way I know it belongs to me. She's almost hypnotized by it and I take the moment to thrust my palm into her arm that's holding me up, right where it's locked at the elbow. There's a satisfying snapping sound as she screams out and I drop about a foot to the ground as she releases me. The fear in her eyes is palpable as she holds her arm and tries to figure out how to finish this fight with a broken right arm. I touch my neck and clear my throat in a ladylike way that I think Liz would appreciate.

"I'm doing this because I can," I say simply.

○

Lola stands over me, reveling in her victory. She leans in and picks me up by the neck, the way I had picked her up mere moments ago, showing me how quickly the tables can turn. I have this strange feeling that it's a lesson I'm not going to have a chance to remember. She stares at me for a moment and, looking into her eyes is like looking into an abyss that I can't understand. I'll never be able to reason with her, never be able to understand her.

She pulls me close to her and then just launches me. For a second I think I'm flying, like her, until I realize that she's just thrown me. I realize this because I start falling. Fast. Like a star headed back to Earth. I brace myself for a fall that's likely to break my neck, but I hit water. Hitting the water at that speed doesn't feel unlike hitting solid ground though and my broken arm cries out a thousand times harder than before. But I'm conscious; I'm alive. I get my bearings and swim one-armed in the direction I deem the surface is. I break through breathless, the rain pelting the water powerfully, and see I'm in the Hudson River – the George Washington Bridge down from me maybe half a mile. My mind boggles at the strength it must take to throw someone that high and far, and I nearly have a breakdown when I try to examine why she can do so many things I cannot. Things that haven't even occurred to me. Like flying. Well, they're going to have to start occurring to me now.

Something like Lola can't exist. Not without something like me. There has to be someone to stop her. I have to stop her. And as frightening as the concept of her is, it's almost a relief. It's like finally having a big, blinding light illuminating my path. I finally have a purpose. Something I'm designed for. I'm almost smiling as I pull myself out of the river, grabbing onto slick rocks, wet sand, trees and grass – whatever solid thing I can touch.

I'm strangely optimistic, maybe just because I'm not dead already, until Lola kicks me in the face, breaking my nose for a second time, and sending me back forty feet into the Hudson.

●

I kick her in the face, more out of frustration than anger. But when she goes flying back into the river I suddenly know how to kill her. When I see her float to the surface face-down I fly across the river and kick her in the back of the neck. She chokes and gags and starts sinking again. Before she goes too deep, I reach into the water and grab her shirt. I fly back toward the shore, dragging her in the water behind me. When I feel her feet catching on the riverbed I stop and stand in the water, straddling her, anchoring my feet into the sand and rocks below. She's coming around, her eyes blinking slowly and her mouth gasping. As I put my hands around her neck and push her head under the water, the rain pelting us both, thunder rumbling all around us, strikes of lightning illuminating the sky angrily – I talk into her head.

<*Lemme know how it looks on the other side, yeah?*>

Her eyes get big as she goes under, locked on mine and I wonder if she's been as nervous about the idea of drowning as I have been. We're so resilient, it seems like it would be kind of horrible. Like you might die and come back a couple times before your body gives out.

And that's pretty much how it goes.

She kicks and fights me, and breaks at least one of my ribs as she struggles, but then, almost suddenly, she dies. I feel it. The life goes out of her, a limpness that cannot be faked. But I hold on just the same and a minute or two later I feel her fighting me again. I take little trips inside her head, reading her mind, bathing in her fear. But I pop out every time I think she's gonna die. I'm not sure that's something I want to know about so intimately. Not yet at least.

It takes more than half an hour and at least five cycles to drown her.

But eventually she stays down for more than ten minutes and I know it's over. I feel her mind go dark, like someone simply flipping a switch in a once bright room.

I let her go.

And the storm stops.

As quickly as it started, it's over – the sky clearing as if it never happened.

She floats to the surface. Her eyes open, her face blue, her tongue lolling out of her mouth grotesquely. I turn around and wade through the waist deep water. Once on the shore I watch her body drift downstream toward a giant bridge. I wring the water out of my hair and flinch at the pain in my ribs.

I have a slight twinge of something. Similar to what I felt in the trailer, regretting killing Delia before I knew what was really going on. I didn't really know Bonnie's deal either, but after the fight she put up, there's just no way I could have let her live. I barely beat her today and she couldn't even fly, or read my mind, or heal at will, and she didn't have the stone. Who knows how strong she might have become in time? Despite the twinge, I know I did the right thing.

I sit down on the rocks and watch the river for a good half hour before I feel my strength return enough to fly a long distance. For a moment, I think I see an old woman on the opposing riverbank washing bloody clothes against the rocks, the river impossibly red with blood. When I blink, she's gone, as is the blood from the river. I reach up almost unconsciously to touch the stone and realize it's gone too, along with Liz's chain. I pull at my cat suit and look on the ground around me to see if it's simply fallen off.

"Damn," I say to myself looking at the river and somehow knowing that it's in there somewhere. I jump in and tear frantically at the water, checking the shore and even diving down into the deeper areas a few times looking for it. Once I get my head together I stand still and reach out for it mentally, hoping it will call to me as it did in the museum.

Nothing. It's gone.

I drag myself back onto the rocks and sit very quietly, trying to figure out what this means for me and all my plans. The stone would obviously have been helpful – it makes me stronger and faster, and even more invulnerable – but its real strength was in its ability to find Bonnie, and now she's dead. I don't need to find her anymore, so it's fine. I'll go back to L.A., and Liz and, well, I don't know what. I guess I'll do whatever I want. Maybe I'll burn the state of Nevada to the ground and bathe in diamonds.

I consider flying through a few floors of the Empire State building on my way home, dropping a few tourists from the top King-Kong-style, but decide to save it for my next trip to Manhattan. Gotta leave something for next time.

PART III:

i was meant for the stage

●

I touch down at the Malibu beach house triumphant. I'm still pissed I lost the stone and have been cursing off and on the entire way back to L.A., but I've convinced myself that since Bonnie is nice and dead it doesn't matter as much.

I throw open the front door grandly. "Honey, I'm home!"

Liz is curled up in a ball on the couch sobbing quietly through her gag.

"Awww. Were you worried about me?" I ask. Liz looks up incredulous, but shifts her expression to calm. She's kinda tough for a prima donna. I pull the gag off her mouth and she looks at my bare neck.

"Where's my necklace?" Is the only thing she has to say.

"Sorry," I shrug. "Lost in battle." I uncuff her and she lowers her head. She rubs her wrists lightly, her shoulders curling into little round shapes. "Hey, I'm sorry, okay," I say. "I certainly didn't lose it on purpose." I look down at her, miserable and trying to disappear into herself. "I lost the stone too," I offer gamely. I poke her in the shoulder. "Hey, you pick whatever you want to eat, I'll go get it," I say trying to perk her up. Liz doesn't look at me, but lifts her right wrist, ready to be handcuffed again. I decide not to cuff her and drop the handcuffs on the table. Liz looks at me surprised. "I've got to learn to trust you sooner or later," I say, shrugging. And she breaks into a huge smile, which in this moment, seems totally worth it. "So what do you want to eat?" I ask again.

"Sushi," she says.

I stick out my tongue and make a face. "Ick," I mumble.

Liz almost smiles again. "Don't be so ignorant, Lola, give something new a try," she says.

"Whatever. I'll be back in thirty minutes." And then look back at her and add, "Be good."

"What else would I be?" she sighs to the empty room, but I hear her anyway.

Nearly an hour later I'm wrinkling my nose as Liz devours raw fish and some smelly kind of soup. I bite into another pizza slice and try to concentrate on her plan.

"I don't know Liz, kinda sounds like you're trying to get me killed."

"Well, I'd be happy to hear your ideas, Lola," she offers back at me.

I chew on my slice quietly for a minute before answering. "So basically, you're saying, rather than recruiting a bunch of dudes to be my gang of minions, I should just like, go and take over an existing gang?"

"It'll be faster," Liz nods, placing some pink fish on her tongue.

"Yeah, faster at killing me," I mutter reaching for another slice.

"What are you so afraid of? You're practically invincible and always bragging about your power."

"Yeah, but I wasn't lying in your office when I talked about being killed before. It's not that hard to kill me, I'm just pretty good at coming back. But a lot can happen in that down time," I pause and eye her warily. "And don't get any bright ideas," I say, pointing my pizza at her. Liz looks into her soup.

"Wouldn't dream of it," she answers. "Besides, why bother? You're bound to die sooner or later, from malnutrition. Have you ever even eaten a vegetable?" she asks pointing her chopsticks at my pizza. I lift the lid on the box, showing her the pie.

"Hey, this totally has olives on it. That's a vegetable...right?" I say, doubting myself at the last minute.

"Olives are fruit."

"Well that's just as good," I say. Liz rolls her eyes at me. She's getting pretty brash for a right-hand man, but I take that as a good sign. She's getting comfortable. We're bonding even. When I leave the house she still gets grouchy, even though I've given her a long leash so she can swim in the pool and I bring her sushi a bunch more times – even though she knows I hate it – but she's still all 'why do I need a leash this,' and 'why can't we leave the house that'. If she wasn't the brains of my operation and my only friend I probably would have launched her off the patio and onto the rocks long ago. But she is, and so I don't.

It takes less than a week to locate a crew worthy of me and my big ideas. I find one that has lots of henchmen. Most of them dissatisfied with management, making it ripe for takeover. It's funny, but the new crew I've picked out kind of look like my Vegas crew, bigger, tougher, and there's way more of them, but all the same elements are in place. It's easy to see who's in charge, who the guy in charge trusts, who the heavies are, and even the fall guys and bag men. Apparently, crime is all about the same wherever you go.

I watch them from the rafters of their 'hide-out' for two nights before deciding to introduce myself.

Liz is nervous, as she is anytime I leave her cuffed and gagged for an extended period of time.

"Do we really have to do the gag, Lola, I thought we were beyond that?"

"Sorry Liz, but I don't know how long I'll be gone."

"But Lola, you said, you said I'm supposed to be your right-hand man, and your friend even, how is that supposed to happen if you can't start trusting me?" she asks. She has a point. I lay the gag down on the dresser.

"All right," I say, "But understand me. This is a test. You betray me Liz and I won't be satisfied with just killing you – no matter where you run. Understand?"

"Yes," Liz says seriously. "I understand." I smile at her, happy that we're finally evolving. I spin around showing off the cat suit.

"How do I look?"

"Smashing," she replies sarcastically.

"Be nice," I warn, looking for my black gloves.

"Are you going to take anything?" she asks.

"What do you mean? Like a nice bottle of wine? It's not a housewarming party, Liz."

"Of course. I meant more like a donation of some kind. Something to show them what you bring to the table."

"You seriously want me to give them something? Other than the opportunity to be my henchmen?"

"I just think you'll have an easier time convincing them that you're their best bet if you show them what you have to offer them. The superpowers are impressive, of course, but guys like this, I think they're probably not too interested in a woman boss – superpowers or no. If you can show them what you can bring to them – riches, power, whatever – I just think you'll have an easier time." She shrugs. I stand with my hands on my hips considering her idea. She is, of course, the brains. I pull four big duffels out of the closet, two filled with cash and two filled with jewelry and loose stones, mostly diamonds.

"Cash or jewels?" I ask Liz, surveying the bags, hands on my hips. Liz's eyes bug out at the overflowing bags.

"Jesus," she breathes. "I suppose the jewelry has more visual impact."

"Jewels it is," I say, kicking three of the bags back into the closet. I zip up the duffel and turn to Liz. "That it?" I ask.

"I suppose," she says shrugging noncommittally. I pull the strap over my shoulder and check my watch.

"Okay, see you in a few hours."

"Good luck," Liz offers. I turn in the doorway.

"You mean that?" I ask.

Liz pauses and then looks me in the eye. "I do."

"Hmph," I grunt.

I take off from the patio, anxious to be done with this next phase of Lola's World Domination. Less than ten minutes later, I'm climbing in through the skylight while the men below me laugh and joke. I set myself and my bag of goodies on the rafters above the main table they're all congregating around. I nearly fall asleep waiting for Mr. Head Honcho to arrive, and when he does, there's little change in the attitude around the table. I'll definitely have to whip this group into shape. I let them go on for what feels like forever before I finally lose patience. I put the bag strap across my body and drop from the rafters to the far end of the table. To their credit, several of them have guns drawn on me by the time I launch myself off the table and behind the boss. I put my hands on either side of boss man's head and snap his neck. He slides impotently out of his chair. I look at the rest of the table.

"Boys, do I have an offer for you," is all I get out before all hell breaks loose.

Bullets are flying and every single dude in the room is yelling out something different. Totally unorganized. This behavior is just not going to fly under my rule. I run around the room so fast I'm nothing but a blur, knocking people out and taking guns – breaking a few fingers in the process – before stopping at the head of the table again and letting the guns clatter to the cement floor below me. A few bullets have grazed me, mostly by pure luck, and I've got one lodged in my shoulder. I figure I should use it to my advantage. "Now boys, you don't want to kill me, I'm just what you need to take this little operation to the next level, but just so we can be clear here, you can't kill me, so you might as well stop trying and open your goddamn ears." I pull back the edge of my cat suit and show my bullet wound and concentrate for a long moment on pushing the bullet out of my shoulder and healing the hole in my flesh. The bullet plinks onto the table delicately. There's some gasping and cussing and at least three of them cross themselves. Now that I have their attention, I levitate, hovering in the air gracefully as I break one of the machine guns over my knee. The gasping and cursing and crossing doubles, maybe triples. "So who's in charge now that I took out this dumbass?" I ask, pointing with a handgun to the dead boss on the floor. There's a long pause, and then some idiot stands up.

"I am," he says.

I shoot him in the head.

"And now?" I ask, looking around the table at bowed heads. Someone clears his throat, "Yes?" I urge.

"Um, you?" he offers tentatively.

"Correct!" I yell out happily. "Now here's the thing, guys, any of you are welcome to leave, the last thing I want is an unmotivated, uncommitted crew, but I'm not shitting you when I say I have the ability to make you rich and powerful beyond your wildest dreams. In fact, here's a taste." I pick the duffel up off the ground and dump the contents out on the table. It looks like a pirate treasure piñata busted open. Diamonds and other precious gems skid and scatter across the table. They seem pretty impressed – even if they don't want to be – and I mentally remind myself to thank Liz. I can see a few fighters in the group though, and I steel myself up for the confrontation.

"You freak bitch," comes a growl from the left side of the table. "You just killed my brother and you think you can buy me off with diamonds?!"

"Well, maybe not you," I say, and put a bullet in his head too. I look at the rest of the group. "That bullet was for calling me a freak, which, though I may well be, is certainly not up to any of you to decide," I sneer. A tentative and shockingly large hand near the end of the table raises.

"Yeah, you, uh, big hand."

"Miss, no disrespect, but what ARE you?"

"Honestly Knuckles? I've got no goddamn idea but does it really matter? At the end of the day, I'm just the girl with the plan to take over Los Angeles."

O

I wake up with one foot in the water, my body beaten and bruised, rocks cutting into my back, wet sand in my hair. It's dark out, early morning, I think, and when I sit up my body screams.

There's water lapping at my right hand so I pull my hand away from the water in something resembling slow motion. I scoot toward some large rocks and lean against them, breathing shallow breaths so as not to cause any more pain to my poor body. Up the river a few hundred yards, is the George Washington Bridge.

I have no idea what day it is or how I got here, or even how long I've been here. My mind races trying to grab onto something solid, but everything slips away.

I realize I don't know my name.

I lay there for hours, until the sun is high and my clothes and the wallet I found in my jeans are dried out. There's no identification inside, which is epically annoying, but there is some money and a MetroCard for the subway. I've also got two keys in my pocket. They look like house keys. It gives me hope that I have a home. The thing I don't get is that obviously not everything is gone – I recognize the George Washington Bridge and the Hudson River, and I know that if I head inland, east, I'll hit a subway station at 168th Street, which will take me downtown. How is it possible to know all of that and not know my name? I examine my clothing and pockets again. Sneakers that look like they've been drowned, jeans, and a white t-shirt. There's also a silver I.D. bracelet, but frustratingly, there's not actually a name on it.

It looks like it was rubbed off years ago.

When I'm sure I can stand without falling over I pull myself up and sit on a boulder. I stare at the sun on the river trying to make sense of why I would have been in it. Something shiny caught on rocks just under the water catches my eye and I stumble over to it and pull it out. It's a thick silver chain with a broken clasp, tangled up with a large flattish piece of broken stone, nearly the size of my palm. It seems crude on first glance but really it's quite finely carved. If it wasn't broken it looks like it would be three open interlocking circles. A solid circle in the center joining three on the outside. The center is intact and there's an intricate carving of a crow on it. I don't know if I'm hallucinating or what, but it feels like it's singing to me, like it belongs to me and as I hold it, I swear I feel stronger, that my muscles hum and my aches lessen. I close my hand around it and am suddenly assaulted with a thousand images all at once. Red-haired women, epic battlefields, a river dark with blood, a wolf, three black crows that turn into a sky of them, eels sliding over one another in water. None of it makes sense or feels like me, but it's familiar just the same. The images are gone almost as quickly as they came. And once gone I'm left again with no images or memory. Unfortunately, the black dots in my brain where I suspect memories used to be will not vanish as easily as the bruises seem to. I pocket the stone and chain and climb toward civilization, hoping that as I walk through the city, the fog will clear and I'll find my name and maybe the answers behind what I was doing in the Hudson River.

I take a train headed downtown as something feels right about it. But sitting in my seat, every time I close my eyes, I see my fist flying into some stranger's face, over and over again until I can't tell if it's the bones in his face breaking, or the bones in my hand. There's a lot of blood. When I open my eyes I'm relieved to find there is no stranger, no blood, and no crushed bones, just the normal train and the empty blackness of my mind.

I look at my sneakers, which are barely holding together, they're so muddy and damp. The gap in my memory widens, eating up bits of my brain. I look at my hands laying peacefully in my lap; they don't look like the hands of someone with no memory. I turn them over and see them bloody again, slamming repeatedly into the same stranger's face. I'm stirred away from my hands by the sound of someone entering the subway car from the one in front of mine. I don't look up to see who it is as I'm too busy checking my real hands for possibly imaginary blood. But then I realize he sounds wrong.

Sounds wrong? What does that even mean?

I try thinking about my shoes and hands again, but there is a strange fire filling up my chest. I look down to see if I am, indeed, on fire. There's nothing there. I put a palm to my heart; there is no real heat, it's imagined. Something is very wrong but except for my chest on fire, I feel an odd calm. I look up at the new passenger's face as he moves through the train toward other cars. His face and bones and blood are the same ones I've been seeing on my hands. This makes me feel less calm.

I wish I could remember my name.

There's something happening now at the back of the car. People are rushing toward the front, toward me. There's a lot of noise, some screaming.

The fire in my chest continues to rage and I suddenly feel like I can see straight into the stranger's heart. The stranger on the train has very bad plans for us all. I rise from the orange and yellow subway seats – yellow that I think reminds me of the color of my mother's kitchen when I was little. After I was done being little everything was painted grey, I think. I shake off the strange feeling of a memory and try to follow the stranger. I move against the traffic of flesh, making my way for the man at the back of the train.

The man has a woman by the neck. He waves a gun wildly like a character from a movie. I walk toward this man with his gun, and this woman with her packages. He doesn't see me at first. This is good, because I can look at them a lot, see everything I need to see. The woman is older, maybe seventy, and she has much to live for. I get closer and I can see grandchildren in her eyes. She carries a loaf of fresh baked bread; it looks like strawberry bread. I didn't know there was such a thing as strawberry bread. I wish she could teach me how to bake bread.

She is not ready to go.

She should not go.

I will not let her go.

His hair is greasy and falling in his eyes, and I can see from the redness there, that he's very tired. He's strong. Tattoos on his forearm around the woman's neck are intersected with veins. The kind of veins that come from going to the gym all the time, riding bikes up steep hills, and getting into bar fights. But this is good for me. This makes it okay for him when he sees me walking towards him, because he doesn't worry about a girl. If I were a boy, or if he were a weaker boy maybe he would have shot me by now. Somehow I know this. Why do I know this? It doesn't matter how I know.

I know.

I know that I am a little bit pretty which makes men smile and not worry about me so much, and although I am tall for a girl, I am still only six feet, which is smaller than he is, so he doesn't worry about me. He just yells at me. Tells me to sit my ASS down. He emphasizes ASS like he really likes to say it. I shake my head. He yells at me some more. Sit my crazy bitch ASS down.

He drops the old woman and she falls to the floor in a pile of fragile bones – alive and kicking, full of life, out of the way. I'm close now. I don't know what will happen if he shoots me. What happens to rocks when they get shot? I don't actually know, but surely other people on this train might be hurt if he fires, even if it bounces off me like some kind of impenetrable trampoline. So when he turns to check his back, to see if he is being set up, I feel my right fist clench. It feels strong. Powerful. I know I'm strong. I don't think anybody has ever told me, it's just something I know. There's power there. I can feel it running though my veins, through my arm, into my chest where the burning began. He turns back to me and sees my eyes. For one moment I think he knows what's going to happen, but it's too quick for him to feel bad about it. My fist comes straight at his face and his neck makes a sharp snapping sound as he falls back onto the train floor.

My name is Bonnie Braverman.

●

While the henchmen build a loft apartment for Liz and I in the existing warehouse space, I take her shopping. She's been stuck in her abduction clothes for weeks now and I hope that this will both curb her overall grouchiness and solidify the bond we've been forming. Of course, for the trip out she has to be dressed in an oversized Lakers t-shirt and shorts that don't fit either. I also make her wear a baseball cap I lifted off of one of the henchmen and an old pair of my chucks, so she's none to pleased about that. According to Liz, rayon has not touched her skin in twenty years. Yawn. She can be such a freaking snob.

I'm taking her to the Glendale Galleria because it's big and crazy and despite being less than fifteen miles from Beverly Hills, it couldn't feel farther from it if it tried, and I know Liz will feel this too. If I'm honest, this is my final test for her. We're on the verge of making a big play for L.A. and I need to know she's fully with me. If today goes well, nothing can stop us.

It doesn't start well.

"I don't want to fly there," she says crossing her arms, looking ridiculous, but nicely incognito in the ill-fitting clothes.

"C'mon Liz," I roll my eyes. "It's by far the fastest way to travel."

"I don't like it and you know it," she says, her foot tapping, her arms still crossed. "If this is supposed to be my 'big day out' then I don't see why I have to fly," she says. I roll my eyes again, even harder.

"FINE!" I go back inside the warehouse. The two henchmen that look exactly the same are the first ones I see. "Hey! Heckle, Jeckle, get over here," I shout, gesturing for them to come to me. They look at each other and then behind them, hoping that I'm not pointing at them and then put their heads down and shuffle over. "Bring the town car around to the back gate, you're going to be taking her highness and me to the Glendale Galleria," I say. They scuttle off and I shout after them as an afterthought. "No guns! I don't need us getting pulled over today!" They literally drop their weapons on a table and run from the room. I return to Liz who's standing by the warehouse door.

"Happy now?" I bow to her.

"Hmmph. It's a start," she says.

"You know, Liz," I say. "You are just unpleasable."

"That's not a word," she says, lifting up her chin so she can look at me from under the baseball cap.

"Whatever," I say dismissing her with a wave of my hand. The henchmen come around the corner in the black town car and Heckle jumps out to open the door for us. Apparently, Jeckle is the superior driver.

"Thank you, Davis," Liz says as she steps into the car, somehow still dainty and graceful even in a gaudy oversized Lakers t-shirt and chucks. I get in behind her.

"Who the hell is Davis?" I ask as we settle back against the leather. Liz points at Heckle in the front seat.

"He is."

"That's Heckle," I say.

"I don't know why you won't just learn their real names," she sighs. "It's not very respectful.

"Are you kidding me? There's hundreds of them, I can't remember all those names."

"But you rename them anyway, so you have to learn all the names you give them – it's the same thing."

"Not really. Besides, if I get the name I gave them wrong it doesn't matter to me, and they know to obey when I point anyway," I say, waving my hand.

"I think it's just your way of dehumanizing them," she says.

"Whatever, Liz. I don't want any backseat theraping today, alright?"

"That's also not a word."

"While we're at it, can you cut it out with the grammar-Nazi crap. Leave me be already!" I shout. But she's smiling and so am I. The relationship probably looks dysfunctional to some – okay, everybody – but the truth is I get a lot of fun out of sparring with Liz. She pretends she doesn't, but I think she doth protest too much, or whatever the saying is.

At the mall, we leave Heckle and Jeckle in the car. This is girl-bonding time and I'm pretty sure it shouldn't come with two dumb henchmen in tow. The mall is crowded for a Tuesday morning, but would be considered empty for a weekend, which is just about what I was hoping for. Plenty of temptation for Liz, but not too much confusion for me. That's one thing about super-senses – and super-hearing especially – it can be hard to separate out all of the noise. Once inside, I hold up my hands to her.

"Well, where to? You're the boss today." Liz checks the mall map and points straight ahead.

"That way," she says and I shrug and follow her dutifully. We roll up outside something called Nordstrom and already I'm complaining.

"Liz, c'mon, this looks like an old lady store." She cuts me a look that could probably kill if I was any less awesome.

"This store has *Burberry*," is all she says before signaling for me to come along with a wag of her finger, heading for the escalator. By the time I reach her on the second floor she already has a handful of items slung over her arm. I finger the tag on a white silk blouse she's holding and almost lose my breakfast.

"Three hundred bucks!? For a white button-down shirt?! Are you kidding me?" Liz doesn't even look up.

"What do you care? You can afford it," she says.

"There's a difference between can and should," I mutter. Liz stops flipping through the racks and looks up at me, her expression one I've never quite seen before. There's something soft and pained in it, less defensive and controlled than usual.

"I thought you said this was my day, no expense spared?"

"I…" I'm about to say something cruel or sarcastic, but that look on her face kills it. "Yeah, yeah it is. Get whatever you want. Besides, things are about to get real busy and we're not going to have time for this kind of thing, so you should get whatever you need, and as my right-hand you should look the part," I say, dropping the price tag. Liz beams for just one moment and then looks away and continues adding to her already monstrous pile. I walk away from her and call Jeckle.

"Yeah, boss?"

"Yeah. Have Heckle bring me the other envelope of cash I left in the car," I look at Liz, nearly blotted out by the pile in her arms and weaving drunkenly toward the dressing rooms. "I'm going to need it."

"Sure thing, boss."

"I'm somewhere called Nordstrom."

"10-4, boss," he says. I hang up and follow her to the dressing room. Three hours and more than twenty thousand dollars later we're finally checking out. I watch the clerk carefully pack up the pieces. A high-necked, sleeveless, backless white silk blouse; a low-cut, light blue, sleeveless silk blouse with some ruffles or something along the neckline; a cream-colored silk blouse – the bitch really likes silk – and light pink cashmere sweater. There's also a dark grey wool skirt; a pencil skirt in three different colors – navy, black, and light grey; a silky cream-colored pantsuit; two pair of black pants; a charcoal trench dress; a black and grey checked trench coat; a handful of scarves and belts; some silver jewelry; six pair of heels, two pair of boots; a t-shirt and a pair of skinny jeans. I look at Liz as the two hundred and fifty dollar jeans get folded up.

"You don't even wear jeans," I say.

Liz sniffs. "How do you know?" she says. I look at her, eyebrow raised. "Fine. I don't. But I thought I'd try them out." I can't decide whether I want to kiss or kill her. Who just 'tries out' a two hundred and fifty dollar pair of jeans? Only my Liz.

"Whatever," I say, sighing. I survey the pile as I hand the cash to the clerk, whose eyes triple in size at the sight of a wad that big. "You sure know how to shop," I say, watching the clerk re-count the cash.

"Yes, it's funny," she says. "Nobody has ever really taken me shopping before. I mean, not since I was a child. I've always really taken care of myself. I didn't know how I'd feel about being taken care of, but it's kind of nice." It's a big deal, I think, that she says this to me, and so I acknowledge it by not saying anything. I don't want to break the spell. I take three of the bags and Liz takes one. On the way out of the department store, Liz talks me into buying a fifteen hundred dollar black leather motorcycle jacket and a two hundred dollar grey t-shirt for myself. She must be rubbing off on me. The jacket is badass but I regret the t-shirt almost immediately. Two hundred bucks and it will probably disintegrate the first time I kill a freaking henchman in it.

I buy a few pairs of jeans and some non-two hundred dollar t-shirts elsewhere in the mall. While shopping for bras and crap like that, Liz and I accidentally end up buying almost identical robes – mine a dark grey silk and hers a soft lilac – but otherwise exactly the same. One of us is definitely rubbing off on the other. Since the robes are silk I'm inclined to think it's Liz rubbing off on me. The smell of delicious fast food wafting from the food court has my mouth watering.

"I don't suppose you're going to be willing to eat anything here," I say, gesturing as we walk by.

Liz turns her nose up as expected, then, with a tone that suggests she doesn't really care one way or another says, "Well, I suppose I'd be willing to eat a corn dog if you're hungry." I laugh out loud.

"A corn dog?! You?! I'd pay to see that." Five minutes later I'm sliding her a twenty and watching her devour two corndogs and a lemonade from Hot Dog On A Stick.

"Guilty pleasure," she says, shrugging, and then adds, "We should get something to go for the henchmen, they must be starving." It's the first time she's called them 'the henchmen' and my heart swells with pride.

On our way out I see the mall management offices, security staff and all, and decide to take a chance. I drag Liz into a game shop across the way and then, absorbed in all the toys, ask her to get me a pretzel from the kiosk directly across from the offices, not ten feet from mall security. Liz barely fusses, which alarms me, as it seems like something she would complain about, but I let her go anyway. It takes a lot of concentration to block out the screeching kids and numerous voices between us, but with effort I'm able to hone in on Liz's voice.

"One pretzel please, butter no salt," she says to the clerk.

"$3.05," the girl says, shifting her weight. There's a long pause and my heart catches in my throat.

"Don't do it, Liz, don't do it," I whisper, waiting for her to speak.

"Is there something wrong ma'am?" the girl asks. There's another long pause and then Liz's voice.

"No. No, sorry. I couldn't find my money," she says, handing the clerk the twenty. I watch as the girl makes change and gives her the pretzel. As Liz walks back to me – pretzel in hand, the baseball cap partially obscuring her face – I try to understand her expression, another one I've never seen before: it's defeat. I've won.

The ride home is long and silent as Jeckle fights the traffic and Heckle hands him bits of corn dogs and fries from the doggie bag Liz insisted we bring along.

o

As I run away from the subway and the sound of that man's neck snapping on the train I'm besieged by memories or at least I hope that's what they are. I'm running, headed for a park, rain pelting me unkindly, not unlike the memories, jabbing me with their truth – ugly and pretty both. I remember a whole life in seconds.

I was a blank slate, a person with no memory or place in time or space.

And in a blink, I'm Bonnie Braverman – a whole person with a whole life. It's the name. It all comes as soon as I know my name, as if all of me is somehow tied to that name. The memories both drown and embrace me; I want to be glad for it, but now my parents are dead. A moment ago they could have been anyone and anywhere and now suddenly they've been dead for nearly thirteen years and I'll never see them again. But there's also strange relief. Not knowing who you are is a certain kind of hell. I don't know if a person can understand how much of who you are is based on who you have been – what you have done and not done – until it's experienced firsthand. They are inextricably linked.

And so, sitting on a park bench in the rain as people run for cover all around me, I'm crying because I've remembered that one of my only friends in the world was killed just for being my friend. It's a moment that I can't forget. Won't forget. It has to mean something; I need it all to mean something.

And along with remembering my dead parents and dead Bryce I also know that I have a brother, Jasper, and I'm in love with a boy named Clark, and my friends, Liesel and Ben, expected me back, probably days ago, maybe more – I don't know how long it's been. But most importantly, I remember there's a girl named Lola and she's just like me – but twisted, like looking at a reversed version of myself. And all that can matter now is finding her and stopping her, making sure that everyone I have left is safe from her – and maybe more than that – maybe making sure that everyone everywhere is safe from her.

But where to begin? I'm no detective. Having superpowers hasn't made me Batman.

No matter. Now that my path is clear there is nothing that can move me from it. In some bizarre way I feel I owe Lola some thanks for killing me. In killing me my memory was lost and when it came rushing back it was so easy to see what was important. Clark. Liesel. Ben. Jasper. The memory of my parents and of Bryce. Doing what's right. Finding out who and what I really am and doing exactly what I should have been doing all along.

Lola has no idea what she has unleashed.

●

Bonnie's drowned face swims in front of me. Ever since I killed her she's been showing up in my dreams. So far it's always just what I did to her, over and over again, with a few added effects I don't understand. The horror on her face is real though, just as it was. I've wished a lot of times since I killed her that the water hadn't been so clear that day, or that I'd held her lower so that I couldn't see her face. In the dream, after I've drowned her for the millionth time, she's still not dead. I watch her come alive, rising from the water, thick black eels writhing at her feet. I spring on her again and drive her deeper into the water. Across the river I see the old woman, oblivious to us, washing dark red clothing against sharp rocks. The sky fills with crows, nearly blotting out the sun, their wings beating madly above us. When Bonnie dies again, when I see the light wink out of her eyes, the crows fall from the sky like rocks, like a giant sheet of rocks. Hitting the water and the beach with incredible velocity. The eels float lifelessly to the surface all around us and I feel short of breath. And as I drag myself back to the riverbank exhausted, she stands up again.

The dream is on an endless loop.

I look around the strange room and remember where I am — the new loft apartment in the warehouse. Liz and I moved in yesterday. I picked a few of the slightly more gifted henchmen to be my 'management team.' And after a rough patch, in which I had to kill a few more of them for insubordination, we're about ready to take the training wheels off.

But I dream of Bonnie every night. The bitch just won't go away. And I'm starting to think it's more than just guilt or something. Like maybe it's a sign. Like a sign that she's not all dead and decomposing in the Hudson River. I stumble out of my dream and my room, pulling open the sliding wall separating Liz's bedroom from my own.

"I think Bonnie's still alive," I say, plunking myself on the edge of the bed. Liz kicks at me and I slide off the bed and onto the floor.

"G'way," comes from under the fluffy duvet.

"Liz. Get up," I say, yanking the covers away from her.

"Lola. Stop. I'm tired," she complains, curling herself into the oversized Lakers t-shirt and a small corner of the sheet (she forgot to get a nightgown at the mall).

"Liz, did you hear me? I don't think Bonnie's dead," I say, sitting back on the edge of the naked bed. Liz kicks at me again fruitlessly and then sits up with a dramatic sigh.

"Why do you think she's alive?" she asks exasperated.

"I've had these dreams about her – all the same, or at least similar."

"It's probably guilt," Liz says, pulling the duvet back onto her from the floor.

"It's not guilt," I say.

"You sure?" she asks muffled again.

"Yes. Why would I feel guilty? No, it's like a sixth sense or something."

"Okay, whatever, it's a sixth sense then," she says. "Go back to sleep." She offers unhelpfully, closing her eyes and curling back up tight like a bug. I chew on my lip.

"You don't believe that."

"No, but I'll pretend to if you'll shut up about it," she says smiling grimly.

"Bitch," I smirk, slapping her ankle lightly.

"Ow," she says, as I leave the room. I grab a Clif bar from the kitchenette and nibble it while perching on a stool. I jump up and go to the edge of the balcony. Gigantor is on watch at the bottom of the stairs, leaning on the railing, one hand resting on the machine gun hanging from his shoulder.

"Gigantor," I shout down the stairs.

"Yeah, boss?" he says, snapping to attention.

"Get Lou over here," I say. Gigantor thinks for a second too long. "Now," I say sharper, and the giant man rushes out of the room below me. I go back into the bedroom and put on my robe. I kick Liz lightly on the butt. "Get up Liz, I'm serious this time," I say. Liz groans but dutifully crawls out of bed and pulls on her lilac robe. She stumbles into the kitchen and starts some coffee. I get dressed and when I come back in she lifts the carafe up, silently offering me a cup. She always does this even though I never say yes. "You know I don't drink that crap," I say. She shrugs her shoulders as if she couldn't care less and pours her own cup and then curls her legs under her in a chair next to me at the kitchen table, waiting patiently for whatever happens next. Lou shows up with a polite knock on the banister since we have no door.

"Hey, boss, what's up?"

"Sit down," I say, gesturing to the chair at the other end of the table.

"You want coffee?" Liz asks, ever the hostess.

"No thanks, Liz," Lou says, lifting up a hand.

"Liz, this isn't a freaking breakfast meeting here. Can you let up with the coffee already?" I snap. Liz rolls her eyes. I look back at Lou. "I've got a special assignment for you. Pick a team – three or four guys plus you, maybe Lenny, Rocco, Knuckles, eh, not Knuckles, it's a finesse assignment, take some of the smarter guys – maybe Curly, Moe, and Larry – but guys with no record 'cause you're going to be flying to New York," I see Liz raise an eyebrow, but I ignore it. "Also, we have anyone that can draw?" I ask. Now Lou's the one to raise an eyebrow.

"Uh, yeah boss, Elliot – I mean, Big Tony – he can draw pretty good, went to art school or sumthin' on a football scholarship, but he dropped out when he lost his ride," he says.

"Great. Get your team together and send Big T over here."

"You uh, gonna tell me what this is about, boss?"

"Eventually." I pause. "Get going." I add, watching him hustle out of the room. Liz continues to sip her coffee and not say anything.

When Big Tony shows up I give him the article about my stone and have him create a detailed drawing of it. Then I describe Bonnie to him. It takes us three tries but on the third we nail it. Lou's right, he's good. Too bad he's just a dumb thug now.

Lou comes back with Rocco, Curly, Gordo, and Bud not long after Big Tony leaves. It's not exactly the dream team, but you work with what you've got. Liz comes out from her bedroom still in her robe – her hands stuffed in the little pockets – and goes directly to the kitchen for more coffee, which she, of course, offers up again. Rocco is the only one to take her up on it; I'm pretty sure he's got a thing for her. I've noticed him checking her out and chatting her up. I snap my fingers at him. "Hey, this isn't your own little personal coffeehouse, Rocco. Get over here." Rocco joins the line. I hand Lou the two drawings. "Alright, boys, assignment number one: find this. It's made of a rough heavy stone, it may have a thick silver chain with it. You should start looking in and around the Hudson River, a few hundred yards above and below the George Washington Bridge. Then start checking all the pawn shops and, you know, whatever underground action there might be," I pause thoughtfully. "Assignment number two: you should look for this girl. Her name is Bonnie Braverman and she may have the stone. If she has it, it's even more important that you get it." I pause again, not sure how much to tell them about Bonnie. "She's like me," I say quietly. Lou leans forward a bit.

"What's that, boss?"

"She's like me," I say, looking at them. "Strong and fast. So don't mess around with her. Take her by surprise, get in and get out," I add.

"Um, boss?" Lou starts tentatively, probably afraid his tongue's going to be ripped out, since I did do that to a henchman once. "How on Earth we gonna find her? I mean, New York City, is like, huge." The others nod lightly.

"Set her up. Start something somewhere in the city. She'll show up. It worked for me once before and she's nothing if not predictable," I say. Everything's really quiet and then Liz sips her coffee loudly and they all look at her. She doesn't raise her eyes from the cup but pushes a thick envelope of cash across the table.

"Get going boys, there's a flight you can catch out of LAX this morning," Liz says. Lou grabs the envelope and starts down the stairs, the rest following him. Rocco is last and pauses at the landing. He looks back at me and takes something small and white out of his pocket and leaves it on the railing. I walk over to see what it is and some kind of horrible dread overtakes me. A part of me knows that this little piece of paper is going to change my life. That the tiny contentment I've gotten as head of this new makeshift family is going to evaporate like dust when I touch it. At the same time, I know it's impossible to leave it alone.

It's a note.

Bonnie,

You must help me – and all of L.A. Lola is building an army and she's keeping me hostage. Please come and put a stop to this madness. She's sick – she needs help – but I think at this point you're the only one who can stop her. She gets more powerful all the time, it seems. Our base is located in a warehouse in downtown Los Angeles somewhere between Alameda and Virgenes. Please come as soon as possible.

Dr. Elizabeth Grant.

The paper flutters in my fingers as I try to calm the tremble in my hand. The corners of the world pucker and peel back revealing black everywhere. I put my hands on the railing to steady myself. For a minute my head reels and fireworks explode behind my eyes. I put a hand to my face, digging my thumb and pointer finger into my eye sockets lightly, as if I can wipe away what they have seen – today, this minute, or maybe further back, maybe all the way. Delia, Adrian, Felice, Lena, Joan, Bonnie, and now Liz. I hold the banister and it bends and crumples under my grip. My eyes snap open.

"Liz!" I call.

"What?" she yells back from somewhere in the loft.

"Come out here," I say. I hear her grumbling to herself, but she emerges dressed in her linen skirt and silk blouse from the day I abducted her. She hasn't worn it since before we went shopping.

Until today. Today, she chooses to wear it.

"Well, I haven't seen that outfit in a while," I pause. "Special occasion?"

Liz sniffs. "It just called out to me today."

"I wonder why," I say, holding up her white note between my fingers briefly and then letting it fall to the floor. Liz's eyes pop just for a second and then lower, following the note to its concrete resting place.

"Lola-" she starts softly.

"Save it, Liz," I say, looking away from her. "Man, you're a shitty therapist," I whistle.

"I thought I was your right-hand man?" she offers almost lightly.

"Well, you're shitty at that, too, I guess," I say to her, resigned. If I'm honest with myself she's been defiant in her own way all along, but I've so wanted to believe that it was just a friendly evolution for us, that our relationship had changed from just therapist and patient, kidnapper and kidnap-ee. "I would have thought you of all people – my therapist – would know what this would do to me, Liz – betrayal by my inner circle. You know everyone I've ever known has betrayed me."

"Maybe I did know what it would do to you," she says, a little bit of steel in her voice.

"What? So now you've got a death wish?"

"Maybe just for you," she hisses, looking up at me, as much steel in her eyes as her voice now. I've never seen this look in her eyes before but I match it.

"What? You suddenly think you can take me?" I ask.

"Not in the way you think," she says, the edge in her voice sharpening. I don't really know what she means, but nothing much matters anymore. I walk over to her and see that despite her hard eyes and voice, her blouse is shivering against her skin and a light sheen of sweat covers her neck and chest. I'm standing so close to her that her hair is tickling my face and I can hear her racing heartbeat as loud as thunder in my ears.

"You've hurt me horribly, Elizabeth," I say, my lips nearly touching her ear.

"As you have me, Lola," she returns, her voice breaking over the words. Standing so close to her that it's almost as if we're dancing or making love, I raise my hands to either side of her face. Her skin is soft and damp now with both our tears. "Lola, don't-" she begins, but before she can finish the sentence, I turn her head sharply to the left, and a little cry comes out of me as I do it.

The crack of her neck snapping is the saddest, loneliest sound I've ever heard.

I'm holding her up – her weight falling into her feet, her toes dancing lightly over the concrete, suspended only from her head, my hands pressing into either side of her skull. Her face looks like a doll's, her eyes still open wide, blank and blink-less, staring into me, glassy and lonely. There's a softness in their chocolate brown color that I've never noticed before. I catch a sob in my throat and let her drop. She falls into a silky little pile – pretty and worthless. I slide down against the wall, like the air has been siphoned out of me, and stare at her – all akimbo limbs and finely tailored clothing – for hours.

Something breaks in me.

Maybe for the first time, or maybe again. Maybe for the last time. I don't know. Nothing makes sense; nothing matters.

I walk into the kitchen and dig out a bottle of vodka. I drink it all and then I drink the next one. All the while, Liz sits in her little dead pile and stares at the floor unblinking. After my third bottle I grab her by the wrist and drag her towards the loft's edge. I pick her up and hold her for a moment, almost like I still love her. I touch her ear – the last ear I whispered into – and rip it off her head.

It comes off with surprising ease and I put it in the pocket of my robe.

I lift her over my head and launch her onto the concrete floor below, pieces of her breaking like expensive plates.

Gigantor stands below the loft, an automatic weapon in one hand and his other nervously clenching and unclenching as he stares at her broken body on the floor. He looks at me and then down, unsure if he's going to be thrown too for witnessing the very private crime. "Get rid of her," I say to him. "And make sure I'm not bothered for the rest of the day." I add, walking away from the railing. I hear him scuttle out of the room to get assistance and I take as many bottles of vodka into the bedroom as I can carry, drawing the heavy drapes behind me.

I don't know how much time has passed, but I'm lying on the floor staring alternately at Liz's ear and the industrial-sized ceiling fan, when Delia shows up, looking all ghosty and pale, still in her green bathrobe, the edges charred, I guess, in homage to the fiery crash that killed her. She strolls into the room as if she's never left, as if she isn't the reason my whole life and everything in it is fucked in the first place. She stops mid-stride just before stepping on Liz's ear and then draws back, a horrified smile on her face.

"Oh dear, Lo, I almost stepped on your BFF," she says, dramatically stretching her leg over the ear and then spinning across to the other side of the room, facing me, hands on her hips. I toss an empty bottle in her direction and it flies right through her and crashes into the concrete. "That's not very nice, Lo," she says sweetly. "Don't blame me for losing your temper and killing your only friend," she says, reaching her hands to the sky.

I turn away from her, take one of the broken bottles into the bathroom with me, and slit my wrists.

○

I go to the depths of Inwood Hill Park – the oldest and most alone place I know of in Manhattan – and teach myself to fly. It takes nearly a day and much of it is really, really not pretty, but I finally get it and explode into the sky like I've been fired from a gun.

Hovering over the city I'm blown away by its beauty. It's my city and I want to take care of it. I want to make sure Lola never touches it again.

Afterward I walk all over the city, reconnecting with it. Rebuilding a bond that I hadn't even realized I'd missed. Long after sundown and deep into the evening hours something powerful calls me north. I'm downtown, in the financial district of all places, when it happens, but I take off in that direction as soon as I feel it, running at first and then, eventually taking flight mid-run. It's fantastic.

A few minutes later, after weaves and turns throughout the city in an attempt to pinpoint the location, I arrive on a small, quiet block with an all-night corner-diner, its lights burning with a kind of loneliness, desperately beating back the night. The fire in my gut tells me this is it.

When I arrive though, there's nothing.

No robbery in place.

No 'bad man with a knife.'

Nothing.

Just me and a handful of other sad little souls sitting around, keeping the darkness at bay. The waitress nods at me and I smile to put her at ease. I sit at the counter and order a black coffee, because it sounds strong and dark. I sit quietly, head down, drinking, just like everyone else, trying to think what went wrong. Where was this bad sound that called to me from so far away.

What has gone wrong? I concentrate, see if I can seek it out. I hear the sound of a mother clicking her spoon nervously against a saucer, the sound of her child up too late and screaming out at odd intervals and squirming against the vinyl of the booth. The sound of a toilet flushing and a zipper being zipped, the unpleasant smell from the same room. The sound of a cough and the water faucet not coming on and hands not being washed. The sound of the waitress whispering 'I love you' into her cell phone and smoothing her skirt before coming through the swinging kitchen door to refill cooling coffees. The sound of the cook, way in the back, with nothing to cook so late at night, sitting on an overturned bucket and reading a book, his finger pulling at the page anxiously before it's time to finally turn it. The sound of a couple in the very back booth, very much in love – or very much in the throes of making up – cuddling together on one bench, each with a strawberry milkshake in front of them, half-finished, their bodies so close it is more like seeing, hearing, feeling one person instead of two.

Everyone – even the couple, though not split from each other - seem split from the world. As if this diner is the only place on Earth awake. Or maybe we aren't even on Earth anymore. Maybe we're all in some abandoned space station truck stop in the empty universe on a space road to nowhere.

I sit, confused, drowning myself in the bitter warmth for a good five minutes before I start to feel the heat in my chest again. With the heat comes the inevitable nausea. Not as strong as the first time, but it must be showing on my face because the kind waitress comes over and touches my hand.

"You okay, honey?" she asks, genuinely concerned. I look past her to the man walking into the diner. And there it is.

It rises off him like the stench of barnyard animals packed together in summer heat. I think even the waitress feels it a little bit because I see gooseflesh bump up on her delicate skin where she has reached out to me, and her breath catches somewhere in her throat. She shakes it off though, smiles like a consummate professional, and moves to greet him. But I grab her arm, a little too hard, perhaps.

"Don't," is all I say, never taking my eyes off him. She's surprised, but her instincts must be good because she doesn't panic and she doesn't pull away from me. I look away from him only to gaze into her eyes. She looks back at me and understands on some level. She nods almost imperceptibly and gives me a crooked half-smile, pouring a little more coffee, her hand shaking just enough for the glass carafe to bang lightly against my ceramic cup. He's walking toward me, and I feel myself tensing up, trying to figure out the perfect math equation that's going to make this all go away.

I'm over-thinking, for sure.

He sits down at the counter, one stool away. I can reach out and touch him if I want to. Something about him reminds me of Lola, but I can't put my finger on what. He turns over his coffee cup on the saucer, silently soliciting service. The waitress, 'Pam,' according to her nametag, stands uncertainly in front of me. I nod at her lightly to go ahead and she slides the short distance over to him and wordlessly offers up the coffee. He shakes his head no and points to the decaf carafe, which has just finished brewing at the other end of the counter. Pam nods politely and fetches the decaf for him and dutifully pours. I wait as if balancing on the edge of a razor blade, unsure if one way or the other is better to fall, but certain that standing directly on the blade is no damn good. When she's done Pam's gaze flicks over to me briefly and then she retreats to the kitchen.

I'm racking my brain trying to figure out how to play this. The sound coming off of this guy is so intense it feels thick between us. I wonder, for a moment, if he can feel it too.

When the burning hot liquid hits me in the face I had no idea it was coming.

Where the hell my great senses were to avoid that I have no idea.

I don't know how much time has passed before I get myself back together, it can't have been long, but it feels like an eon. I've never been burned like that before and it's horrible, almost worse than the drowning. It feels like somehow my body is both dying and rebuilding itself at once. I don't remember screaming, but when I finally look up everything has gone to shit. I'm not where I should be if I fell off the stool, but I don't know why anyone would have moved me. It seems like things shouldn't be this bad if I was only out for a minute and it shouldn't have taken longer than a minute for me to get myself together after the boiling water. But then I feel my forehead.

I think he shot me in the head.

Sure enough, I look up at my reflection in the chrome of one of the stools and I can see the wound slowly healing itself, a raised red scar where the bullet must have entered and a smattering of blood on my face mixed with the grotesque, healing burned flesh. "Sonofabitch," I say to myself. I'm suddenly offended and pissed that he would just shoot me in the head. It seems very planned and I don't understand what that means. But there's enough screaming that I'm forced to turn my attention back to the chaos in the diner.

The man has moved away from me and, of course, because nothing is ever easy, he has the child in one hand and the child's mother literally under his boot. I don't know how long he's had them this way, but long enough that the diner is eerily absent of the child's screaming and he's turning a bit blue as he dangles from his own little hoodie sweatshirt.

There's a gun on the counter, which he must have used on me, but he also has some kind of automatic weapon. Looking at this man, paying closer attention to him, I realize that unlike the junkies I've dispatched in my past, or the petty thieves and thugs, and even the would-be rapists, this man is something different. There's something more deliberate and thus scarier about him. It doesn't feel as if I've just been called to the scene of something horrible. It feels like I was drawn here, deliberately. I shake off the paranoia look at my burned hands to see the flesh knitting itself back together again like magic skin. It doesn't feel good, and it looks terrifying. I get an idea.

At first I crouch a bit and cover my face, thinking he'll let me get a bit closer if he believes I'm badly injured. I motion to the man in the booth and the couple to stay down. I look directly at Pam and she grabs the cook by the front of his shirt and pulls him with her below the counter. The man is already screaming at me. I open up my arms as I walk toward him, so he can see my face knitting itself back together. This must be a horrifying enough sight on its own, but then I spread my arms wide. I am filling up the space with my whole being, trying to cover every inch of the space with my body. He becomes more insane with rage with every step I take. The child is looking very blue and the mother is now screaming despite the boot on her neck, screaming for the life of her child, for her own life, for fear of the man above her, and maybe even in fear of the scalded girl knitting herself back together and coming closer.

Eventually, the man will have to drop the boy in order to shoot that gun. There's no way he can manipulate that kind of weapon efficiently with one hand. As the child falls I think about dashing to catch him before he hits the ground and taking the gunman out after he's gotten off maybe one or two harmless shots. But in my delusions of heroic grandeur it's occurred to me that those one or two bullets could go anywhere and everywhere, ricocheting like they have minds of their own, injuring or killing wherever they land. It's better I stay where I am. The boy will survive the short fall to the ground, I'll draw the gunfire, and take out the gunman after a bullet or two land gently in my leg.

Well, that was the plan.

Instead the 'gunman' turns out to be an 'expert gunman.' When the first bullet hits me it feels not unlike the way the fire feels in my chest when I feel the bad sound, but times ten. I'm shocked. The second bullet feels less like fire and more like a razored spear. Three and four, cause tears to spill out from my eyes uncontrollably. Five rips at my throat and I scream. Or maybe that's the rest of the diners screaming. Six feels like it grazes my spine and seven feels like it lodges there. My legs feel funny after seven, but they continue to obey me. Fortunately for me, every shot he takes, he makes, so there's little to no ricocheting going on. Unfortunately for him, the more hits I take the angrier I get and no matter how many bullets I take – number eight gets me in the hand – I never stop moving towards him. Nine gets me in the left knee, which is excruciating, but by the time eleven gets me in the pelvis I'm close enough to put my bullet-ridden hand around the barrel of the gun. When I do this he stops and looks into my eyes, really looks into my eyes. I think he sees his own death right there, or at least a picture of how it is going to be for him when he's done, when the world is done with him.

I scream through my torn throat at him as I have never screamed in my life and I wrench the weapon away, flinging it with deadly accurate precision at the opposite wall. It buries itself nearly a foot into the concrete, sticking out of the wall like good modern art. He falls to his knees like he's going to beg for his pathetic existence. For the first time the mother is free and she scoops up her boy and dives behind the counter with him, shrieking the whole time. I push the gunman to the ground and crouch over him, my own blood pouring off of me in huge swathes. I crush his hand, breaking every bone he's got, ensuring that he will never again be picking up a gun. He curls up into a fetal position and I stand up to look at the diners.

"Is everyone okay?" I croak, my voice tearing as it tries to repair itself and bleed to death at the same damn time. Pam is the first to stand up.

"Um, yes," she says. The cook stands up next to her and nods, still in shock. The man in the booth raises his hand as if to agree and the couple in back, in tears of joy more than horror, I hope, cry out that they are both fine.

"The boy?" I croak again. Pam looks down behind the counter.

"He's going to be fine. He's breathing fine."

"And her?"

"She'll be okay."

"Good." I nod and look down at the man weeping at my feet holding his hand like a baby with a splinter. "Did someone call the police?"

Pam raises her hand almost guiltily. "I did," she says, swallowing hard.

"Good," I say again. I turn to leave and a small sound leaves Pam's throat.

"Um, what about him? What if he tries to get away?"

"Oh, don't worry about him. He's coming outside with me." Looks of confusion cross their faces. I grab the gunman by his foot, drag him outside, and with everyone watching me I fly up to the roof of the diner with the gunman in tow. Just imagining their faces brings a smile to mine. I guess, I've outed myself, but it feels kind of nice. On the roof, I hang him by his belt off the neon sign. He can't stay there forever, but the police are getting close and they can get him down easily enough, probably.

As I turn to go I see three men hovering in the shadows. Something feels off about them being there and I consider going over to explore the issue further, but just then the ambulance and police cars come hurtling around the corner and so instead I disappear into the lightening sky.

I don't know how long I fly – just savoring the incredible feeling of being up there, all alone, full of freedom – but when I crash back down to Earth (landing continues to be much more difficult than taking off) I find I'm in the alley behind Clark's apartment. I guess unconsciously he's who I most want to tell everything to. I sit down in the alley, aware that it's pretty disgusting on the ground, but my clothes are already shredded and filthy anyway. My once white t-shirt is now a muddy, old blood color, and riddled with bullet holes. The jeans and shoes aren't much better. My wounds have gone a long way toward healing while I flew around, but I decide to concentrate to see if I can finish up the process as I saw Lola do before. Sure enough, after a handful of minutes of focus I find the wounds disappearing. It's a shame I can't do the same for my clothing. After half an hour or so I'm as good as new, or as close as I can get. And all I want in the whole world is to see Clark.

●

I wake up naked in the bathtub in two inches of my own cold blood instead of water, my neck twisted painfully against the tile, my wrists healing nicely, pink scars all that's left of my savage cutting frenzy.

I should be happy to be waking up in my blood. It's what I figured would happen: it's what has happened every other time I've tried to kill myself, though, never so viciously before. Still, I should have expected it. But it's now I realize – not when I did it – that this time I really didn't want to wake up. That this wasn't yet another of my tests to see about adding to the, 'things that are awesome about being me' list, but rather a genuine suicide attempt. Not that I really thought it would work, but somewhere inside, I guess, I hoped it would. There's something extra-desperate about the fact that I can't even kill myself.

And that I've probably killed the only other person on Earth that maybe could have.

I drink some more and I don't slow down until everything looks blurry and watery.

I take my old cat suit out of the top drawer and rub it against my cheek. I pull it on and walk around the room a little bit trying to get some joy from it. But nothing comes. Liz's ear laughs at me from the chair in the corner. I can't really remember what it felt like to love the feel of the suit against my skin, to feel more powerful inside it. Now it just feels like ordinary material.

I climb into the bed and finish the rest of a bottle of Tequila, hoping it will be enough to knock me out. I'm both wishing and worried that Delia's going to show up again. I don't know why I've never seen her before now, why she would choose now to finally show herself. Maybe she just likes to see me unraveling. And I am.

Unraveling.

I can hear my henchmen whispering about it in the warehouse below me. I don't care. I'll kill them all if I have to. There's no limit to what I can do. There's nothing to be afraid of now that Liz has been taken from me.

I curl into my sheets with the bottle of Tequila and wait for Delia to reappear. Maybe she can hand me some magic key of destiny, the launch codes I've been missing all along. When I pull the bottle to my lips I notice it's empty and toss it at the ceiling fan. It breaks on the blades. Shards of glass rain down on me as I close my eyes.

Even before I'm asleep she's there. Looking like she did the day she died. The day I killed her. Drunk even before I poisoned her, wearing that beat-up old green robe, her blonde hair wild and unkempt, her fingers picking at our old threadbare couch. I hated that couch. She looks tired to me now. I didn't remember her looking that tired before. Lame, sure, but not so tired. Maybe it's just me that feels tired.

I decide I'm going to talk to her today, and she's going to answer me.

"Delia!" I scream, even though she's barely four feet away. She looks at me with lazy drunken eyes, annoyed but also humored by my loudness.

"Yes, Lo?"

"I want answers!" I scream again, pounding my fist onto a wooden side table so hard that it splinters into bits. Delia pushes deeper into her couch and pulls out a bottle of Jack, like it's a magic couch full of bottles, and hands it to me. The wallpaper behind her is covered with images of crows and wolves and eels. I don't remember it. It must be new.

"How about a drink instead?" she offers. I'm about to scream again, but a drink actually sounds pretty good and so I hunch up my shoulders like I don't really care and take the bottle from her.

We drink there, together, each from our own bottle, watching cartoons on the tiny television, laughing at all the same parts for what feels like hours. When I look up again the couch is empty. Someone's calling my name from outside the trailer. Have I always been in the trailer? I walk outside clumsily, shielding my eyes with one hand from the always-bright Nevada sun. Bonnie is standing there calling my name. I'm annoyed she's alive, but more annoyed that she's bothering me, and I'm also pretty convinced she's the reason my mother has disappeared.

"Stop bothering me!" I say to her, letting the door slam shut behind me. I go back inside but my mother is still gone. I take her place on the couch and work on finishing the bottle while the cartoons roll by. The entire time, Bonnie stays outside calling my name like a schoolyard bully taunting me 'LOLA...LOOOOOO LLLLLAAA.... LOLLLLLLAAA....' and I curse under my breath at her until my drink is gone. I search in the magic couch for another bottle, but apparently it's a trick only my mother can do because I come up with nothing but pennies and razor blades. I click off the cartoons and go back outside to shut Bonnie up, but when I step out of the trailer, it's no longer Nevada, it's the river where I drowned her – but she's nowhere to be seen. Below me is the water's edge and Bonnie's face swims just beneath the surface. She looks like a ghost, like a flat image projected under the surface, but when I poke at her watery face she is spongy and real. I draw back and blink, trying to erase her.

When I open my eyes again the fan is spinning above me, glass is sprinkled all over me like fine sugar, and Delia is sitting in a chair, legs crossed, doing a fine impression of Liz.

"You certainly haven't done much with my power, considering how badly you wanted it," she says, standing and walking across my room in her bare feet, crunching across the glass almost gracefully. My mother was never graceful.

"It's maybe true that I jumped the gun a little bit," I admit.

"A little bit? I was practically killing myself anyway, you couldn't just wait awhile, you little twit?"

"Yeah, well, I'm, like, progressive, or something." I say stubbornly.

"Hmm. I'd say it's more like sadistic."

"Oh...and you, you were a saint, I suppose? I mean, would it have killed you to give me a goddamn hug, or make me a freaking peanut butter sandwich?"

"I don't know, do you think you could hug someone right now? How about making me a peanut butter sandwich?" she asks, hands on her hips like the know-it-all she always was. I throw another bottle at her and she disappears. I walk into the kitchen defiantly and open the cupboard to make a peanut butter sandwich, but all the cupboards are filled with alcohol and broken glass. I scream at the top of my lungs and break at least ten bottles before collapsing on the floor, the minions' whispers drifting up into the loft like the incessant buzz of insects.

I don't want to dream of Delia again so I haven't slept in a day or two. I sit on the grungy bed sheets, Liz's ear placed delicately in the chair opposite me.

"You see," I say to the ear. "It's not my fault. Delia made me this way. Whatever power I got from her, it made me this way. There's something broken about it. It's not my fault I hurt people."

The ear sits quietly in judgment of me.

"You know, I don't have to talk to you," I say, crossing my arms over my chest and looking away. The ear is silent. It always wins these battles of will. It's so superior, just sitting there all soundless. "I don't even owe you an explanation," I say. "It's not like you can understand what I'm dealing with even if I do explain it to you."

Liz's ear plays its cards close to its chest and continues to say nothing.

"You know I can find someone else to talk to, right? You're totally replaceable," I say nonchalantly. I'm bluffing, but then I suddenly realize — as if a light bulb has clicked on over my head like a cartoon — that Liz's ear is replaceable. I sneak away from the ear and toward the loft stairs but realize I'm naked. Knuckles is standing at the bottom, mouth agape, his expression one that suggests he is considering gouging out his eyes before I do. I point at him and bellow, "Turn around!" He gulps audibly and faces the concrete wall. I run back to the bedroom and pull on the black cat suit. I yank my wild unwashed hair into a ponytail and put on a pair of green flip-flops. I look in the mirror and realize something is missing. I riffle through a duffel bag on the floor and pull out the first necklace I ever stole. It's huge and sparkly. I put it on and it shines, even in the dim, unnatural light. Perfect. I grab a never-before-used dusty ass phone book off the concrete floor and tear a few pages out. I stuff the pages down my suit and as I head back to the front door, Liz's ear asks me where I'm going.

"Uh, nowhere. Just out, gonna run some errands. You know, the usual, maybe pick up something to eat, you want anything?" I ask, trying to cover my tracks. The ear doesn't answer. "Okay then, see you later," I say gamely, waving and walking to the stairs with a considered casual air. Knuckles is still facing the wall. I walk past him without acknowledging him and head to the back parking lot. When I get there my bike is nowhere to be found. I spin around on the nearest guard. "Where's my bike!?" I scream. The guy's eyes are like plates.

"Your bike, boss?"

"Yes, my freaking motorcycle!"

"You uh – you never uh, had a motorcycle here, boss," he says, stepping sideways away from me as if he's going to make a run for it. I pin him against the building by his neck.

"Of course, I did. I've had that bike since I was 12!" I scream. His eyes are rolling back in his head and his tongue is lolling out. I don't know what he's trying to say but whatever it is he's wrong. And then I remember that I never did get my bike after I left LACMA. I had forgotten all about it once I got the stone. I slap my hand to my forehead and laugh. "Sorry. My bad," I say, dropping him to the ground. He gurgles and spits. A couple other henchmen look on in horror. I smile at them and take off into the sky. My flip-flops fall off almost immediately. Once in the sky, I take out one of the phonebook pages and flatten out the crinkles as best I can. The closest address is for a 'Stern, Oscar, PhD.

Dr. Stern's office is in a new strip-mall and there's only a few other spaces rented out. A Starbucks at the opposite end, a clothing store of some kind in the middle, and a copy and ship place next to the Starbucks. There are only six cars in the entire parking lot, including one in front of Stern's office. I set down in the alley behind the strip mall and adjust my cat suit before pushing through the door and into the air-conditioned space. A little bell chimes when I come in and a voice calls out somewhere from the back. "Hello? One minute please-" it says. There's the shuffle of papers, the clicking sound of a filing cabinet closing. and a middle-aged, slightly soft looking gentleman in a white button-down shirt emerges from the back. I can see confusion in his face, but he covers. "Well, hello. I'm Dr. Stern. Is there, something I can do for you?" he reaches his hand out and I shake it, uninterested.

"Lola," I say, distracted. I'm too busy looking at his ears to pay attention to much else.

"Lola. Okay, what can I do for you?" he asks, standing awkwardly in his own reception area. I gesture to his office and he nods. "Of course, of course, have a seat," he says, motioning me into his office. "I have to warn you," he begins, following me inside, but leaving the door open. "It's after my regular office hours, I must have forgotten to lock the front door," he adds, looking back at it good-naturedly. "But, what can I do for you, would you like me to schedule an appointment for you at some other time?"

"No," I say. "Now's fine."

"Well, I'm sorry Lola, but I'm not really open now-"

"It's alright. I just need your ear," I say, staring at his right ear like it's on the menu.

"Excuse me?" he says, standing up from his chair. "I think maybe you should go. If you'd like to come back during my regular office hours, we can talk then."

"And I need your ear," I say. He walks past me towards the door.

"I don't even know what that means, but it's time for you to go," he says, getting nervous. As he passes my chair I jump onto his back. He screams. I grab his right ear and yank it off. He falls to the ground in a lump. It's so quick even I can't believe it. He's not actually dead, just passed out, though if he doesn't wake up soon he's going to die from blood loss. I take a tissue from the box on his desk and clean off the ear. I put it in the little breast pocket inside the cat suit and walk out the door. There's still only six cars in the parking lot and nothing has changed and the whole thing took less than five minutes. That fish in barrels thing really is a saying for a reason, I guess.

Back at the loft the new ear won't talk to me and Liz's ear laughs at me for thinking I can do better than it.

I leave Mr. Stern's ear in an old pizza box after unsuccessfully ranting at it for twenty minutes with no response.

o

I wait across the street from Clark's apartment for over an hour just watching the dark windows. He's not there. It's so late, nearly two in the morning, and so my mind races. Wondering where he could be. Pangs of jealousy and insecurity assail me. When I finally see him come up the street, my heart skips a beat for sure and I step back into the shadows around me and lean against the stone of a building as if it alone can keep me upright. Is it possible I've already forgotten a little bit how handsome he is, how much I love him, how much he once looked like he was wearing my future, like in looking at him was the only way I could even imagine a future worth having? He jogs up the stairs, a book under his arm and a late night coffee in his hand. He disappears into the building. I watch the windows from the street and feel both comforted and tortured watching his routine, everything the same, except no me. He opens the window near the kitchen since it catches the best breeze. He washes his hands in the kitchen sink, drying them on a green towel that hangs on the stove.

I close my eyes and can almost see him pulling off his sneakers with his feet and tripping over them as he flops into his favorite chair, the leather one by the window.

I take a breath and step out of the shadow to cross the street, but curse and step back. I shouldn't drag him back into my mess, but I can't help it.

Love is stupid, I suppose.

A neighbor is going into the building and holds the door open for me, perhaps recognizing me. He does a double take at my appearance, but like a true New Yorker minds his own business. With surprise I realize it's only been a few weeks since I left him.

It feels like so much longer.

So much has happened.

I stand outside Clark's apartment door for another ten minutes trying to gear up the courage to knock, wondering how it's possible that being in front of his door was completely common not so long ago and now it seems like a different reality entirely — one that I ache for but am also somehow simultaneously glad to have put away, it feels good at least to be honest in my life, about who and what I am. But that honesty doesn't make me yearn for him any less. I listen to his breathing through the door, to his sighs and movements, the scratching of his temple with his left hand the way he does when he finds something funny or perplexing. I can hear Joan jumping around on the hardwood, playing with shoelaces or toys or dust in the air, mewing happily. Clark says 'no' to her twice, gently, and I can hear him trying not to smile in the word. I knock softly, breaking the spell of happiness that is just listening to them.

"Coming," Clark says through the door. I feel the heat of him through the door and inhale sharply. The lock and chain tremble as they come shooting off and he flings the door open as if afraid I'll disappear. I have this whole sentence prepared in my head, this whole thing I'm planning to say, but he moves so quickly pulling me into him that I don't even have a chance to start. He kisses me and I can't do anything but kiss him back, fall into him and everything he stands for. I don't want to mislead him, but I can feel that he doesn't care about any of that, and suddenly neither do I.

We're a tangle of arms and legs all the way to the bedroom – hands pulling at zippers and buttons, flashes of flesh being exposed in fits and starts. One of us manages to push little Joan away with a sock-covered foot long enough for the other to shut the bedroom door. Clark reaches to pull off my t-shirt and suddenly realizes it's covered in blood and bullet holes. He pauses momentarily and my mouth is still open, waiting for a kiss.

"Um, are you okay?" he asks, looking me up and down and really seeing the horror of my clothing for the first time.

"Uh, yeah. It's not my blood, well, not all of it," I stammer.

"Oh, okay, good," he says, before kissing me again. We fall together onto the bed and it's like he's devouring me, and I wonder how it can feel so wonderful to be devoured.

Afterward, we lay together, his body against mine, the flush of our hot skin pressing together, fitting perfectly, like the puzzle pieces I never quite believed in. I whisper to him. "You know I can't come back, right?"

"Yes," he breathes into my neck and hair, barely audible. Maybe audible to only me.

"But you know I love you more than anything, right?" I half ask.

"Yes," he breathes again. I turn around to face him, making our puzzle-piece bodies fit together differently, even more perfectly. His eyes look different than I remember. "You look different," he says, kissing me before and after the words.

"So do you," I say.

"A lot has happened," he says. I smile, not knowing if he means for me or for him or for the world, and not caring.

"Yes," is all I say. I fall asleep there with him, not for long, just long enough to remember how delicious it is. I have a small, sharp dream of my mother. It's unlike dreams I have had before. This one is insistent and pressing, fast and blunt. She says only five words and it feels like a vision beamed into my head more than a dream. I sit straight up, startling Clark, who had drifted off too.

"What is it?" he asks, looking around the room as if there is something with us.

"I just had a dream, or something," I say, pivoting my legs off the bed and plunking my feet on the floor, his warm arm falling away from my hip. I reach for my t-shirt and remember it's a mess. I go to my old drawer – which is blissfully still full of my clothes – and pull out new jeans and a t-shirt.

"What was the dream?" he asks, sitting up and rubbing his eyes, reaching for his glasses on the table.

"It was my mother, she said…'The Book. Get The Book'."

"What does that mean?" Clark asks, as confused as me.

"I don't know, but I have to go. I have to ask someone that might know." I pull on the jeans and look for a spare pair of sneakers in his closet while Clark pulls on sweatpants and half hops to the bedroom door. Joan comes diving into the room as the door slides open and she dodges past Clark's feet and runs to me. I like to think she remembers me, but she's probably just curious. I reach down and pick her up, nuzzling her in the crook of my neck. She swats my nose.

Clark comes back in the room and turns on the television. On the news is the report of my diner rescue. He points to the television with the remote still in his hand.

"This is you, isn't it?" he asks, sitting next to me on the bed. "They've been running it over and over."

"Yes," I say, trying to own it, to be unwavering.

"I'm really proud of you," he says, pulling his eyes from the flickering screen and looking into mine.

"Thanks," I say back, smiling hugely. It feels nice to be recognized and supported, for him to be proud of me for something I'm made to do, as opposed to all the things I've tried to make myself be good at.

"Are you sure you can't do this and also stay with me?" he asks genuinely. The idea is so tempting I can taste the edges of it in the corners of my mouth.

"It's not so simple. There's this girl," I begin.

"Yes?" he prompts.

"Well, she's like me. But she's all bad where I'm good, and she just, well, nothing gets in her way and she would come through you like tissue paper if she knew what you mean to me. She," my voice breaks. "She killed my very good friend right in front of me. So she can't know. And the only way to be sure she doesn't know is for me to not have you at all."

"Where is she? How will she know?" He wants the answers to be different, and so do I.

"I don't know where she is," I say, and Clark starts to protest but I cut him off. "It doesn't matter where she is, she can be here so fast, you can't believe it. When I fought her before, she realized she could slow me down by hurting civilians and so she just started grabbing people from a bus and throwing them into the air like they were balls to be juggled. And I didn't even know those people. Imagine what she might do to someone I love. I don't have to imagine it, I've already seen it," I say, remembering Bryce's beautiful face still in my hands. I pet Joan and Clark is silent for a moment.

"People on a bus?" he says to the room more than me. "That thing, a week ago, uptown, that was you and her?"

"Yes. She killed me. Drowned me actually, in the Hudson. I woke up later on the riverbank. I'd lost most of my memory. I didn't remember about her, I didn't remember anything, but when I used my powers it all came back," I say. Clark nods again. There's another long pause between us. We're pausing a lot. It's hard to find safe things to say to one another.

"So, what will you do? You'll just spend your whole life not having anyone you love so that this girl won't hurt them?" he asks. I shrug hopelessly.

"Maybe. I have to think of what to do about her. I doubt she'll leave me alone, maybe she'll kill me again. I don't know. I haven't figured it out yet. I'm going to find my brother, he's my best hope of finding whatever this book is," I say, realizing how lame it sounds as I say it. Clark is quiet for long minutes before he speaks again.

"Well, if you haven't figured it out yet, maybe there's still a chance for us." I don't correct him, but I should. He shouldn't spend his life waiting, hoping, for me to come back. But I'm selfish just like anyone and the idea that he might wait for me is like some kind of perfect treasure that I can lock away inside. It's too precious not to cling to, and so I don't say anything. I just kiss him and we lay together with Joan playing over us and under us and in between us until I can't bear it and know I'll never leave if I don't go right now. I get up and finish dressing. In the living room I notice that there are newspapers and sheets of printed-paper strewn all over the room, articles and printouts pinned up on the walls. It looks a bit like a crazy person lives here. There's also no trace of Jake or Ryan, I wonder briefly if they left because Clark seems like he went nuts, or because Clark wanted to be alone the same way that I did. I walk over and look at some of the articles and headlines. They're all about me, some of them are highlighted and circled, and little notes are scratched on the side.

It turns out everyone is a better detective than me.

I look back toward the bedroom and Clark is leaning in the doorway.

"You figured it out even before I told you?"

He shrugs and smiles his boyish smile. "I'm no dummy. Once the thing on the train happened, it was pretty easy to go back and remember things about our life that never quite made sense. And once I thought it – well, it just sounded right. There was always something special about you. I knew it from the first time I laid eyes on you." He looks at me intently and I wonder if he's going to say it. "And it wasn't in the bookstore. You're the one that saved me from getting hit by the train." He pauses. "Aren't you?" I nod silently and look back at him, my eyes wet. "Thank you for saving me," he says simply.

"You're welcome," I say, a smile spreading slowly across my face.

"Besides," he says, walking over and pulling one of the articles down and looking at it intently. "The girl I loved had disappeared. I wasn't going to just go back about my business," he says. We're quiet for a long, peaceful moment, him watching me, me staring at a room wallpapered with the good I've done. It's a great gift he's given me and he probably doesn't even realize it. He walks over to me and holds me for a long time. I break the embrace because I have to. It feels like cutting off a limb.

"Her name is Lola," I say quietly as I pull away. "The girl's name is Lola. and I don't mean to scare you off blondes, but she's a blonde, tall, almost my height, very slender, long legs, icy blue eyes.

If you see anyone like that trying to get close to you…well, don't let them, okay?"

"Sure, sure," he says lightly. "No leggy, blue-eyed blondes. You couldn't have picked something easier?"

"No, I'm afraid leggy blondes are off the menu for the foreseeable future," I say, smiling playfully, grateful for this strange, perfect moment of normal. I kiss him a last time on his warm mouth and duck out the door before either of us can say anything else sad and horrible.

On the roof of Clark's apartment building I sit cross-legged with the stone in my right hand and concentrate until I feel like my brain is about to explode through my ears.

Eventually, I feel the stone leeching my power away and I almost break contact because it feels like it should be wrong for it to take from me, but something about it also feels natural and so I follow my instincts and stick with it. At first all I see is this bright beating dot, like a heartbeat, and then I see a much smaller one, at least ten times fainter, almost unnoticeable. I ignore it for the time being and focus on the larger beat and suddenly, even though my eyes are closed, I see Lola before me. My eyes snap open in alarm but when I look around it's just the New York skyline and the rooftop. I glance around anxiously and close my eyes again. The image is wavering and gauzy, as if projected onto a watery surface. Lola is sitting in a dark room, staring at a blank wall. Her face is a mask I don't understand except that it reminds me a little bit of myself. I yank back, away from her slightly to try to pinpoint where the room is. It's somewhere on the west coast, Los Angeles, somewhere in downtown L.A. by the looks of the big buildings. I pull myself back even farther and look again for the smaller dot. Once I lock onto it, I reach out and pull toward it with all my strength, and with a snap I find myself staring at a flickery image of Jasper. He's bent over a book, studying intently. I look around his living room and then pull back until I'm outside. It's the same house from when I tried to visit, last June.

I stare at the stone. As I relax I feel my energy and strength pouring back into me.

So, the stone can find Jasper and Lola. Surely the stone is how Lola first found me, otherwise she would have come back once she realized I wasn't dead in the river. What do the three of us have in common? The question boggles my mind as the

immediate answer seems like nothing. Unless. Does Jasper have
superpowers? No, surely not. Surely, I would know, surely I would
have sensed something when I saw him. I wrack my brain. What
do Jasper and I have in common? Parents. Dead parents. Blood.
  Oh.
  Blood.
  What if we share blood with Lola? Could she be related to
me? To us? My mind reels with the possibilities. I have to find the
book. I push it all away from me and stand up. I brush myself off
and look around before taking to the air at a speed that I hope will
avoid any curious onlookers. I have to admit, puzzles, nightmares,
and Lola the serial killer be damned, the flying is freaking fantastic.
I don't know if I'll ever get used to the freedom of it. It's so
glorious that I curse the years I wasted not knowing I was capable
of it. I fly toward Jasper, toward the beating of his heart, which I
can now feel almost in time with my own.

●

  I go out and take four more therapists' cars in a desperate
attempt to find a less judgey replacement. I only stop because
they're all stupid and won't talk back to me. I leave them with Dr.
Stern's ear in the old pizza box and go back to fighting it out with
Liz's ear.
  Every fight ends with broken bottles and suicide attempts.
  I waver between trying to drink myself to death and bathing
in hallucinations, or dreams, I can't tell which. Sometimes it's
Delia, sometimes it's Bonnie. Once it was even Adrian. Adrian
driving in a red car, fast across a blank desert highway, singing along
to the radio and smiling his lopsided smile. I try to talk to him and
then I'm even sitting in the car next to him, trying to see if he'll say
words back to me, but he can't hear me, or doesn't want to. I
finally give up and content myself with sitting next to him, my hand
close to his thigh, the wind blowing my hair back. It feels like so
long ago that I could have enjoyed something so simple. When I
turn to ask him another question he's pointing a gun at me and
shoots me in the stomach without saying a word.
  I wake up on the floor with a bit of glass jammed in my
neck.

I'm a little surprised actually, that I'm able to heal with the glass still in my neck. I had jammed it in there and left it there on purpose, half-hoping I wouldn't wake up.

But, here I am.

I pull the glass out of my neck and blood blooms across my skin. I grab the closest thing, which turns out to be my cat suit, and press it on the wound to slow the bleeding. The cheap material does a crap job but it's better than nothing. My body is saturated with alcohol and that, combined with the loss of blood, has the room swimming. I lie down on the floor, still holding the cat suit to my neck and reach for another bottle. They're all empty though. I hear the henchmen chattering through the floor; they're all freaked out. They wonder, if I killed Liz who might be next. It unnerves them. They're also getting restless; I don't send them out on enough missions, and though they're all about as rich as any normal person could ever want to be, they've begun to doubt that I have a master plan. I'd take offense – because I totally do, like, have a plan – but even I know I'm stalling. I close my eyes for a moment and when I open them Bonnie is standing over me. Crows fill the room behind her, throwing their shadows onto the walls like magicians. I blink hard twice and she doesn't go away.

"Hello Lola," she says, smiling. "Nice to see you again." I open my mouth to speak but she crouches down and puts a finger on my lips. "Don't worry. I'm going to take care of everything," she says. "Just let go and I'll take care of everything." I close my eyes and push the black fabric closer to my throat. Some part of me inside is incredibly relieved. When I open them again she's bringing a sledgehammer straight down toward my head.

O

I stand outside Jasper's door for fifteen minutes before I can will myself to knock. I'm in such a hurry, yet I feel like a little kid, rooted to the ground, unable to move. When I finally knock it sounds hollow and sad. I try to smooth out my lame t-shirt and jeans combo. I shouldn't be worried about making a good impression considering what's going on right now but I almost step back off the porch and onto the dirt and grass, and seriously consider running for it. The door opens and seeing Jasper standing in the doorway is like seeing my father as he was the day he died. He looks glorious and I'm afraid touching him will cause him to vanish. I forget all about my stupid clothing. He steps out onto the porch, and then onto the grass a few feet in front of me. He breaks into a smile and I see we have the same smile. I'd forgotten about that. I mirror him, unable to contain my joy at just seeing him, even though we both know the situation is as awkward as it can get. I'm about to speak, but he goes first.

"I was expecting you much sooner," he says.

"I came once before," I say. He's surprised. "I watched you teach some kids for a little while, but I-" I don't know what to say. "I'm sorry," is all I can come up with.

"If anyone has things to say sorry for, I'm pretty sure it's me," he says.

"We both know that isn't true," I say, staring at the concrete steps. There's an awkward silence between us, the kind of silence that had we been a different brother and sister, might be warm. But we're not that brother and sister; we've been robbed of that relationship, and we look at our shoes and kick at the dirt as if to prove it. I break first, which is still a pretty new development for me. "Did mom leave anything for me?"

"She did. I have them inside," he says. I'm startled by the ease at which I'm answered, as if I expect to negotiate a maze and defeat a Minotaur in order to receive my prize.

"Can I see it, or them, whatever?"

"Yeah, yeah, sure," Jasper says, stepping inside the house and motioning for me to follow. "Come in, Bonnie." It's the first time I've heard him say my name in almost thirteen years. It sounds unimaginably lovely. I choke out a pathetic response.

"Okay." It's funny to be eighteen years old and have superpowers and still wish that your older brother would pick you up and hold you and protect you forever. He's just as I remember him: still strong, but vulnerable, with kindness pooling in his eyes. He's always been, and is now, an eccentric blend of both my mother and my father, while I remain so singularly my mother's, that it's painful to me. I've come to accept this, but I ache to have something of my father in me as well – like the things I can see in Jasper, the way he moves and clears his throat, his eyes and skin – all my father. It's like some kind of schizophrenia to stand next to both of these men I loved tied up into one person, and yet feel emotionally as if Jasper and I are still miles apart, forever separated by that horrible day on the road.

I survey his living room. It's nice and comfortable, but somewhat Spartan, a trait I suspect we share more from growing up in group homes and less because of our shared blood. Jasper walks me into a small home office of sorts and moves a box out of a deep closet. Behind the box is an old trunk I recognize instantly. He drags it out along with several dozen actual bunny-sized dust bunnies.

I remember the trunk. It had lived in my parents' bedroom at the foot of the bed, though I'd never seen it open, or even unlocked. Jasper pulls a silver chain out from under his t-shirt with some keys on it. I recognize the chain as one my mother had worn all her life, including the day she died. I finger the ID bracelet in my pocket and take it out to show it to him. Jasper raises his eyebrows at me. "I'd forgotten about that bracelet. I'm glad you've had it," he says, bending down toward the trunk with one of the keys from the chain around his neck.

"You keep that on you always?" I ask. Jasper nods.

"Ever since I looked inside the trunk," he says. I swallow hard. He's looked inside. I can't help but wonder now what he knows, about me, about our mother. I envy him the knowledge. Jasper looks away from me. He hesitates when putting the key in the lock. "I, I'm sorry I didn't come get you, especially after looking in the trunk, but I…" he pauses, uncomfortable. "I had a few bad years. It took me awhile to get myself together, and by then I couldn't find you. You were like a ghost – your trail vanishing the day you left the home. Eventually, I had to just believe that you'd find me, and here you are." He looks up at me, and my eyes are threatening to spill over with tears but I blink them back. He clears his throat and starts again. "I barely understand a fraction of what's in here, but I hope it makes more sense to you." He turns the key and opens the lid. I realize I've been holding my breath, unsure what to expect. Some part of me seems to expect my mother's ghost to materialize out of the ancient trunk smell. Instead, the first thing I see is a big leather-bound book, at least twelve inches by twenty inches and massively thick. I kneel down and touch it to make sure it won't vanish. Laying on top of the book are several pieces of old jewelry and next to the book, the knee-high leather boots that my mother had always worn. I finger

the old, coffee-colored leather of the boots. "You remember
them?" Jasper asks. I look up, my eyes wet.

"She wore them always, or at least that's what I remember."
Jasper nods in agreement.

"She did. All the time," he says, rolling his eyes like an
embarrassed teenager. I pull them out of the trunk and onto my
feet. Despite their age they're in excellent shape, and fit as if
they've been made for me. I stand up in them, feeling taller and
stronger already. Jasper's breath catches in his throat. "Jesus. You
look so much like her," he says. I smile.

"Thanks," I say. Jasper stands up.

"Okay, well, I'll um, leave you alone. Just let me know if
you need anything." Despite my desperation to be near him, to
understand him, and to have him understand me, I'm grateful to be
alone with the trunk, with my trunk. My mother's giant silver and
red ring sits on top of the book, and I put it on the middle finger of
my left hand, where she had always worn it. I clutch my fingers
together into a fist and feel the power coursing through my whole
being. There's nothing magical about the ring, except that it was
hers. There's a necklace too, a long silver chain with a charm. I put
it in my pocket along with other jewelry I don't recognize: two
more rings one with a blue stone – much older and likely more
valuable than the red one, and a simple silver band. There's a small
stack of pictures tied with a pink ribbon, and a stack of letters
addressed to my mother tied with a black ribbon, and it's all so
delicious and inviting – but the book is the thing. I can love the
boots desperately, and yearn to spend days poring over pictures and
letters, but I still know the book is the thing. I feel pulled to it, not
unlike how I feel about the stone, which is practically humming in
my pocket right now. As I reach for the book I see that there's
something else in the trunk.

It's the other piece of the broken stone. I reach for it and
realize it, not the book, was what was calling to me. I take the
smaller broken piece and match it up with the larger stone in my
pocket.

It fuses together instantly and the power of the whole stone
nearly knocks me backward. The energy surging from it is
intoxicating.

"Unbelievable," I breathe, marveling at the impossible
happening before my eyes and in my own hand. I clutch the stone

tightly and put it in my pocket, turning my attention back to the book. While the stone is obviously what calls to me, the rational part of my brain still knows that the book will hold the answers I need.

The thick leather cover creaks as I pull it open. The first page is delicate and feels like dried butterfly wings. Across the top in large and elaborate calligraphy is only the word BRAVERMAN. The pages are brittle and I pull them forward with all the gentleness I can find in myself. There are pages and pages of text, filled top to bottom, in dozens of different hands – I assume dozens of my ancestors. I flip forward and am taken aback when I see my mother's handwriting – lovely and looping cursive, beautiful but concise. She used to write me notes on the napkin that she put in my lunches, I had forgotten all about them. I shake myself out of the memory and stare at the pages – I'll be able to learn so much about her – all the things I'm supposed to know. I want to hunker down and drown myself in the whole book from beginning to end, but I don't have that kind of time. Not now. I thumb toward the back, to where my pages should be, and I find an envelope with my name on it. It's my mother's handwriting again. I open the envelope and pull out the delicate sheets of paper. It's dated the day she died. Her words flow over me like water breaking on stones.

Bonnie

I'm so sorry I had to leave you so early. I had hoped we'd have more time together. Here are the things I would have told you, had we had the chance.

As you've probably figured out by now, you're a little bit different, like I was, and like your grandmother and great-grandmothers before you. We come from a very long line of powerful Braverman women. And there are others – women we call our Others – they are from the LeFever line and have been around as long as we have. They're like us, connected to us somehow, almost like the opposite of us. It's hard to explain, and I don't understand it all. Most of the written history has been lost over the years. and much of it destroyed when we emigrated to America, as I understand it. But your Other, if you don't already know, is Lola LeFever, the daughter of Delia LeFever, and I'm sorry to say that from what I know of Delia…and even from what I know of you, she's probably a very strong one. We're always a little different, but always much the same, and our strength always seems pretty proportionate to our Other's strength. And you, you're something special and if you are, so must

Lola be. You see I wasn't much, I was pretty quiet and my other, Delia, who you may know about by now, she was pretty quiet too. We almost even became friends in a way. I was selfish. I wasn't good at being who I was supposed to be. I led a quiet life, even before I fell in love with your father, but after that, well, I was just selfish. I couldn't give him up. We had Jasper almost right away and I felt guilty for years, sure that I was not doing what I was supposed to be doing, not being who I was supposed to be. Out of guilt I attempted to make things better by reaching out to Delia, seeing if we could come to some agreement. We did, and as far as I know she's kept her end of the deal, she did for the first seven years at least, I'll have to trust her that she honors it when I'm gone.

But you see, I didn't feel guilty anymore once I was pregnant with you. Because — I knew that you were what I was supposed to do with my life. That you were going to be better and stronger and more important than I had ever been, and that made my selfishness really its own kind of destiny. I was merely a vessel — a way for you to come into the world. I knew what you were going to be was important from the first time I felt you inside of me. And you were everything I had imagined.

Destiny doesn't always come when it's convenient or when you think it should. It comes when you're ready, whether you know it or not.

I know you've struggled, but that's how it is when you have exceptional power…the road is harder I think. I'm sure you won't even remember the little things you did when you were young. You were the strength and power and goodness I didn't know that a child, even a Braverman child, could be. You were beyond me before you even took breath.

So, here's what you should know. You can fly. If you haven't tried it already then do it right now because it is the single greatest gift we're given…although perhaps that's just my personal opinion, since I was never much for all the fighting.

We're incredibly strong and fast, and can heal just about any wound. When you're getting really good at being you, you can heal at will and speed your healing, and even make yourself invulnerable in a variety of ways. We cannot be killed. I drowned once when I was seventeen, and woke up safely on the beach four days later — it was the most amazing thing — though avoid it if you can, it was a particularly unpleasant experience. We've also got great internal radar. Trust it, as it can put you where you need to be when you need to be there.

And the symbol. There's a powerful stone that can increase your powers, certainly enough to give you an edge, it makes it possible to locate your Other, or anyone connected to us by blood, no matter where they are. There's a small broken piece of the symbol in the trunk. The LeFevers do not know we have it, haven't known for centuries. The other piece was lost by Delia in our last battle together in Los Angeles, when we nearly brought down a mountain and afterward agreed to make peace. Because of our agreement we both allowed the stone to remain lost. This was a bit disingenuous of me since I still had a small piece of the stone, but I had no intentions of using it unless Delia broke our arrangement. If you need it – if things are desperate and you can find the other piece, making the stone whole again will make it more powerful than ever. The stone will also allow you to read your Other's mind when you're in close proximity. It's how I knew that ultimately Delia didn't want to fight anymore. But here's something the LeFevers have never figured out about the symbol, and you will not find it written anywhere, in fact, I take a great chance writing it here, and you should destroy this letter once you've read it…but I believe in this case the risk is necessary. The power is not in the actual stone, but in the symbol. Do you understand?

And this brings us to the last thing – how we die. First you should know that when we're pregnant with our daughters, the next Braverman, we're at our strongest, even more powerful and impossible to kill than usual; nature's way I guess of protecting the next in the line, but once she's born, the power mostly leaves us. It's not like it goes away entirely…our instincts are still sharp and we are always faster and stronger than anyone else. But there's no more lifting cars and jumping buildings, or flying. And we become vulnerable in a way we have never been before - vulnerable to things like bullets, car crashes, and long falls.

And when we die, the full measure of the power passes to our daughter.

And here's the most important thing for you to know. The dying has nothing to do with you. You can't do anything to stop it. And it happens whether or not you do everything wrong or everything right.

So you have to forgive yourself for becoming something amazing once I died. It's not your fault; it never was and never will be; it was nothing you did; it is just your very existence, which is both necessary and beautiful, so you can't be feeling regret about that.

Let the guilt go and be the amazing woman I've always known you would become.

I love you.
Mom

I wipe tears off of the letter, afraid I'll smear her words, almost all I have of her. A wave of relief passes over me that is almost as powerful as the sadness, relief that she has left words that unburden me finally of that day on the road, when they died and I lived. I don't think I knew until just now how heavy those burdens had been to carry. I feel like a new woman – the woman my mother believed I would become.

I close my eyes and set the book aside. The stack of letters are addressed to my mother, from Delia LeFever. I pull one at random from the stack and read it.

Scarlett

You're right about why I agreed to this shit plan of yours – it's for Lola. By the time I was born my mother Aveline was crazy as a shithouse rat. Maybe she was always like that, but I doubt it. You know as well as I do what this life does to us. Maybe part of me needs to believe that she didn't start out like that. Her battles with your mother Jean couldn't have helped. She was a terrible mother to me, and I hated her. But waiting for Lola to be born, I have to say, I hate Aveline less. I understand her and her pain a lot more than I ever thought I would. I already love Lola, but I also catch myself resenting her, maybe hating her a little too. Does this happen to you with Bonnie? Probably not, you and all your goddamn "goodness", it probably never even occurs to you. But really, you're telling me the first time you wanted to fly away from everything and found you couldn't...you didn't resent Bonnie just a little bit? For holding all your power in her tiny, useless hands? Again, you and yours and all your goodness probably prevents it from even occurring to you...bitches.

I've been staying awake nights lately, wondering about that actually – why you and yours got the good deal and me and mine got such a bad one. You ever think about that?

Delia

ps. I do love her, Scarlett. Love being such a foreign concept to me, it's pretty hard to miss it when I feel it. I feel it for her. She may be the only thing I've ever loved. Time will tell if I can show it better than it's been shown to me.

I lock the trunk back up, though I don't know why as I'm taking the contents with me – the book, letters, and photographs under my arm, the boots on my feet, the jewelry in my pocket and on my finger. When I walk into the kitchen, Jasper is sitting drinking tea. I sit across from him.

"You want some tea?" he asks, gesturing to his cup.

"I'd love some, but I have to go," I say. "There's some stuff I have to do. There's this girl-"

"Delia's daughter, Lola. She's after you?" he asks, concerned.

"Yes, well, sort of. She killed me once already. I don't know if she's coming back. The book's going to help – thank you so much for taking care of it."

"Of course," he says and then after a pause. "She killed you?"

"Oh yeah, she handed me my ass, and then drowned me about half a dozen times."

"Jeezus."

"Yeah. Totally." I lay the silver chain with the keys on the table.

"The trunk's yours too – you keep it," he says.

"Will you hold onto it for me? I'll be back for it."

"So, you're going to come back?"

"Of course. You're my brother."

"I just thought, you know, I figured you blamed me for not coming to get you when I turned eighteen."

"You were just a kid."

"But I should have come anyway."

"I wouldn't have."

"Yes you would," he says. I pause and smile.

"Agree to disagree?" I ask gamely, holding out my hand.

"Sure," he says, reaching out and shaking my hand, as if making a sibling pact. I push the chain with the keys towards him. He shakes his head. "Oh, you should keep the chain and keys, and there's more, I mean, it's not like the book, it's not important to um, what you are or can do, but-" Jasper wrinkles up his mouth unsure and stumbling over how to define me. It's like he's trying to not offend me, but to simultaneously acknowledge that he gets that I have some stuff going on that the average eighteen year old doesn't. It's sweet. It feels like what a regular brother would do.

"What is it?" I ask.

"Well, there's some money, not a lot, not life-changing money or anything, but it could help you, y'know, go to school, or travel, or settle down or something. I used mine for school, but there are no restrictions on it or anything. There's also a small beach house and some land in Maine."

"Maine?" I say, my ears perking up at the sound of the word.

"Yeah, it was passed down to mom from Grandma Jean I think...we went there a few times when you were really little, do you remember?" he asks.

"I remember," I say. I have a home. A home that wants me.

"Well, it's yours," he says, smiling.

"Isn't it ours?" I ask.

"No. They left me the house in Pennsylvania, which, I hope you don't mind, but I sold. I just, it was too painful to be there," he explains, eyes downcast. There's a little pinch inside me about never getting to see the yellow kitchen I keep thinking I remember, but I had never imagined that the house was still ours anyway, and so the pinch passes quickly.

"I understand," I say. We both must look pathetically sad sitting at Jasper's kitchen table, heads bowed, remembering our dead parents and wishing for the years we missed with each other. Jasper speaks up, breaking the melancholy.

"So, the long silver key is the trunk, that little one is for a deposit box in Philadelphia, and the two others go to the beach house," Jasper reaches behind him to a kitchen drawer and pulls out a thick white envelope and hands it to me. "The deed and everything you need is in there." I peek inside the flap and then put it with the pictures and letters on top of the book. He stands up suddenly from the table and leaves the room. I sit quietly for a full minute and am about to call out to him when he comes back into the room with a small duffel bag. "Here, take this. Put the book and all that stuff in there so it doesn't get damaged or anything," he says responsibly, kind of like an older brother should sound. I smile up at him and take the bag, filling it with the book, letter, pictures, jewelry, deed, and my old sneakers. I put the keys in my jeans pocket.

"Thanks," I say. "For everything."

"Do you really have to go?" he asks, seeming hopeful.

"Yeah," I say, smiling. "But I'll be back." I stand up from the table and he does the same. Just as I'm about to swing the duffle over my shoulder and walk away, he reaches out and embraces me. It's more powerful than I could have imagined. Sloppy tears fall out of my eyes and onto his t-shirt. He releases his grip slightly and we separate. I can't wait to come back. I hope I get the chance to.

●

The sledgehammer never comes down though. There's no Bonnie, there's no sledgehammer. There's nothing. It's just me, my bloody cat suit pressed to my neck and an ugly red raised scar where I'd pulled out the glass earlier. I breathe deeply a few times, my heart still caught in my throat, before reaching into the covers behind me for another bottle. I drain half of it before I feel steady enough to stand.

I stumble-walk into the bedroom to look for Scarlett's letters, to read them for the thousandth time, to try to imagine who she was, who Bonnie was, who Delia was. I don't really know how much longer I can go on like this, afraid of all the ghosts, killing a body that won't be killed.

Delia comes to me again, dancing around in her old green robe. She's a bad dancer.

"That's because you never saw me with power, my dear," the Delia vision says to me.

"I'm sure it didn't look much different," I mumble.

"Well, I never started drinking until you came along and took away everything that was amazing about me," she says with a little smirk.

"Yeah, right," I say, not believing a word.

"Really. You think you're so great and powerful, but I never touched that stuff you're failing to kill yourself with until I was faced with losing all my power," she says cruelly. I look up at her as she dances around the room.

"I don't believe you," I breathe. She bends down to me and whispers in my ear.

"Believe it my darling daughter," she pauses. "Here's something I know you'll believe, since you always expect only the worst of me," her lips nearly touch my ear. "I always knew you would be no good, and I tried to get rid of you when you were three months along." She pirouettes into the other room and yells back. "Of course, it's not that easy! We don't always get to decide. It decides for us, whether we're ready or not!"

I close my eyes, hoping she'll go away forever. I'm sorry I ever decided to talk to her in the first place.

I place Liz's ear on the chair in front of me, and I'm sitting on the bed, trying to form what it is I really want to say. Our therapy sessions need to go better if I'm going to get out of this funk and back onto world domination, especially before my minions stage a revolt and I have to kill them all and find new ones.

"Aha!" I yell at the ear. "I know!" And I pounce off the couch and rummage through a pile of junk in the corner until I come up with Scarlett's letters to Delia. I toss them over my shoulder one by one searching for the right one. "Aha!" I yell again when I find it. I drag it and myself back to the couch and begin reading aloud to Liz's ear.

"There's this part in one of her letters that makes perfect sense, and really just, like totally justifies the fact that I killed her...hold on, lemme find it," I skim the pages, mumbling as I read the words. "Here it is, -

'we all have our own demons I suppose. And you're right about Bonnie – I don't resent her – and I'll be honest, it didn't ever occur to me as you said it wouldn't. I'm sorry if that upsets you. I can understand why you might struggle with it, Delia. It's a strange thing the day that baby is born and so much of you goes with it. But I think, maybe you just have to see it as not leaving you so much as carrying on through her. Try to focus on that.'"

I look up at Liz's ear from the crumpled letter in my hand. "So what do you have to say about that?" I pause for the ear's reaction. "I KNOW, right?!" I laugh, crumpling up the letter in the process. "She TOTALLY resented me, she even admits it here, to this stranger – her goddamn arch nemesis for Christ's sake! Which, while we're on that subject, why wasn't she trying to KILL her!?!" I look over at the pile of letters. "Let me show you something else!" I dig through the pile again, tossing the letters everywhere and talking to myself. "Not that one, not that one, no, no, no..." I eventually give up and slump against the wall. I look sideways at Liz's ear. "You see, it's not like having a stranger in my head – these things I feel but don't want to feel – because it's my whole body that feels it. And really that doesn't sound right either because while it feels like a stranger, the truth is it's always been there – for as long as I can remember, long before I got the powers, just lurking under the surface of me, and it's just like the powers freed it

— so if it's always been there, how can it be anything but me?" I ask. Liz's ear just sits there staring at me. I kick it off the chair and it lands over in a pile of broken glass. I stare at it for a few minutes before crawling over to it on my hands and knees. "I'm sorry," I say to the ear. "Do you forgive me?" She doesn't answer. I'm prone on the floor whispering into Liz's ear, clenching a shard of glass, when I hear a henchman clear his throat.

Moe stands in the doorway, a machine gun in one hand and a big white box in the other. "Uh, boss?" he asks carefully.

"What?!" I snap, dropping the shard of glass innocently beside me.

"Uh, we're uh, all set up for your meeting," he stammers.

"You lose the coin toss, Moe?" I ask, while putting Liz's ear back on her chair. Moe looks like he almost throws up in his mouth at the whole nightmarish scene. I slap my hand over the neck wound still leaking blood.

"I uh, don't know what you mean, boss," he says nervously.

"You think I don't know what you guys are saying about me? I've got freaking super-hearing, you moron. I hear EVERYTHING," I shout, as blood seeps out of my neck and between my fingers.

"Uh sure, boss. We know, we-" he loses the sentence and I lose interest and cut him off with the wave of my hand. I'm about to scream at him to leave me alone when I realize he's still holding a big white box tied up with a bright red ribbon. "What's that?" I demand, pointing with my free hand. Moe offers it forward carefully, as if feeding a lion.

"Uh, we um…we didn't know if you'd want this…"

"Who's it from?" I snap, my patience fraying at all edges even as I reach for it.

"It's from Liz, boss," he says. I draw my hand back slowly.

"What do you mean?" I breathe.

"Miss Liz, she got this for you for your birthday coming up, but it just showed up today, we were going to wait 'til your birthday but we thought since, well, we thought you might want it now." Seconds and minutes break off in my head like stones. I feel nothing – that's a lie, I feel everything and it's unbearable.

"You want I should leave it?" Moe asks.

"Yes," I say. "Leave it and tell them I'll be down in a minute." I pick at the red ribbon for a minute looking between

Liz's ear and the box. Finally, I slide the ribbon off and lift the lid. Inside is a completely badass leather cat suit – just my size – and a note. I pull open the tiny envelope and take out the small, thick white card inside. I turn it over and read:

"L.

Get some taste.

L."

I chuckle and look back at the suit. There's something dripping onto it and I realize I'm crying.

I strip naked and consider the suit. It doesn't look as comfortable as the other, but even I know it's more impressive. It will also look great with my leather boots. I concentrate for a moment trying to heal my neck wound, which should only take a second, but the alcohol in my system must be slowing things down. Finally after a few minutes of intense concentration and an insane headache, I'm able to stop the bleeding. In the bathroom, I wash the blood off my body and pull the suit on. It fits perfectly and makes me feel like I have a part of Liz still with me. Well, other than her ear. It also makes me feel a bit more put together, but I almost don't recognize myself in the mirror, so I smash the mirror to bits with my fists. I get little shards of glass buried in my hands and so I take another few minutes to heal my hands back up, pushing the glass shards out into the sink. I don't bother to wash my hands a second time. Who do I really need to impress? My headache rages now, pounding onto the walls of my brain, not unlike how I just pounded on the mirror. Ironic. Or something.

When I come downstairs, they're all a little grumbly and still whispering like I don't have freaking super-hearing. They're still especially freaked out about Liz and the whole ear situation, but several of them are impressed with the leather outfit. So, there's that. Anyone who says women gossip more than men hasn't met my damn henchmen.

"All right, shut up," I say, raising my hands in the air. "I know you're all itching for some real action, something beyond the small stuff we've been doing, so I hope you're actually ready for it." I snap my fingers and gesture to Jeeves who pulls out a map of downtown Los Angeles. I lean over and explain everything. The henchmen have never been more serious, which I appreciate.

O

When I return to my apartment, it's late and I go through the fire escape, more out of habit than anything else. Liesel sees me from the hallway and runs to the window. I climb in awkwardly struggling with the bag and the small opening.

"Oh my god!" Liesel cries out. "Are you okay? I've been so worried!" I feel shameful; I'm a terrible friend, I should have called her to at least let her know I was okay. This whole having friends thing is still pretty new to me, I'm crappy at it I guess. "Did you lose your keys? Where have you been? Are you okay? Where's Bryce?" Liesel's questions tumble out so fast I can't answer them. So I just answer the only one that matters.

"Bryce is dead," I say. The air comes right out of Liesel and she sits on the bed, her cheeks visibly paling.

"No," she breathes, her eyes fill with tears and then spill freely over her cheeks.

"Yes," I say. "It turns out there is someone else like me out there – but she's not a good guy. Her name is Lola LeFever and she killed Bryce right in front of me in Central Park. Broke her back, nearly broke her in half."

"Oh my god," she says again. "I read about the thing in the park, they haven't identified Bryce to the public, just listed her as a Jane Doe. I, I can't believe she's dead.

"I'm sorry Liesel, it's my fault. Lola did it to get to me, if she hadn't been with me-" I can't finish the sentence.

Liesel raises her hand to stop me. "It's not your fault. It's Lola's fault, I just, you know, it's a lot," She's quiet for a moment and then after a deep breath, looks at me, "That was almost a week ago, where have you been since then?"

"She killed me too. Drowned me in the Hudson, a bunch of times actually. I woke up several days later, but I'd lost my memory." Liesel sighs and covers her face with her hands, she's overwhelmed. I know how she feels. I tell her the rest and we end up in the kitchen drinking tea and arguing about whether or not I can stay with them at the apartment. "I can't do it, Liesel."

"You have to stay Bonnie – I won't have it any other way."

"No. It's too dangerous. If I'm not putting Clark in danger by staying with him then I'm not putting you and Ben in danger either."

"Bonnie. This is what friends are for, to help in times of trouble, what is more trouble than this?"

"I won't pretend it's not tempting, but I just can't. We're not playing games, here. Bryce is already dead," I say firmly.

"I know. I know," she says, rubbing her forehead. "But it doesn't matter, I couldn't live with myself if I left you alone at a time like this."

"And I can't live with myself if I get you both killed!" I shout.

"But it's not your choice, it's mine."

"You're so goddamn stubborn," I hiss.

"Yes, I am. Equaled maybe only by you," she says, crossing her arms. I sit back in my chair, stretching out my legs.

"Fine," I say. Not intending to actually stay, but at least not willing to argue the point anymore.

"Nice boots," she offers, and then adds lightly, "I didn't really think you'd have time for a shopping spree what with all you've got going on."

I smile back at her across the table. "Aren't they amazing? They were my mother's," I say, rubbing a finger across the smooth leather.

"I guess that's why they look like they belong to you," she says kindly, her eyes shifting to the large duffel bag. "What else did you get, anything that will help?" I open the bag and pull out the book. Liesel's eyes light up.

"Do you mind if I look at it?" Liesel asks, reaching for it with her delicate hands.

"Of course not," I say, watching her crack open the old leather binding.

"We'll have to get it translated. What is this? Celtic?" she asks, her fingers running over the words. I look up from the bag and turn to her.

"What do you mean 'translated'?" I say, shaking my head in confusion. She opens up the page and points to the wall of text.

"Wait, you can't – can you read this?" she asks incredulously.

"Of course, what are you-" I pause and look at the page and realize that it's in another language. I hadn't even noticed because for some reason I can read it as if it was written in a language I've read my whole life.

Liesel whistles long and low. "Wow. That's incredible." She turns more pages and runs her hands over the beautifully shaped words. I sit down next to her.

"I didn't even notice it," I say quietly. "What language is it?"

"I'm not sure, it looks kind of Celtic to me, or maybe Irish Gaelic? I really don't know. I can't believe you can read this. I mean, if it's Celtic, that's like a dead language at this point, it's been hundreds, I think, maybe even a thousand years since it was used."

"And I know it as well as I know English? That makes no sense," I say, shaking my head.

"A lot of stuff about you doesn't make sense," Liesel says. "I think we just have to accept that premise and move forward."

I smile at her broadly, loving that someone else in the world doesn't care that I don't make sense. I never thought in my life I would get to have a friend like Liesel.

The next morning, I'm still in research mode with the book. Liesel had made a compelling argument that I didn't have any time to waste in figuring out what I am and how to defeat Lola, and that I'd already come here and so if Lola was going to find them anyway, wasn't it safer if I was there to help protect them? I couldn't argue with that, although now I was nervous about my idea of leaving Clark alone, and Jasper. Who could have guessed one day I would have so many people important to me that there wasn't enough of me to go around? Liesel has been bringing me tea and keeping my spirits up and I've been reading all morning with little result. I reach to turn on the bedside lamp and in my frustration smash it to bits.

"Oh crap," I say, eyes wide, mouth hanging open. There's a giggle from across the room.

"So, you don't so much like that lamp?" Liesel says with a smile. I turn to see her tiny frame in the doorway.

"Liesel, I'm so sorry. It wasn't like, an important antique or anything, was it?" I ask lamely.

"Just Crate & Barrel – no loss." She steps forward and hands me a fresh mug of tea.

"Thanks," I say. "Watch your feet." I take the mug from her and gesture to the glass strewn across the floor. Liesel crawls up onto the foot of the bed. "You want to bring me a broom so I can clean it up?" I ask.

"In a minute," she says and gestures to my book. "What's wrong – is the book not helpful?"

"No, I mean, yes," I sigh. "It's amazing – I'm learning all this incredible stuff about my mother and grandmother – all of them, going back nearly 200 years. But it's just about their lives, so while it's fascinating and personal and priceless, it's like reading chapter twelve of a history book, and what I really need is chapter one, you know?" I massage the bridge of my nose.

"Hmmm. Makes sense, I guess," Liesel says. "Have you learned anything you can use?"

I look up. "I've learned that we don't live very long."

Liesel looks down. "Oh."

"Yeah, I think the oldest of the ancestors I've found so far was in her early 40s when she died."

"Early 40s!?! My god," Liesel breathes, looking up at me

"Yeah. Not exactly inspiring."

"What kills them?" she asks, touching one of the pages.

"Different things, but they all seem to know when they're going to die."

"How do you mean?"

"Well, look," I flip to the end of the book, to my mother's chapter and hold the book toward her and then remember that it's all in Celtic. "Oh yeah," I say, and pull it back on my lap. "Here, I'll read it, it's the very last passage…

"It hangs over me like pregnant clouds, my fate all bound up in them, about to break loose. I always knew it would be this way, my mother warned me that I would sense it when my time was up, but I never imagined it like this. I don't know what I thought – I guess that I would only feel it right before it was supposed to happen, that it would feel normal and "right", but it's been nearly a day now of it pressing on me. Feeling so closed in and all I can think about is how much I want to stay. I woke up in the night sure of it and it hasn't lessened for a moment since. It's torture. Not just the not knowing how it will come for me, but the worry that it will take some of my family with me. I've been pushing James and Jasper away ever since I felt it, hoping to keep them safe from whatever takes me. Of course Bonnie will be safe no matter what, there's some small comfort in that at least."

I stop and Liesel inhales sharply.

"Jeez. That's intense."

"Yeah, there's a lot of intense in here," I say, closing the book, "But not a lot of facts. I mean I still don't know who or what we really are...or where we come from, although the Celtic obviously points to a more specific area and maybe time period. But there's no information about the stone."

"What?" Liesel prompts.

"I do know that my great-grandmother, Audra, fought in World War II."

"That's amazing."

"I know. It's pretty cool. There's lots of that stuff – these women – my ancestors – they were all so different and amazing and yet they were all so alike too. Just like me. Sometimes reading their thoughts feels like reading my own. But I'm still not learning how to beat Lola. In fact, the little I have learned about 'the Others' is that they're not killable – the same way that I'm not."

"But, your mother died...and her mother before her...if you're not killable, then how?"

"It seems that once we have a daughter we lose most of the power. So when my mom had me, it made her vulnerable to being killed."

"So does that mean that the...the Others, are born at the same time as you?"

"It's not exact, but close. All of the dates here list the births within about a year of each other."

"How old did Lola look? Was she your age?"

"Well, I wasn't really paying much attention as she kicked my ass across New York, but yeah, she seemed close to my age."

"So wait, if your mother died when you were six and she didn't have her powers since you were born, and you were too young for a long time to really use your powers, then there are these long periods of time where a Braverman and a LeFever have power, and then long periods of nothing...why would it be like that?"

"I don't know. Maybe it's like in agriculture."

Liesel cocks her head at me.

"You know, like fields that lie fallow for seasons to rejuvenate, maybe the power has to rest or something. Recharge," I shrug. Liesel laughs, her eyebrow raised at me.

"Okay, farmer Ted, whatever you say."

"Shut up," I say tossing a pillow in her direction, smiling.

"So, what are you going to do?"

"I don't know," I say, massaging the bridge of my nose again. "I thought about going to the library or trying to find a historian or something, but I don't know, I don't think I'm cut out for all this detective stuff."

"Maybe you should try thinking more outside the box," Liesel suggests.

"How do you mean?"

"Well," she starts, pausing and touching pages of the book. "You've got these artifacts that you know are tied to whatever you are – and especially the stone, which you've said feels powerful to you – I don't know, it seems like maybe all the answers are already inside you, and you just need to figure out how to unlock them, y'know?"

I look at Liesel, stunned. She'd make a way better Batman than me.

"What?" she asks.

"You're just brilliant," I say. "I don't know what I'd do without you." I hug her suddenly – spilling both of our teas in the process – and dive off of the bed in a jumble.

"Watch the glass!" she calls out.

"Too late!" I say, already in the hallway, two pieces jammed in my bare foot, little drops of blood dripping onto the hardwood as I hurry down the hall to the kitchen where I'd left the duffel bag. As I dig through the bag I hear Liesel calling Ben to bring her a broom, and Ben gently cursing as he stumbles upon my blood trail. In a minute I have it in my hands. The stone.

Maybe it's the key I needed on the island.

Only one way to find out.

●

You'd think from all the screaming that it isn't going well, but actually I couldn't be more pleased. I'm surveying everything from an awesome penthouse suite we took over early on in the center of downtown L.A. It gives me a massive, sweeping view of everything and in tonight's case that includes about twelve square

blocks of my own territory. For a bunch of glorified morons, my
boys are doing pretty well. We hit in the early morning hours so
there would be fewer people in what is more of a commercial
district. My boys did a great job recruiting from the downtown
area, so we already had a lot of people on the inside, which helped
immensely. And I've got a whole parking garage full of hostages to
use as bargaining chips. As long as Bruce Willis isn't hiding out in
my city, I think we're good.

We set fire to everything a block out from the edges of my
territory, and L.A.'s finest are so far mostly busy doing damage
control. They haven't even bothered much with us yet, which has
given my boys plenty of time to set up. Moe shows up in the room
panting, ruining the peaceful survey of my lands. "What?" I ask,
not looking up. He tries to speak but has no breath. "Moe, you've
got twelve seconds to come up with a sentence and it better not
start with 'um'," I say.

"Yes, sir, boss. The boys are asking what we do when the
city cuts the power?" he breathes.

"Why do you think I kept hostages?" I ask.

"Oh," he says, almost deflated.

"You can go now," I say, waving my hand at him. "Send in
Jeeves."

"Yes, boss," he says, shuffling out. Jeeves shows up
moments later.

"You wanted to see me, boss?"

"Tell me when the news helicopters arrive," I say.

"They just have, boss, I was actually coming to tell you.
They're keeping a pretty wide berth but they're there, six of them, I
think."

"Perfect," I coo, pulling up the hood on my new leather cat
suit. "Let the boys know I'm going out and I don't want to be hit by
any goddamn friendly fire," I say, opening the door to the roof
deck.

"Got it boss," he replies watching me disappear into the
roof garden. Jeeves is right; there are at least six news choppers just
outside the perimeter. I fly up into the air and hover above my new
home.

"Hmm. Which one should it be?" I pose to myself,
nibbling on my fingers excitedly. This is really my debut to the
world, so I want it to look just right. A FOX News chopper floats

dead center in the group. I shoot into the night and pull up just short of the FOX team. The looks on their faces are priceless. Over the blades I can hear a shrill blonde woman inside yelling. "PLEASE TELL ME WE'RE ROLLING…ARE YOU GETTING IT?!" The cameraman is telling her to shut up, the pilot looks like someone kicked him the groin. I hover in front of them, making sure everyone gets plenty of footage of me, and then I unceremoniously thrust my foot, heel-first, into the glass window and metal base of the helicopter. The force sends it toppling end over end and it crashes into the Harbor Freeway below. It explodes on impact and I look at the other choppers on either side of me, their news teams staring, mouths agape. I juke toward the next closest team and the pilot jerks the controls wildly, smashing into another chopper, which spins out of control and then crashes into the freeway on its own. The three remaining news teams beat a hasty retreat and I smile and do a civilized little golf-clap for myself. I have a feeling I'm going to enjoy the coverage. Perhaps, I'll have Jeeves make popcorn.

Around mid-day the following afternoon, the power is cut. It doesn't seem like a big deal since the sun is high in the sky, but it'll start to get hot without the air conditioning soon – not to mention all the other crap that you need power for. So I pick one lucky girl from my stable of hostages in the parking garage, and pin a nice, polite note to her shirt:

Dear City of L.A./Power Companies/LAPD/FBI/Whoever:
Turn my power back on. Every hour it's off after 4, I kill a hostage.
Sincerely,
The King of Los Angeles

I have her escorted safely to the perimeter.

At ten minutes to four I have Jeeves bring me three hostages selected randomly. I stand them in front of me in the penthouse and offer them all bottled water. None of them take it. At exactly four o'clock I ask Jeeves to turn on the lights. He flips the switch and nothing happens. I grab the guy in the middle – some suit – and drag him out to the roof deck with me. I survey the skyline and pinpoint what looks like the command center the LAPD and FBI have set up on the edges of my borders. I grab the suit by his fancy lapels and launch him at them like he's a giant lawn dart. I shade my eyes, watching his trajectory across the sky. My aim is super badass and he crashes through one of the command center trailers like a fleshy bullet. My men with binoculars hoot and holler in celebration while the other side shouts orders and screams obscenities. I brush my hands together, satisfied, and go back inside to wait with the other two hostages for five o'clock. At five Jeeves tries the lights and they're back on. I send the other hostages back to my hostage warehouse unharmed.

I laze about the rest of the day, shouting occasional orders and taking an informal survey of the loot being brought in. One of the great perks of our location choice is that it includes, pretty much in its entirety, the Los Angeles diamond district. The men are exceptionally pleased with what they pull off those streets. I have them pile everything up into the penthouse by type: piles of cash, piles of gold, piles of platinum, piles of jewelry, piles of loose gems (diamonds get their own pile), etcetera. It's pretty freaking impressive and the way it all shines in the sun (except the cash of course) is deliciously satisfying. Most awesome of all is that the boys bring me a present halfway through the day. An ornate and somewhat ridiculous throne for me to sit on. It's all carved wood and gilded in gold with a lushly cushioned back and seat. I'm a bit dainty in it; obviously it's built for a large man, but I love it anyway. It's huge and fits well in the room after I have all the existing furniture removed. I take Liz out of my pocket though and wish for a place to keep her close to me, her own special place. I send Jeeves out for another chair, a smaller, more delicate chair to go by my side. Despite the use of the word 'delicate' I think he's still hoping it's for him. A handful of minions arrive two hours later with a gorgeous glass and red velvet throne. It's much less grand than mine, but beautiful and important in its own way. I motion for them to set it down to the right side of mine and they do. They shift around uncomfortably and then escape while I walk up and down eyeing the new seating. Finally, I take Liz out of my pocket and place her on the chair. I take a few steps back and cock my head. "Do you like it?" I ask.

"Uh, of course boss, it's great," Jeeves says.

"I'm not talking to you, Jeeves," I snap, annoyed. He looks around confused. And then hurries out with the rest of them. I sit next to Liz and together we survey our awesome domain and riches. Not bad for a couple days' work.

When it's dark I decide to firebomb the forces outside our borders to give my men time to start on my outer wall. I know none of them are looking forward to the hard labor of building a wall all around our borders – they're getting lazy already if you ask me – but it's been the plan all along and they know it. So I swing a satchel full of grenades over my shoulder and go out onto the roof deck. I take off into the air, above the clouds and then once I'm outside my perimeter I drop down close enough to see all the LAPD/FBI sawhorses circling my lands.

Once overhead, I just start pulling pins and dropping the grenades from the sky. At first I'm a little too high and some are detonating before they hit the ground, thus making my attack totally ineffective as anything other than an annoyance. But I drop lower to maximize the impact. The screaming tells me I've got it just right. I do a few passes around the perimeter, dropping a dozen on each side of my borders. Back at my penthouse, Jeeves is watching the aftermath from the window with some binoculars, along with two other thugs whose names I don't know.

"That ought to slow them down," I say happily, dusting off my hands as I come back into the front room.

"Nice work, boss," Jeeves says while the other two henchmen duck out conspicuously. There's dust and grime on my leather cat suit and I step into the bedroom and strip it off, pulling on one of the silk robes I brought with me.

I fling the suit at Jeeves. "Have this cleaned," I say, moving towards my throne, excited to check out the view of L.A. on fire from my new seat. Jeeves looks at me with his head cocked. "What!? Your name is Jeeves for chrissake, you're SUPPOSED to do these kinds of thing," I say. He turns to leave. "And don't bother me unless there's an emergency, I need rest," I say with finality. The elevator doors snap closed behind him and I go into the kitchen for a drink, or fifty.

I tell myself I'm drinking because tomorrow's my birthday, and because despite the fact that I'm only about to turn seventeen, I feel a hundred and seventeen. But really I'm drinking because of everything.

○

It's a hell of a lot easier to get to the cottage in Maine when you already know where you're going. Also, when you can fly.

It takes me only a couple hours, instead of the better part of a day, and with the stone in my pocket the intense tug of the place is ratcheted up considerably. I can zero in on the place like I have high-tech radar now, even if I didn't already know where it was.

I set down in the expanse of trees near the cottage and walk across the rocky beach up to the porch, slowly, paying close attention to how crisp everything feels and sounds, tastes and smells. Compared to last time, when everything was like faint, pale memories, this is like vivid 3-D. The carving on the house is undeniably the symbol from my stone, and as I touch it with my fingertips a now familiar jolt of power courses through me. I draw back and bite my lip.

I pull the house key from my pocket and unlock the front door. It squeaks open and dust swishes around on the hardwood floors as the ocean breeze comes in with me. The moonlight does a good job of illuminating the house and the rooms spark old memories. Despite the small feel of the cottage from the outside, inside, there are soaring wood ceilings and to left is a small kitchen with a nook of windows overlooking the sea, I have a flash of my mother sitting there with a book in morning sunlight. Directly in front of me is a wood stair, leading up to the second floor. I walk down a hallway toward the back of the house and realize it's actually the front. There's a porch here and an old gravel drive. I peek in all the rooms and closets, hoping for more treasures from my past, but the house is painfully empty, with only a few pieces of furniture, that give off nothing particularly powerful when I draw my hands across them. I go back to the ocean side of the house and climb the stairs to the second floor. At the top, the space opens up and there's a window seat that overlooks the water and an unobstructed view of the island. Just looking at the island is like taking a lightning bolt to the chest. As magical as the house is in my memory, I'm here for the island.

At the water's edge I watch the island, silent and dark. Last time I swam there, and although there was something natural in that, something full of memory and even something baptismal about it, I don't have the luxury of memory lane. I've wasted enough time as it is.

From the sky it's easy to drop down directly onto the symbol as the full moon lights up the large polished stone like a landing pad. As I land I feel a whoosh of power surging up and through me, imbuing me with strength and who knows what else.

I take the stone out of my pocket and compare it to the stone below me. The designs are exact and the two stones hum in concert with one another as if they wish to be joined. But there's no magic treasure map hidey-hole in which to place the stone, turn it counter clockwise, and reveal all the secrets of the universe or anything. I want there to be, but there just isn't. I search for the better part of an hour before I give up realizing there's no easy answer, like in the movies.

I lie down on the stone, depressed and worried. I really thought this was the answer. I feel drained and hopeless, and within minutes I can feel myself sprawled across the symbol, as if I've never slept before, my stone clutched in my hand.

She's standing before me and at first she looks as solid as the stone beneath me, not feathery and soft like she always is in my dreams. But as she moves I see her split into more women, she splits and splits and splits, it seems like countless times, until I am surrounded by flickering, half-translucent Braverman women. All strong shoulders and red hair. They're all dressed differently, marking different time periods and they all have something about them that defines them uniquely. Making them different than me, different than my mother, yet the same too. I try to absorb them all, to see and learn everything, but before I can even begin to count them or understand their meanings they shuffle back behind my mother's image like a deck of cards, like a thousand thinly sliced paper dolls all propping each other up. With the women behind her, my mother's image becomes more solid, more opaque again, and she speaks to me as clearly as if she had never stopped. Her voice is dark and smooth, like tinted glass, and it slides over me, like love.

"We have no answers for you," she says, her eyes piercing right into me, responding to a question I haven't bothered to think up, let alone ask.

"I, I didn't ask anything," I say.

"We all had the same questions once. The questions are always the same," she says, emotionless, as if she is not my mother, but a hybrid of all the Bravermans that ever were. She doesn't acknowledge that I have spoken. "You have come to us and we cannot help you, there is no help. We are your mother, we are you, but we cannot help you from where we are. What you do, you must do alone," they say.

"What must I do?" I ask, confused by the soliloquy. It's as if they are talking to something that is not there, as if they are an ancient tape being played on a loop.

"It is *geis* to help. Prohibited. It is beyond our power, it is beyond our desire. You must make things right," they continue, without acknowledging me. I sit still hoping there is something useful on this tape from beyond. "You cannot be killed; she cannot be killed. It's the way things are. It cannot be undone. It cannot be unlinked. In over a thousand years it has never been undone. You must find a way to keep things as they are supposed to be. She can never die; you can never die. We can never die. It's the way for all time. It cannot be unlinked without desire."

"But I totally have desire," I mutter to myself, barely acknowledging the seemingly useless tape women now. As I say it, my mother pulls from them, toward me, her body arching to me as they struggle to drag her back into them. She looks even more like my mother than before, more real and human, and I can see she is concentrating very hard to make me see her this way, to separate herself from the deck of ancestors.

"You must not do this, Bonnie. You must promise me you will not do this. It's dangerous. It will have consequences. It will change everything, more than just you and Lola - everything." She is snapped back from me and into the fold.

As they shuffle themselves, I see something in the background, very deep, behind the last of the paper-women. A field filled with giant stones. The image flickers like an old timey film, and a woman, a huge, powerful woman, tattooed nearly from head to toe is wearing the stone as a necklace and raising her hands up to the moon, almost as if she's making a request. A large group of women and girls surround her, all different shapes and sizes. I can't see any of their faces, as they are bowed in supplication, or trained on the woman and the bright moon. One woman with bright red hair kneels at the center of the circle. There's a brilliant, pulsating light and when it clears the girl in the circle has fallen and so has another girl, one with pale blonde hair, whose body is now slumped half-way in and half-way out of the circle. The giant tattooed woman has vanished. But as I lean forward to see more, to understand what I'm seeing, the paper women shuffle in front of the scene.

"No," I say. "Let me see! Let me understand!" I plead. A woman, very much not my mother, one I haven't seen before, dressed in thick chainmail and dull silver battle armor, comes to the forefront.

"That is not for your eyes. None of this is for your eyes. Keep the balance, that is what you do. Always do we fight. Never do we kill." She disappears into the deck again.

"YOU WILL NOT DO THIS!" they boom suddenly in unison almost as if deviating angrily from their looping soundtrack. But I've heard all of the tape already and I try to ignore them, thinking hard about what has been said and not said, about what I have glimpsed beyond them. The women suddenly flicker and burn out, vanishing entirely. It's dark all around me now, almost as if the moon itself has gone out – the trees, my only company in the clearing. What does 'it cannot be unlinked without desire' even mean?

"What are we?" I ask the stone below me. It says nothing to me. I look up at where the moon used to be and shout at it. "WHAT AM I?" my voice tears at the atmosphere, the power of it shocking even me.

"We have been called thousands of names," a layered, guttural voice says, reverberating up through the stone. I spin around looking for the paper-women, but I am alone. Just the moonlight and the stone, the voice echoing off the rocks and trees. "Badb, Macha, Nemain, Rhiannon, Aine, Danu, Banshee, Nigheag Na H-ath, Buanann, Epona, Medb, Valkyrie. There are endless names," the strange words echo inside of me, completely foreign and yet somehow icily familiar. They feel like the blood in my veins. There's a flash of white and a lightning strike pierces the stone. When I open my eyes there is a woman before me, not like the flickering paper-women of before, but a woman, flesh and blood, solid as I am. It's the same tattooed woman from the field. She looks less like my mother or me, and more like some version of us all concocted in a place where dreams meet nightmares. Strange markings cover her skin and though the stone is still in my hand it is also tied around her neck. Her eyes are wide, black pools, inhumanly large, and her hair writhes, as if alive. She is so close that her breath is hot on my cheek. She radiates power and fear and love. She pushes into me, so we are nearly eye to eye. I try not to blink, afraid I'll miss something.

"WE ARE A GOD. WE ARE THE MORRIGAN," she says, and the volume of her voice nearly blows out my eardrums. She draws back slightly and as she does so another lightning strike hits the stone and her form shifts into three giant black crows that tear into the night sky and disappear screaming.

●

Delia, Bonnie, and Liz run around the penthouse, like ghosts, attached to leashes glued to my hand. They haunt me and taunt me and sometimes bring their friends – Lena, Joan, and some of the boys whose names I've long forgotten. It's ironic that the only ghost I want to see is Adrian, but he doesn't come since he's the only one I haven't managed to kill. My last tie to life, to redemption. The only person I've ever cared for that I haven't utterly destroyed.

I'm starting to think I might be a little crazy.

But on the plus side, I've figured out that I really don't need to eat to stay alive, which should totally go on the 'list of things awesome about being me', but I've forgotten what the other things on the list were, so I don't bother to add it. I talk to Liz's ear all day long, often gesturing at the ghosts around me, trying to make it understand how hopeless it all is.

I've had at least four, maybe five bottles of tequila today in continued celebration of my awesome-victory-slash-birthday when the penthouse elevator slides open. I assume it's Jeeves or some other random minion, but I'm immediately pissed because I can hear it's nice and quiet outside, so I know there are no emergencies. I drag my way toward the elevator prepared to hand someone their head.

My heart almost stops when I see it's a flesh-and-blood Adrian standing in front of me.

"A-Adria-" is all I get out before he shoots me in the stomach. I stumble forward, doubling over and he stabs a needle in my bare arm. I look at him and he does it again. Everything swims in front of me and I'm gone.

○

When I open my eyes it's dusk, which means I have lost at least a day. The ground around me is wet as if I have been rained on but I remain dry. The stone is still in my hand, but when I touch the delicately carved edges of the crow, it feels hot. The ridges in the stone below me feel hot as well. Was it all just a dream? It didn't feel like a dream. And what dream lasts nearly a day? I feel like I have been given a gift, but I'm not entirely sure it's a gift I want. The women and their riddles reverberate in my head. "We are The Morrigan," I say out loud to myself and the woods. "What the hell is a Morrigan?"

●

I wake up bolted to a cement floor, my hands bound behind me with some kind of customized metal mittens that look and feel like something from a sci-fi movie. Something's wrong with my hands as I can't really feel them inside the mittens, which bothers me, but I figure they must still be in there or I wouldn't be attached to the floor. Blood is seeping rapidly from me via a hole in my stomach, and I can't seem to concentrate on the wound to heal it. The alcohol thinning my blood isn't helping any, but I also see several puncture wounds in my bare arm and I remember being drugged. I don't remember about seeing Adrian's face until I hear his voice.

He's in the room with me and I'm shocked that I didn't sense it. The drugs and the drink, I guess. This must be how Delia felt all the time. No wonder she didn't ever want to play with me. His voice comes from a corner behind my left shoulder, at least fifteen feet away, maybe twenty.

"Lola," he says again.

"Yeah," I say, clearing my throat, trying to hide any feelings I have about his voice in the raggedness of the word.

"So, how ya been mi niña?"

"Honestly? Been better, and I'm not even talking about this sci-fi-bolted-to-the-floor-shit you've got going on here," I say.

"It took me forever to find you. Gave me plenty of time to come up with a decent plan."

"I'm sure you needed it."

"What, like I'm stupid? Like you're a rocket scientist?"

"No, no, we're both stupid as rocks, but at least I've got super-powers. I suspect this will not end well for you and I'll probably just continue being stupid."

"Not end well for me? Hmmm, like it didn't end well for Felice, is that the kind of thing we're talking about?"

"I mean if you're into that it can be arranged. You got a tire iron on ya?"

"You bitch," he says, a little spittle hits me on my left shoulder.

"She took my bike," I say.

"Your bike!?! Are you kidding me?"

"No Adrian, I'm not kidding you. After setting me up to get caught, maybe killed, and then killing me and dumping me in the desert, she stole my bike. It was the last straw. Something broke in my mind and I fucking broke her. I don't think you're on any kind of high moral ground here."

"She was my sister. What else could I do?"

"Yeah, real damn heroic. You deserve some kind of shiny medal."

"You shot me."

"And yet, you deserved so much more."

"I couldn't have saved you. I tried to save you the first time. I was destroyed that they left you there, especially after what you did, throwing me over that fence. But there was nothing I could do. And the second time, you were going to kill my sister. What was I supposed to do?"

"Uh-huh. Sounds like a lot of excuses, is there a point in our future, or can you just get a move on with trying to kill me?"

"Trying? Oh, I'm gonna kill you. The difference between Melvin and me is that I know there's something wrong with you. I'd never figured out exactly what, but watching you lately has made it pretty damn easy. So I'm not taking any chances. I spent a long time looking for you, preparing myself for this. And then I had to sit and wait, which was even more excruciating," he spits. I look up from the floor.

"Waiting? What do you mean waiting?"

"I've been watching you for weeks, I had to wait until you were vulnerable."

"So, you were on the inside all along?" I ask, genuinely shocked. Adrian smiles proudly.

"One of the boys for a while now," he says, beaming at me.

"Sonofabitch," I say to myself, feeling betrayed again, but not sure who I can blame.

"Yeah, I should have made a move after you killed Liz, you freaking lost your shit after that," he says, almost to himself. I level my eyes at him sharply.

"You don't talk about her."

"Sore spot, huh?" he says gleefully, almost laughing. "Yeah, once you took her ear I knew you were gonna crack. Lots of talk amongst the boys after that."

"SHUT UP! JUST SHUT THE FUCK UP!" I scream, feeling like I can almost tear the flesh from his bones with the power of my screams. "You don't talk about her, you don't talk about her ear!" I shout. Adrian smiles again, happy that he has gotten to me this easily.

"Oh, that's right, you don't talk about her ear, you talk to it," he chuckles.

"Shut up," I say quietly, imagining ways to shut him up myself.

"At first I was pissed you killed her, because I wanted to do it, but I've seen that it's much better you did it yourself."

"She betrayed me," I seethe.

"Sure. Sure, she did. They all do, right?"

"They do," I whisper, more to myself than to him.

"You ever wonder if it's you that makes that happen?" he asks, pacing lightly in front of me.

"No," I say.

"Convenient," he says, ticking his head to the side.

"Yeah, well, at least she didn't cry and whine like your sister," I say, narrowing my eyes. But before I have a chance to look up and see what effect my words have had I feel something hit me in the back of the neck and it snaps. My head lolls hard to the side and my body slumps to the floor, hands still anchored. As I die all I can think is that I'm pretty sure he hit me with a goddamn tire iron.

○

There's something about finding out you're a god that makes you want to go see your ex-boyfriend. And I don't even mean just for bragging rights. More in the hopes that someone can bring you down to earth and maybe pet your hair and tell you that it's all going to be okay. I try to resist going as I don't want to further confuse the issue, but even as a supposed god, Clark's pull on me is impressive. I miss him. Especially now that he knows about me and that there are no secrets between us, the draw of him is greater and more perfect than ever. So when I get back into the city, instead of going straight to Ben and Liesel's, as I should, I make a stop at his apartment.

I land on the roof, asphalt and tar pulling up a bit in my wake, I still really need to work on these landings. The second I hit Clark's floor pins shoot through my entire body alerting me to something horrible. My stomach lurches hard to the right. I put a hand on the wall, steadying myself, trying to clear my head and prepare myself for whatever horror might be awaiting me. As I turn the corner to Clark's apartment I see his front door is pristine, as if nothing in the world is or ever has been wrong. I walk up to his perfect door and turn the knob hard to the right, snapping the locking mechanism inside. I push the door open slowly, willing everything to be as pristine inside.

The apartment is destroyed. It looks like my worst nightmare.

It looks like Lola.

A small cry escapes my throat as I survey the damage — furniture overturned and torn, television and window smashed, a lamp, on, but tangled in its own cord, lying helplessly on the floor, broken glass littering the hardwood like diamonds.

I'm moving slowly toward his bedroom when the room explodes into bullets. They sink into my back by the dozens and as seamlessly as if they're imbedding themselves in a piece of putty. I go down hard, my face smashing into the glass-covered floor with a wet, crunchy thud.

I wake up to Joan's rough tongue licking my cheek, her plaintive mews in my ear. I'm not sure how long it's been, but the apartment isn't swarming with police yet, so that's good. I push myself up off the glassy floor, creating a thousand more tiny cuts in the process. Joan skitters back from me and I crack my neck. I think it must have broken on impact with the hardwood. Bullets and shell casings litter the floor around me. I feel my back and thighs – they're healing fast, but could use some help. I hear shouting in the hallway and sirens in the distance. I have to get out of here, but first I have to figure out how she found him. I go into the bedroom looking for any clue as to what might have happened. But everything is so ransacked that I can't make sense of it. On my way into the bathroom, I trip on one of my own sneakers and as I do I see something sticking out of the sole. I pull back on the rubber and edge out a small flat microchip with a wire attached to it. Even I have seen enough television to know that it's a trace. How long have I had this? And why? I curse myself for doing something as meaningless as changing shoes at his apartment the last time I was here, a simple act that may have signed his death warrant. I take the trace to the bathroom and flush it. A quick check of my current clothing reveals no other surprises and a quick check of the apartment reveals no bodies of people I love.

I'm about to flee the apartment via the fire escape when I realize that whoever tracked me could have been tracking me when I went to Jasper's or back home. I search frantically for the house phone, which has been yanked clean off the wall. But Clark's mobile phone is still here, sitting inside his nightstand drawer, charging innocently. I dial Jasper's home number in Philadelphia. He answers on the third ring, and his voice sounds like music.

"Hello?"

"Jasper? Thank god. Are you okay?"

"Who is this?" he asks, more annoyed that anything else.

"Oh, sorry – it's Bonnie – are you okay?"

"I'm fine," he says, pausing, confused. "Are you okay?"

"Yeah, I'm fine. You need to get out of the house."

"What?"

"I'm serious – get out now. Go to a friend's house or a hotel – and call me at this number later to let me know you're somewhere safe," I say rushing my words as the sirens seem almost on top of me now.

"Bonnie, wait, does this have anything to do with the news-" he begins, but I cut him off.

"I'm sorry, I have to go – get out of the house, now!" I hang up the phone and scoop up Joan. Sirens are filling the street and there's movement in the building. I open the bedroom window leading to the fire escape and put Clark's mobile in my pocket, as I do, I realize the stone is gone. "They took the stone," I breathe, the realization hitting me like a thousand new bullets. The sound of footsteps charging up the stairwell sends me out the window onto the fire escape and I take to the air a split second before the police break down the front door.

●

My neck is all messed up when I wake up. I feel like ass. Adrian is crouched in front of me, head cocked.

"Amazing," he says.

"Tell me about it," I say, leveraging myself awkwardly back into a sitting position and cracking my neck a few times. He backs off when I sit up and I realize for the first time that he's afraid of me. He's doing a good job of covering it up, but now that I've sensed it, it's so strong I can almost swim in it.

"So, we could do this all day then," he says, smiling. His smile is just as beautiful as ever and I'm epically pissed at myself to realize that there's a tiny little butterfly beat in my heart at seeing his face. "Is that – what are you thinking?" he asks suspiciously. He was always good at reading my face.

"I'm thinking that I'd like to do that to you and see how long it takes you to wake back up," I say. He smiles again and I close my eyes. "How long was I out?" I ask.

"A few hours."

"Not too bad then," I say, happy that he's proving to be even stupider than I am. Just as I think it though he plunges another needle into my arm.

"Hell. Would it kill you to warn a girl?"

"In this case, I suspect it would."

"Good point," I say, grimacing. I don't know what he's giving me, but it's powerful. Almost immediately my vision blurs slightly and my thoughts feel thicker. With the alcohol almost gone from my system though, it's more manageable. I play it up a bit, try to keep him from thinking he needs to give me more.

"You know I loved you, right?" I say, slurring my words a little bit more than necessary. He blinks and sits down, leaning the tire iron up against the side of his chair. The sound the tire iron makes dragging against the concrete is horrible. I like it.

"Yeah, I know you loved me."

"I mean, I still love you," I say, not sure whether I mean it or not.

"Doesn't matter."

"You're mad I killed Felice…" I let my sentence drag out. "But don't you think she deserved it, maybe just a little bit?" He pulls back horrified and not trying to hide it.

"No. No, I don't think she deserved it. What she did was wrong, but she didn't deserve to be tortured and killed," he says. I look at him in mock horror, hoping it comes off as somewhat genuine.

"I didn't torture her."

"What do you mean, I saw her body, she looked terrible. I dream about it every night."

"Listen, I'm not saying it was pretty, I'm not saying she enjoyed it, I'm just saying it was fast. I didn't torture her or anything." This information changes nothing in him. It's as if he's been listening to a decades old family story his whole life and he was just offered hard evidence it's all bullshit but he's decided to believe the myth anyway. He shakes off my words.

"I can't believe anything you say."

"Sure, I understand, I'm just saying, if it eases your mind at all, I didn't torture her. She was scared, yes, but she died fast." He turns away from me and I look at how I'm bolted to the floor, trying to determine if there's anything that can be done about breaking the ring that holds the mittens down. Without the drugs, I think I can snap the thick metal cable, but not slightly depowered and trussed up like this. I look up innocently just as he turns around, tossing my hair away from my face and giving him my best slightly drugged smile.

"You can say whatever you want to me, it's not going to change things."

"Of course not," I say, nodding as if he's just informed me that he won't be taking an umbrella with him since it's not raining outside. There's a long pause between us. "You know, you're the only guy I've ever been with."

"Is that supposed to impress me, or please me, or something?"

"No. I just thought you should know."

"Okay," he says. He picks the tire iron up again and I close my eyes. I kind of think he's going to break my neck again, like maybe he's testing my limits, like I do, like maybe he's going to see how long it takes me to heal this time. But I give him too much credit; he's not that clever.

Nevertheless I'm shocked when he drives the tire iron through the unhealed wound he gave me earlier. The pain is excruciating.

I guess I black out again, or die again, I'm not sure which. I'm not sure there's a difference.

O

I head home to make sure Ben and Liesel are okay. Clark's already gone and Jasper is safe, at least so far, so Ben and Liesel are the only other people in the world I love, so it stands to reason they're the only other people that are in danger. I land on the fire escape outside Liesel's bedroom and wrench open the window. Liesel sees me, or perhaps hears me from the hallway and comes running.

"Bonnie!" she shouts as I climb through her tiny window. She rushes over and grabs my hand as I angle my long legs through the small space, nearly smashing Joan against the sill in my awkwardness. Once inside, I collapse on the bed. Joan is damp with my blood and tears, mewing angrily at either being wet and bloody, or having nearly been killed, maybe both. "What's wrong?" Liesel asks, sitting next to me and trying to look past my hair and into my tear-stained face.

"Clark is gone," I choke on the words. "I went to his apartment and it's completely destroyed," I say. Liesel looks at the back of my shirt torn open by the bullets, and covered in blood, my skin still riddled with half-healed bullet wounds.

"What happened to you?" she asks.

"There must have been someone still there. They shot me about a thousand times. I never even saw them. But when I woke up they had taken the stone, which can only mean that it was Lola, or someone working with Lola..." I trail off miserably, trying to shush Joan with haphazard strokes on the head. Liesel nods, but her face crinkles up with concern, sadness creeping into the corners.

"Have you seen the news?" she asks, the corners deepening.

"No, why?" Even as I hear the words come out of my mouth I know it's Lola. What else could it be? Liesel takes me by the hand into the living room, where Ben sits in front of the TV, his eyes wide, his cheeks pale. The TV is on, but muted. I plunge ungracefully onto the hardwood floor and watch the news reports come in from Los Angeles. There's actual grainy night footage of Lola, in flight, kicking a freaking helicopter out of the sky.

"Oh my god," I say, setting Joan onto the floor, where she begins to lick herself clean.

"Yeah," Liesel says quietly.

"How long has this been going on?"

"It started a few days ago...right Ben?" Liesel asks. Ben nods silently and Liesel continues. "So, it must be, I don't know, maybe, three or four days now?"

"Oh my god," I say again. Cursing myself for taking so long with all my damn soul searching. My dream vision thing must have had me out for days, not just one night. "How many people have died?" I ask, my voice catching quietly in my throat.

"A lot," she says, lowering her head.

"I think it's 1231 at last count," Ben says. "Including law enforcement," he adds quickly, never taking his eyes off the television. Liesel kicks him. "Ouch!" he laments, rubbing his shin and then looking at me. "Oh, sorry Bonnie. It's, it's a lot of people. Mostly law enforcement at this point. It was actually under 500 and they thought mostly civilians that got caught in the crossfire as she was taking over, but then on the first night she just went batshit crazy and flew over the FBI and LAPD perimeters dropping – well they're saying they were grenades. There's a lot of really gruesome footage. She's also got hostages, they think."

"What!?" I say, swinging my head around to face him.

"Yeah, there's some 1600 people unaccounted for and they think she's using them as hostages. Like the first day they cut the power, and she sent one out with a note pinned to her shirt to have it turned back on or she was going to start killing people. They called her bluff and she killed some guy. Threw him from inside the perimeter into one of the FBI trailers. She must have thrown him half a mile. They haven't even been able to identify the guy yet. So far no more hostages have been killed as far as they know, but they don't know if she's feeding them or using them for target practice or what because she's not talking. She's just kind of announced herself as the King of Los Angeles and she's even got her people building a wall," Ben says pointing to the screen where you can faintly make out what looks like a wall being built partway inside Lola's perimeter.

I hold my head in my hands. What have I done? I've lost the stone, Clark is kidnapped, or dead, which I can't even bring myself to consider, and I've allowed all these people to be killed and captured. It's so much worse than anything I've ever allowed myself to imagine. But I don't know how to stop her. I don't know how to fly in there and just shut her down. She was more powerful than me before, and though I've certainly learned a lot since we last tangled, something tells me she's learned more. Ben breaks into my thoughts. "Here's the thing though," he begins, pointing at the TV screen again. "I don't think she's there anymore." He sits forward squinting at the screen, one finger placed contemplatively on his chin. My head snaps up.

"What do you mean?"

"Well, at first, it was like she couldn't get enough attention, you know? She takes over this section of L.A., she sends out a note proclaiming herself King, she kills a hostage, she kicks a helicopter out of the sky, she drops grenades on the LAPD and FBI – all in the first 24 hours – but now, she hasn't shown her face in the last, almost 48 hours. I really don't think she's there," he looks up at me." Why would she leave?" I ask. They shrug their shoulders and we all turn back to the television. There's nothing new to report though, it's the same repeating cycle of footage since I first came in the room. Liesel says what I'm thinking, probably because she knows I'm afraid to say it out loud.

"Do you think she has Clark?"

"She must, it's the only thing that makes sense," I say, as if any of this makes sense, and because I will lose my mind if I even think about him being dead for one more second.

"What are you going to do?"

"I'm going to fucking kill her," I say, simultaneously thinking it and meaning it for the first time.

●

When I come to this time I play possum for the better part of two hours. It's excruciating to stay perfectly still like this, and is maybe the most patient I've ever been in my entire life. Lying there, pretending to be a corpse, a tiny slit of my left eye open and watching Adrian watch me, which he's not as diligent about as I would have expected. I try not to think about how beautiful he still looks to me.

Eventually I half-cough, half-choke and feign my rebirth. I'm feeling pretty strong. Not like I should be, but I can feel my body working its way back from the brink. I sense it's pretty pissed at me for how I've been treating it. Whatever – it's got me, I've got it, it's about all we've got – I don't suppose it's going to betray me at this point in the game, it's the one thing that won't.

"Welcome back," Adrian says with a smug look.

"That was mean," I say.

"I could have just left it in there," he says, waving around a tire iron caked with my congealing and partially dried blood. "I wonder what would have happened if I'd done that? Maybe we'll have to see next time."

"We can see; I doubt it will kill me. My body's got a great survival instinct."

"I can't disagree with you. But I think I've got a way to get rid of you for real when I'm ready."

"Oh yeah?" I look down at the floor, pretending to busy myself with rearranging my stiff limbs. I don't want my face to give anything away if he says anything legitimate.

"Like I'm gonna tell you," he says.

I sigh, feigning disinterest. "How long was I down that time?"

"About the same."

Jesus he's dense. That means my healing time was nearly cut in half. If I can stall him on giving me the next dose of drugs, maybe I can avoid a third time hitting the mat. I concentrate on healing myself in the form of cleansing my blood, which I've never really tried before and is difficult enough without making small talk to distract my would-be killer. It's all much harder than it sounds.

"Has it ever occurred to you that there's something worse than killing me and something that could potentially benefit you more, well, more directly at least, than simple revenge?" I ask. He looks genuinely perplexed. I sigh and spell it out for him. "You don't think the government might be interested in something like me? Might be interested in paying someone to bring me in? You could single-handedly stop the chaos is Los Angeles, be a hero to the city, and simultaneously solve dozens of open homicides. I'm sure the government would be more than happy to ship me off to some underground lab where they can run tests on me until I die. In fact, I think that works out on the revenge tip pretty well too." I watch him pace the floor, seemingly deep in thought. It's whole minutes before he speaks again.

"The problem with that," he begins. "Is that I think you'd get out. I think someone, somewhere along the way would screw up and you'd get out, and I think you'd make it a point to come after me and kill me. Maybe torture me to make up for whatever happens to you in the meantime. I think I wouldn't have a good night's sleep for the rest of my life, no matter how much money they gave me or how long my life lasted," he says. I nod, acknowledging that this is probably true.

"Good point. I hadn't thought of that," I say. Adrian smiles out the side of his mouth.

"Of course you did. You're just trying to trick me."

"No, no, I really hadn't thought it through."

"Sure you didn't. You know, you're no rocket scientist, Lola, but you're smarter than you let on sometimes. Maybe even wise beyond your years," he says while going to the briefcase in the corner and preparing a new dose of whatever elephant tranquilizer he's using on me. The irony of my situation, after what I did to Delia, does not escape me.

Fortunately, by the time he fills up the syringe, I'm pretty sure I can take him.

He comes closer and as he draws up to plunge the needle in my arm I steel myself for the puncture. When he hits my skin the needle snaps off violently and I know I've got it. I didn't know if I could do that, but sitting here I suddenly didn't see why not. Adrian looks at my eyes, shocked, and then hears the clang of metal. A flash of confusion passes over his face and I smile up at him briefly before swinging my body around and nailing him in the face with my metal bound hands. I watch him look at the broken ring dangling impotently from the bottom of the mittens, where I've ripped it out of the concrete, before he faints dead away.

○

I go into my bedroom to pull myself together. I change into some new jeans and a clean white t-shirt, trying to avoid a few of the still raw wounds. Afterward I sit on the floor, my legs crossed, hands laying on my thighs and focus all of my energy into healing the rest of my injuries. It takes a lot of my strength, but it's worth it. I sit there for a long time after, just trying to think about all the balls in the air: Lola has taken over part of Los Angeles, hundreds, maybe thousands have died, and perhaps thousands more are held hostage. She may or may not actually even be there running her own operation. Someone has kidnapped Clark, and stolen my stone. It's a safe assumption that Lola has or will soon have the stone again. That will make her stronger and faster and enable her to find not only me, but probably Jasper, since I was able to find him with it. There's nothing left to do but to take her out, if that's even possible. Everything I've seen and read says 'no', from the paper-women to the book, but they wouldn't object so strenuously if it wasn't even possible, right? The idea of killing Lola frightens me to no end. Not because she doesn't deserve it, but because I'm afraid of what happens if I kill her. My mother said it was geis. Prohibited.

What happens to her if I kill her? What happens to me if I kill her?

We're clearly linked, the same in some fundamental way that I still don't understand. Does she just go away if I kill her? I suspect it's not that simple. That seems to fly in the face of the idea of there even being a Lola and a me in the first place. What happens to the world when there's no more balance? It seems wrong. I'm afraid of it. And not just because I don't want to die. I feel a thousand years of instinct telling me to be afraid of it. Those women, my ancestors I guess, straight up told me it was impossible, and my mother warned of consequences. Also, I'm something called The Morrigan. Is Lola also The Morrigan?

Liesel comes in. "You okay?" she asks.

"Not really."

"Anything I can do?"

I'm about to say no when I realize that just simply knowing what The Morrigan is might help. "Actually, yeah, can we Google 'The Morrigan' on your laptop?" Liesel wrinkles her forehead at me but goes to get her laptop without a word and is back in under a minute. She pulls up the desk chair and types as she talks.

"What's The Morrigan?"

"Apparently I am," I say.

"Seriously?" she turns away from the light of the screen to look at me.

"Seriously," I say. Liesel turns back around and types. We end up on Wikipedia. Of course.

"The Morrigan..." Liesel begins and then pauses.

"What?" I urge. She clears her throat.

"'The Morrigan is a figure from Irish Mythology that was once considered a goddess'," Liesel reads and then looks back at me, her eyes huge in her tiny face.

"Keep going," I say. She clears her throat again.

"'She is associated with sovereignty, prophesy, war, and death on the battlefield. She sometimes appears in the form of a crow,'" Liesel pauses and looks back at me. "Didn't you-"

"See them constantly," I say. "Keep going."

"It says here it can also takes the form of an eel, a wolf, and a cow, and can be connected to fertility, wealth, and the land. The Morrigan is a triple goddess, the most common combination being Badb, Macha, and Newain. The Morrígan means 'terror' or 'phantom queen' or Mórrígan meaning 'great queen' and has been associated with the Banshee, Furies, and the Valkyrie. Shit. The Valkyrie," Liesel says. She looks at me over her shoulder again. "Jeezus, Bonnie."

"I know," I say. "Is there anything else? Something about the stone or her death or anything?"

Liesel scans and scrolls. "No," she says. "I mean, there are tons of things referenced here, but no, nothing neatly summarized. Damn." Liesel swivels around. "How did you know you're The Morrigan?"

"Well, I had some kind of dream or vision or something and some woman, maybe she's the actual Morrigan? Or the original Morrigan? She said to me 'We are a God. We are The Morrigan'."

Liesel seems to be at a loss for words, and I'm there too. I rub my temples and Liesel comes over to sit with me. She puts a tiny hand on my broad shoulder and pats me almost like I'm a cat, trying to soothe everything away. It's nice to feel that someone loves me so unconditionally, to love back, to have known bona fide fairytale-like true love with Clark, and reconnecting with Jasper. It's a lot to live for, and I'm afraid to lose it.

But if Lola has her way, there will be no peace, for me, or mine, or anyone. I close my eyes and think of all the things I have seen and what they add up to. The stone, the bird on the stone, the crows the day my mother died on the road. Three of them standing above me, watching me. The mark on her wrist when I took off the bracelet.

And suddenly I get an idea about how to maybe even the odds a little bit.

●

Adrian is passed out and so I set to work on getting these weird mittens off. I can't seem to get enough leverage with my hands behind my back to just strong arm them off and so I step my legs through until my hands are in front. My legs are long, but so are my arms and so it works pretty easily.

I try to ignore the fact that I still can't feel my hands.

Once the mittens are in front of me, it's a simple matter of brute strength to break them down. First I force them apart and once my arms are separated I just start punching the concrete walls until they start disintegrating. It's another five minutes and the building sounds like it's going to come down around us before I get the first hand free. As the metal falls away I see why I can't feel my hands.

He's crushed them to pulp.

They look not unlike Felice did, bits of bone sitting in strange-shaped bags the color of my flesh.

I scream almost loud enough to bring the building down. They haven't been healing all this time because I've been focusing my energy elsewhere. I spend another five minutes getting the second glove off and finding my left hand in similar condition. I go to Adrian's briefcase and see all the treats he had planned for me. Among other more interesting things in the case there's a set of regular cuffs. I don't know what the hell he thought he was going to do with these but they work for me. With much difficulty – my hands still useless to me – I maneuver Adrian over to the distorted but still intact metal ring cemented into the center of the floor. With even more difficulty, I manage to cuff him to it. Just his one hand to the ring is all I can manage, and probably all that's really necessary. I make sure nothing – including the tire iron covered with my guts – is within his reach, and sit with my back against the cement wall, legs crossed, facing him, laying my little flesh bag hands on my thighs and focus on my healing like I haven't in a very long time. I don't know how long it will take to fix my hands, but neither of us are going anywhere until it's done.

My hands are better before Adrian comes around. As a matter of fact, I start snapping my fingers in his face to help wake him up. When he's conscious enough to realize that the tables have turned, a darkness settles over his face that almost scares me.

"Nice try with the hands," I say, snapping my fingers a few more times in case he missed it before.

"It was worth a try. I would have preferred to do it while you were conscious, but I was worried you'd get out. Clearly, I was right to be concerned," he says, lifting his bound arm off the ground and tugging the handcuffs against the metal ring. "I don't suppose I'm getting away with a leg wound this time."

"No, no I don't suppose you are."

"A boy can hope."

"You really shouldn't bother."

"Y'know Lola, despite all my preparation, I kind of knew it was going to go this way. I knew the only chance I had of killing you before you killed me was if I just did it, right off the bat, before you even regained consciousness."

"You're probably right," I say. "So Adrian, if you don't mind my asking. Why didn't you just do it?" I pause and then echo his words of a moment ago. "I don't suppose a girl can hope that, after all this time, it was love."

"Would that stop you from killing me?" he asks.

As much as I want to hear it from him, I can't bear to stoop and lie to him. "Not this time."

"I didn't think so. It wasn't love, though I did love you once," he says.

"Gee, thanks," I pause, "So, what was it?"

"Just the revenge, I think," he says shrugging his shoulders, seemingly resigned to his fate, like he actually accepted it long ago. "I've been looking for you for so long, always with only one thing on my mind. And you know, I think I've been planning to die this whole time. Knowing that I wanted to hurt you, but also somehow knowing it would be the end of me."

He can't possibly know how hard that last sentence hits me. It shocks even me how much I relate to it.

"I understand what you mean."

"You do?"

"I really do."

"That's kind of nice, then."

"Yeah, yeah it is." The gun has been sitting between my legs as we talk. Now I just casually pick it up and shoot him in the head with no warning. I don't do it to be cruel, I do it so he won't be afraid like Felice had been. I do it to be merciful.

Part of me does still love him.

He falls slowly to the floor, slumping at first and then his head hitting the concrete with a wet thud. There's surprisingly little blood. My aim was good. He's lying there, staring at me with his eyes open and I lie down too, so I'm looking right at him for a while. Except for the distance between us, I can almost imagine it's like those long days we spent in bed together, just staring at one another. Eventually, I curl up in a fetal position and close my eyes to focus on purging my body of the rest of his animal tranquilizers and whatever alcohol might remain, also a general clean up of miscellaneous wounds, which are many. I cry for a long time too, not just for Adrian, but for myself. I realize now, lying there with him, that killing Adrian has also killed the last soft parts in me. It's all hard now without him. I'd thought killing Liz was the last of the soft parts, but I guess I'd buried some softness for Adrian deep inside, and now that's gone too. Adrian was my last chance. The last person I hadn't killed, the last person I cared for, the last shred of whatever humanity I had left.

All gone now.

And it makes me sad. Sad for me, and sad for the world. Sad for everything that must be coming now.

I wake up a few hours later and it takes a moment to realize where I am, but it comes flooding back like a painful dream and I try not to look at Adrian's body. I stretch my arms and stand up. I test my legs and crack my neck. I have no idea where I even am. I open the door to the room and am alone in another room, a large abandoned basement in a building somewhere. I look at the door to the room I'd been in. It's an old fallout shelter. There's an exit at the far end of the basement, when I go through it, a bright warm sun assaults me. A Los Angeles sun if I've ever seen one. Looking around I recognize street names. "Sonofabitch," I smile. We're still in my L.A. territory, barely two blocks from my penthouse.

I take flight immediately to survey my lands and what has been going on — and likely wrong — in my absence. I can't have been gone more than 48 hours but I can tell from the air, that edges are fraying. It looks like my henchman have managed to lose ground on both the northeast and southwest sides of my border — pushing us back almost two whole streets on each side, and the wall only partially built on the north and west sides. "Sonofabitch," I breathe again, setting down on the roof. "Jeeves!!! Moe!!!" I scream down the hallway from the roof deck to the floor below. The door flies open a moment later and Jeeves appears, out of breath and shocked.

"Boss! Where've you been?!" he asks.

"I've gotta better question for you, Jeeves — what the hell happened to my borders?!" I scream, gesturing to the horizon around me.

"We uh, had some, um, setbacks," he starts, looking down at his feet sheepishly.

"Setbacks!? It looks like we're pushed clear back to Fourth Street on the northside!"

"They sent in the air force or something, boss, really had us on the run."

"Where's Moe?" I ask, irritated.

"Moe's dead, boss. So's Big Tony, Trapjaw, Shipwreck, Odd Job, Tweedle Dumb, Pinky, Number 2, Alfred, Heckle, and a bunch of others. We re-grouped though, boss – the boys did good," he says, head still lowered. I bite my lip and feel the gears in my head churning as hard as they can.

"All right, all right. Bring me Vince, and um, whoever the replacement leaders are – I forget all the names I gave them. Bring them here now, we need to get this shit straightened out."

"Okay, boss," Jeeves says, pausing on his way out. "Good to have you back, boss." The door slams behind him and I chew on my thumb a bit.

"Yeah, yeah," I can't help but feel pretty uninterested in all of this now. Like it never occurred to me until now that half of my enjoyment was doing it with Liz, or knowing that Adrian was out there somewhere. I'm so alone now. Surrounded by idiot minions with fake names I gave them from movies, comic books, and cartoons. None of them care about me, and I don't care about them. This whole adventure seems so pointless, but I also don't know how to give it up. Something unnatural drives me to try to have everything, even as my will to have it ebbs away from me.

Before Jeeves can get the team up to the penthouse though, the air force shows again and Jeeves comes scurrying back, ready to pee his pants, pointing, and freaking out. Apparently they were pretty scarred by whatever happened with the air force in the last two days. "Where's my cat suit, Jeeves?" I ask between clenched teeth.

"On your bed, boss," Jeeves says, crouching and trying to be invisible to the planes screeching around the edges of my L.A.

"Get me my minions, I'll be back in a minute," I say, stripping my clothes off as I walk.

Zipped into my cat suit and feeling slightly more at home, I take off into the air, muttering about my worthless henchmen and their pea-sized brains. "First they let Adrian in, now they can't even hold our borders for two days. They're completely freaking worthless. I have to do everything my damn self," I'm still grumbling about it when I pull up next to one of the jets flying around my airspace. I smile and do a little salute, and as the eyes of the pilot widen to saucers I wind up and punch her goddamn plane out of the sky. The force of it takes a chunk out of the side, but more importantly, it sends the plane awkwardly toward the ground, crashing dramatically into a huge parking garage and much more, just outside my borders. My hand is all torn up from the punch and I focus on it for a minute trying to heal it quickly before the other two get a lock on me. I should have brought some gloves.

I hover in the air watching my beautiful destruction and feeling slightly better about everything as my bones knit back together. I turn midair, intending to do the same to the other two jets headed my way, but find they've launched some kind of missiles at me. I take off, trying to elude them but they must be heat-seeking because I can't lose them no matter how I dip and swerve. I launch myself into the upper atmosphere, trying to outrun them. I go higher than ever before and then make a right angled turn high in the sky and light out over the ocean, swooping low, low enough that both missiles crash impotently into the sea, exploding underwater and sending surfing size waves towards shore.

Before either of the jets can get a bead on me again I take the fight directly to them. Flying up beside the first of the two remaining and I use a similar maneuver as I did on the first and just punch it out of the sky, but this one I punch up instead of down, hard, like my best uppercut ever, and it spins out of control with the impact. After nearly taking out two buildings the aircraft veers towards the ocean and ditches into the sea moments after the airman ejects himself.

I work on healing my hand again, while the third jet zooms past me to the right. It seems unsure of itself, probably waiting for bad orders about procedure or some such bull. For the last one I decide to get creative. I rush to catch up with it and then get in front of it, right in the airman's line of sight. I kneel down on the front of the plane and punch a hole in the cockpit. Still on my knees I tear pieces of the plane away, slap the sidearm out of the pilot's hand, and wrench him from his seat, dropping him unceremoniously out over the city. The plane, unmanned, crashes somewhere out over the valley. I don't see where. I don't care.

That ought to shut things down a bit on the 'resistance' front.

I'd love to say I return to my lair full of hope and conquering hero crap, but while the henchmen are definitely happy, I'm just not feeling it.

The penthouse is a mess of broken glass and shredded high-end wallpaper, which I guess means I was literally tearing into the walls before my little adventure with Adrian. I should thank him for shocking me out of my drunken suicidal stupor, but I'm feeling something different now. Something lonelier, something sadder, something deeper. When my New York team finally returns to the nest I'm grateful for the distraction. I'm sitting on my throne, examining my hands, when they step out of the elevator. Before they even get into the room I know they have my stone – it's calling to me, almost cooing. Singing a sweet and delicious song about power. And it fills me up inside a little bit, getting into the hollow nooks and crannies. I look at Liz's ear sitting on the smaller throne I call the 'Queen's Throne.' "Do you hear that?" I ask, pausing for her answer. "How can you miss it?! It sounds like what a sugar and diamonds milkshake would sound like!" I say, clapping my hands, almost giddy. The ear says nothing. "Pft," I say. "You can't hear for shit."

Lou comes in first, followed by Gordo and Bud. Two of them are missing, but I don't remember their names. Maybe Bonnie killed them. Nah, that doesn't sound right. Gordo is dragging some guy I've never seen before around by his neck. I really don't care who he is, I just want my goddamn stone.

"You have it?" I ask Lou before he can speak. His eyes drift unconsciously to Liz's ear sitting next to me on her throne. "Yeah, it's Liz's ear, it's all that's left, you wanna make something of it?!" I yell.

Lou looks away from the ear, down at his shoes. "'Course not, boss."

"Where's my stone?" I demand again. Lou takes it out of his pocket and steps forward, reaching it out to me, unsure. I snatch it from his hand and the power pours into me, filling me up with everything I've been missing. Maybe not the same things I've been missing, but at least it fills me up with something. It's different now though, even more powerful and intoxicating. I look down at it in my hand and realize it's whole. So that's why the power is so intense, almost tangible. I feel like throwing everyone out and stripping naked and bathing in it. "Wow," I finally say, breathless.

"We uh...we did good?" Lou says uncertainly.

"Yeah, Lou. You did good." But that perfect happiness can't last for long and I'm not done questioning them. "So what happened, and what took you so long?"

"Well, um," he begins looking around at his cohorts, "We did what you said, boss. We looked for the stone in the Hudson but we didn't find anything, and then we looked all over the city, all the diamond districts and museums, and underground, but we found nothing. So then we did what you said and Rocco went into this diner to rob it or something, and sure enough boss, she showed up. He, uh, didn't find the stone on her before she woke up, but we managed to get a trace on her and we followed her around. One a the places she went was her boyfriend's apartment, so, we, uh, kidnapped him or whatever, and Gordo stayed behind in case she came back. But because of our prisoner or whatever, we had to drive back instead of fly, plus, well, LAX, Burbank, and Long Beach are all shut down anyway. Then when we got to the borders, well you didn't exactly make it easy to get back inside, boss. It's like world war three out there y'know," he trails off, hoping for a chuckle for his lame joke before starting up again, but nobody is in the mood. "Anyway, by the time we figured out how to get back in Gordo here was calling us to tell us he was on a flight to Vegas with the stone. So we waited for him to show, and then when you pulled that stunt with the jets we figured it was the perfect time to get back inside, and, well, here we are," he says, smiling proudly but tentatively.

"Boyfriend?" I ask, not even looking up from my stone. Lou motions to Gordo who pushes the stranger forward. He stumbles and falls to one knee, which is awesome cause it looks like he's bowing to me, as it should be. "Who's this?" I say, barely acknowledging him.

"He belongs to Bonnie," Lou says proudly, at which my head snaps up.

"So she is alive," I seethe.

"Not anymore," Lou says straightening out his suit cuff. "Gordo put about a thousand bullets in her back – she went down hard, and she had the stone on her that time, so he took it," he smiles. I cut him one of my most dangerous looks.

"You freaking moron," I say, sighing.

"Huh?" he asks his voice cracking a bit.

"I told you she was like me. There's no way Gordo killed her with bullets in the back," I say.

"But...she went down..." he tries again

"Lou. Do you think Gordo could kill me with a thousand bullets in my back?"

"'Course not, boss," he says, a little too quickly, as if he's considered and discussed it, which I'm sure he has.

"Then she's not dead!" I scream so loud that they all cover their ears with their meaty hands, even the boy-shaped present in front of me. None of them look up when I stand, instead choosing the dark, glass-littered carpet. I shift my stone from hand to hand and circle the stranger kneeling before me, "You say this one belongs to her?" I ask gently. Lou clears his throat, no longer excited to be the spokesman.

"It's her boyfriend. His name's Clark, he's some kind of law student or something," Lou says, never raising his eyes. I put my index finger under Clark's chin and force him to rise from his knees. He's taller than me once he's standing, taller than all of us except Gordo actually. He's handsome, chiseled in the face like he's the superhero. Black hair like crows' wings and warm chocolaty eyes that remind me of Liz. He's on the slim side with broad shoulders. Nice.

"Clark," I say, tasting the name on my tongue.

"Lola," he says calmly and I hear my henchmen suck in a collective breath. They've never heard anyone other than Liz say my name.

"You know me?" I ask, surprised but going for polite, demure, maybe even flattered.

"No more than you know me," he says stoically.

"Oooh. Mysterious," I say turning to my team. "Nice work, henchmen. As you can see," I say, gesturing to Liz's ear. "A lot has happened while you've been gone, and Liz having...left us, I'm in dire need of a new friend, so this will do nicely." They don't know what to do with the praise and so just continue staring at their shoes. A silver glint in Lou's shirt catches my eye and I motion for him to step forward. "Your necklace," I say, and he takes it off and hands it to me. It has a large silver cross on it and so I unclasp the lock and take the cross off. I throw the cross over my shoulder and it imbeds itself in the wall above my throne like a Chinese star. I thread the chain through the stone and put it back on my neck where it belongs. "Ah, that's better," I say, smiling. I turn back to the group. "All right, Lou, you should hook up with Jeeves. You're back in charge once he brings you up to speed, but he's been doing well, so make him your second in command, or whatever. The rest of you, do whatever Lou says." I look at them and they stand there, looking like they're waiting for a cookie. "Go!" I bellow, and they nearly run out of the room. I turn my attention to Clark. "Well, let's find out if your girlfriend is coming to get you – shall we?" I say, sitting on my throne and crossing my legs primly. Clark looks at me.

"You know that guy's name is Matthew, right?" he asks. I look up distracted.

"Who?"

"That guy you call Lou. His name is Matthew," he says.

"Oh him," I laugh. "I gave them all new names – henchmen-appropriate names – long ago." I pause waiting for him to respond. He waits a long time and I stand up and walk over to him. "I wonder what we should name you," I say whispering into his ear. He raises an eyebrow at me.

"You're totally nuts, aren't you?"

"Probably," I say casually, and then smack him with the back of my hand and send him flying across the room. I stare at his now less impressive frame crumpled a bit against the exposed brick wall. "Let's see if B's on her way to rescue you, eh?" I say, sitting back on my throne and focusing all I've got into my stone. It pulls the energy out of me like last time, but without too much fuss the internal radar pops up and I'm able to search out her beat-beat-beating heartbeat, somewhere over Ohio and advancing surprisingly fast. "Looks like a showdown," I giggle out loud to the ear and the boyfriend.

Nobody answers me.

o

I'm shooting across the country at record speed, even for me. Clark's face and the possible thousands of unknown faces of Lola's hostages and victims driving me. I don't slow down until I'm above Los Angeles. From the sky it's easy to see her location and the damage she's caused. I hover well outside her borders and consider my options. First priority is to get Clark out of harm's way so she can't use him against me, then find and release the hostages, if there are any. But for either of those things to happen Lola has to be out of the picture, at least temporarily.

There's one building towering above all the rest. Unless she's a moron, that's her location; the best, highest position from which she can survey all that's going on in her created kingdom. So, that's my play. I thought I'd be scared, standing here, planning to take the fight to her, to maybe be killed by her. Again. And maybe for good this time

But I'm not.

Despite the women's warnings that she cannot be killed, I can't help but feel some kind of destiny has brought us both here, and that it will play out as it should. That something has an endgame in mind for us beyond what either of us are capable of imagining. And if that means my death, so be it. But I'll fight tooth-and-nail to keep it from being the case. For the first time in my whole life I'm feeling like I've got a lot to live for.

I take a deep cleansing breath and fly with everything I've got at Lola's penthouse windows, sonic booms breaking behind me like music. As I get close I can make out her shape, and Clark's slumped one a few feet away. I gulp hard and push it from my mind. I crash through Lola's windows like a meteor from deep space and she has a split second of recognition before I hit her full on in the chest. The force of my impact sends her flying through the windows on the other side of the room.

I don't wait to see where she lands, but make a quick left turn in the room while still in flight and scoop Clark up in my arms, escaping out the way I came.

●

When I come to from Bonnie's blow I'm shooting through the air backward a mile over Santa Monica.

"Jeezus," I say to myself and the sky and the clouds, trying to bring myself to a stop in midair. I hover there and feel my chest to make sure she hasn't left any fist-sized holes. It's a lot more power than she had last time. "I guess the bitch learned how to fly," I say to myself. I check to make sure I'm still wearing the stone, and it's there around my neck, feeding me its power. Even if she's learned a few tricks, the stone should still make me more powerful than she is, especially now that it's whole. I reorient myself towards the penthouse and head back. I'll kill the bitch for good this time. Already the sky is rumbling with thunder, pregnant with another epic storm.

O

I set down with Clark far outside Lola's borders and away from the authorities. He wakes up just as we're landing.

"Omigod. You can fly," he says. I smile broadly.

"Awesome, right?"

"Totally," he says, awestruck, his feet touching the grass. He looks around. "Where are we?"

"A park somewhere in L.A., somewhere well outside Lola's borders," I pause. "I hate to leave you here but I can't stay. I have to go back and take care of her. Will you be okay? Can you get home?" I ask. Clark looks around the peaceful park.

"Of course. But should I wait for you?" The thought is so optimistic I can hardly bear it.

"No. No, you should get back to New York. Far away from all of this. I...I don't know what's going to happen. I might not be back."

"Don't say that. I know you can beat her," he says. His confidence in me is touching. I smile and kiss him lightly but he pulls me in for more. Imbuing me with his own love and strength.

If it's a last kiss, it's a good one.

My heart swells with love for him as I leave him staring after me, waving from a perfect patch of grass.

●

When I fly back into the penthouse, the henchmen are staring out the hole Bonnie made coming in. My throne is broken into splinters. Liz's throne is intact and her ear is unharmed. I pick up the ear and am about to put it in my pocket when I hear sonic booms outside the window. I turn toward the sound but it's too late and her fists crash into my back with such velocity that I go flying out the same hole all over again, and I lose consciousness all over again too.

○

This time when Lola goes flying out of the window I turn on the onlookers. I know there's not much time. Already the rain has started, the thunder and lightning strikes. All of Los Angeles feels like Armageddon.

"Hey, boys. Where are the hostages?" I ask politely, while dusting off my hands. Two of them look at one guy. And he shrugs his shoulders innocently. Suckers. I rush to his side and hang him outside the broken window by his neck. He breaks in less than ten seconds.

"Downstairs in the parking garage," he scratches out between hyperventilating breaths. I bring him back in and set him down on the floor. The other two have their guns drawn, but they don't really look committed.

"Don't even try it," I warn, stepping forward. As I do, something squishes underfoot and I look down to find a severed rotting ear on the floor. One of the thugs sucks in a breath as if I've broken the greatest of rules. I pick up the ear and hold it up to him. "What's this?"

"That's Liz," he says.

I hold it up, one eyebrow cocked. "Um, it's an ear," I say, confused.

"It uh, it used to belong to this woman named Liz. She was Lola's friend, has been with her since the beginning."

"What happened to her?" I ask, holding the ear away from me.

"Lola killed her," the other one says.

"What? On purpose?" I ask, looking back and forth from them to the ear. They nod. I cock my head. "Damn." If she's doing this to even her closest friend she's even further gone than I thought. I put the disgusting ear in my pocket – it might be useful – and turn back to Lola's thugs drawing myself up powerfully. "I suggest you guys get out of here. Your 'king' isn't long for this world, and I'm not going to look kindly on anyone that's still waiting for her to come home when I get back." I motion to the walkie-talkie in thug number two's hand. "I'd send out word to everyone. Some of you might even be able to sneak through the FBI lines and escape." They look at me for about two seconds and I crack my neck while staring them down. At the sound of the crack they run full tilt out of the room, two of them dropping their guns in the process. I follow them out to the hallway and then fly down the stairs toward the garage.

Already word has made it to the ground floor and I see Lola's people hightailing it for the borders. There are huge doors leading towards the parking garage and the handles are linked by a thick chain and massive lock. I snap the lock and remove the chain. When I push the doors open, letting in the light, I hear people scuttling away. The stench is incredible – piss and feces and body odor – but I don't smell death, which is good. There's a breaker box outside the garage and I fling the switch turning on the overhead lights. People scream. You'd think the dark would be more scary than the light, but I suppose any change is frightening. Inside, I see at well over a thousand men, women, and children, all in various states of dehydration and starving, but alive. A man in front shades his eyes from the light and looks at me. He yells back at the people behind him.

"It's not her. It's someone else," he says.

Someone in the back shouts out. "Is it one of the guards?"

The man in front looks me up and down. "No," he says. I hear a collective sigh of relief. "Who are you?" he asks and then tentatively adds. "The police?" I smile and step out of the way of the door so they can move past me.

"No, I'm not the police. But you're free. Please help each other and make your way together south, I think that's your best path out. Some of Lola's men are still out there, but the police and FBI will see soon enough that they're abandoning their posts. Stay together and stay calm and you should all be fine," I say, moving to the exterior door and propping that open as well. Sunlight pours into the hallway and the hostages move toward it as if they are one. The man who has been speaking for the group pauses in front of me as they head toward the street.

"Will you come with us? Will you stay with us?" he asks. I open my mouth to tell him that I can't when I'm lifted away, Lola having grabbed me by my neck. We're flying together. She's driving us forward, her hands around my neck, my back curled and legs dangling as we reach epic speeds. She's screeching something so loudly I can't make out the words. Finally on the third try, I realize what she's saying.

●

"WHERE'S MY EAAAAAAAR!!!!!!!!!!!" I scream at her with such intensity that I think it's tearing a hole in the universe. She's blinking like she doesn't understand my words and if it wasn't for the fact that I can't find Liz's ear I would just bury her at the bottom of the ocean right now. My henchmen have abandoned me and from the sky I can see police and FBI pouring over my borders and into my lands. Plus, the bitch freed my smelly hostages. I couldn't hate her more, and I don't know why she's so goddamn strong. I should easily be overpowering her since I have the stone. There's a giant building at the end of this alley and I'm going to wedge her so deep inside the rock that she'll never see daylight again.

I push forward harder and then pull up a second before impact. She goes shooting through the building, crashing through exterior walls and then interior walls, and even through people's cubical walls like a character in a cartoon. Unfortunately, the building is inside my borders so there are no little worker-bee office-drones to accidentally get beheaded as she rockets through their workspace. I stand on the street and stare through the hole she's created with her monstrous back. She's soooo broad shouldered. Maybe she'll go all the way through.

O

I might have gone clear through to the other side, but I regroup and get my feet down. The floor shudders underneath me, carpet and floorboards and insulation bunching at my heels as I screech to a stop. I'm at least a hundred feet inside the building, a nice clean me-sized hole through everything between she and I. She's seething like some kind of wild animal and something about her looks wrong. Even more wrong than before. I brush the rubble from my shoulders and talk to myself. "Hi, Lola, how've you been? Well, I hope. Yeah, it's great to see you, thanks for leaving me for dead in the goddamn Hudson River." It's good this office is abandoned or people would be looking at me like I'm nuts.

I dust myself off and levitate off the ground a little bit, taking a brief second to peek inside Lola's head, which opens like a flower for me. I pick up a lot of useful stuff, not the least of which is that she truly has been driving herself mad. Once I've got what I think I need, I hover lightly above the ground preparing to attack. I take off at bullet like speed back through the hole in the building.

Let's see if she can take as good as she gives.

I hit her like a goddamn train and she goes shooting into a building across the street. She doesn't go through the wall as I did, but she's wedged so deep in the wall she's going to leave a little snow angel shape in the stone when she gets her ass out.

I have to get her away from the hostages, and frankly, out of the city. I can't give her the opportunity to use innocent people against me and so I take off into the air, straight up, hoping she'll chase me when she's able to extricate herself.

●

My body is a couple feet deep into the building and deep cuts all over are gushing blood. I'd anchored myself carefully for her hit, I hadn't expected her to be able to throw me once I was prepared, not with the stone on me. Perhaps, I've underestimated her. I untangle myself from the rock and stand up gingerly, shaking the rubble from my suit. I spend a handful of seconds healing a broken leg and realize she's just as dumb as she used to be if she thinks I'm going to follow her. Instead, I fly toward the Santa Monica pier and all the delicious tourists and beachgoers that await me there. Even with the storm tearing up Los Angeles and the city on relative lockdown I'm sure I can find some stragglers. She may have my ear, but I have innocent civilians all over this city.

Before I've even done anything, people are running and screaming and acting like morons and so I swoop onto the beach and scoop up soggy tourists and fling them into the sea. They make this delicious squealing sound as they head toward the water, but there's no equally delicious splash sound and so I look over and, of course, Bonnie has showed up and is plucking them out of the sky as quickly as I can throw them. I stop on the beach to watch her do-gooder handy work. The people are fleeing like rats and I put my hands on my hips and wait for her to join me.

"Nice work," I say nodding my head in genuine appreciation of the smoothness of her new moves as she sets down lightly in front of me.

"Thanks," she says, pausing, looking around the chaotic beach. "We can't do this here."

"I actually think this is the perfect place to be doing this."

"No," she says firmly, looking down at me, acting like she's the boss of this, of us.

"You're not the boss of me," I say, annoyed at myself for the unfiltered nature of the sentence.

"And neither are you of me. We. Don't. Do. This. Here," she says again, emphasizing THIS and HERE. This is definitely a different Bonnie. Thunder rumbles and lightning flashes across the ocean behind her. There's no confusion in her, no hesitation. She looks like how I used to feel. Why don't I feel that way anymore? Also, she seems like she's glowing. I know that sounds stupid, but it's almost like she's radiating power. I feel small and dark in comparison. And since I have the stone that's even more backwards than it should be. She rolls her tongue in her mouth like she's about to speak. "It's beneath you," she finally says.

"What's beneath me?"

"Using innocents as a shield. Why are you afraid of a fair fight?" she asks. That stings. I'm not that interested in things being fair, but I don't like the idea that she thinks I'm using it as a crutch.

I stretch my back dramatically, but casually, like a cat. I'm wasting time trying to think of something clever to say when she blurts out, "I have your mother's letters."

I'm blinded by rage and swing my fist at her face. She dodges it, but not entirely and I catch her just enough to knock her down, but not to imbed her ass in the moon as I was hoping.

"Jesus Lola," she says brushing herself off. "I meant I have them and I can give them to you," she says. I look at her suspiciously as she massages her jaw lightly.

"What do you mean you'll give them to me?"

"I mean I have them and I can give them to you. You should have them," she says. I steel my shoulders.

"I don't want them," I say.

She talks inside my head this time.

<Sure, you do>

"Don't tell me what I want and don't TALK INSIDE MY HEAD!" I scream at her at such a volume that all the windows across the street from the beach shatter. We both look around a little shocked at that. The area is surprisingly empty thanks to the rain, wind, thunder, lightning, and maybe the two psychotic superheroes beating each other up. It looks like an apocalyptic landscape all around us but I can feel eyes staring at us from the buildings and the pier. I'm pissed she's mastered both the telepathy and the flight and I throw a little of my energy toward blocking her out of my head before making the connection that she's talking in my head, without the stone. Why can she do that? It's the stone that makes that possible. I look at her, my eyes narrowed. "Wait, why can you do that?"

"Do what?" she asks innocently.

"Don't play with me. Talk inside my head. Why can you do that without the stone?" Bonnie shrugs her shoulders. The gesture enrages me and I swing my fist at her, hoping to knock her entire head off her stupid shrugging shoulders. She doesn't even dodge the punch, but catches it with her hand. It must hurt like hell but she does it. And more importantly she's taken me by surprise.

"Lola," she says, drawing me closer, my fist covered with her hand. "Let's talk about this. It doesn't have to be this way," she says quietly. As we're standing there together I see why she's matching me. She has the symbol of the stone tattooed on the underside of her wrist. The thick black markings radiate power at me the same way the stone does.

"What the hell is that?" I spit, looking at the symbol. She stares me down.

"You know what it is," she says. I curse to myself. That would explain the equal strength but she still seems stronger than me. And glowy. What's up with the glowing? It seems I am going to need every edge I can get. I relax my body.

"Okay," I say. Her guard is still up.

"Okay what?" she says suspiciously, one eyebrow raised.

"Okay, let's talk," I say, shrugging. She begins to release my hand and as she does so I grab her wrist and fling her around as hard as I can, sending her careening towards the Ferris Wheel on the pier. She goes crashing through it like a ragdoll and falls into the sea, the wheel coming down on top of her.

"I love drowning that bitch," I cackle, hovering over the ocean and watching the few remaining bystanders scream their heads off as they escape into buildings along Ocean Avenue. I'm so busy being pleased with myself I don't notice the ripple in the water beneath me and when she hits me from below, surging up out of the water like one of those crazy, jumping great white sharks, I nearly black out from the force of it. We fly up into the atmosphere, powered by Bonnie alone, my body bent in half where her shoulder is digging into my stomach.

"Lola. Please, you can try and kill me again if that's what you really want, but can't we talk first? Can't you tell me why you feel so determined to kill me. What is this really about?" She's talking softly and she sounds like what a mother should sound like. This makes me even angrier about everything. I separate myself from her shoulder and she allows it. We hover in the sky, arguing.

"About?! Are you fucking insane? I don't have to have a reason to kill anyone, least of all you. It's just what I am, it's what I'm supposed to do. You got all the good parts and I got all the dark bits and that's how it is….it's how it always has been, and it's a complete crock of shit, you and yours having it so easy, while we're all suffering. You having a goddamn heart-to-heart with me is not going to make it 'all better.'"

"I know," she says. "But I don't think that it has to be this way, I think our mothers tried to do it differently…"

"I don't have a mother!!!!" I scream wishing I could tear the sky in two with only my voice. "I kill you because I kill everything. I kill you because you're the only thing that can kill me and I can't have that!"

○

Floating above the ocean with her, it's clear that she's not going to give up until I'm dead. Any fantasies I've harbored of us both living out our days in peace is ridiculous. And I can't allow her to kill me again; she's shown an incredible disregard for human life and from the looks of her I'm not sure she's not a bit insane.

Which I get. Thinking about how the power feels like is inside me and then imagining what it must be like for her – all twisted and dark. Well, it must be hell. I've had a hard time with it and mine comes almost entirely with good, for Lola it's the opposite and it must be horrifying. And with her the way she is, I feel like she'll bring that hell to Earth if given half the chance

There has to be a way to get us out of the city, away from people, so she can't keep using them against me.

And floating there with her, I finally have a good idea.

●

Bonnie looks down at the ocean below us and then toward the beach and the city. She looks sad, but I don't want her looking sad; I want her looking angry. "I won't stop until I've killed you, Bonnie," I say. She looks back at me with something soft in her eyes. I think it might be pity. And if there was anything to piss me off more than I already am, it's a look of pity.

"I know," she says. While still hovering hundreds of feet above the ocean she reaches out to take my hand. I slap it away and in the process she manages to get her arms around me. She wraps her arms around me tightly and launches us both up into the atmosphere with such speed that I'm stunned. I struggle but her positioning is good and I can't get the leverage to wrench free.

While we fly she's whispering in my ear. I don't know what she's saying but I know that I'm going to rip out her vocal chords the first chance I get. I think she's singing a song into my ear, but I don't know the words.

We go so fast that everything around us is just a bright blur that I can't focus on. Maybe she's taking us up into space – will our bodies explode in the vacuum or will we dance on the moon? Maybe her plan is to kill the whole line, to kill us both. All the Bravermans. All the LeFevers.

And actually, on some level, I can totally get behind that. It would be a relief almost.

I close my eyes, waiting for them to pop out of their sockets with the pressure.

But the pop never comes, and when I open them everything is a bright golden-brownish blur. I have no freaking clue where we are. But she suddenly starts driving us back down towards the ground, hard and fast. I can't get any leverage to stop us and at the last second she leaps away from me, simultaneously propelling me even faster towards the ground and managing to change her own direction. Oh she's gotten gooood, is all I have time to think before I hit the ground like a small meteor. The impact is like an explosion and I lie at the center of the hole I've made in the Earth, healing my parts before even attempting to even crawl out. Above me, sheets of lightning flash in the sky. Faint drops of rain hit me. When I finally slither out of the hole, she's standing on the edge of my crater, hands on her hips as if waiting patiently for me.

"You bitch," I spit.

"Yeah, well, at least I didn't drown you six times and leave you for dead," she says.

"Four," I say, under my breath as I crawl out of the pit, the dirt already becoming muddy in the increasing rain.

"Huh?"

"I only drowned you four times."

"I'm pretty sure it was six."

"Well, you were pretty incapacitated, I really think I was paying more attention."

"Really? Really? You think I wasn't paying attention while I was being repeatedly drowned?"

"How about we split the difference and call it five."

"Fine. Five it is."

"Fine." I cross my arms and look at her wondering what the grand plan is, if it wasn't to kill us both in outer space. And then I see where we are.

The Nevada desert.

About a mile from my goddamn trailer. I can see it in the distance, the aluminum roof glinting like a slab of glass in the sun. I look back at her,

"You bitch."

"Sorry Lola. But I had to get us away from people."

"You could have dropped us anywhere in the desert, you had to bring us here specifically? You're a fucking bitch."

○

"I'm pretty sure I'm the less bitchy of the two of us, Lola." I say, an edge to my voice I wasn't expecting.

"Don't count on it," she snarls back at me.

I shrug my shoulders. "I don't know what you expected; every time I run into you you're throwing innocent civilians into our battles."

"Innocent? Those people are not innocent. Nobody's innocent these days."

"All right, but you're not trying to punish them for their crimes, you're just using them to keep an advantage over me." I pause for effect. "You're a coward." The word seems to sting her a little bit, maybe because she knows it's true, or maybe because she doesn't believe it yet and I'm shattering some protective shell she's built around herself. I expect another witty barb to come flying my way, but instead she comes at me physically.

The force of her shoulder in my chest cracks at least two ribs, and we go flying a few dozen feet before we hit the dirt in a thud. I sense a different kind of fight than the last one we had and am proved right when Lola pulls my hair. I screech and kick her off of me. She goes soaring backwards and lands on her ass a few feet away. I've healed my ribs before she picks herself up and hovers over the ground. She takes off into the air and I call after her. "I'm not coming after you, Lola!"

"No problem," she calls back. "Reno's only thirty or forty miles away. Imagine the cowardly damage I can do there." She takes off like a streak of light into the sky. Blasts of lightning and thunder in her wake.

"Damn," I curse, kicking at the dirt. "So much for that great idea." And take off after her.

●

I smile when I hear her curse and come after me. She's no rocket scientist either, it turns out. That said, I've no idea what the hell to do with her. I'm pretty confident about the strength thing being a bit unequal now and I need to find a way to even the odds.

She's right on my heels by the time I get to Reno, I can practically feel her breath on my neck. I put my clenched fists out in front of me and fly right through the "Biggest Little City In The World" sign, which I've always kind of wanted to do, even before I knew I could fly. Sparks and pieces go flying everywhere as the structure collapses to the street. Bonnie's forced to stop and rescue a bunch of tourists too stupid to run when the debris falls toward them. I laugh like the maniac I've become and veer off course, crashing into the corner of Circus Circus and taking a big chunk of it with me. Bonnie's caught up to me again however, so I turn slightly and crash through the thirteenth or fourteenth floor of the Silver Legacy. I'm bathed in green as I go straight through it, almost as if it wasn't there, crashing through walls and wires, doors and stairwells. Bonnie still follows me, so close and accurately that she doesn't crash into anything, just follows perfectly in the hole I've made for her. When I reach the hallway I turn up and fly through floor after floor. Crashing through everything slows me down though, while Bonnie just drafts me, so by the time I get to the roof, she's got my foot. We climb out of the roof hole together, into the rain, but she's on me before I can even get all the way out. She smashes my head into the tar of the roof over and over again. I black out on the fifth or sixth smash and wonder if she's ever going to let me wake up.

○

She won't be out for long and so I'm determined to get her out of Reno while I have the chance. I stand up and drag her the rest of the way out of the hole and look around. I pick her up by the ankle and begin swinging her around like an ice-skater.

"We're. Not. Doing. This. HERE!" I shout as I check my internal map and let her go. Security bursts through the door and onto the roof just as she goes into orbit and I follow suit.

When I catch up with her, she's right where I want her to be and on track to crash right where I want her to crash, if she doesn't wake up first. I shield my eyes as her back crashes into the edge of a cliff and she drops a hundred and fifty feet to the ground, landing in the pile of metal.

●

I wake a split-second before hitting the ground but am unable to stop myself and land roughly on some sharp pieces of metal. I can't believe for a minute that she's managed to get me out of the city until I realize exactly where I am, inside Delia's destroyed old car at the bottom of our cliff. I see a tiny bit of bone from the corner of my eye and scream at the top of my lungs before bursting through the partially intact roof towards Bonnie.

She doesn't even flinch. "We're not doing this where people are," she says, a clap of thunder punctuating her words. "If you want to try to kill me, you're going to have to do it out here. That shouldn't be too hard for you, should it?" she says, her eyes shifting almost imperceptibly to the car.

"You know that's the car that I killed my mother in?" I screech. "You get that from taking a little trip inside my head?"

She nods. "I thought maybe it'd give you some perspective."

"On what?!"

"On us. On what we are. Were you happy after you killed me? 'Cause I'll be honest, you seem like a disaster area since I saw you last."

"I wasn't happy after I killed you – but maybe that was just because you WEREN'T REALLY DEAD!" I scream.

"Well, whatever. Have you ever bothered to think about what happens if one of us dies?"

"Yes, I've thought about it a lot. You'll be dead, and I'll be unstoppable."

"Maybe," she says thoughtfully.

I sigh through the rain, tired of being wet. "What does that even mean, 'maybe?'"

"Well, I don't know for sure but I'm willing to bet it isn't that easy. There's two of us for a reason," she says, motioning between us. "I don't know if the world will bear just having one of us, whether it's the good guy," she pauses, "That's me by the way, or the bad guy, which I'm sure you know, is you." She's being all 'funny' which is annoying the crap out of me. I'm about to kill her again and, as always with people, she's just not taking it seriously enough.

"I don't think the world's that smart," I say.

"You sure you're willing to risk it? What's the harm in just leaving things the way they are? The way they're supposed to be?"

"So, you're just going to let me keep on killing and doing what I want to do?" This gets her and there's a long pause before she answers.

"No, I guess I can't do that."

"Well, okay then. Unless you're ready to let me walk away and go about my business, which so far totals killing thousands of 'innocents' as you like to call them, I suggest you put up your fucking dukes and all that." I stare her down and she looks away. She looks pretty sad and contemplative. It's a minute before she answers me.

"Okay then," she says and she raises her hands like a boxer. It's finally on. We're finally going to duke it out like we were meant to.

Naturally, I throw the first punch.

o

Her first punch is good and catches me across the jaw. My head rolls back and my jaw slips out of place, but before she can hit me again, I catch her hand and force her backward, pushing my jaw back in place and using a tiny bit of my energy to repair it. She resists my weight and swings again, knocking me onto my back twenty feet away on the dusty desert floor. She comes closer and I sweep her legs out from under her. We're both scrambling to get up.

I don't want to do this with her, but she won't be reasoned with. She's like a wild animal that's learned to kill and won't ever stop. And she's in pain too, I know that much from being in her head. Her mind is a dark place that I can't and don't want to understand. But the one thing I have come to understand is that it's not entirely her fault. She's made horrible choices, but the same way I'm driven by something beyond me, so is she. But what she's driven by is mean in a limitless way I don't think I'll ever really understand. It's some kind of cosmic joke and we're only pawns. Selfishly I'm afraid of what happens if I really kill her. What do I become? The world is most definitely out of balance if I kill her

352

and so what does that mean? If I really believe that the world wants balance, then maybe I won't be able to kill her. I don't know. I don't know what will happen. Maybe the whole world will unravel on itself, but I don't have a choice, she's given us no choice, and so I come at her and give back as good as she gave to me.

When I punch her, there's a crack of thunder and flash of lightning across the whole sky and instead of her jaw just coming out of joint, it shatters. I'm surprised that I'm able to break hers when she hasn't been able to break mine. The stone and the symbol should pretty well even us up.

And then it hits me why I'm stronger than she is.

I'm pregnant.

As soon as I think it, I know it's true. I'm stronger, faster, and more resilient than I've ever been before, and Lola's having trouble keeping up, and it must be because I'm pregnant.

Some part of me cries out NO.

That I'm too young, that it's not what I want, not yet at least. That it's too much too fast. That it should be my decision and mine alone, not the decision of some ancient power that's possessing me.

But other parts of me feel almost at home in the destiny of it all, that it makes sense, that in a way I should have seen it coming. The larger pictures for all of us, not just me and my little life and the way I want it to be, but Lola and me, and this larger idea we seem to be a part of. The words from my mother's letter echo in my head: "It doesn't always come when it's convenient or when you think it should. It's a strange kind of destiny that we don't seem to have any say about, but it brought you to me and for that I can never be too frustrated by it." And she's right, that's exactly how I feel. Like all my nerves and fear about throwing myself into having a real life, everything has led up to this moment, everything has put me on this path, so that I would be right where I needed to be here and now. As if something is pulling my strings from behind a curtain. It's maddening, but it seems so perfectly laid out now that I see the resolution, that it's hard to truly be angry about it.

All the emotions I've experienced in my life wash over me in this one wave, leaving me drenched in miracles and prophecy.

And now I have an even bigger reason to defeat Lola – not just to defend the world from her and to save myself – but to protect my child. To ensure my child lives. I can't worry about the repercussions are of killing. I don't have a choice; she'll never stop coming for me, for us. I wish she would just stop fighting me long enough for us to think things through, to talk it out, but she's like pure, wild instinct and she's coming at me again with her still-broken jaw before I can even form words.

I throw my fist into her with everything I've got and it sends her shooting backward with incredible velocity, back into the sharp wreckage of her mother's old car. I follow her into the charred metal and pin her down, some of her mother's bones bright in the sun beside us. I put my hands around her neck. It feels wrong and also right, and I can't seem to help myself from squeezing harder.

Tears slide out of the corners of my eyes hitting her on the face and in her dark blonde curls. "Please Lola, please," I beg, wishing that none of it had to be this way, begging her to just slow down, to listen, to talk to me, to just stop and be still. "Lola please," I say my voice breaking with sobs. "Please, just let it go." And as I say this I realize what the women meant by 'it cannot be unlinked without desire.' Lola has to want to give it up. It's the only way for me to kill her, it's the only way either of us can be killed, we have to want it. We have to truly want to be released from The Morrigan.

●

She's crying and her tears are falling on me, enough so that I can't tell which are hers and which are mine. Behind her, miraculously unburned, is the Dodgers cap I put on my mother the day I killed her. I blink at it. A deep and powerful sadness seeps into my bones. Bonnie is begging me to let go. I have no interest in letting go for her, but for me, suddenly for me, it feels like there's nothing to hold onto anyway. This power has been killing me almost since the day I took it and I just don't want it anymore. Letting go seems like the most powerful thing I could do.

And so I do.

I just let it all go.

And it feels glorious.

○

"Please just let it go, Lola," I cry, our faces damp with tears. And then suddenly...
 ...she does.
And once she's powerless, my hands just squeeze right through her neck, and her head comes off in my hands. Her whole body goes limp under me – the struggle and life just falling out of her, the light in her eyes going dark so quickly I can't believe it. I collapse backward onto the melted seat, Lola's head in my hands, her body sitting next to me in the car like some kind of unfunny comedy routine. There are so many things to think about. My baby, and Lola's death, and what any and all of it means. I've got so many emotions from elation to sorrow that there's no time to stop on just one. And then it overcomes me...

◐

At first it's just unbelievable power washing over and through me.
I feel like I can eat the sun.
No, not only eat the sun, but eat it and crave more, snacking on stars and whole planets afterwards.
The blood that I have felt since I can remember, the blood boiling through my veins is so intense, so palpable, that I feel it's going to start leaking out through my skin, unable to be contained in my basic and oh so human body. I know what they meant now about gods. About being a god. I reach up to my cheek to brush away a tear and pull back a bloody hand, the blood is leaking out of me, pouring out of my eyes and stretching my body to unheard of shapes and lengths. I stop crying, hoping that I can hold everything inside. There's a literal vibration inside me as the power takes root, moving things around and making room for itself. My chest feels filled beyond capacity, ready to burst with power. I press on the bones of my ribcage as if I can hold it all in through sheer willpower alone. It's agonizing pain, feeling the power try to find a home in a body that was already full, but as my body bends to the power, shaping itself around it, I also feel myself enveloped by all

Lola's memories and Delia's. Aveline, Hedy, Barbara, Amelia, so many names – all of Lola's ancestors. They break over me so fast that I can't count them all. With the names and faces comes a wave of darkness, redrawing the lines in my head that have brought me both such comfort and such frustration. I can feel the lines as they pick up from their comfortable, worn places in my mind and lay themselves down in new places, places they have never been before.

I'm horrified to realize my fears coming true inside me, the consequence my mother spoke of. The *geis*, the prohibited action. What was prohibited was joining the power. It will change everything. Now I understand.

Of course killing Lola will change me.

It has to change me. There can't be such a wild imbalance in the world. There cannot be me without Lola and there cannot be Lola without me. This is what she didn't understand, or maybe she did. Maybe she understood it better than I ever would have.

So everything changes in this moment. Not only for me, but for my daughter and all the other daughters that will come after her.

All the lines that have ever been drawn for all the Bravermans and all the LeFevers are changing. Lola's desperation to be the only one, to destroy everything, has brought us to this.

And now I am the only one.

We are the only one.

And since there is only one, we will have a new kind of balance. We. I find myself thinking in terms of 'we'. As Lola and her ancestors take root inside me, making a home for themselves inside their ancient enemy, it feels for a moment like all my Braverman ancestors and all of their LeFever counterparts are standing on opposite sides of my brain ready to wage a war. I grip the sides of my head, praying that my skull can contain them and all of their incessant talking, arguing, and warring. We cannot war with each other anymore, because now we're the same, the way we maybe always should have been. Though I fear the idea of 'me' slipping entirely into the background as I become something new I can feel them slowly calming, coming to peace inside us and accepting this new shared life and body, understanding that we have no choice.

Lola's head slides from our hands and I know it's all over because she's in us and there's no way to undo that. I also know that it couldn't have been done if she hadn't wanted to let go.

I stand up from the car and look at the desert around me. Everything looks different now, but also the same, like two drawings layered on top of one another, each making the other more complete. I consider burying Lola's body, but instantly know, maybe because she's inside me now, that she wouldn't want to be under the dirt. I take Liz's ear out of my pocket and put it in Lola's already cool hand.

Part of me is so angry with her for bringing us here, for not being able to accept the natural balance in the world, the way that things are supposed to be, one dark and one light, keeping a forever balance. For putting me in such a terrible position of killing her and destroying that balance. But part of me feels a love for her too. A love for all of the Lolas and what a terrible hand they've been dealt. And an understanding of the madness that would drive her to me, that would feel the need, the pounding never-ending ache to either kill or be killed. It's in me now, and so it's finally easy to understand.

And maybe this was both our destinies anyway. Maybe after all this time the world has realized that its Bonnies and Lolas were not such a great balance after all and it's ready to start with something new.

I'm sad for my baby girl, my baby that will be both of us. Like we are now, she will be equal parts Lola and equal parts Bonnie. Equal parts Braverman and LeFever. She will live her whole life with that duality. It will seem normal to her and I'll never be able to make her understand how easy it had really been for me, once upon a time, to just be good. But in her difference she will also be better than me. More than me. A girl king, destined to be the only one.

I put a hand on where she must be inside of me — barely a seed, a tiny little sea monkey of a thing — and feel so much joy I can't quite believe it. I think the Lola part of me is a little grateful. Like maybe she would never have been able to understand such pure joy if not inside me. As I walk toward the horizon my only thoughts are of my baby girl and that I'm going to stay with her as long as I can, so that she can learn everything I've learned, so that she can have real hope for what she can do in the world. So that she can become what none of us have really been able to become.

A new kind of superhero, a real one.

EPILOGUE

Eight Months, Two Weeks, and Six Days Later

The midwife left an hour ago, beaming as if we had just been doubly blessed. Happy in her ignorance. I still haven't spoken and Clark has wisely left me alone. I can see him out by the water, he knows what this means just as I do.

We're cursed.

Because there's two of them. Not one. Two.

Perfect and magnificent, but two.

Though I've told myself that it doesn't necessarily mean what I think it does, deep down, I know. I know that this is what my mother meant when she said there would be *geis*. Consequences. She didn't mean for the power, for the world, or even for the changes that would come to me, she meant for my future daughters.

The Morrigan force will split again.

It will pour into my two innocent daughters and everything Lola and I endured months ago and everything she and all her ancestors sacrificed in giving up the power has made no difference. I've taken Lola out of the equation, but in the end it has changed nothing.

I have beautiful twin girls sitting in front of me, just waiting for the Morrigan power to split again – damning one of them and making enemies out of sisters.

ACKNOWLEDGEMENTS

First and foremost to my family – Mom, Dad, Scott, and Dave, who were always incredibly supportive, especially considering how long this took, and who always want good things for me, even when we don't necessarily see eye to eye on what those things are. And to Adam who knows (and frequently lets everyone else know) that he's pretty much responsible for this book making it into your hands. To Shelti who made me an aunt (yes!) and to little Luke, who I plan to spoil mercilessly.

Jose Rodriguez - advisor, mentor, and friend, who probably had no idea I was going to be so troublesome to mentor, but who never stopped believing in me and hopefully knows that I never would have made it half this far without him.

Huge thanks to my writing group "The 33rd Street Writing Collective" (aren't we fancy?) – Sarah Ulicny, Marta Ficke, Jon LaPearl, Rob Brieslen, and Andy Peters – great writers and friends all. Whatever Adam may like to believe, this book also needed you guys in order to happen. Though not part of the "Collective" I also have to thank Erin Jade Lange – the best YA beta reader (and friend) a writer could hope for. I'm not really sure how I did anything before I met Erin – it must have been terrible – good thing I can't remember!

Steven Malk and Ty King from Writers House, who were absolute champs through an exhausting revision process and without whom this book would probably have been left in a drawer long ago.

Artist Stephanie Hans, who not only created illustrations more beautiful than I ever could have dreamed, but also read the book and loved it, which is, I suspect, why her illustrations ring so powerfully true for everyone who sees them. Jon LaPearl and Sarah Ulicny who both edited this beast of a book for a pittance. Quite a sacrifice when you understand that I hate and despise commas and pretty much refuse to learn about them – sorry guys!

Ross Campbell and Keegan Xavi, devoted and beautiful friends of mine that fought me every step of the way when I tried to make a change they thought lessened the book. Eternal apologies to Ross for not being able to give him the ending he wanted so desperately (it involved ice-cream and skipping and happiness in general). Also Meredith McClaren, another wonderful artist who has become a valued friend and co-conspirator toward world domination.

To all the fantastic folks at Coral Graphics and Berryville Graphics who helped pull the Limited Edition Hardcover together, their genuine care (and excitement) for the project made the experience so much more manageable (and enjoyable) for a rookie like me. Particularly wonderful were: Pam Dillaman, Kelly Bassford, the army of awesome prep folks, Claire Giobbe, and of course, Karen Gache.

Special thanks to Marc Glick, a most unexpected early reader who made me smile more than he'll ever know, as well as Jason Anthony who had such wonderful words for the book at a critical time. To Josh Chaplinksy and Brooke Gardner who read very early drafts of this book and didn't laugh in my face (which would have been devastating, even though it would have been an entirely appropriate response). Also, rather late thanks to a handful of awesome folks who really went above and beyond: Lewis Smith, Adam Thourne, Ryan Hull, Karl Foster, Max Bliss, Ryan Fitzgerald, and Bill Zajac.

To Sue who has been an advocate and friend for so long I don't remember what it was like before we were pals and to Maddy who tries to remind me that not all Canadians are sweethearts (even though she is both Canadian and sweetheart). To Fiona Staples, Rebekah Isaacs, Emily Carroll, Karen Mahoney, and Cassandra James, phenomenal artists all, and people so generous in sharing their time and talent to help a fellow artist on her way. Special thanks to Brian Wood and Scott Snyder – insanely talented writers that both inspired me and encouraged me with wonderful regularity.

Last, but certainly not least, to Richard Cameron, the best boss a person could hope for, a boss that is both friend and cheerleader. You have to be a pretty amazing person to do everything in your power to help someone else, even when you know that their success is going to majorly screw up your own life. Richard is this kind of person.

SPECIAL THANKS TO ALL KICKSTARTER CONTRIBUTORS! YOU GUYS MADE THIS BOOK POSSIBLE – DON'T EVER FORGET IT!

5 Minute Marvels, A. Haggerty, A. K. Tosh, A.I. Ruiz, Aaron Hunter, Aaron M. Fisk, Aaron M. Krivitzky, Abigail Gruchacz, Adam Birkner, Adam Rajski, Adam Sypnier, Adam Thoume, Adam Weiler, Adrian lilley, Ahmed Bhuiyan, Aida Escriva-Sammer, Aimee Kuzenski, Alasdair Stuart, Alejandra Quintas, Alex Kidwell, Alex Scigajlo, Alex Wong, Alexa Dickman, Ali Grotkowski, Alice Lyall, Alicia K., Aliou Diallo, Alisa Bishop, Allison Post, Almitra Corey, Alvin Dantes, Amanda Clare Lees, Amanda Dreyer, Amanda Power, AN Bengco, Andrea Marie Brokaw, Andrew Corbett, Andrew G. Davis, Andrew J. Peters, Andrew Seles, Andy Jackson, Andy P, Andy Taylor, Angela Davis, Angie Batgirl, Anis & Alexis Mojgani, Anna Gaffey, Annabeth Leong, Annie Golden, Anonymous, Anthony Kolb, Anthony Martinez, Arabella & Thomas Benson, Ardo Omer, Arthur Clemens, Ashley Durham, Ashley L. Wright, Ashton Blackley, Aunt Mary and Uncle Laird Tucker, Aurélien Gaillard, Austin Alexander, Ayo Næsborg-Andersen, B Eileen Carter, B. Jeremiah Youll, B. Parran, Bailey, Baron Alexander Mansfield, Belinda & Raul, Ben Caldwell, Ben Cohen, Ben Durbin, Ben Rabin, Ben Rankel, Benjamin Smith, BJ Dowd, Bonnie and Betsy, Bonnie Clyde, Brad Dancer, Braden, Bradley Grehan, Brandon Eaker, Brandon Schatz, Brandon! Williams, Bree Bridges, Brekke & Rin (For Kerowyn), Brendan Tihane, Brett Weldele, Brian Chastain, Brian Cronin, Brian Jacobson, Brian Kelly Hahn & Rebecca Hahn, Brian Lyons, Brittany Cole, Brittany Miller, Brittany Uhlich, Bronson Luke Jarrard, Bryan Massengale, Bryan Q. Miller, C.L. Stegall, Caanan Grall, Caitlin Lustig, Carl Rigney, Carly A. Kocurek, Carly Whitaker, Caroline Pinder, Cass Somerton, Cassandra Rose, Cassie Kingsbury, Cat, Catie Coleman, CCR, Cecelia Larsen, Charles Benward, Chelan Sweeney, Chibi, Chris Beatty, Chris Kaiser, Chris Schinaman, Chris Vance, Chris Vincent, Chrissandra Porter, Christian Berntsen, Christopher Wilde, Cindi Weatherington, Cindy Grant, Clay Wager, Cliff DaSilva, Clint Mitchell, Colby Taylor, Corky LaVallee, Courtney Grimm, Craig Blackwood, Craig E., Craig Johnston, Crystal Weaver, Cynthia

Ramey, Dad (on behalf of Camryn), Dale Amann, Damien Swallow, Dan Grove, Dana Kyle, Daniel Campisi, Daniel Miller, Daniel Romberg, Danielle D'Adamo, Danielle E. Sucher, Danny Pettry II, Darrah Rippy, Dave Hill, Dave Levine, Dave Rezak, David Clark, David Earl Gauley, David Golbitz, David R. Sanderson, David Ramsey, David Sanchez, Dean Hacker, DeAnne Millais, Dee Pirko, Delia Gable, Dennis H., der Wolpertinger, Derek Handley, Derek Meier, Devin R Bruce, Diana Wadke, Dominique Dzioba, Dorothy P., Doug Bissell, Drew Blueberry, Eamon R. McIvor, Ed Watson, Eldritch, Eleanor Russell, Elise Vist, Elle Skinner, Ellen Cerpentier, Ellie Landry, Elliott "Mechanistic Moth" Sawyer, Emily Beth, Emily Paliszewski, Emily Richards, Emily V. Nisbet, Emma Rothapfel, EmmJ, Eric Bacon, Eric Smith, Eric Tilton, Erica McGillivray, Erica_Jane_MP, Erin Cunningham, Erin Jade Lange, Erin Thomas, Eruvadhril, Evil Hat Productions, Ex-bestfriend, F Dunne, Fatima Min Rivas, Fawndolyn Valentine, Felomena Li, Ph.D., Fenix Boden, Forrest Simmons, Francesco Policek, Frank "Grayhawk" Huminski, Fraser Simons, Frederick Melhuish III, G Davis, Gabriel Schlesinger, Gary Ault, Geoff Henao, Geoff Urland, Geoffrey E Voss, George William Harris, Grace Ausick, Graeme Burk, Grant P. Hayward, Greg and Julie Hatcher, Greg McElhatton, Griff Maloney, Gwen M. Nelson, Hannah Karahkwenhawe Stacey, Henry Roenke, Hideous Energy, Hina Ansari, Holly Braithwaite, Hooper Triplett, Hutch, Hwan Cho, Iain Bex, Ian Mond, Illicit Cookies, Imani J Dean, Isaac Yañez, Ivan Yagolnikov, J Mitchell, J. E. Tetzloff, J. Robert Deans, Jack Cheevers, Jack Connell, Jacki Hayes, Jacob Kernohan, Jacob P. Rutberg, Jacole Baker, Jacque Mox, Jacqueline Shekell, Jakob Orion Pfefferkorn, James Abels, James Daily, James Jandebeur, James Leask, James Roffino, James Roland, James Traino, Jamie Nooney, Jamilla Emerson, Janelle Asselin, Janette Kinney, Janna Hochberg, Janne T, January Hooper, Jaslyn Shand, Jason Barry, Jason DeWitt, Jason Enright, Jason Grimes, Jason Oren, Jason Paulson, Jason Roop, Jay Collins, Jay Emond, Jay Kominek, Jeff Chong, Jeff Gahres, Jeff Hitchcock, Jeff Metzner, Jen Tracy, Jen Van Meter & Greg Rucka, Jenjen4280, Jenn Ong, Jennifer Conrad, Jennifer Huynh, Jennifer Martin, Jenny Tzahi, Jens Eschholz, Jeremy L Mosher, Jeremy Tidwell, Jeremy Whitley, Jeric Pereda, Jerry Sköld, Jess "Kika" Green, Jess and Steve Kuiken, Jesse Matonak, Jesse McClusky, Jessica Andersen, Jessica Watkins, Jessie Dawn Trubiano, Jessie Zimmer, JHG Hendriks, Jill D'Agnenica, Jim Ecco, JK Parkin, JLO, JMD, JNH, Jody Sollazzo, Joe Wagstaff, Joey Esposito, Joey Lindsey, John P. Christie, John S Dean, Jon Christianson, Jonny Rice, Jono Chan, Jordan N. Harris, Jordan Stacey, Joseph D. Compton, Joseph D. Payne, Josh Bazin, Josh Bullock, Josh Chaplinsky, Josh Rector, Josh Schroeder, Joshua Ingram, JP Sauers, Juan Manuel Haces Valdez, Judi Corvinelli, Julie Johannessen,

Julie Wenzel, June St.James, Justin Corwin, Justin Hirt, K. Barrett, K. D. Eddinger, K. L. Janca, Kaizoman, Kalen Rixon, Kara Sjoblom-Bay, Karen F, Karen Gache, Karen Mahoney, Karen Monaghan, Kari Sanders Merritt, Karl Foster, Karl Hailperin, Karl The Good, Karol Callaway, Karsten Franke, Kat Trabert, Kate Ray, Katharine Gilstrap, Katherine L. Gallagher, Katherine Schramm, Katheryn Phillips - for Cammie & Leah, Kathryn O'Farrell, Kathryn Tom, Katie McCamey, Katje van Loon, Katrina Kleman, Katrina Lehto, Kaydalia, Kaylie McDougal, Keegan Xavi, Kelly Aziz, Kelly Gillespie, Kelly M, Kelly Shields, Kelseigh Nieforth, Kelsey Liggett, Kelsey Travis, Ken Blakey, Kenneth Lynch, Kenneth Stull, Kevin Bates, Kevin Guzman, Kevin Hallagan, Kevin Vodka, Kiel Cross, Kieren Medley, K.J. Rollins, Kimberly Keating, Kin Wong, Kristen Jernigan, Kristin L. Brooks, Kristine Roper, Kristy Baker, Kurt Anderson, Kyle Baker, Kylock, Lara Eckener, Laura Ewing, Laura Gramlich, Laura MacDonald, Laura Wesley, Lauren A. Perkins, Lauren Burke, Lauren R. Delos Reyes, Lawrence McClurkin, Lewis Dix, Lewis Smith, Lexie C., Lianne McIntosh, Lim Si Hui, Lisa 'The Mouse', Lisa Higgins, Lisa Hunt, Lisa M. Rabey, Lisa Thomas, Lisje, Lito Hernandez, Liz Cady, Liz Crissey, Lizzie S, LM, Locutus, Logan "the literary bandit" Riley, Loo Yuxian, LRFeldman, Lucia Capano, LuckySu, Lucy Welch, Luke, Luke Read, Lyle Skains, Machine Age Productions, Mackenzie Williams, Maddie A Smyth, Maddy Beaupre, Heili & Madis Sillard, Magdalena Moore, Margaret M. St. John, Maria Ey. Luihn, Maria Larraga, Marie Simmons, Marina Müller, Marissa Dakay, Marissa Miller, Mark A. Chapa, Mark Kadas, Mark Nunnikhoven, Marta Ficke, Mathilde Sachiko Bouhon, Matt Berk, Matt Riggsby, Matthew Bogart, Matthew Brodie-Hopkins, Matthew K Branin, Matthew Lambert, Matthew Laurier, Matthew Stewart, Matthew W. Ellison, Max Bliss, Megan C. Sullivan, Megan D, Megan Purdy, Meghan Asaurus, Meghan Smith, Melanee W., Melanie Stapel, Melinda Beasi, Melissa Dominic, Melissa Krause, Melissa Twinn, Melissa Visitacion, Meredith Jeanne Gillies, Merily Roots, Mia Zachary, Micah Griffin-Lundy, Michael Backs, Michael Bast, Michael Busuttil, Michael D. Blanchard, Michael D. Harvie, Michael Ellis, Michael Feldhusen, Michael Kaplan, Michael M. Jones, Michael May, Michael S. Grissett, Michal Kopecny, Michelle Chan, Miguel Antonio Alderete, Mike Skolnik, Ming Doyle, Mischa Wolfinger, Monica A. Caples, Muneera Mak, My Bergström, Myrah Fisher, N. Weninger, Nadia Cerezo, Nafmi Sanichar - van Herwijnen, Natalie, Nathan Monson, Nathan Olmstead, Nathan S., Nathan Skiba, Neil Richard, Nick "Where's the Beef" Marino, Nico Kolstee, Nicole "Bitmap" Lorenz, Nieske Vergunst, Nilah Magruder, Nino Gortayo, NY Coopers, Olav Beemer, Oliver Juang, Osvaldo Cruz-Rodriguez, Patty Wong, Paul Allor, Paul F. Lerman, Perfektion Design, Pete Griffith, Pete Hurley, Peter Christensen, Peter

Souter, Phil Wait, Phillip O'Connor, Pippi Ardennia, Pira Urosevic, PJ Grant, PJ Hambrick, Poet Mase, R. Zemlicka, Rachel Brandt Fisher, Rachel Leon, Raja Elohim, Ralph Mazza, Ramsey Frye, Rebecca Putnam, Rebecca Turner, Ren & Mally Cappelli, Rey Morales, rgscarter, Rhel ná DecVandé, Rhiannon K., Ria Nightscooter, Richard Cameron & Alexa Aron, Richard Majewski, Rick C., Rick Jones, Rita Contois, RJ Gonzales, Rob Loxterkamp, Robert Bieselin, Robert E. Stutts, Robert Goodwin, Robert J. Plass, Roberta Miller, Robin E. Cook, Robin Harman, Roderick Taylor, Ronny H. Ringen, Rosanne Girton, Ross Campbell, Rubiee Tallyn Hayes, Ruth Bedder, Ryan Eickholt, Ryan Fitzgerald, Ryan Hull, Ryan K Lindsay, S. Barnes, Sabrina Hollinshead, Samanda b Jeude, Samantha Kappes, Samuel and Zachary Kaplan, Samuel Douglas Miller, Sara Yoon, Sarah Bryars, Sarah Hudkins, Sarah Rae, Scott A Evans, Scott and Shelti Thompson, Scott Carlson, Scott Gable, Scott Hutchinson, Scott Johnson, Scott Puckett, Scott Steussy, Sean Gerlach, Sean McAdams, Seeley James, seraangel, Serene Careaga, Seth Rosenblatt, Shane Isaacson, Shannon Lynn, Shawn Poulen, Shelby Norris, Sid Quilty, Silvernis, Skye McAllister, Sonia Harris, Stacie Joy, Stan Yamane, Stephan Szabo, Stephanie Franklin, Stephanie Gunn, Stephanie Hodge, Stephanie Kingsbury, Stephanie Rice, Stephanie Sears, Stephen Paradis, Stephen Ward, Steve Sunu, Steven McManigle, Stuart Fleming, summervillain, Susan Adami, Susan Fang, Susanne Ferebee, Susanne Fischer, Sveta Bogojevic, Sym Cas, Tamme & Marshall Thompson, Tammy Graham, Tammy Ryan, Tania C Richter, Taylor R. Martin, Teresa Potter, Tess Nara, Thacher E. Cleveland, The Conway Family, The Tampa Nagels, Theo Van Duyn III, Thomas Giles, Tiarne Romey, Tiela Garnett, Tiffany Leigh, Tiffany Reynolds, Tim Hanley, Timothy Donohue, Tina B, TK Read, Tlegg, Tom 'Ace of Spades' DeSantos, Tom B., Tom Ciaccio, Tom Ladegard, Tony Peterson, Tonya Lobato, Tori E., TQ Broens, Tsutako, Tyler 'Doc' Barnas, Tyler Dunn, Tyler Jirik, UncannyDerek, Upekha Bandaranayake, UQ Women's Collective, Ursula Jean, Vera Thijssen, Victor Reutermo, Victoria Donnelly, Victoria Eden, Victoria Fletcher, Victoria Kalemkeridis, Weiss Hall, Wendy Smith, Will Hochella, William Clyne, William Zajac, Wolftrest, Yan Basque, Zach Smith, Zoe L.

KELLY THOMPSON has a degree in Sequential Art from The Savannah College of Art & Design. Her love of comics and superheroes have compelled her since she first discovered them as a teenager. Currently living in Manhattan with her boyfriend and absolutely no pets. Kelly aches for a kitten, or even a goldfish. She has a name already picked out, suitable for either. You can find Kelly all over the Internet where she is generally well-liked, except when she's detested. This is her first novel.

www.1979semifinalist.com

www.thegirlwhowouldbeking.com